THE WAY THE WIND BLOWS

Dr. Crandall —
With Sincere Thanks!
Geoff McLeod

GEOFFREY MCLEOD

The Way the Wind Blows

rev. 8.03.2016

Copyright © Geoffrey McLeod 2016

Printed in the United States of America

* * * * *

Disclaimer

This is a work of fiction, a product of the author's imagination. Any resemblance or similarity to any actual events or persons, living or dead, is purely coincidental. Although the author and publisher have made every effort to insure there are no errors, inaccuracies, omissions, or inconsistencies herein, any slights or people, places, or organizations are unintentional.

* * * * *

Cover artwork by Geoffrey McLeod
Interior formatting by Debora Lewis arenapublishing.org

ISBN-13:978-1536999990
ISBN-10: 1536999997

TABLE OF CONTENTS

Acknowledgments

I am indebted to my fellow Marines and to friends in law enforcement that provided comments, suggestions, and an example for life. Jane Yolen's Book, *Take Joy, a Writer's Guide to Loving the Craft* provided the inspiration to get started and keep going. Friends Jim and Ellen Herman stuck with me from the beginning. High school classmate, Beverly Albrecht, was a constant and valuable critic. Bisbee author, Debrah Strait, patiently offered wise criticism that kept me focused. Former Attorney and Law Professor, Gary Ramaeker, provided valuable insight into some of the legal aspects, as well as helping me to better define my characters. My sister, Sue Powell, always an encouraging supporter, read every one of the early versions. Friends and neighbors in my community also provided valuable insight.

Appreciation must also go to my publisher, Debora Lewis of Arena publishing. Her expertise is priceless for self-published authors.

In spite of drawing on the wisdom and experience of professionals in various fields, I remain responsible for plot, characters, and details in the story. The errors are mine. In references to law enforcement and military personnel and procedures, no disrespect is intended.

1

The War Years

On the plane from Okinawa bound for Viet Nam, Rob Simpson listened to the chatter.

"Nothing to worry about," one of the green replacement troops said. "After that peace treaty in Paris last month, all we gotta do is hang out and chase them good lookin' broads. A tour like this will be a piece of cake!"

Lounging in the seat next to Rob was a lean, weathered Marine. His collar bore the insignia of a Staff Sergeant. Steel gray eyes in constant motion didn't miss anything. His big roman nose was crooked. The firm set of his jaw indicated that he didn't waste a lot of energy smiling. The uniform was as seasoned as the man. This was not his first tour.

Rob leaned toward him, "What about that cease fire, Sergeant, any truth to that?"

A quick glance at Rob told the veteran everything he needed to know. His voice was hard, "None - just bullshit talk. No reason to go in the first place and no plan to get out. Charlie's been fighting this one on his own turf for generations. He's committed and he's damn good. He won't quit 'til he's dead, or we're gone. Nobody gives a damn about us."

"I do," Rob replied.

"Why the hell should you care?"

"My brother died over here."

The Sergeant nodded at Rob's name tag, "Simpson, huh."

"PFC Rob Simpson, Sergeant," he replied and extended his hand.

Turning slightly, a big hand closed on Rob's with a powerful grip. Rob saw the name tag and his eyes lit up, "Staff Sergeant Tarkenton, Staff Sergeant Willy Tarkenton," he said.

"Yeah, big fucking deal," Sergeant Willy mumbled. "Where the hell do you know me from?"

"My brother wrote about you in his letters. He said you were brave, tough, one of the best."

"At least he was honest," Sgt. Willy muttered and Rob liked him immediately.

When they stepped off the plane and onto the tarmac at Da Nang, the wise cracking Newbies got their first taste of reality. Rows of metal coffins were waiting to be loaded on the plane they had just departed.

Newbies were assigned to their units and sent into hell. Rob was assigned to Sgt. Willy's company. Hauling his gear, Rob boarded the chopper with Sgt. Willy and several others. They were bound for their own hell. The air was hot and humid, with threatening clouds, thumping rotors overhead, and dense jungle flying past beneath the skids.

As they approached the position, Sgt. Willy leaned to Rob, "When we land, keep your fucking head down and haul ass. There's snipers out there lookin' for fresh meat."

The bird was on the ground only long enough for the men to offload with their gear and supplies. Dead and wounded replaced them, and the bird was off. Sand bagged bunkers with bare chested Marines lounging over automatic weapons glanced at Rob and the other Newbies and chuckled. The salts and short timers ignored the Newbies. Experience taught them that they had to trust the new Marines, just don't make friends with any of them. It was easier lose someone you didn't know.

Rob's new home was a plywood and canvas hooch surrounded by sand bags. The humidity was sweltering. When the wind came from the wrong direction, it didn't smell very good either.

On the ground, inside the compound, Sgt. Willy changed. Staff Sergeant William J. Tarkenton was on his third tour in Viet Nam.

Rob was three months out of boot camp. No more friendly chit chat. He was a hard ass, not letting up on anyone. He was especially hard on Rob, not allowing a slack moment or a single error. Rob had to learn quickly.

"The greatest danger you're going to face is overconfidence and not being prepared for the unexpected," Sgt. Willy told Rob. "Even inside the wire ain't secure. The enemy out there is hardened by generations of war on his own turf and he's damned good!"

That was not the same impression that others had, but Sgt. Willy survived and many others had not.

The intense training paid off. Rob got through the first fire fights without a scratch. Careless members of his platoon got a free ride home, severely injured or dead. After each mission, Sgt. Willy debriefed his men and then singled out Rob for his harshest comments.

"He likes you," a short timer said after an ass chewing with Rob as the recipient.

"I'm glad," Rob replied. "I'd be in deep shit if he didn't."

"No, you'd be dead if he didn't like you," and Rob knew that was true.

Summoning Sgt. Willy to his tent, the young Second Lieutenant pointed at the topo map, "Tonight, I want you to take a recon patrol to this point and determine what the Viet Cong are up to."

"Not good, L.T.," Sgt Willy interrupted and covered a broad area of the map with one huge hand. "Charlie owns this turf. We already know that. Sending a patrol out there at night would be suicide. Whoever dreamed up this operation had their head up their ass."

The lieutenant glared at the veteran, "This is my operation, Sergeant, and I already cleared it with battalion. You just follow orders!" and he dismissed Sgt. Willy.

Rob was in his hooch cleaning his rifle when Sgt. Willy stomped in with a disgusted look, "Fucking asshole," he mumbled. "Second Lieutenants ain't good for nothing except target practice."

Rob grinned, "You don't have much use for officers, do you."

"It ain't that. I don't have any use for leaders that can't lead. Get this, Simpson, we always follow orders. Right up until the shooting starts. After that you're on your own, rank means nothing. Only quick reactions, a cool head, and wise decisions matter," he snarled and handed Rob a list.

"Drag these sorry asses over to my hooch. We've got a patrol tonight and I want to brief all of you."

When Sgt. Willy outlined the operation, he didn't tolerate any discussion. He ended the briefing with this ominous warning, "You people pay attention tonight and keep your shit together. If you do, you just might come back alive. I don't think all of us will."

After the squad departed, Rob lagged behind. Sgt. Willy looked him over, "Are you scared, Simpson?"

"You bet your ass I am," Rob replied.

"That's good. If you ain't scared, you'll never make it. You just do your job and don't screw up, or I'll kick your ass!"

Turning away, Rob was leaving when Sgt. Willy stopped him, "Are you afraid of dying, Simpson?"

Rob didn't hesitate, "No! I'm afraid of not doing my job. I'm afraid of letting the people down that depend on me. I want to complete this tour and go home so I can take care of my wife and our baby."

The wiry Sergeant grinned, "Then you better plan on staying alive if you intend to accomplish all that shit. Staying alive will give you experience for the next time...in case there is a next time."

Returning to his hooch, Rob wrote a quick letter to his wife. He hoped it would not be the last letter he ever wrote, and then they were off.

The night patrol consisted of a handpicked squad. Passing through the concertina wire that surrounded the hilltop, they were alert. Barely able to see the next man, they moved toward their objective. The humidity was stifling, promising more rain. It was dark and still under the canopy. Shadowy, irregular shapes faded into trees and dense undergrowth. Rob was well trained, but he was scared stiff.

It happened quickly. The thick silence of the jungle suddenly shattered with the flash of AK 47 fire, the deadly sound of bullets thudding into bodies. Point man, Lance Corporal Withers down in the first volley. Sgt. Willy instinctively returning fire. An instant later Rob did the same. Adrenaline and training replaced fear. Staying alive took precedence over being a good husband and father.

As if in slow motion, the muzzle blasts seemed to linger in the dark. The sharp report of rifle fire became a staccato drum roll. The radio operator was down, dead in that first volley of fire. Moving erratically, Rob fired his M 16 until it was empty. No more magazines. Dropping to the ground, he groped for another weapon.

He found another weapon and fired until it too was empty. There was a shape rushing at him. Reacting instinctively, the empty rifle made contact. The weight of a lifeless body. On hands and knees searching for another weapon. Nothing. Rob jerked the Kabar from the sheath on his hip. A shape, close and threatening. Rob thrust his knife deeply into the bulk of the body. A flash of light illuminated his attacker's face. It was a boy...maybe 14 or 15. Dead on Rob's knife.

No time for remorse. Move and watch. Another VC with his weapon. Kicking at the man's knees, he fell. Rob stabbed and felt his blade go home.

A sound... and activity seemed to stop. The sky burst into a bright light that created grotesque, wavering shadows and shapes through the trees. In the instant of silence, he was surrounded by the sound of men dying. Sgt. Willy writhing in pain, Kaczynski down, but alive.

Have to get them away from here.

Forcing his way through the heavy underbrush, Rob carried Sgt. Willy back to the compound. He called out for a Corpsman as he entered the perimeter. Lowering his mentor to the ground, he grabbed another rifle and magazines.

"Ambush," he cried. "We need reinforcements!"

Without regard for his own safety, Rob charged back through the tangled growth. He fell several times and regained his feet quickly to continue his forward rush. With the fighting ahead, he slowed and darted from tree to tree. There was a shape rising ahead of him, preparing to fire. The heavy bullet thudded into the tree next to him. Firing directly into the afterglow of the muzzle blast, the man fell.

With smoke, gunfire, whistling shrapnel, and mass confusion, it was too hot even for a Corpsman. Again and again, Rob fought his way to the killing zone. The smell of gunpowder and smoke mingling with the brassy taste and smell of blood filled the air. In that mayhem, Rob's world became a frightening, lonely place.

Then it was over.

With his torn and stinking uniform sticking to his body, soaked with sweat and covered with blood, Rob returned to the compound. Staff Sergeant Willy's prediction was frightfully accurate. Twelve men went out that night. Four survived. In spite of Rob's heroic efforts, Sergeant Willy was not one of the survivors.

Looking up, the Corpsmen working on the wounded, prepping them for the chopper, were getting blurry. Corpsmen were tending Rob's wounds and attaching IV's. The motion of the Huey and the sounds slowly faded. The odors were gone, and when Rob awoke, he was in a military hospital. The doctors had removed the metal. The medals might come later. The terrible memories of that firefight would haunt the survivors for years to come.

From the hospital, Rob wrote letters home. He learned that Helen had given birth to a healthy son and named him Robert. He began writing two letters, one to his wife and the other to his newborn son.

Promotions come quickly for Marines with Rob's leadership ability and combat experience. Following a brief return stateside, he was sent back to Viet Nam. For this tour, newly promoted Sergeant Simpson was attached to a group that wore civilian clothing, riding on helicopters with the pilots of Air America. The pilots were good, almost an extension of the bird. They not only could, but did go anywhere, any time. That was a comfort to people like Rob.

When Saigon fell to communist forces, Rob was there, and again, when the US merchant ship Mayaguez was seized by Cambodian forces. His daughter Patricia was born while he was gone. When it was over, he went home to a country he didn't recognize. No one cared what he did for his country. He was reviled for the uniform he wore. Like many before him discovered, the transition back to civilian life was more challenging than learning how to fight.

Before he was released, Rob was summoned to Washington, D.C. for a meeting with President Ford. Helen did not join him. She was cold and indifferent to the honor.

With his Honorable Discharge, Rob moved his family to Los Angeles and went to work for a Mercedes Benz dealer as a technician. Hard work, natural ability, and attention to detail were well rewarded. Those skills provided a higher standard of living for his family. It allowed him the pleasure of watching his children grow.

But Rob's war was not over. The deadly skills that made him so valuable in combat didn't go unnoticed. The CIA convinced him that his country needed him. Covert assignments took him to places that didn't show on most maps and under circumstances that never reached the news media. Rob's lethal expertise was utilized by intelligence agencies in Washington, D.C. Those agencies never spoke of his actions and any official records of what they required of him were labeled 'Top Secret' and filed.

'Taking human life is not a natural act,' Sgt. Willy often said. Rob knew that, but kill or be killed superseded any rational thought. The memory of his friend Sgt. Willy visited him often. The only thing that helped him retain any semblance of sanity were the words Sgt. Willy had spoken, *'We all have to die Rob, some sooner than others. In war, it's just a job. Do your best, get back alive, have a good night sleep and leave it out there. Whatever you do, don't take it personal.'*

In the end, he realized the absurdity of his efforts. He was being used to further political agendas that had nothing to do with protecting home, family, and country. Remembering Sgt. Willy's words of wisdom, *'Bein' dead ain't patriotic,'* he refused the agency's last request. It was time to put some semblance of a normal life together with his wife and children. Purchasing a home in Tucson, he went to work at the Mercedes dealer.

But still, terrible and unbidden, the memories of war haunted him. Rob struggled with the desperate need for someone to talk to, someone that could listen without judgment. Even his former comrades could not fulfill that need. They had their own ghosts to deal with. Many of them dealt with those horrors by hiding in drugs or alcohol. With a wife and family, Rob couldn't do that.

Rob put away his uniform with the medals and awards from his military service. Tours in the service of his country had taken him away from his family and prevented him the pleasure of watching his children grow, but the strain was most apparent in his relationship with his wife. She blamed Rob, and not the government, for his long and frequent absences. Helen didn't make it any easier. She told their children that his travels to exotic foreign places were his choice.

2

BARBEQUE AND GOLF

The summer monsoon rains in Arizona mean relief from the heat, but by August that relief begins to fade and the blistering heat is accompanied by increased humidity. It affects people differently. Relationships can heat up with passion or hostility. Rob wasn't finding much passion at home. Hoping to temper the hostility, he suggested inviting a group of friends for a barbeque. Helen agreed and sent their kids to her parents for the weekend.

John Giraldi was a manager at a local department store. By his own standards, he was indispensable. He bragged how he was being groomed for rapid advancement to upper management because of his extraordinary abilities. Tall, tan, and slender, his wife Jenna was pleasant and attractive.

Dave Grierson was Rob's co-worker and closest friend. Shaving regularly was something he avoided. Proper English was completely foreign to him, but his salty, straightforward speech always cut through the bullshit. What Dave lacked in vocabulary, he made up for in honesty.

His wife Sandy was two years younger than Dave's 32 years. Her short auburn hair surrounded an open, friendly face. She was pretty, but strangers never credited her for wisdom after they met her husband.

Chuck Stuart was a hard looking, tattooed, biker type with a government job that he didn't discuss. His wife, Samantha, was a petite, professional, real estate agent. Blonde hair, blue eyes and winning smile helped make her successful in her career. These two personified the idea that opposites attract.

"Are you guys up for a round of golf tomorrow?" John asked as the men gathered around the barbeque grille. "I thought I'd show you how the game is played."

"Shit," Dave muttered, "Who the hell is going to teach you? If one of us filled in your score card you wouldn't even come in fourth."

While Rob tended the steaks, the discussion of Giraldi's integrity continued. There were some that would have backed down from Giraldi's arrogance, but Dave Grierson was not one of them.

Before the conversation became too heated, the wives returned from the kitchen with their individual masterpieces. As soon as the steaks came off the grille, everyone took their places at the table, ate too much, drank too much, and enjoyed the afternoon. Before leaving, the men firmed up plans for golf.

"That was a nice afternoon," Rob said after their friends left.

"Yeah," Helen replied. "I'm tired; I'm going to bed."

When Rob got into bed and put his arm around her, she pushed him away, "It's too hot," and turning her back to him went to sleep.

The following morning while Rob was getting his clubs ready for their golf game, John called, "Hey man, I'll have to pass on golf today," he said. "They need me at the store. It's obvious they can't do without me."

Before leaving, Rob asked, "Do you want me to pick up the kids after golf?"

"Yeah, that way I can get some work done around here. If you took them out for hamburgers, I wouldn't have to cook."

After the golf game, Rob picked up Robert and Patricia at their grandparents. Tucking one under each arm, he led them out to the car, "What do you kids think about hamburgers?"

"Can we play goofy golf after," Patricia asked as she scrambled into the car next to her father.

"Yeah, Dad, you played golf today, can we do that too?" Robert chimed in enthusiastically.

"We can do that, but you'll have to go easy on me. You have to remember, I'm an old man."

They both looked up at him and laughed, "You aren't that old, Daddy!"

Fast food for his children wasn't Rob's first choice, but miniature golf with his children was something he enjoyed. Listening to their squeals of delight, he watched their youthful enthusiasm as they made their way through the obstacles.

On the way home, Patricia snuggled under his arm and looked up at him, "Do you have to go away again, Daddy?"

"No, Honey, that's all done now. We've got a lot of time to make up for."

"Oh, good, I'm glad," she said and leaned back with a content smile.

Robert was watching the exchange between his father and sister, "I'm glad, too," he said.

The war, the hard times, were behind him now. Rob looked down at his two children and sighed. He was content. Finally, he could share the precious growing years with them.

3

MANUEL JESUS ORTEGA

She couldn't have been more than 15 or 16. Ragged, dirty, scared out of her wits, and very pregnant, she stumbled into the border crossing at McAllen, Texas. The senior Border Patrol officer was a hardened veteran, but he had a daughter. The girl looked up at him and collapsed in pain. Risking his career, he carried her to his duty vehicle. With lights flashing and siren wailing, he drove to the closest hospital.

The hospital staff did all they could, but there were complications. The mother lived only long enough to see the birth certificate that gave her son citizenship in the United States.

The owner of a local sporting goods store, Jorge Martinez, took the child to be raised as his own. The boy was named Manuel Jesus and assumed his guardian's family name. Manuel grew up tough in a brutal environment.

When Manuel was 12 years old, his 15-year-old stepsister was raped by a neighborhood gang member.

Jorge Martinez was infuriated and vowed revenge, "The police don't protect honest, hard working people like us," he told Manuel. "They won't even find out who did this to my daughter and punish them. I want you to find out who did this to her."

The following day, Manuel provided the name to his guardian. Julio was an older boy with a bad reputation.

"There's ways to take care of people like that." Jorge said. "It's time you learned."

Leading Manuel to the warehouse where he stored excess inventory in large containers, Jorge opened a hidden trapdoor. Descending into a dark tunnel, he led Manuel along the passageway. A trap door opened into another warehouse.

"This is Mexico," Jorge grinned.

Young Manuel was impressed, "Then we came under the river?"

"This was very expensive to build, but it's like all the others along the border."

Gesturing to one side, Manuel asked, "What's in those boxes?"

Without reply, Jorge gave him a harsh look.

"It must be drugs," Manuel said. "But what do you have to trade for it?"

Jorge laughed, "Manny, what do I sell in my store?"

Nodding with understanding, Manuel replied, "Guns and bullets."

At an adobe ranch house outside of Reynosa, Manuel was introduced to Senor Salazar, the owner, and several of the vaqueros. "These men will teach you what you have to do, Manny. Pay attention and learn well."

Jorge gave one of the vaqueros a large pistol and several boxes of bullets. He explained what he wanted done. The man looked at Manuel and then at the pistol. His evil smile showed missing teeth, "Bueno, Senor Martinez," he muttered and took Manuel roughly by the arm.

The first time he fired the heavy pistol, Manuel was startled by the loud noise and recoil. He realized its potential at once. When Manuel grew tired of shooting at tin cans and bottles, he shot a neighbor's dog so he could watch it die.

"It happens too quickly," Manuel said. "When I shoot Julio, I want to watch him suffer."

"No!" Senor Salazar said sharply. "A wounded man, like a wounded animal, is too dangerous. It must be done quickly, and you must be sure."

With a cold smile, Senor Salazar handed Manuel a sharp machete, "If you cut off his head, they will not suspect one so small as you."

The toothless one was a cruel and dangerous man, but he was a good teacher. He made Manuel practice with the machete using bales of straw. It was difficult and Manuel became angry when the men laughed at him. He would show them.

Manuel found a small calf in the trees. There was not as much resistance when he struck with the machete. A living thing was much easier to kill than straw bales.

Making his way home along the smooth floor of the dark tunnel, he thought about the vaqueros. They were cruel and dangerous men, but they feared and obeyed Jorge. That was power; the kind of power Manuel knew he would possess one day.

Manuel discussed the plan with his guardian and they made preparations. Several days, later Julio found Manuel waiting for him.

"What are you doing here, *puta*?" Julio snarled.

Without speaking, Manuel took the big pistol from under his shirt. Pointing it at Julio's face, he pulled the trigger. Julio fell dead on the sidewalk. Manuel reached into the bushes for the razor sharp machete. He severed Julio's head and laughed.

Later that same day Manuel was in a car with all his belongings and on his way to Arizona. The long drive gave Manuel time to think about what he had done. He felt no more remorse for killing Julio than he had felt for the dog or the calf. He thought of how easily the bigger and stronger boy had been eliminated and it pleased him. It was a valuable lesson. Anyone that caused trouble could be silenced.

After being driven to a modest house in Douglas, Arizona, he was introduced to Arturo Ortega. Manny lived in the Ortega home and started high school that fall. Mr. Ortega introduced him to the family business. Manny was eager and learned quickly. He had little regard for American law and none for women. The law was a joke to be manipulated or ignored. Women had only one purpose.

The senior Ortega was a wise and powerful man with important connections on both sides of the border. Manny learned how Mr. Ortega used those sources to his advantage. As a high school student, Manny was willing to provide new customers for the drugs coming out of Mexico. He met influential men across the border willing to pay well for the services of young girls. By arranging for drugs and spending money, Manuel was able to provide the girls for them.

By the time he graduated from high school, Manuel was becoming financially successful. He never filled out a job application and his driver's license was purchased under a fictitious name. For all practical purposes, the Manuel Jesus Martinez-Ortega who graduated from Douglas High School no longer existed.

4

JUDY WHITBY

With her nose pressed against the window, Judy Whitby watched in wide-eyed fascination as the Santa Fe rolled into Flagstaff, Arizona. It was like the brochures from the Chamber of Commerce, only better. Beyond the city, a mountain rose up to 12,637 feet. The city was over 6,000 feet above sea level! Back in Duluth there was nothing that high.

The young man who joined her somewhere in New Mexico still babbled on about his many fine qualities. He seemed to be the ultimate authority on the subject. Judy had neither the time nor the inclination to question that authority. This was her stop and it was time to get off the train.

She was gathering her belongings when he interrupted her, "Maybe when I'm in town I might give you a call. I could show you a good time."

Judy didn't respond.

"Why don't you give me your phone number?"

"It's in the phone book."

"Cool, I can look it up. What's your name?"

"That's in there too," she smiled.

"Excuse me," she said, and with her purse and backpack, pushed past him.

Stepping onto the platform, she felt a twinge of anxiety. She was alone in a strange town further away from home than she had ever been. Her suitcases beside her, the train she had been on for the last two days already moving. She wasn't sure how to get to campus, or how to find her dorm. She took a deep breath of the cool mountain air, touched the pendant at her throat, and smiled.

Her thoughts drifted back to the time when she was eight years old. She was at Voyageurs National Park in northern Minnesota with her father. On the second day at their campsite, Judy found a strangely shaped stone and showed it to her father, "Daddy, what's this?"

John Whitby was not the kind of father to simply answer a question and pass up a teaching opportunity, "What makes it unique, Sweetheart?"

"It's different, Daddy. It doesn't look like the other stones. It looks like someone made it this way."

"I think you're right, but what would someone do with a stone that came to a point like that?"

After studying the stone in her hand for several minutes, she looked up at her father, "It might have been a tool," then she brightened, "Is it an arrowhead, Daddy?"

"I think you're right, but there aren't any Indians around here, are there?"

He watched with delight as she considered that fact then looked back at him, "No, it must be old."

"Maybe, but how are you going to find out?"

She did find out. As a reward, the arrowhead was her Christmas present that year. It was cradled in a silver clasp that her father made and hung on a silver chain.

There were other experiences where Judy's father instilled an insatiable curiosity and determination to discover the truth. Opinions were not good enough for her. She needed to know *why*. If the museum or library couldn't provide a satisfactory answer, she did her own research and wouldn't quit until she was satisfied.

As she grew older, her fascination with Native Americans grew and when it was time to choose a college, she chose Northern Arizona University. It was in the heart of Indian country.

A dark haired man wearing jeans, boots, and a cowboy hat slouched against the building, the only person in sight. He looked like a real

Indian, Navajo or maybe Hopi, she thought. Both were in this part of the country, and that was why she was here.

"Excuse me, sir..."

"Sir?" he grinned as if the title was a joke. He looked her over quickly, "Must be a student," he grunted.

"Yes sir, can you tell me how to get to the college?"

"Too far to walk. You better take taxi."

"Where do I find a taxi?"

"You wait here," and he was gone.

A few minutes later, a battered sedan drove up with 'Flagstaff Taxi' on the door.

"Goin' to campus, little lady?"

"Yes sir... how much does it cost?"

"Couple o' bucks," the driver replied as he got out of his cab and started to help with her luggage.

He was a strange man in an unfamiliar town and when she hesitated, he grinned, "Nothin' to worry about, young lady. I ain't lost a passenger yet."

He had an honest face and a friendly smile. He looked like he could be trusted, but just to be sure she asked him to put her luggage in the back seat beside her. He chuckled quietly and did as she asked.

"My kids went to NAU," he said. "Good school. You must be a freshman, what made you choose NAU?"

"The anthropology professors, they're supposed to be good."

"You won't be disappointed... which dorm are you in?"

She told him and he began a nonstop monolog about the benefits of NAU and Flagstaff. Much of it she already knew, but he added to her knowledge with local tidbits.

"Why isn't the meter turned on?" she asked suddenly.

He glanced over his shoulder and chuckled, "Makes it a little easier on the pocketbook."

Her suitcases looked like they'd had some use, and the way she asked about the fare, he must have figured she wasn't rich.

"I'll flip 'er on in a mile or two," and he did.

Taking a longer route, he pointed out landmarks, stores, restaurants, and other businesses she might want to be aware of and made comments about each of them. It was all valuable information and she made mental notes of his comments.

"That one's yours," he pointed when they arrived at a series of dormitories. "It's a bit of a walk. Will you let me help you with your bags or are you still wonderin' about us folks here?"

"I think I can manage, but thank you. How much do I owe you?"

"Like I said, couple o' bucks."

She took two one-dollar bills out of her wallet and looked at the driver. He was once a big man, but worn with middle age and graying hair that tufted out from under the battered cowboy hat he wore. His face was lined with well-earned wrinkles and his eyes were honest. She unfolded another dollar bill and gave it to him, "Thank you, sir, for the ride and the information. I appreciate that."

That single dollar bill was a lot of money to her. Refusing it would have whittled away a piece of the independence she was learning. He looked up at her with understanding, "Thank you, and good luck," he said, got back into his cab, and drove off.

Judy looked across the grounds toward her dorm. It was a long way and she began to wish she had accepted his offer. Young people were all around, some carrying loads to the dorms and others returning for more. If they could do it, so could she. She had a backpack, her purse and two large, heavy suitcases. She arranged her load and started off.

Another student going in the opposite direction saw Judy struggling with her suitcases and stopped, "You've got a lot there. Let me help," and without waiting for a reply he took her suitcases and started off.

He showed her the way to her dorm and carried her suitcases up to her room. He set her bags down and was gone before she could thank him. One of her roommates was already there. The other two arrived shortly thereafter and they began to set up their room. Then it was time to call and report her safe arrival. She found a pay phone and made her first collect call home.

"Hi Mom, it's me."

"I'm glad you called, Honey. How was the trip?"

"The trip was boring, but Flagstaff is super! It's so beautiful up here, even better than the pictures. My roommates are really neat girls and all three are from the west."

Then her father got on the phone, "Hi Precious, how's my girl?"

"I'm fine. I'm so thankful you let me come here. This is going to be a great opportunity."

"Do you need anything?"

"Not right now. I think I can walk to all my classes. The scholarship covers most of what I need and my roommates and I talked about sharing some of the other expenses so that helps."

"We're proud of you, but we miss you. Here, I'll put the kids on. I love you."

"I love you too, Dad."

12-year-old Sarah got on next, "Hi Judy. What are the boys like? Are they different than the guys at school?" Sarah considered her older sister an authority.

"I don't know, Sis," Judy laughed. "I just got here and I don't know any of them yet... but I'll let you know."

Eight-year-old Brian was next, "Did you see any cowboys or Indians?"

"I saw some men that looked like Indians," Judy said, "but they were dressed like cowboys with hats, jeans and boots."

When classes started, it wasn't anything like high school. The lectures were long and filled with details. Homework demanded extra time and concentration. Judy thrived at the challenge. Because of distractions in the dorm, she spent most of her time in the library where it was quiet.

Several of her classmates lived in Flagstaff. They invited her to their homes for dinner regularly and introduced her to trails on the mountain. At Thanksgiving, when her roommates went home for the holiday, Judy was invited to share the festivities with one of her new friends. When winter came, she went skiing. It gave her an opportunity to ask about college men.

"Most of the guys in my high school were pretty immature or boring. What are the guys like here?"

"Hardly any difference, just older and a little more aggressive," Mary Jane grinned. "Not much chance of finding a husband if that's what's on your mind... unless you're willing to lower your standards."

"I came to get an education not a husband!" Judy laughed. "I know what I want in a man, so I can wait."

"The decent ones are hard to find... good luck!"

Christmas break came quickly that first year, and Judy was anxious to go home and spend time with her family. There was so much to tell that couldn't be done during her Sunday night phone calls. At home, Sarah pestered her about boys, Brian was curious about cowboys and Indians, and her mother, Marianne, was concerned if she was getting enough to eat and sleeping regularly. Then it was time alone with her father.

"Is there anything you need?" her father asked.

"I have everything I need, but what about you and Mom? It's expensive with me being so far away and I know this is a difficult time for you. Sometimes I feel I should have stayed here and gone to Junior College. I could have gotten a job and helped."

"No, Honey, we've been over that before. We've saved up for this for a long time and it's what you want. I'm looking forward to the day when I read your name in the National Geographic. I'll brag to all the guys at work that the anthropologist is my daughter. So how are your grades?"

"I got straight A's and I'm going to be on the Dean's list," she said proudly. "My professors even want me to tutor some of the other kids."

Her father smiled and hugged her, "They'll be asking you to teach the classes next! I'm proud of you, Honey."

After returning to school, she allowed herself time on weekends for hiking and an occasional double date. She wasn't impressed with the guys she met. No one could match her enthusiasm for the outdoors. None of them could keep up with her hiking.

Close to the end of the year, several girls approached her with the idea of renting a house off campus. It made sense: if they shared expenses, they could save money.

When they found a large rambling house, Judy was chosen to negotiate the terms of the lease. After meeting the girls, Edward Baumgartner, the future landlord, seemed willing to adjust the rent to something they could afford. Judy tried one additional tactic.

"If we take care of the yard and paint the inside do you think you could lower the rent just a little?"

Mr. Baumgartner considered the idea and agreed to lower the rent.

"That includes the utilities, doesn't it?" she asked hopefully.

Mr. Baumgartner paused. With an approving glance at the six girls, he smiled, "All right, I'll do that... and I suppose you want me to provide the paint too."

"That way it would be the color you want," Judy said with an innocent smile.

5

DIVORCE

The whirring of air tools and the chatter of voices filled the air when a stranger entered the shop and approached one of the technicians, "Are you Rob Simpson?"

Wiping his hands on a shop towel, Rob extended his hand, "Yes sir, what can I do for you?"

The stranger ignored the gesture and stuffed an envelope in Rob's hand.

"What's this?"

"Consider yourself served, sucker," the stranger said with a sarcastic grin, "Divorce papers and a restraining order. You'll need a sheriff escort to pick up your stuff!"

Rob stared in disbelief as the arrogant punk walked off.

Approaching Rob, Dave jerked the unlit cigar out of his mouth and asked, "Who the fuck was that little turd?"

Rob slumped against his workbench and handed the papers to his friend to read. Rob was stunned; it was totally unexpected. He called Helen and tried to reason with her.

"Just sign the damn papers and leave us alone," she told him. "The only time I want to see you is in court!" and she hung up the phone.

Helen was unwilling to compromise or negotiate; she wouldn't even let him speak to the children. As reality settled in, he was devastated.

The process was bewildering, brutal, and expensive. When it was over, Rob found himself living in a tiny apartment. Helen got the kids, the car, the house, and all its furniture, along with child support and spousal maintenance. Rob got the bills. It was as one-sided a decision as it could have been. His dream of family life with his wife and children was shattered. Every effort, every compromise, simply hadn't worked. It never occurred to him that it wasn't his fault.

It wasn't long after the divorce that the truth became clear. John Giraldi divorced his wife, Jenna, and moved into Rob's former home with Helen. John tolerated Rob's children but he had little use for them. This situation lasted barely six months before John lost his job.

"It's just a little misunderstanding with some of those idiots in upper management," he told Helen. "They don't realize who they're dealing with! I'll straighten this out real quick and show them who's right."

The matter was soon corrected but not the way John described. He went to court and then to prison for embezzling funds. In the meantime, he had depleted most of Helen's assets and left her with no recourse but to sell her house or get more money from her ex-husband. She decided to take Rob back into court to have her alimony increased.

When Rob was served with the papers for an adjustment to the divorce decree, he was reluctant to use the same attorney. He was discussing the matter with his friend Dave, when one of Rob's regular customers joined them. Attorney J.J. Rabinowitz owned two Mercedes. Rob was the only person allowed to work on his vehicles.

"You look discouraged, Rob," he said. "What seems to be the trouble?"

"Ex wife," Rob said and handed the papers to J.J. "She wants more money."

After glancing over the paperwork, J.J. asked, "Do you have an attorney to represent you?"

"I wasn't impressed with the one that handled the divorce," Rob said. "It looks like I'm going to get screwed again."

"I can look into the matter for you," J.J. said with a serious look. "Many times a reasonable settlement can be reached without the necessity of a court appearance."

Rob shook his head, "I'm not sure I can afford it, J.J. The last time I ended up paying for my attorney as well as hers. The way that turned out, I could have saved a lot if I just showed up with my checkbook."

"That's not always the case, my friend," J.J. smiled. "You have a little time before you have to respond. Let me look into this and see if there is a reasonable alternative."

"I appreciate that, J.J., but I don't want to put you out."

"Rob, I don't trust anyone else with my cars. In addition to being an excellent technician, I know I can rely on you to be fair. Don't worry about the money; I'll handle this on a pro bono basis."

After J.J. left with Rob's documents, Dave had a question, "What the hell does pro bono mean?"

"It means free," Rob replied and went back to work.

The Rabinowitz firm, in addition to his associates, included a unique group who were loosely referred to as 'Research Staff'. This group spent little actual time in the office. They were investigators. Their job was to uncover anything that might help a case. They were very good.

Several days later, J.J. called Rob, "I'd like for you to come to the office, Rob. There are several matters we need to discuss before we respond to Helen's attorney."

"Can't we just discuss it over the phone?"

"No, there are some very serious considerations that we have to address. Can you come by the office tonight after work?"

"I'll be there."

After work, when Rob came into the office, J.J. offered him a chair and sat quietly before he began.

"We need to respond to the motion from Helen's attorney, Rob. My staff came up with some information that we need to discuss. It isn't pleasant, so I hope you can bear with me."

"None of it has been pleasant so far," Rob said and eased into a chair.

"I want you to understand that none of this is a reflection on you as a husband or a father. You're a good man, Rob, you just chose the wrong woman."

"Helen doesn't seem to agree with your opinion."

"This is about her, Rob, not about you. You have to understand that. If you don't agree, I won't go any further."

Rob shrugged, "I don't know where you're going with this, but go on."

"When did you ship out for Viet Nam?"

"April 1973."

"And you were gone for 18 months?"

"Yes sir."

"When was Robert born?"

"March of '74..." he answered and fell silent. It was the first time Rob ever considered the implications.

"I had my people check out some of your military history."

"A lot of the stuff I did is classified."

"We have ways to access those files," J.J. continued. "You have skills that very few men possess. I want you to promise me you won't do anything foolish."

"I'm not proud of the things I did, but what I did, I did for my country and under orders. Giraldi is a low life bum but he's getting what he deserves. I could take him out and nobody would know, but he isn't worth the effort. Helen and her attorney aren't worth it either. The kids need a break, and so do I. I just want to get this over with and get on with my life."

J.J. continued quietly, "Her attorney feels he can justify an increase in alimony. In order to prevail, we have to prove otherwise. What that means is the first trial was a fraud because it didn't disclose Robert's paternity. We have documents and witnesses that can attest to that."

"Is it really necessary to make that public?"

"That depends on her attorney, Fielding. If he's smart and looks at our response, he should talk to Helen and try to negotiate or drop the matter. If he chooses to go ahead, then this will have to come out."

While Rob sat quietly, J.J. continued, "There's more, Rob. It pains me to have to be the one to tell you, but you have to be prepared in case you have to go on the stand. I don't know of any way to prepare you for this. It involves your daughter, Patricia."

Rob looked up, "Just go ahead and say it."

"We uncovered evidence of drug use by Patricia. We also discovered that Helen is complicit in pornographic movies involving Patricia."

Rob responded quietly, "I can't let that one slide, J.J."

"I understand that, Rob, but let me finish.

"Giraldi was behind that, and he's currently in prison for another matter. He's aware that charges are pending against him regarding Patricia. He's willing to deal by revealing the names of his accomplices..."

"So he'll get out on bail or plea bargain and be out in no time," Rob interrupted.

J.J. smiled and held up his hand, "He won't get bail, and in cases of child pornography, even the best of deals doesn't amount to a lot. He gave up a lot of names in exchange for a reduced sentence."

"Then what happens?"

"Patricia wasn't his only victim. What Giraldi thinks he's getting, and what he is getting, are worlds apart. The FBI is putting its case against Giraldi and his accomplices together right now. The others will come out after the first trial. The plea bargain only applies to Patricia's case. If Giraldi lasts a year in prison, he'll be lucky. Inmates don't treat child molesters kindly."

"Isn't there some other way so this doesn't come out in public?"

"Like I said, I'll give this information to Fielding. It will be up to him."

"Will the kids be there, if it goes to court, I mean?"

"I'll see to it that they are excluded from the courtroom."

Shaking his head, Rob replied, "How could I have been so stupid? I must look like a fucking idiot!"

"No, Rob, you were only too trusting. Honest people like you find it hard to conceive of people that deceitful. She was unfaithful to you even while you were in Viet Nam. That was easy because you weren't around. It's something even your friends won't tell you."

"When all this comes out, what do I tell my kids?" Rob asked.

"There's no easy answer for that. Unfortunately, Robert isn't your..."

"No," Rob interrupted, "He has my name. He is my son, just like Patricia is my daughter. I have to find a way to help them through this."

"I respect that, but I must warn you, Rob, the hearing isn't going to be easy on either one of you."

Rob stood, "Didn't figure it would be," he said and nodded at J.J., "You sure put up with a lot of bullshit in your line of work don't you?"

"That's true Rob, but sometimes we get to help good people and make positive things happen. It's just a matter of deciding how to go about it and that's the hard part."

Even after negotiations, Fielding and his client felt comfortable going to court. Entering the courtroom with her attorney, Helen was confident that she was going to conclude the day well compensated. Fielding looked at Rabinowitz with a smug grin and they took their place in the courtroom.

Fielding produced his evidence to justify an increase in alimony. Then for the next hour, the judge listened intently to Rabinowitz' witnesses and considered the documents presented. Fielding had not prepared well for this hearing and it showed. His cross-examination and objections were less than compelling.

When Rabinowitz continued, the judge interrupted him and called a recess. He summoned the attorneys into his chambers. Closing the door, he directed counsel to be seated. From behind his desk he started with Rabinowitz, "Your witnesses have made some serious allegations out there. And your documents tend to show there was fraud committed on the court during the trial."

"Yes, your honor, and there is more to come."

Leaning back in his chair, the judge steepled his fingers with his eyes boring into J.J., "Well?" he said.

Rabinowitz briefly summarized the information regarding drugs and Helen's complicity in the pornographic movies involving her daughter.

The judge glared at Fielding, "Were you aware of any of this?"

Shifting uncomfortably, Fielding did not reply.

With a disgusted look, the judge continued, "I'm not at all happy with this fraud situation. We can reopen this case based on misrepresentation of parentage, or you can talk to your client and try to reach an agreement with opposing counsel."

He turned back to Rabinowitz, "Do you have anything to add?"

"Yes, your honor, a few words about my client."

With the judge's approval, Rabinowitz briefly summarized Rob's military career and covert CIA activities. It painted a comprehensive picture of Rob Simpson's lethal capabilities.

When J.J. concluded his comments, the judge turned to Fielding, "When Mr. Simpson learned about his wife's infidelity, I would say we're fortunate he didn't take matters into his own hands."

"Your honor," J.J. interrupted, "I've known my client for a number of years. He served honorably in the U.S. Marine Corps. He earned the Congressional Medal of Honor. That is not something he would do. He came to me to resolve this matter as peacefully as possible."

"I would certainly hope so," the judge replied then leveled his finger at Fielding, "Are you sure you want to go back out there and be responsible for Mr. Simpson discovering what his wife has done to his children?"

"Well...uh," Fielding stammered, "I...I think I need to confer with my client, Your Honor."

The judge dismissed the attorneys with a wave of his hand.

Fielding met with his client, then with J.J. After reaching an agreement, they explained it to the judge and he approved. When court reconvened, the judge asked counsel to recite their agreement for the record. Then he addressed the parties, "Mrs. Simpson..." he began.

Helen was indignant, "My name isn't Simpson, my name..."

The judge interrupted, "Thank you, ma'am, but I have heard enough from and about you."

After ascertaining that the parties understood and were in agreement, he rendered his decision. Attorney fees and costs were awarded to Rob. Helen retained custody of the two minor children for the time being and would continue to receive child support. Alimony was reduced to zero.

Then the judge added a few choice words of his own, "Mrs. Simpson, your behavior as outlined in this proceeding, is and was inexcusable. Although neither attorney has suggested it, I feel it is my duty to direct child protective services to investigate your fitness as a parent and determine if it is in the best interests of the children to remain in your care. If that report is unfavorable, additional proceedings will be forthcoming."

Slamming his gavel, the judge stormed from the courtroom in disgust.

Fielding led Helen from the courtroom in tears while Rob sat with his hands clenched, staring straight ahead. J.J. stood beside him, watching his friend.

He put his hand on Rob's shoulder, "Son, I know this has been hard on you. I'm sorry we had to handle things the way we did. Under the circumstances, I think the judge was generous. Maybe now you can get on with your life and find a way to deal with your bitterness."

Rob stood, "Thanks, J.J." he said and shook his friend's hand.

Leaving the courtroom, Rob stepped out into a cold January afternoon and sat on one of the benches outside. J.J. was right. The proceeding was not pleasant for anyone.

6

BACK TO COLLEGE

After spending the summer working two jobs and saving every penny, Judy returned to NAU for her sophomore year. In addition to class work, now she had to worry about making sure the rent would be paid on time and all the things she promised Mr. Baumgartner would be accomplished.

There were duties and responsibilities to be agreed upon, cooking, cleaning, painting, and yard work. The other girls agreed that they needed a plan and elected Judy as their house leader. She would delegate those responsibilities.

Once the semester started, Judy's roommates tried to fix her up with dates, but she wasn't interested. The demands of college were far more important, but she did miss hiking. Then Heather introduced her to a tall, good-looking student she knew.

"Judy, this is Craig Ditmore, he's from Phoenix."

"I'm sure Heather told you about me," he said confidently. "She said you like to hike. How about getting together this weekend for a short hike?"

Judy hesitated before she agreed to go with him. She was anxious to get out hiking once again.

"I'll pick you up about nine on Saturday. I know some good day hikes."

Craig arrived after 9:30 in his new Corvette. He was late and Judy wasn't interested in his car. It was awkward to get into and didn't leave much room for their packs. Except for Alice, Judy's roommates were impressed with his good looks and new car as they watched through the window.

"Who fixed her up with *him*?" Alice asked angrily.

"I did," Heather said.

"Why did you do that? Judy's a decent girl. Craig is only after one thing and once he gets that he dumps the girl!"

"It's about time someone put her in her place," Heather said with a smug grin. "She thinks she's so smart, thinking she can run everything. Craig will educate her."

"She's not like you," Alice fumed. "She deserves someone better than him!"

The hike was shorter and less strenuous than Judy would have liked, but it was an outing. On the drive back to her place, he asked her to have dinner with him. Like most cash strapped college girls, Judy wasn't about to turn down a free meal. She would have settled for pizza, but he took her to an expensive restaurant.

Over the next several weeks, Craig spent time and money trying to impress her. There were occasional hikes, but too short, not the kind she preferred. Craig had a different agenda, and Judy wasn't interested.

With Christmas parties all over campus, Craig tried to convince Judy to go with him, "There's this big party on Saturday night and my buddy Daryl doesn't have a date. If you can fix him up with one of your roommates, we can double date. What about it?"

Judy was reluctant, "I'll see if any of them are interested."

Alice was the only girl at home that night.

"That's Craig," Judy said. "He wants me to go to a Christmas party with him and his buddy Daryl, but Daryl doesn't have a date. Are you interested in going?"

"They're both jerks," Alice replied, "But we can use a break. If we go together it might not be a problem, but I want to get home early."

"So do I," Judy agreed and went back to the phone.

"Alice said she'd go with us, but we'll need to get home early so we can finish up our term papers before the break."

"Good, we'll pick you up at seven."

It was cold and snowing when Craig and Daryl arrived shortly before eight in Daryl's car. Both of them had been drinking. It was not an auspicious beginning.

Cars were parked down both sides of the street in front of a big house. Multi-colored Christmas lights sparkled in the falling snow. From the outside, it looked inviting and helped set the mood for the holiday.

"This might not be so bad after all," Alice said.

"It does look like Christmas," Judy agreed.

Their opinions changed as soon as they were inside. Alcohol and drugs were in abundance.

Alice was concerned, "If I knew ahead of time that it was this kind of party I wouldn't have agreed to come."

"I don't like it either," Judy agreed. "I'm sorry I got you into this. Just don't drink anything, and stick close. We better find a way to leave early."

The party rapidly got noisier and more boisterous. Some of the girls were acting wild and didn't protest when they were ushered down the hallway to where the bedrooms were. Both Craig and Daryl were drinking steadily and getting more aggressive.

"This is getting out of hand," Alice said.

Judy agreed, "See if Daryl's sober enough to take us home."

While Alice approached Daryl, Craig swaggered over to Judy, "Hey baby, what do you say we take a walk down lover's lane." He grabbed her arm and started toward the hallway.

Judy tried to pull away, "No way, Craig. You're drunk and I'm not going anywhere with you!"

"You stuck up bitch," he slurred. "You run around wiggling your cute little ass and thinking you're hot shit. I wasted a lot of time and money on you and I expect something in return. If you ain't going back there, I'll fuck you right here."

He was unsteady on his feet, one hand on her arm and a beer in the other. Judy was frightened and angry. Swinging her free arm, she caught him off balance and knocked him off his feet. Craig sprawled on the floor with his ears ringing and a red welt on his face that would last for days. Judy burst through the stunned group. She grabbed Alice and their coats on the way out the door.

Alice was laughing, "Good shot Judy! I don't think he'll bother you again!"

Judy's hand still stung as they hurried to the street, "I hope they don't come after us."

"They'll have lots of time to think about that," Alice said. "It's a long walk home and if they do come after us, we'll be in trouble."

"It's cold too, we'll have to walk fast to stay warm."

One of Craig's friends was helping him to his feet, "I told you before man, you should stick with the dumb chicks. They don't fight back."

"I'll get even with that bitch," Craig muttered and spit blood on the floor. "She won't get away with that!"

His friend laughed, "Guess you missed that movie where the broad gets even with the guy."

"Yeah, 'Fatal Attraction', boiled pet rabbit!" another said.

"Or bashed up Corvette," Daryl added.

"She wouldn't dare do anything to my car," Craig said.

"Are you sure? She looked pretty pissed off. I wouldn't put it past her to get even."

Craig looked worried, "You gonna let me lock my 'vette in your garage?"

After half an hour in the cold, Alice and Judy's confidence began to falter. The snow was increasing and the wind in their faces was getting stronger. When a car pulled to the curb ahead of them, they panicked. It was a snow covered old sedan with bumper stickers plastered across the back, *Peace, No More Nukes, Save the Whales,* and other more graphic and less politically correct comments. They started to hurry past until Judy saw the sign on the door and stopped. It was barely legible. *Flagstaff Taxi* had earned another year of fading.

The window was down, "Are you ladies all right?"

"We're going home," Alice said.

Judy leaned over and looked in the window. The cowboy hat was replaced with a leather pilot's hat with sheepskin earflaps, but he had the same friendly smile, "I know you," she said.

"Told you I never lost a passenger," the driver replied. "You'll keep my record intact if you ladies get in and I can close the window. I'm not as young as you are and the cold gets to my arthritis."

Alice was shivering, "How do you know him?"

"He's took me to campus when I first came to town. He's right, we better get in."

As soon as they were in his cab, the driver rolled up the window and turned his heater on high, "Where to, ladies?"

With her teeth chattering, Judy gave him the address, and the driver chuckled, "That would have been a long walk."

They rode in silence with the wipers scraping twin arcs across the windshield, smearing the wet snow, before the driver spoke again, "I'm not usually this nosy, but you really got me curious. What were you doing walking in this weather?"

"We were invited to a party," Judy said. "It was pretty wild, drinking, drugs, stuff like that."

"How did you ever end up at a place like that?"

"We went with a couple of guys."

"And they decided if you weren't going to party with them they weren't going to take you home?"

"One guy was tryin to drag Judy into one of the bedrooms and..."

His foot was off the accelerator instantly and he looked in the rear view mirror, "Did they hurt either one of you?" he asked before Alice could finish.

Alice giggled, "No, but she knocked him on his ass!"

The driver chuckled, "Good for you! Do you think any of them are going to try anything?"

"I don't think so."

It was quiet again until Alice spoke up, "Hey, why isn't the meter running?"

"Sometimes I forget," he said and flipped it on.

When they arrived at the girls home Judy asked how much the fare was.

"Couple o' bucks," he said.

"But this was much further than from the depot to campus."

"Really, I didn't notice."

"You're very kind and you really helped us out, we wouldn't have made it home if you hadn't stopped."

Turning in his seat, he smiled, "Does that mean you're starting to trust some of us folks out here?"

"Well, not everyone."

"You must mean your dates for the evening," he said.

"Yes sir."

"Where was that party anyhow? I might swing by and see if I can pick up a couple more fares."

Alice gave him the address as they got out of the cab. Judy dug in her wallet for money. She handed a five-dollar bill through the window.

"I'll get your change," he said.

"No sir," Judy said. "You really helped us. Thank you."

Leaning in the window, Judy kissed the stubble on his cheek, "Merry Christmas."

He grinned bashfully, "You're welcome... Merry Christmas to you too."

Four days later, Judy was buried in her books when Alice interrupted her, "You've got a phone call, Judy."

"Can you take a message; I've got to finish this paper."

"It's long distance."

The only long distance call would have to be from home, but it was the middle of the week. No one called unless it was something serious. She hoped her brother and sister were all right. They sometimes did crazy things. Then she felt a sense of relief. No, whatever happened, Dad could take care of it. He always did.

"Hello, this is Judy."

There was a pause before her mother spoke. Judy barely recognized her voice. "Hi Honey... I've got some bad news... your father had a heart attack..."

"Oh no... please no," Judy gasped in horror, "Will he be all right?"

"No..." Marianne choked. "He... he died..."

Judy slumped to the floor in shock as the phone fell from her hands. Her body convulsed with anguished sobbing as her world collapsed. It was several long minutes before her thoughts turned outward. She took a deep breath and picked up the phone.

Trying desperately to sound strong, she asked, "Are you all right, Mom? Do you have someone with you?"

"The kids are here... it was just such a shock."

"I'll be home as soon as I can... oh Mom, what are we going to do?"

7

A Sad Christmas

In spite of the holiday, not many people headed for Duluth in winter. It required several plane changes before Judy arrived in Duluth late the following night. Her childhood home felt cold and empty when her mother met her at the door and hugged her, "I'm glad you're here, Honey. I still have to make the funeral arrangements."

"I'll help, Mom. Dad would want us to be strong. We can do it together," Judy was at the limit of her emotional control.

Walking into the house together, they found Sarah standing in the hallway. She looked as if she had been crying since the day of the heart attack. Brian was sullen and sat in another room.

Judy tried to hide her own grief and concentrated on supporting her mother and siblings. The funeral was painful. When she watched her beloved father's coffin being lowered into the frozen ground, Judy lost her composure and wept.

Without her father's presence, Judy's home felt empty when they returned later that day. Their Christmas tree, filled with handmade ornaments accumulated over a lifetime, could not cheer them up. Beneath the tree were the brightly wrapped gifts as they had been every year as far back as Judy could remember. Marianne tried to cheer up her children.

"Brian, Honey, why don't you turn on the tree lights? It always makes things brighter."

"It's nothing but a dead tree... just like everything else around here!" he said and stalked from the room.

After the sad Christmas, Judy spent time alone with her mother, "I don't think I'll go back to NAU, Mom. It would be better if I stayed here and helped you."

"Sit down, Honey," Marianne said.

The time had come for a serious talk. She sat facing her daughter and held her hands, "Very few people in life have specific goals, and even fewer manage to attain any of them. All your life you've surpassed every goal you ever set for yourself. Give yourself credit for what you have accomplished."

"I should have chosen a different major, something I could use after graduation to get a decent job. Who's going to hire me? I don't have any marketable skills, and other than a few field trips, I don't have any experience."

"That's not the way to measure success, Judy," Marianne interrupted. "That's using someone else's standards. This is your life and your dream. Set your own standards.

"You're not a quitter, Judy. You never have been. You've got one more year before graduation. What's your next goal, a Master's degree?"

"Well, yes but..."

"Then do it!"

"But we can't afford that."

Marianne laughed, "That never stopped you before. Just make it happen."

"You make it sound so easy, Mom."

"It's not, and you know it isn't. It's hard work, give and take, negotiating every day of your life. Your father showed you that by example, and he lived it."

"I miss him, Mom," Judy said softly.

"I do too, Honey. Your father was the finest man I've ever known. He loved all of us unconditionally. He's still here... in my heart, and he always will be.

"I would have wanted more time, but things didn't turn out that way. I'm just thankful for the time we did have, and I've got you three kids. Some day you'll find a man like your Dad and you'll understand."

Judy laughed bitterly and told her mother how Craig tried to attack her, "Is that the way men are, Mom?"

"Of course not," Marianne replied. "There are men like your father and there are others like Craig. You're a smart girl, Honey. You know the difference, and you know what you want. It's going to be a pretty remarkable man that ends up being good enough for you."

Judy returned to NAU after New Years. The remainder of the semester passed rapidly. When summer came, she went home to work and save money for her senior year. At the end of summer, she boarded a plane for her return to Arizona.

Arriving back in Flagstaff several days early, Judy got her bike from Mary Jane and began searching for an apartment. After a number of unsuccessful attempts at finding a vacancy, Judy was becoming discouraged. She was leaving an apartment as two younger girls were arriving.

"No vacancies," Judy told them. "I already checked."

The petite brunette used her pen to eliminate another apartment on her list, "That's six so far. Have you got a list or are you just looking?"

"I've got a list, but it's getting shorter, and I'm starting to get tired. It looks as if everything close to campus is already full."

"Let's compare our lists so we don't waste a trip where one of us has already been. I'm Angie Romero from Douglas, Arizona. This is Beth Jablonski from Nebraska. We were in the same dorm last year."

"I'm Judy Whitby from Duluth, Minnesota. I rented a house with five other girls last year. I got an uncomfortable feeling about the landlord, so I thought I'd try an apartment."

"What's your major?" Angie asked.

"Anthropology," Judy replied. "I sometimes go on field trips so I'm not always home. What about you?"

"I'm a business major," Angie said.

"Political Science," Beth replied with a cocky grin. "I thought I might run for president."

Angie consulted the lists while they got acquainted. "Between the two of us we've sure eliminated a lot of apartments. What's this one at the bottom of your list with a question mark, Judy?"

"That one sounded pretty good, but it's out a ways. I thought I'd wait 'til after lunch to check that one out. I'm riding my bike."

"You're riding a bike, and you've already been to this many places!" Angie said with a surprised look.

"I try to conserve wherever I can. I've been able to manage so far."

"If this last one sounds so good, why don't you leave your bike here and take my car."

"Are you sure you don't mind?" Judy asked.

"I don't mind," Beth grinned. "It'll be nice to have someone else to talk to for a change!"

The apartment was on the opposite side of campus. Judy approached the manager, "I'm looking for a one bedroom or a studio for the school year. Do you have any vacancies?"

The manager shook her head, "I'm sorry, but we don't. We're pretty well filled up at this time."

Judy thanked her and started to leave.

Angie crossed another name off her list and started to follow Judy. They had just reached the door when the manager called to them, "Are you three together?"

"Well, we..." Beth said.

"Yes we are," Angie interrupted.

"We do have a three bedroom apartment left. Would you like to see it?"

After a quick consultation, they agreed they'd like to take a look. The manager grabbed a key and started toward the remaining vacancy. Before they reached the apartment, the manager learned the girls' names, where they were from, and their majors.

The complex was large, well lighted, and maintained. The vacancy was on the ground floor and not very far from the parking lot. Close to the door was a bicycle rack and Judy smiled. Now, if there was enough room for three of them and if they could afford it.

"This unit is furnished and all utilities are included except cable TV. Laundry facilities are in the common area, but you're expected to keep it clean," the manager said as she unlocked the door and showed them in.

The manager watched the three girls as they explored the apartment. When Judy went to the kitchen and gave it a thorough inspection, the manager was pleased. It was apparent that these three girls were serious students.

She handed the key to Judy, "You girls think it over. I have to get back to the office. Lock up when you're through and come back to see me."

Beth flopped down in a chair and smiled, "I like it!"

Angie stood by a desk and glanced out a window, "Me too. What about you, Judy, do you think the three of us could tolerate each other for a year?"

From the kitchen table, Judy looked up, "I take my studies pretty seriously, and I try to keep quiet. I'm not much for parties, at least on school nights. I had enough of that before."

"Do you have any objections to having a guy for dinner once in a while," Beth asked.

"As long as he's decent and no drinking or drugs," Judy said.

"Beth's pretty good about that," Angie chuckled. "If she gets carried away, we can throw her out!"

"I wonder if we can afford it. This is a pretty nice place," Judy said apprehensively.

"If we split it three ways and work out something for groceries we might be able to," Angie said. "Can you cook?"

Judy laughed, "I've got a brother and a sister. You can ask them!"

After locking the apartment, the three girls hurried back to the office. The manger explained rent and deposits. It fit the girls' budget and they completed the applications. The manager asked if they had local references.

Angie and Beth were in dorms the previous year and that wasn't much help. Judy's experience with the house and five other girls might not have made a favorable impression either.

"Is there anyone locally who knows you and could provide a reference?" the manager asked.

"There's a girl that I know pretty well," Judy said. "I used to spend holidays with her and her family."

"Do you have her number?"

"I don't have it with me, but it's in the phone book. Their name is Mellenkamp."

Raising an eyebrow, the manager picked up her phone, and dialed a number from memory.

"Hi Theresa, it's Louise," she said as soon as the call was answered.

"I'm fine... say, I have a young lady here that wants to rent an apartment. She says she knows Mary Jane. Her name's Judy..."

"Yep, she's a red head all right," Louise said and listened for several minutes with an occasional acknowledgement, then hung up.

"She said if you don't like the apartment, you can stay with them. I think that's good enough for me. You'll need to pay the first month and the deposit. How did you want to handle that?"

After a brief consultation, there were three checks on the manager's desk and the girls had their apartment. Angie did the driving and the rest of the day was spent moving in.

8

LIFE GOES ON

After the hearing, Rob lost contact with his children. It was rumored that Robert joined the Army. Patricia remained with her mother and they moved in with Fielding.

It was time to start over. A small home on the east side of Tucson and a new Toyota 4Runner started the process. Weekends were spent hiking and camping. Several nights a week, Rob attended Pima Community College. Getting an education beyond his high school diploma was important to him.

Except for an occasional barbeque with his closest friends, Rob spent his time alone. Although he seemed content with his solitary lifestyle, they worried about him. Gatherings at his new home, allowed them to keep an eye on him. It might have been because Rob grilled outstanding steaks. The wives handled the side dishes. They banished the men to the patio with their beer and did their magic in the kitchen.

"You know, man, I finally figured out why you go to them night classes," Dave was saying as they gathered around the grille. "I've seen the way those teeny boppers dress on campus. There ought to be a law against showing that much flesh, but you don't even seem to notice. Do you need your eyes examined, or are you studying to be a damned priest?"

Rob chuckled, "Did it ever occur to you I might want to get a degree so I could get a real job and wouldn't have to put up with guys like you."

Chuck shook his head and grinned while Rob turned the steaks.

"Naw, I'm serious man. Don't you think it's about time you started to check out the chicks? My old lady's got lots of friends she'd like to introduce you to."

"You're a lucky man, Dave. Your wife is a fine woman, but I don't know why she puts up with you. She could do a lot better."

Dave laughed, "I know, but don't you tell her that."

"Don't tell me what," Sandy asked as she and Samantha brought out a salad with tomatoes, lettuce, and avocado. There were chips with salsa, jicima, limes, margaritas, and more beer.

"He doesn't want me to tell you what I did with all the money I won on the damn lottery," Dave said as he snatched a piece of jicima.

"Well you certainly didn't spend it on charm school or English lessons!" Sandy laughed.

The heat of the day was following the sun down into the Tucson Mountains when the feast was cleared away. Subtle colors flowed in and out of the canyons in the Catalina Mountains, constantly changing hue in the fading light. It was peaceful. Rob looked at his friends and smiled. Sandy nestled under Dave's arm and looked content. Samantha sat next to Chuck and held his hand. That image of happily married couples reminded him of what was lacking in his life.

"It's been quite a while since your divorce, Rob," Samantha said. "Do you ever think about dating?"

"No, I believe all the good ones are already married. Ladies like you two are sure a lot different than Helen," Rob said. "She had me fooled from the start. I never suspected anything. This guy Fielding she's living with now was her attorney. He isn't much different than Giraldi, he just hasn't been caught yet."

"I'd be happy to drop a dime on him, buddy," Dave offered.

"That's not necessary," Rob said. "Guys like that usually go out of their way to screw up. When he does, she'll be out looking for someone else."

"You were pretty young when you got married, Rob," Sandy said. "You've changed a lot since then."

"You're a lot wiser than you give yourself credit for," Samantha added. "You know what's important to you, and you know what you want."

"She's right," Chuck said and put his arm over his wife's shoulder. "Both Dave and I could have been in that same situation, but we were fortunate enough to marry some pretty spectacular women. Someday you'll find a woman with the same interests as you."

"Just give her a chance," Samantha told Rob, but she was smiling at her husband. "That's what Chuck did."

Finding a decent hiking companion was disappointing. Very few shared Rob's enthusiasm and no one that could match his grueling pace when he hiked. Consequently, he did most of his hiking solo and exploring the 'Sky Islands' of southeast Arizona. Hiking alone, quiet and alert, he often saw wildlife that most experts claimed were either extinct or nonexistent in the area. In the Chiricahua Mountains, he watched a Mexican Jaguar feeding.

Hiking in the Tortolita Mountains north of Tucson one weekend, he made a startling discovery. Stopping for a drink of water, he noticed something out of place in the dirt at his feet. Stooping to pick up the oddly shaped piece, he discovered it was a broken piece of pottery. As he studied it, his curiosity grew and he wondered where it had come from. Searching the immediate area, he found several more pieces.

Discovering the pottery sherds added interest to his hikes, and before long, he had a sizeable collection of various sized pieces. The Amerind Foundation east of Tucson helped him identify what he had collected, but they warned him of the laws that protected Native American artifacts. When he found an intact Hohokam pot partially buried in a dry riverbed, the temptation was too great. He knew that the next hiker in the area would take it and try to sell it. This artifact was too priceless to be lost to an uncaring retail environment. He made notes of the surrounding area with map coordinates and detailed sketches. Carefully packing the precious artifact, he took it home, built an airtight display case, and put it in his bedroom closet. As soon as he could, he would deliver it to the Amerind.

Bit by bit he increased his library of Native American reference books, and added courses to his studies at Pima Community College. The business courses were boring, but necessary. The Native American studies were fascinating.

In the summer of 1992, Rob worried that he was getting soft, forgetting skills that served him well in the war years. He wondered if he was still capable of living off the land, and traveling long distances undetected.

There was a way to find out.

With two weeks' vacation, he left the 4Runner in his garage and took a bus to Truth or Consequences, New Mexico. Getting off the bus, he made his way west across Interstate 25 and into the Gila National forest on foot. Ten days and 300 miles later, he slipped back into his home unnoticed. He was pleased with himself. He wasn't getting soft after all.

"What did you do on your vacation?" Dave asked when Rob returned to work on Monday. "You're lookin' pretty smug."

"I went for a hike," Rob replied with a satisfied grin.

"No shit, I figured that much. You couldn't have gone very far though; I went by your place and saw the 4Runner was still there. So, where did you go?"

"You wouldn't believe me if I told you."

"Try me..."

"I took a bus to T or C and walked home," Rob replied casually.

"You're right, I don't believe you," Dave laughed. "I figured you'd have one of those teeny boppers from Pima hidden away in your house."

"If I did, you'd be the first to know."

Humming softly to himself, he raised the hood on the new Mercedes and went to work. Rob was content, he was finally beginning to enjoy his life once more.

9

MANNY'S EMPIRE

Douglas, Arizona was too confining for someone with Manuel Jesus Ortega's ambition. Deciding that a large metro area would provide better opportunities, Manny moved to Phoenix. The large population base provided access to many more customers for the product and services he provided. Pretty, young, college girls without money and a habit didn't object to his system of barter.

As Manny's business and profits increased, so did his ambition. He didn't think competing with the large, established networks would be a problem. Phoenix was a big city. There was room for all of them.

Then he received an anonymous phone call.

The message was polite and explicit. There was *not* room for all of them.

Manny began exploring alternatives. Connections on the supply side of his business were still good, but he needed his own market. His quest led him north to Flagstaff where there was only one small time dealer who had other interests, and a need for ready cash. That was a good place to start.

The large house and well-kept grounds were surrounded by an impressive stone wall.

A distinguished looking, middle-aged man answered the door, "Mr. Baumgartner, my name is Manuel Ortega. I understand you know of secure rental properties where one might not be disturbed."

"I'm sorry, but my rentals are only for students."

"I'm not a student," Manny said. "I'm a businessman like yourself, and I'm in a position to invest in your operation."

"I don't need any help," Baumgartner answered indignantly and started to close the door.

"I'll be precise," Manny interrupted. "You don't have a reliable source for a certain product, and you're currently in need of financial assistance. I'm able to provide both."

Baumgartner hesitated and looked carefully at his visitor. The name was familiar in certain select circles, "Maybe you should come inside so we can talk."

Once inside, Baumgartner explained his operation, "I have a few houses that I rent to co-eds at reasonable rates. Some of my tenants like to experiment with drugs. On a small campus like this, that can create a problem. If the wrong people discovered their drug use, they could be removed from campus. Those girls require a discreet source."

"I can be discreet," Baumgartner smiled. "Sometimes the need of my clients exceeds their ability to pay. In addition to being discreet, I can be generous. I offer them a simple solution. For a few hours work in my studio, I'm willing to forgive their debt."

Manny was intrigued, "What kind of studio?"

"I make movies. Lots of people like watching pornographic movies with young college girls," he grinned. "My tenants are willing to provide that sort of entertainment in exchange for a few drugs."

Manny was pleased. There were details to be worked out, but by appealing to Baumgartner's need for ready cash and a safe supplier of drugs, Manny took on a new venture. Moving to Flagstaff and keeping a low profile satisfied the Phoenix people.

Through Baumgartner's connections, Manny met Hector Gonzales. As a junior on campus, he was a bright young business major. Hector could prove to be valuable. He knew how to transfer large sums of cash without attracting attention. Hector's new car and spending money became part of his new 'Ortega scholarship'.

10

JUDY'S SENIOR YEAR

Her senior year was a blur of hard work and new discoveries. Field trips into the surrounding countryside fascinated her. Native American history was no longer stories in books. She was walking where they walked and touching the soil that provided the ancient ones sustenance.

In a cooperative effort with the Museum of Northern Arizona, her class was working an area close to Walnut Canyon National Monument. Cold and covered with dirt, she sifted soil samples, determined to find something of value in her carefully staked area.

"What are you wasting your time with that for," one of her classmates laughed as he stood above her. "There ain't no pottery sherds in that. It's just black dirt!"

Brushing her grubby hair from her face with an even dirtier hand, she glared at the intruder, "If you paid attention during lectures, or read something besides Playboy, you'd know this is too deep for sherds."

She transferred a handful of dirt into an empty container, "This layer is charcoal! If there was any pottery here, it would be closer to the surface."

"What do you mean charcoal, it's probably just volcanic pumice," he sneered.

Judy shook her head in exasperation, "If you can't tell the difference by now, you're wasting your time, my time, and Professor Shreveport's time. Go back to your own area and leave me alone!"

"Damned amateurs," she muttered under her breath as he stomped away. She labeled the container and set it beside several other carefully marked containers. Digging in her pocket, she took out her notebook and a pencil and carefully recorded her findings.

The leaves were turning, and fall was in the air, "Are you going home for Thanksgiving," Angie asked.

"No," Judy replied. "I can't afford to go home. Mary Jane's family invited me to spend Thanksgiving with them. I'll wait until Christmas."

Beth's eyes lit up and she grinned, "Is that because Mary Jane has a cute brother?"

"No, Beth, nothing like that. Her family always invites me over for the holidays."

"I can't figure that out, Judy," Beth continued. "You haven't been on a date all semester. I know at least a dozen guys that want to ask you out."

"You go out all the time, Beth. Maybe she's more selective than you are," Angie teased.

"I can't help it if the guys find me irresistible," Beth chuckled. "And I'm not afraid to let you meet them either. Why don't you ever bring your dates to the apartment so we can meet them, Angie?"

"Because you're so irresistible," Angie replied with a twinkle in her eye. Then she looked at Judy, "She's right you know. A pretty girl like you has to have a guy somewhere. Is there someone back in Duluth?"

"No, I really don't have time for that," Judy said. "I have to keep my grades up for my scholarship. All the guys I've met just want to party or talk about themselves, and I haven't met one yet that really likes the outdoors."

Beth laughed, "None of them can keep up with you, Judy. You run up those hills faster than most people come down! It must be because you ride that old bike of yours everywhere."

"My bike keeps me in shape," Judy said. She was quiet for several minutes before she looked up, "You know, the other thing that's important to me is meeting at least one man that isn't afraid to show a little respect for women. The last man that took time to hold a door for me was my father."

"Then maybe you should date somebody's father," Beth teased.

"No, Beth, she has a point," Angie said and turned to Judy. "I respect your standards, Judy. Too many of us settle for far less," she added quietly and went back to her studies.

Angie's reply aroused Judy's curiosity. Was there a deeper meaning to her comment?

With excellent grades and three years of classes, Judy's strong character showed. She had her own ideas, and disagreed with some of the theories that were being taught. When she questioned Professor Shreveport during his lecture, he responded harshly.

"That's the way it is!" he stated. "If you disagree, then you better be able to prove your point! I've been doing this for almost thirty years, and I know what I'm talking about! When you've got thirty years experience then you can disagree with the facts!"

"I don't believe all the facts are available yet," Judy replied defensively. "More research needs to be done..."

"Then you get out there and do the research," he interrupted. "Until then, sit down and be quiet. You're disrupting my class!"

She slumped into her seat while an ominous silence filled the room.

The confrontation with her professor was a serious matter. It got worse when she was told to report to the office of the department head. That was not a good sign. Dr. Kenmore had a reputation for being strict. He didn't tolerate any lack of respect for his staff. Would this incident prevent her from graduating?

It was a cold blustery day as Judy pedaled her way to the office of the chair of the Anthropology department. She was apprehensive. Would he dismiss her from class, and suspend her from school? The stern look of the secretary as she directed Judy to a chair didn't help.

The wait seemed interminable, and when she was finally told to go in, she braced herself for the worst. Dr. Kenmore's desk was clear except for the folder he was perusing. One wall was filled with diplomas and certificates of recognition, another wall contained an extensive library. Behind Dr. Kenmore, the gray gloom filtered through the window.

Dr. Kenmore looked up over his glasses, "Have a seat, Miss Whitby," he ordered.

Taking a seat facing his desk, Judy suddenly felt very small and insignificant. She clasped her hands in her lap and realized they were perspiring.

"I understand you created an incident during Professor Shreveport's lecture."

"Yes, sir," Judy replied nervously. "I disagreed with what he was saying and spoke out of line. I meant no disrespect, sir."

"What was the subject of his lecture?"

"It had to do with the Clovis people, where they came from and when. He said they came across the land bridge to Alaska and stayed in the west."

"That is one currently accepted theory. Do you disagree with that?"

"I don't know, sir... I just wondered if maybe they were in other areas," she said meekly. "I was wrong to speak out that way. I don't have Professor Shreveport's experience."

Dr. Kenmore was obviously displeased with her answer, "So you have this theory and nothing to back it up, but you were willing to disrupt his lecture and then wouldn't defend your position?"

"I already disrupted Dr. Shreveport's lecture... I'm sorry, I shouldn't have interrupted him."

Looking up from the folder on his desk, Dr. Kenmore looked at Judy severely, "Is it your impression that everything in our field has already been discovered?"

"No sir... I believe we're still learning about the past."

"If you believe that, then you should be willing to defend your position! You're going to face critics much tougher than Shreveport if you continue in your chosen field!"

The severity of his rebuke startled her. She stared at him uncertainly.

He slapped the folder on his desk, "You're a brilliant student, Miss Whitby, and your reason for being here at the University is to get an education. Contrary to what some people will tell you, the answers aren't all in books! There's more to Anthropology than digging in the dirt for old bones or artifacts. Eventually you're going to have to piece that information together and share your discoveries and opinions. What you're going to find is that in this field most of your peers will be one hell of a lot tougher on you than Shreveport was in class.

"He discussed the situation with me. He was disappointed the way you handled yourself, not because you disagreed, but because you didn't stand your ground! He expected more from you than that."

This revelation shocked Judy. It was not what she anticipated. Was it possible that Dr. Shreveport had been testing her?

"You expressed your opinion in that class, Miss Whitby. That's a safe place to vent unproved theories. You'd never get away with it among your peers without some pretty sound evidence. I'm curious to know how you arrived at your point of view."

Hesitantly, Judy fingered the pendant that hung around her neck. It was her only link to her theory. She took a deep breath, removed the pendant, stood, and placed it on Dr. Kenmore's desk.

"That's all I have, but I think it's significant," she said.

Dr. Kenmore picked up the pendant and after scrutinizing it carefully, said, "This is definitely Clovis, and the setting is some of the finest craftsmanship I've ever seen. Where did you buy this?"

Questioning one of her most treasured memories of her father was like a physical blow. She forgot that Dr. Kenmore was the head of the department, with a brilliant mind and numerous books and publications to his credit. Her anger and frustration were building. It had gone far enough! At this point, she was going to stand her ground.

"I didn't buy it!" Judy stated angrily with her feet firmly planted. "I found that Clovis point when I was eight years old and my father made the necklace for me for Christmas."

He looked at the necklace again before he continued, "So you think that because you found this somewhere beyond the accepted range of Clovis people that it means anything? Where did you find it?"

"Voyageurs National Park in northern Minnesota," she replied without hesitation.

"How do you know some tourist didn't drop it?"

"No!" Judy snapped. "It was in a bank of gravel, and you can see that it's worn from tumbling."

"Did you see any signs of bone or hide or anything else that might have indicated the presence of people?" he asked.

"Of course not! There's no telling what was uncovered when the glaciers receded all across the Midwest. It's the same all over this continent; catastrophic events have destroyed so much we'll never know for sure. There's sites everywhere that are being destroyed today by what people think of as progress. We don't even know for sure what's under Lake Mead let alone what was lost when, or if, the comet created the Gulf of Mexico. What about when Yellowstone erupted, or Lake Agassiz washed out to sea? That's all ancient history, so we can only guess at what really happened. The truth is in the ground where those Native Americans walked and in the stories and customs handed down through generations. The real truth is in the family values of traditional Native Americans."

When Judy paused for a breath, Dr. Kenmore was leaning back in his chair, watching her, and smiling. Defending her position, expounding her beliefs came out in a torrent of words without pause. She was afraid she had gone too far.

"I'm sorry sir," she said with a look of chagrin.

"There's no evidence to back up any of that, is there," he said pleasantly.

"Absence of evidence does not mean evidence of absence," Judy blurted out and this time Dr. Kenmore laughed.

"You're a fan of Carl Sagan too, I see."

Judy felt her cheeks burning, "Yes sir... he isn't afraid to question what many people accept as truth."

"Obviously you aren't afraid to do that either, Miss Whitby. What are your plans after graduation?"

Judy retrieved her pendant and sunk back into her chair, "I don't have any idea right now, sir. I don't have any marketable skills and I don't have any experience."

"What about graduate school?"

"I'd like to do that sir, but we can't afford it. My Mom is a widow, and I have a brother and sister."

"Have you looked into scholarships?"

"No sir, I haven't. I should, but I'm not even sure where to start."

"That's unacceptable," he said firmly and took several sheets of paper from the folder. "Here's a list of available scholarships and other sources of funding for gifted students. Pick up the applications from my secretary on your way out. Take them home, fill them out, and return them to me before the end of the month. I'll arrange for letters of recommendation from your professors. Do you have any questions?"

Judy stared at Dr. Kenmore in disbelief. "Why are you doing this for me?" she asked.

"You're a pain in the ass according to most of your professors, Miss Whitby," he said with a grin. "But you're also brilliant, meticulous, and very refreshing. In some ways, we envy you. We can't rock the proverbial boat, or openly question our colleagues. My career would be at stake if I did, but you can. You'll be ridiculed and often laughed at for your radical ideas... even when you're right."

He stood and closed the folder on his desk, "The way you presented your opinion in here today is what Professor Shreveport hoped to elicit from you during his lecture. That kind of heated exchange would have ignited the spark of curiosity in an entire class, but you missed the opportunity."

Judy stared at Dr. Kenmore with her mouth open. She was stunned, "Thank you sir," she said in an unsteady voice and reached out to shake his hand.

She was partway out the door with the list of scholarships in her hand when he stopped her, "Miss Whitby..."

"Yes sir?"

"About the Clovis people."

"Yes sir?"

"Your views are absolutely correct."

On the long, cold ride, back to her apartment Judy's attitude began to change. Dr. Kenmore warned her about the difficulties she would face if she continued in her field. He also alluded to the respect she had earned from him and his staff. Best of all, he made it very plain that he expected her to continue her education, at least through a master's program.

Two days later, she returned the completed scholarship applications, along with a cover letter and stamped envelope for each of them.

With her newfound confidence, Judy excelled in her classes. No longer hesitant to support her theories, she argued long and loudly to prove her point. Judy was still 'a pain in the ass', as Dr. Kenmore said, and her professors agreed with that observation... but they respected her. She was making dead, dry, history into an exciting, living thing, and it was contagious. Many of her fellow students gladly paid her to tutor them.

In the spring of 1992 with her mother in attendance, Judy graduated Summa Cum Laude with her degree in anthropology and a full scholarship for her Master's program at NAU.

Judy's immediate future was secure. Sarah and Brian could both plan for college. Their mother felt the relief of one less financial burden.

A family outing was in order to celebrate. With two canoes and provisions, the Whitby family spent ten days feeding mosquitoes and exploring Voyageurs National Park.

11

Patricia To NAU

The phone call from Helen was a surprise, "My friend and I are going to take a vacation, and we'll be gone for the summer," she said. "If you take care of Patricia you could spend some quality time with your daughter."

"I'd like that. I miss her," Rob replied, cautious about this change of heart.

"She decided to go up to NAU. You could take her up to Flagstaff and get her settled in."

Now it made sense. If Rob took Patricia to college, it was a way of getting around the court order and into his pocketbook. Rob wouldn't deny his daughter. Books, tuition, dorm fees, and incidentals would be expensive.

When Patricia moved in for the summer, it was a disaster. Late night conversations with her friends, TV, and loud music were more important than time with her Dad. Much to her dismay, Rob curtailed her association with her more questionable friends.

By the end of summer, Rob was frustrated. Teaching values was impossible without a receptive audience.

The drive to Flagstaff was cool at best. As soon as she got into his 4Runner, Patricia plugged earphones into her Walkman and ignored him. The silence gave Rob time to think about his own plans, night classes at Pima Community College, and hiking or camping on weekends. NAU was close to many of the finest National Parks offering unsurpassed outdoor recreational opportunities.

Once they arrived in Flagstaff, Patricia put aside her music and began giving directions, "I've got to meet my friends so we can start planning things. You just drive where I tell you and don't interfere with us. I've got stuff to buy so you'll have to come along."

Rob ignored her insolence. He smiled as he drove. Flagstaff was definitely a college town. The streets, stores, and campus were crowded with throngs of young people checking things out and making or renewing friendships. He watched the young men watching the girls, and the girls making sure they were being watched. The air was crisp and clean. Beyond the city, Mount Humphreys dominated the landscape.

By the end of the day, Patricia was registered, had her class schedules, her books and a place in the dorm of her choosing. Rob felt relieved. He found Patricia with a group of young people.

"Are you about ready to get on the road, Honey?" he asked.

"No, I invited some of my friends to go to dinner with us," Patricia announced. "There's a really cool place where all the kids hang out."

The restaurant was packed with noisy students, poor service, and marginal food. When they finished eating Rob asked once again, "We've got a long drive ahead of us and it's getting late. Are you ready to go?"

"I decided I'm going to stay in the dorm tonight and hang out with some of my friends."

"I thought we agreed to go back home tonight and bring the rest of your things up later."

"What kind of a father are you anyhow?" she snapped. "You should be happy that I'm making friends and getting settled in at my new school!"

Rob took a deep breath and replied, "All right, Patricia, if you'll just give me the number of the dorm I can call you in the morning and we can plan the return trip."

She rolled her eyes in exasperation and looked at him with scorn, "You should know I don't have the number. You can look it up in the phone book, but don't you call too early!"

"All right then, can I drop you somewhere?"

"I told you before, Margie has a car. Weren't you paying attention? You never listen to me! We'll manage just fine without you."

It was an obvious dismissal, waiting for him to leave. Rob let out his breath slowly, controlling his irritation, "I'm tired and not in the mood to argue in front of your friends."

He picked up the check and nodded to her friends, "You kids enjoy your evening. Good night." He left them and melted into the crowd, ignoring the parting comments.

Outside it was quiet, peaceful, and considerably less hostile. He took a deep breath of refreshing mountain air and looked up toward the inviting silhouette of mountains now a dark shape against the evening sky. The silence was broken by a group of young people that followed him out.

"I don't understand why you put up with that bullshit, man," one of them said. "If that was my kid I'd slap the shit out of her."

They weren't freshmen. There was a relaxed and confident air about them.

"That wouldn't have accomplished anything," Rob said. "Besides, it's peaceful out here in the fresh air. She has to contend with herself no matter where she goes."

"I don't get it."

"I can always get away from people like her. She can't."

There were grins and a few chuckles, "That's cool, man. Hey, you want to join us for a few beers?"

"I appreciate the offer, but I think you'd enjoy it more without me, on one condition."

"What's that?"

"Give me a rain check. I'd like to get some input on local trails up here. I'll spring for the beer in trade for the information."

One of them tore a sheet of paper out of his notebook and scribbled a name and phone number on it, "Here, I'm Jack Randolph. Next time you're up, call me. I know a few of the trails here."

"Thanks, Jack. Rob Simpson," he replied and extended his hand while he gave Jack a careful look.

The younger man was several inches taller than Rob, broad shouldered, lean, and wiry with the appearance of one toughened by hard work. He had an unruly mop of dark hair and his face had the rugged look of one who spent most of his time outdoors. Even at his young age, there were creases around his eyes from long hours looking into the sun. His face was pleasant; someone content with himself, confident, and good-natured. He shook Rob's hand and looked up, "That's some grip. You must work for a living!"

Rob nodded and shook the tingling from his hand, "I guess you work too... I'm a mechanic, but it's tough on the bones and joints; makes you old quick. You kids have the right idea. Get your education and make a decent living."

"You got a place to stay tonight?" Jack asked.

"Not yet, but I'll find something... I hope."

"Lots of people in town so most of the motels are full; you'll have to try someplace away from campus. If you can't, we'll be at 'Rooster's'. I've got a couch."

"I appreciate that," Rob said and went to find a motel.

From a nearby table, Judy and her roommates observed the confrontation between the father and his daughter. They listened in amazement after he departed and the criticism continued.

Judy slid her chair back, "I think I'll go over there and start that little twit's education tonight. She needs to learn how to treat her father with respect."

"I don't think he handled that very well," Angie said. "A father shouldn't be that submissive."

"Maybe we should try to catch him and tell him that all kids aren't like that," Judy said. "He should understand that we thought he handled the situation pretty well. He could have created a scene."

"You might think that, but I don't think it would do any good," Beth said. "He just took all that abuse without a sound."

Angie grinned, "If you can catch him in the parking lot, you can ask him if he's a wuss!"

"I don't think I'll put it quite that way," Judy replied, "But we should at least talk to him."

Gathering their belongings, they started for the door. Judy nudged Patricia's chair as she passed. The contents of Patricia's drink dumped into her lap. Sputtering a string of expletives, Patricia spun around to see who had done this to her but saw only the mob of students.

Outside, the laughing trio looked at one another again, "Did you do that?" Beth asked.

"No, did you?" Angie replied turning to Judy.

Judy's wide-eyed look was one of pure innocence, "Not me. Do you think I'd do something so mean to a nice girl like that?"

There was no sign of Patricia's Dad in the parking lot. It looked as if the answer to their question would remain unanswered. The three piled into Angie's car and started toward their apartment, but the discussion continued.

"I thought the way he acted showed a lot of restraint," Judy said.

"Well, he sure is cute," Angie said.

"Yeah, and he's got a nice ass!" Beth laughed.

"Now there's a guy I might go out with if he asked me," Judy said.

Angie was astonished, "You haven't been on a date in at least two years, Judy, and it's not for a lack of offers."

"He's old enough to be your father," Beth interrupted. "Besides, he's married isn't he?"

"I thought the little twit said he was divorced. She said something about her mother being off with her current boyfriend," replied Judy.

"If he's divorced, a hunk like that must have lots of girlfriends. Wuss or not, he's still a good looking guy," Angie added.

"Maybe so," Beth interrupted, "But even as cute as he is, he's got no guts if he'd put up with that kind of abuse in public."

"He's still the one that brought her to campus and spent the day running her and her friends around," Judy said in his defense.

"Besides, he took them to dinner and tolerated all that abuse without creating a scene. He didn't need to do any of that."

"He's probably just a hen pecked sissy and that's why he's divorced."

"I don't buy that. There's something about him."

"Yeah, he's got a nice ass!" Beth laughed.

"No, it's more than that. I think you two have him figured wrong."

"Well, if you're so sure, how are you going to prove it?"

"I'll just ask him," Judy replied confidently.

"You won't do that," Beth laughed in reply. "I'll bet being in the same restaurant with him tonight is as close as you'll ever get!"

"I'll have to go along with Beth on that, Judy. You don't just walk up to a complete stranger and ask him if he's a wuss! Besides," she added, "You haven't even been out with a guy as long as I've known you. Would you even know how to act?"

"Maybe not, but I *will* talk to him. I can promise you that. After I talk to him I'll know who's right about him."

"But he's so old."

Judy glared at her roommate, "That's just numbers, Beth. Age doesn't mean anything when it's the right person."

"Well it may not matter to you, Honey," Beth said, "but I'm sure it's something he'd be thinking about if you threw yourself at him!"

"I don't have any intention of throwing myself at him!" Judy retorted. "I still believe you two are wrong about him, and I intend to prove it to you!"

Angie was quiet before she added her opinion, "So what happens if you talk to this guy and he actually does ask you out or something?"

"I don't know... I didn't think about that."

Angie laughed, "Well, that's one thing about you Judy, when you make up your mind about something you just don't quit!"

When they were back at their apartment and settled in for the night, Judy lay in her bed thinking. There was something about him that intrigued her. He was cute and he did have a nice ass, but there was Angie's comment about their age difference.

What if he did ask me out...but then, what possible reason could he have to consider such a thing?

Then she stopped.

Dad was much older than Mom when they got married and they were happily married right up to the day he died. Older men often date younger women even if it is just to feed their ego. Well, it certainly couldn't hurt to give it a try. What is there to lose?

The following day she heard about his conversation with Jack Randolph and his friends outside the restaurant. He asked about hiking. That gave Judy an idea. She could use that as an introduction to get him talking. She found out where Patricia's dorm was and discovered that it was the same dorm as one of her friends. She left word with the friend to call her as soon as Patricia returned with her Dad.

It was after nine when Patricia's belongings were loaded into Rob's vehicle. He finally coaxed her out of bed and into the vehicle to begin the trip.

"I've got to work tomorrow, Patricia. We need to get you settled in so I can get home before it's too late."

"What about me? I'm the one that has to do all the work. My room is so small and there'll be three other girls in there! No place to invite my friends and I have to figure out where to put my posters and pictures. You should have found a bigger dorm, or made them let me get my own apartment."

"It's school policy for freshmen to live in the dorms for their first year. I can't do much about that."

She started up again once they were on the road, "This is too early, I wanted to sleep in!"

"You can sleep while I drive."

"I could have driven myself if you got me another car to replace the one that got wrecked. Now I'm going to have to beg people for rides or walk. That isn't fair!"

"That little accident of yours more than doubled our insurance. You should have had a designated driver or at least been a little less aggressive."

Patricia had her own version of her accident. It was one that differed considerably from the police report, but Rob had to listen to her views once more. When she finally ran out of things to grumble about, she plugged her earphones into her Walkman, turned away and curled up to snooze.

There was a park-like atmosphere on campus. Patricia's dorm at NAU was in a two-story building surrounded by trees and other similar buildings with broad sidewalks between them that wound to the parking lots.

"Drop me off here," Patricia said. "There isn't any parking place close to the dorm, and I don't want to walk. I'll open my room so you can put my stuff away."

Rob found an empty parking place at the far end of the parking lot. When he arrived at her room with the first armload of belongings, the door was open but Patricia was nowhere to be seen. He deposited the first load on her bed, closed the door, and went back for more. It was going to be a long day.

It wasn't until the third trip that she met him at the door, "Why did you just pile my stuff up like that? Now I'm going to have to sort through these things all by myself!"

"You should stay in here and keep an eye on your things, Patricia. There's lots of people roaming about and you wouldn't want to have anything stolen."

Without waiting for her reply, he went after another load. Returning to his vehicle, he saw that groups of boys from other dorms were helping the girls carry their belongings into the building. Patricia's friends were the same group that had been to dinner with them. Their primary function was listening to her complaints, hanging on every word, and nodding in agreement.

When he brought in the last load, he found that most of her things still lay where he put them. Patricia was busy showing her collection of music and pictures to her friends.

"That's the last of it," he said.

She glanced up with an annoyed look, "It's about time." Then she brightened, "Hey, Dad, can I have some money? We want to go out for dinner tonight. I told them I'd treat!"

Against his better judgment, Rob reached into his pocket and handed her several bills. Her allowance was certainly ample, so he tried to justify this with the idea that it would be her first night alone on a new campus. He knew he was kidding himself. He turned to go and then stopped at the door.

"You take care of yourself, Honey, I love you," he said.

Without looking up she simply said, "Yeah, bye," and went back to her friends.

As soon as he was back outside, he looked at the mountain just now fading blue in the afternoon sun. He took a deep breath of the cool mountain air and smiled. It was a long difficult summer but now there was relief in sight.

He passed groups of happy young people. Many of them nodded politely or said hello. They were a gregarious and content lot. Like Jack Randolph and his group. By the time he reached his vehicle he was thinking ahead to the opportunity of getting back to hiking. He leaned against the rear of his 4Runner with his arms folded across his chest, relaxed, and enjoying the cooler air of the high country. He looked at the mountain once again, and breathed deeply. It was an area he always wanted to explore.

In the dorm room, Patricia watched through the window until her Dad passed out of sight. Turning to her friends, she held up the money her Dad left and laughed, "Finally! He's gone. What a relief! You have no idea what I had to put up with all summer," she said.

"No privacy and him watching everything I did just to make sure I didn't have any fun. All right girls, party time! Who knows where we can score some grass?"

One of the girls knew someone that had connections. Patricia gave her some money and sent her on her way with instructions to bring the other girl back with her. What could it hurt to have another girl at her party?

"It doesn't take you long to find out how to get things done, does it, Patricia?" one of her roommates asked.

"A few questions, a little money, and things happen the way I want them to," Patricia grinned. "Nobody messes with me. It may take a while with some people, but I always win in the end."

"You sure don't like your father very much do you?"

"He doesn't matter. He's just another man. I'm stuck with him because he's family, but that's all right. Did you see how easily he parted with the money, and took us all to dinner the other night? He might wear the pants, but between my mother and me, we're in control."

"How do you get away with all that? My father would slap me silly if I did half the stuff you do."

"He wouldn't dare lay a hand on me!" Patricia snapped. "He's been pulling that Daddy shit all my life. All I have to do is turn on a little charm and he does whatever I want. "

"If that's so, why did you choose NAU? I would think you'd want to be closer to him if he's that easy."

"He was starting to meddle in my affairs. I had some good contacts in Tucson, but they were getting nervous when he started asking questions. We'll get our own network going up here and things'll be fine. You just stick with me and you'll see!"

12

MEETING JUDY

"Hey, aren't you Patricia Simpson's Dad?" a cheery voice asked. Rob tensed perceptibly and was alert for what might happen next. Being associated with Patricia usually meant trouble in one form or another. He turned slowly, "Yes," he replied.

It was a tall, good-looking co-ed straddling her bicycle. She was wearing sunglasses, a light sweater, shorts, and sandals. Long auburn hair glowed in the sunlight. She had an open, friendly smile, and long lovely legs. She was older, not one of those immature kids like Patricia and her friends.

His eyes did a quick appraisal from head to toe and she shifted uneasily on her feet. His eyes lingered for an instant where every other guy's eyes paused when they looked at a girl. Like other girls in that situation, he saw the slight straightening of her shoulders. It took no longer than the blink of an eye, but it formed a permanent and unforgettable image.

She had done that very thing when he turned to face her. He was certainly different up close and face-to-face, wearing a polo shirt, jeans and no jacket. He was much taller than her first impression, over six feet, with broad shoulders, long, well-muscled arms and large hands, sturdy and fit, with a big chest and a slender waist. His blonde hair was a little long for someone his age but it looked natural on him. He had a strong, handsome face, and piercing blue eyes. There was much more to this man than she first assumed. Maybe even a little intimidating.

With a smile that almost radiated confidence, she extended her hand, "Hi, I'm Judy Whitby!"

It was a contagious smile, and he couldn't ignore the offer of a handshake. He leaned forward and took her hand in his. She had a firm grip, firmer than he would have expected, but he detected a slight trembling.

"Hi, yourself," he replied and felt a grin tugging at the corners of his mouth. "I'm Rob Simpson."

"I heard you were interested in finding out about some of the trails in the area."

News does travel fast. Wonder where she heard that.

He gestured toward the mountain and replied cautiously, "I planned to get up there and get a feel for the country."

"It's beautiful," she grinned. "I know a few good day hikes that are short and aren't too strenuous. That way you could get acclimated to the elevation before taking on some of the longer hikes."

She didn't say anything about me being older than her and probably not up to the exertion. She only mentioned the elevation and that's legitimate. Somehow, she learned that I'm a flatlander. I wonder what else she knows about me.

"Do you hike a lot?" he asked.

"Not as much as I'd like. I'm pretty busy with school and it's hard to find somebody that likes to hike and can handle themselves. Good hiking companions are few and far between."

Then her confidence flickered. Her comment sounded too presumptuous.

He grinned, "That almost sounds like an invitation."

Something on her bike suddenly required her attention, and she looked down, "Well... maybe... sort of..."

He looked at her again, more carefully this time. She was slender, and looked like an athlete. Those long, lovely legs were sturdy and well muscled, suitable for hiking, and she had a firm grip as evidenced by the handshake. Satisfied that she might actually be able to handle the outdoors, he waited for her to continue. She fidgeted and seemed nervous, slow in replying. Was she playing games?

"Take off your sunglasses," he said.

"Why?" she asked, looking up defiantly.

"I want to see who you are," he answered looking at her with a steady gaze.

Removing her sunglasses, a quick toss of her head settled long auburn curls. Beautiful blue green eyes with a hint of nervousness returned his gaze.

His quick, measured look probed the very depths of her character searching for truth or deception. For a moment, there was a noticeable twinge of self-consciousness. Rob liked what he saw. She might be nervous, but there was no doubt that this young lady was incapable of deceit. With that single piercing look, he learned more about her than most of her friends knew after years of friendship.

"Are you asking me to go hiking with you sometime?" It was direct a question that left little hedging room.

She didn't need it. "Yes," she replied boldly, looking directly at him.

Her eyes showed that she wasn't kidding or playing games. They also showed that she was in unfamiliar territory, not really that bold.

Rob laughed pleasantly and continued, "I guess you are serious aren't you. Well, that's fine with me because you're right; it is tough to find a good hiking companion. Are you?"

"Am I what?"

"A good hiking companion?" he asked with a friendly smile.

"I can keep up, I know the area, and I'm good company."

It was a good answer. It was honest without bragging and he liked that. "Am I?" he asked.

"Are you what?"

"A good hiking companion?"

"You'll do," she said with a grin.

"Well, Judy, you are the bold one aren't you."

"Not always," she replied quietly and looked back at her bike.

Rob felt his tension draining away as they talked. It must have been the same for her. Judy was a bright, friendly girl, easy to talk to. She didn't hesitate to tell him about her family and her reasons for attending NAU. Rob leaned easily against the tailgate of his 4Runner with his arms across his chest finally enjoying a conversation without hostility. She stood straddling her bike.

"Would you like a cup of coffee or something?" he asked. It slipped out easily and naturally.

There was a hint of surprise in her eyes, "Are you buying?" she asked cautiously.

"I thought I might."

"No thanks."

"What if I let you buy?"

"Nope, only if we go Dutch," she replied and he could tell she was relieved to have a more comfortable alternative, one that didn't require any commitment.

"Well, Judy Whitby you drive a hard bargain. So, do we walk, do I follow you, do you follow me, do we leave your bike here and come back for it, or do we throw it in the back and go together?"

"Will you drop me off at my apartment afterwards?"

"As long as it's in Arizona," he kidded.

It was her turn to laugh and he liked the way her eyes squinted and her nose wrinkled when she did.

"Of course it is, silly. I live in town, but it's getting late and if we have coffee it will be dark before I get home. I don't have a light on my bike."

"Why not?" he asked as he opened the tailgate and lifted her bike in.

He noticed that she watched him with a bit of apprehension. Was she concerned without her means of transportation... or escape?

"Cheapskate, I guess. The light I mean."

"Or you can't afford one?" he asked as he closed the tailgate. Leading the way to the passenger side, he opened the door for her. She paused and looked at him in surprise before she got in. Rob went around and found his door ajar. He was equally surprised.

"Both," she answered as he opened his door. "The light I mean. Hey, thanks for opening the door. Guys don't generally do that anymore."

Rob leaned on the door looking at her without getting in, "I do... all the time," he said seriously. "I don't have any doubts about you or any other woman's ability to open a door for herself. I do it out of respect. You ride with me, I open the doors."

From the corner of his eye he caught a smug grin as he got in, "Your door?" she said.

He looked at her curiously. "Same reason," she said.

He grinned and drove off. This pretty redhead was certainly different than what he was accustomed to. She could hold her own with confidence and without showing disrespect.

She gave directions to a small restaurant that advertised a vegetarian menu and health foods, "I don't care about the food here but they've got good coffee and it's not expensive."

They drank coffee and chatted comfortably, both enjoying the company, discovering their interests in common.

Rob enjoyed her quick wit and found that under that bold front, she was actually quite shy. He also discovered that she was also exceptionally intelligent, able to converse comfortably on a number of subjects. As they chatted, her blue green eyes continued to captivate him. He was glad she had agreed to have coffee with him.

When people began to straggle in and order their dinner, Rob glanced up in surprise. Outside it was full dark. They spent several hours over their coffee and didn't realize how much time had elapsed.

Rob glanced at his watch, "Hey it's late. Would you consider dinner? I've got to eat something before I get back on the road and the company would be nice."

By now, she was relaxed and felt safe with him, but he could see the struggle going on inside. Maybe it was the money and pride, or maybe it was something else.

"No, I better not... not this time."

It was a typical brush off until she reached across the table and touched his hand, "You're very kind to ask."

He turned his hand over and held hers looking down at it. His hand was big and strong and calloused, but surprisingly gentle. Her tiny hand nearly disappeared in his.

"Well, all right," he replied, disappointed.

"Will you ask me again?" she asked quickly and her eyes said she meant it.

"But just not tonight, though?" Her hand was still in his. He looked down and put his other hand on top of hers. "All right, Judy, I'll ask you again some time, but I want you to know that I'd enjoy your company for dinner tonight.

"And I'd enjoy yours. Please don't make this any harder for me. It's been a great afternoon." She took a deep breath and added, "Thank you."

Rob stood and picked up the check, "We can split the bill, but let me pick up the table rent."

Her eyes twinkled, "And I always thought it was called a tip."

They left and she gave him directions to her apartment. It was quite a ways from campus and although it wasn't fancy, it was clean and well kept. It looked like the sort of place a thrifty co-ed could afford. Rob liked the idea that it was well lighted. It looked safe and secure. He unloaded her bike and set it on the ground for her.

"Do you want to come in and meet my roommates? If you don't they'll bug me to death."

It looked as if she was suddenly having second thoughts. "Do they bite?" Rob asked and the humor relieved her.

Judy laughed merrily as she wheeled her bike toward her front door, "No, at least I don't think so. They're girls, just like me."

She locked her bike in the rack and after knocking once, unlocked and opened the door. Her two roommates were watching TV. They were shocked to see Rob coming in with her. Scrambling to their feet, they turned off the TV.

"Angie, Beth, this is Mr. Simpson."

"Rob, Rob Simpson," he corrected as he looked over the roommates. They were younger girls, but they certainly weren't 'girls just like me' as Judy described

"Beth is the blonde," Judy added motioning to a pretty, red-faced girl.

"Hi Beth, Angie, we had coffee, but she wouldn't eat dinner with me," he said with a grin and couldn't help but notice the quick flush on Judy's cheek.

"She doesn't even drink coffee with guys from school let alone strangers," Beth said and then covered her mouth in embarrassment.

"Come in and sit down," Angie said, scurrying to clear a spot on one of their chairs. "We don't have a lot of room but you're welcome."

"No, but thank you. I have to get back on the road. I've got several hours of windshield time ahead of me and I have to be at work tomorrow. I'll be back one of these days, though. Judy promised me that she'd have dinner with me some other time."

The two girls looked at one another and then at Judy. From their surprise, it was obvious that Judy didn't accept dinner invitations regularly either.

"I might even come in and sit down if the offer is still good next time I'm in town."

"It will be," Judy's roommates answered simultaneously, then laughed nervously.

"I better get going. It was really nice to meet you girls," he said as he glanced around their apartment quickly. It was neat and organized except for the piles of books that were obviously new in preparation for the school year.

"It looks as if the world will be in good hands when ladies like you graduate and make your mark in the world. Just remember how important your education is. Good night," he said, and with that, he turned and went out the door. He was surprised that Judy followed him out to the parking lot.

When he opened his door, he turned and she was looking at him with a warm smile and a sparkle in her eyes, "Thank you for the afternoon," she said. "And thank you the ride home, and for understanding about dinner."

"You're welcome. I enjoyed it too. I haven't had such a pleasant afternoon in a long time. I may understand about dinner tonight, but I'll be a little more reluctant to accept no next time," he said. He was serious, but not pressuring... and there were no strings attached.

On a sudden impulse, she threw her arms around him and hugged him briefly but firmly. She stepped back as her cheeks began to turn red, "Will you call me?"

It was his turn to be surprised, "I had every intention of doing just that. Goodnight, Judy."

"Goodnight, Rob."

He watched her standing at the curb in his rear view mirror as long as he could. She hadn't moved and he fought the temptation to turn around and go back.

On the way out of town, Rob drove through a fast food place, got two hamburgers, and a drink. He ate while he drove and couldn't stop thinking about the afternoon with the pretty redhead.

She certainly is different! No dates, no boyfriends and yet she singled me out. She spent the afternoon with me. How did she know so much about me? It was almost like a date! Hell, I haven't been on a date for over a year, no wait, almost two years...or is it three? She's very pretty and those eyes...

If he closed his eyes, he could still see them.

But then she's just a kid, a few years older than Patricia. I'm almost old enough to be her father! It's probably just a lark for her. Nothing could ever come of it. I'd be a fool to think it could.

But her roommates didn't treat me like somebody's father. They acted more like a couple of roommates would act if she brought home a real date for approval. And she hugged me! I forgot how soft a woman could be.

She gave me her phone number and made it a point to be sure I'd call. Maybe I will call her. No, that's just wishful thinking.

But it was a nice afternoon.

By the time he finally got home, it was late. He forced himself back to reality and put Judy in the back of his mind. Tomorrow was going to be a tough day catching up after taking the day off today. Patricia would have been much happier if her mother had taken her up to school. There were all those 'girl things' to do, and according to Patricia, he wasn't much good at that.

Getting ready for bed, he opened his closet, made sure there was a clean uniform for tomorrow. In the corner, he saw his hiking boots. The blue green eyes came back to him instantly. Hiking. She focused on hiking when they talked. How did she know his one weakness? No, it was foolishness. Shaking his head he slid the closet door closed, shutting down the thought and crawled into bed.

For some, the sense of smell is the strongest receptor, triggering vivid memories. It was the lingering hint of fragrance that forced blue green eyes and pretty smile into focus for Rob.

He couldn't sleep that night, thinking about her. Lying in the dark, he realized that there was one unresolved problem.

"All right, I'll call her," he said aloud, and fell asleep.

13

Judy's Reaction

"Good grief," Judy said aloud as she watched him drive off. "Why did I do that?"

Rob was solid muscle and it felt good in his arms even for that brief moment. She was flushed when she turned back to her apartment. A thought suddenly occurred to her. He was polite and courteous to her roommates. He gave them the once over but he didn't scrutinize them as closely as he did when he looked at her. Rob approved of their looks, most guys did, but it was their eyes that told him who they were. Whatever it was that he saw in their eyes was not what he looked for, and saw, in hers. He *was* different

When Judy came back into the apartment her roommates were waiting for her, "All right, Judy, what happened? You were just going to talk to him," Angie began.

"Yeah, is he a wuss like we said, or were you right?" Beth asked.

Angie took over, "You spent the whole afternoon with him drinking coffee and then said you'd have dinner with him some time. Now you're talking about hiking with him? That's not what you said you were going to do!"

Judy slumped into a chair with stars in her eyes, "It just sort of happened. He's so easy to talk to I lost track of time. He asked me if I wanted some coffee, so we spent the afternoon getting to know one another. I mentioned hiking and before you know it, I agreed to go with him."

Then she smiled, "I can tell you this, that guy is not a wuss."

"That part must be true," Angie said. "He sure is a big dude!"

"And he's a lot cuter up close," Beth said, "And really nice."

"After meeting him I don't think I'd have had the audacity to treat him like his own daughter did," Angie said.

For a moment, Judy looked serious, "There's something about him that makes me think there is a definite limit to his tolerance. That kid of his is pretty bad, but he is her father. He didn't need to put up with that, but he didn't put her down in front of her friends. That took a lot of restraint!"

"Why did you walk him out to his car?" Beth asked.

"I wanted to thank him for a nice afternoon," Judy said and then smiled, "And I hugged him."

"You did what!" Beth gasped. "What in the world made you do that?"

Her roommates had more questions and wouldn't let up until they were satisfied. When they exhausted all their questions and felt they had all the details about her afternoon they went to bed.

It was three a.m.

Judy went to her bedroom and lay awake thinking until sunlight streamed through her window. She still wasn't able to sleep. Rob was not only handsome and sexy, but he was a gentleman. She hadn't enjoyed talking to anyone that much, and the way he looked at her made her quiver just thinking about it. She told him things about herself that no one else knew. It just came out naturally and he listened without judgment.

She got out of bed, made breakfast for Angie and Beth, and did the laundry for all three of them. By early afternoon, she did all the ironing and she was tired. She tried to take a nap. She lay on her bed with the phone at her side and stared at the ceiling wondering why she had been so bold. He was so much older than her. What ever possessed her to approach him that way?

He didn't call that night like she had hoped that he would. Angie and Beth could feel her disappointment and tried in vain to distract her. After being up all-night and busy all day, Judy was exhausted. She went to bed early and pounded her pillow in frustration. She was being foolish. Rob was a grown man with a job. He had children almost her age. He was a good-looking guy. He must have lots of girlfriends. What could she possibly offer him?

It was a long and difficult day for Rob. It was hard to concentrate. He was still thinking about the redhead. At lunch, he alluded to the previous day's events to his friend Dave and asked him to stop by the house for a beer after work. Never one to turn down a free beer, Dave agreed. Besides, he wanted to learn the rest of the story. Why, all of a sudden, was there a woman in Rob's life?

Dave took a long swallow of the free beer. It was cold and refreshing, "Okay, man, tell me the story about this chick, and don't give me no bullshit."

Although his vocabulary was often limited, Dave had no trouble asking questions or making a point in simple language that left little room for misunderstanding. Rob liked that.

Rob recounted the previous day's events and how it affected him. He described Judy in detail, "She has long auburn hair, incredibly beautiful eyes, a fantastic body with long tanned legs, and she likes to hike. She's easygoing, fun to talk to, and I feel like we have a lot of the same interests. She's smart as hell, a graduate student in anthropology, and has a great sense of humor. She's a lot different than any girl I've ever met."

Dave sipped his beer, munched on the snacks Rob laid out and listened, asking an occasional question to clarify something and nodding occasionally.

"So what's your problem, man? If she's a graduate student, she's got to be over eighteen. Get her out in the woods and jump her bones. That's what she wants isn't it?"

"Be careful, Dave," Rob said seriously and surprised Dave.

Looking up from his beer, Dave chose his words a little more carefully, "Sorry, man. I didn't mean no offense, but ain't this kind of sudden?"

"Sounds that way, doesn't it," Rob replied. "I can't understand how or why she picked me. There's a lot of good-looking guys closer to her age up there."

Dave laughed, "Hell, man, a good-looking stud like you? How could she resist?"

"I'm probably old enough to be her father."

"So what? It sounds like that isn't a problem for her, so why should it be for you? If she likes hiking as much as you do, and even if nothing else develops, it's no big deal. You're always bitchin' about hiking alone so here's your chance to remedy that. Go for it, man. You're such an obnoxious prick when you don't get out! Go hike with the teeny bopper, get it out of your system, and make it easier for all of us at the shop."

"Well, my friend, like I said, she's different. That's the kind of gal that ought to be married to someone that truly understands what a treasure she is and appreciates her, someone that treats her right. Not some low life son of a bitch that just wants to jump her bones."

The change in Rob's tone was a relief, "You mean like me?" Dave laughed, but he was still cautious.

They continued their discussion through more beer and platefuls of snacks before Dave finally confessed that he had to leave, "My old lady will be pissed off at me and then I'll have a problem bigger than the one you think you've got.

"Look at it this way, man, what have you got to lose? Why not go for it? If nothing else, you'll definitely enjoy the hike. You're always talkin' about that high country anyway."

Rob walked to the door with his friend, "Well whatever happens I appreciate being able to talk about it."

At the door, they shook hands and joined in a bone-crushing bear hug that would have broken the ribs of most people. "Keep me posted on your new lady," Dave grinned as he made his way out to his car.

After Dave left, Rob sat brooding over his situation. Maybe he should call her and explain that it was all a misunderstanding. There was the age difference and he wasn't really interested in a long distance relationship anyway.

When he picked up the phone, the numbers seemed blurry, "Damned beer. Maybe it would be better to wait," he said aloud. "I'll never match wits with her after all that beer."

He was getting ready for bed with just junk food, beer, and no supper. He felt a little light-headed and fell onto his bed to watch the room spin above him.

"Where's that smell coming from? I thought I washed that shirt. Damn, she's beautiful."

In the morning, Rob made a healthy breakfast and felt better. Filling a cup with coffee, he went out to the garage to head off to work. When he opened the door, he caught sight of his dusty backpack propped in a corner. It had lain neglected for months. Deep inside he felt the calling of the outdoors. Dave was right, he had nothing to lose, and he did like the high country. He looked at his cell phone and put it aside.

Better to call at lunch, or better yet tonight. It won't be a short conversation.

After work, Rob took his pack into the house and went through it carefully, making a mental note of what needed to be replenished or replaced. He checked his boots and gathered his outdoor gear together. He filled the duffel bag with the things that he always kept with him in the past and made sure there were extra jackets, blankets, first aid kit, water, and emergency food in the back of his 4Runner just in case. It was almost seven.

The phone rang once.

"Hello?"

"Hi, can I speak to..."

"Rob?" the tentative voice answered.

"Yes... Judy?"

"Hi... how are you doing?" she sounded brighter already.

"I'm fine. Say, you talked about hiking. I was thinking, how about this Saturday?"

She didn't hesitate. "What time? I mean you have a long drive."

"Are you an early riser?"

"Yes I am. How about nine? Can you get here that early?"

"How about eight?" he answered.

"I like that even better," she replied, excited.

"How's school?"

"Good... I'm glad you called. I didn't know if you would. Did I thank you for the good time and the coffee and the ride home."

"Yes, you did. Did I thank you for the same things... and that hug? That meant a lot to me," he added seriously. "I don't get a lot of hugs."

"I've got plenty and you can have one any time," she laughed.

Closing his eyes, he could see the twinkle in her eyes and feel her smile.

Talking got easier and more comfortable as they talked. The way she responded to the conversation, her insight, made him forget that she was also a very pretty girl, and much younger than him.

Changing the subject, she sounded serious, "Rob, I want to ask you a difficult question. I don't want to upset you or give you the wrong idea, but it's something that's important to me."

"Go ahead," Rob said and prepared for the worst.

There was a brief pause while she gathered her courage then asked, "Are you married?"

Her question was followed by a long silence before he answered, "No... I'm divorced, and you're right, it is a difficult question. If you want to pursue that, I'd rather not do it over the phone."

Her question had a sobering effect on him. The conversation had suddenly gone beyond simply getting to know one another. It was more personal, the sort of question one asked when they were considering developing a closer relationship.

"I'm sorry I asked. I thought all I really needed was a yes or no answer but it's not really that simple is it?"

"No it isn't. It makes me feel like I have to explain or justify my failure."

"I don't believe that you failed!" her reply was firm and sharp. "Let's change the subject. It wasn't fair for me to ask such an insensitive question. I'm sorry. Can you forgive me?"

Rob relaxed, "I already did. Seven o'clock?"

"I like that even better," and he could feel her grin once again.

"You seemed reluctant to have dinner with me the other day, so how about breakfast Saturday?"

"You're pretty persistent aren't you?"

"No, I'm sensible. We both need to eat breakfast anyhow and what better time to plan our hike. Seeing as how you're arranging that part of it, I'll buy breakfast. Isn't that a fair trade?"

"You make it hard to say no."

"Well then, if we're having breakfast why don't we make it six? We can look at maps while we eat and wait for it to get light."

"You're impossible!" she laughed.

"Is that a yes or no?"

"Of course it's a yes, but how are you going to get here that early? It's a long drive."

"That's simple. I'll drive up Friday night and get a motel."

When Judy hung up the phone, she wondered about the conversation. Talking about breakfast was where most men suggested spending the night. It sounded as if the thought hadn't even occurred to him. They talked for over an hour and still hadn't said all she wanted to say when they finally said goodnight. Judy fell back against her pillow and grinned. The more they talked, the more fascinated she was. He was different in so many ways from all the guys she had ever known.

14

THE FIRST HIKE

D riving to Flagstaff on Friday night Rob found a motel without too much trouble. School started and there weren't a lot of parents in town. After studying his maps, he turned in for the night. At 5:00 a.m., he awoke and showered. While he dressed, his excitement grew. After months of postponement there was a new trail and a new hiking companion out there waiting for him. There was time to get a feel for the weather and a look at the sky before he picked her up.

To the east, the morning stars were fading into the dawning sky. The wind was cool and he sensed the dampness that told him the chance of rain had increased since last night's report. Setting off at a brisk pace, he walked for several blocks assimilating the surroundings. The few dogs that barked registered on his sub-conscious. It was instinctive.

Today would be the true test. Could she really hike or was that just a story? He hiked with novices before, people who didn't really enjoy the outdoors and weren't capable of taking care of themselves. But this gal rode a bike and had a firm handshake. She was in good shape, but could she hike? He'd soon know.

Returning to the motel, he got into his 4Runner and drove to Judy's apartment. Promptly at six, he pulled into the parking lot and saw her coming down the walk to greet him! Auburn hair tied into a ponytail flowed from her baseball cap. She wore a flannel shirt over a T-shirt, worn jeans, and hiking boots that looked fairly new. She looked ready for the hike from her outfit right down to the excited glow on her pretty face, even prettier than he remembered.

"Good morning," she said with a captivating smile.

"Good morning. You look like you're ready to hit the trail."

"I am," she said, hesitated an instant, and hugged him.

"There," she said grinning. "You said you needed a hug!"

"Always do," Rob saw the blue green eyes that haunted him all week, and smiled, "Thank you."

"My pack is just inside the door. I'll be right out."

She slipped in and brought out a small, well-worn daypack, and a nylon windbreaker. The pack told him she wasn't a novice, but still, her boots looked new. They loaded her things in the back and set off for breakfast. She gave directions and then talked incessantly of different trails, her classes, her professors, and anything else she could think of. Rob smiled as he listened. She seemed even more excited than he was about the prospect of a hike and spending the time together.

The restaurant was set back from the road in a strip mall. It was on the road out of town and didn't look like much from the outside. It was clean inside, the service was good, and the food was excellent. They chatted during breakfast like old friends.

She was still bubbling with excitement when they left the restaurant and started down the road. It was cool with a light breeze, a good day for a hike. White popcorn clouds floated in the deep blue of the high country sky. The trees closed in quickly as they drove, casting the long gray shadows of early morning across the road and flitting over the windshield. Before long, Judy pointed to a side road that led to a dirt parking lot. There were several other cars already there when he stopped and shut off his truck.

"It's a pretty popular trailhead on a weekend," she explained. "Once we get up the trail there's side trails we can take. Some of the locals hike with their kids and dogs. Some use it for jogging, and some start off from here for overnight or even longer hikes. Once you get past the range of the day-trippers I think you could hike clear up to Utah and hardly see another soul."

"We're a little short on time, do you think we could save Utah for another time?" he grinned.

Her eyes sparkled, "Okay, we can do that some other time."

They got out of the vehicle and set out their equipment. Rob's pack was much larger than she expected for a day hike.

She gestured at the mountain, "Are you planning on spending the week up there or did you bring a big lunch?"

Rob nodded at his pack and explained, "I carry a heavy pack to keep in shape. When I do conditioning hikes near home, I load it up with sand. That way when I go on a longer hike the weight of extra gear doesn't come as quite a shock. I've been doing it for so long I guess I don't know any other way."

He made her check her boots and then helped her into her pack. At first, she was annoyed until he made a few minor adjustments and suddenly her pack felt lighter and more comfortable. She helped him into his pack and was surprised. It *was* heavy!

"You have a lot in here. Are you sure you weren't planning to go all the way to Utah?"

"Not today," he teased, "Maybe next time."

Judy chuckled at his reply. He had a sense of humor. It was going to be a fun day.

Leading the way up into the trees, she began at a steady pace. She wasn't sure how the extra weight and the higher elevation would affect him, so she didn't push too hard. It didn't take long to find out.

"I like to push pretty hard at the beginning of a hike," he said as he came up beside her. "As soon as we're away from civilization we can set an easier pace."

He was certainly right about that. Rob stepped out, taking long strides, and covering the early uphill stretch of the trail quickly. Following his effortless, mile-eating pace, Judy was pushing herself to keep up. She wondered how long he could maintain that pace at this altitude and hoped she wouldn't fall too far behind. She was in excellent shape and easily outpaced everyone she ever hiked with. This was different. Rob was like a supercharged mountain goat and she felt a twinge of disappointment. This was not her kind of hike. She knew that she could keep up, but it would certainly hurt tomorrow. She tried thinking of other things as she followed him. What would happen if she hurried up beside him and took his hand? Would that break the brutal pace or would it make him angry?

The trail was wide and smooth, following the ridgeline. There were no trees to break the wind that buffeted them from the west. The day started out cool and if it warmed up any, it wasn't noticeable. At this rate, it was useless to try to pick out landmarks or to keep her bearings. She hoped that Rob had studied his maps enough to keep them from missing one of the crossover trails and getting them lost. Falling into the mindless routine of forcing one foot in front of the other and trying to keep up, she almost forged past when his pace slackened then slowed to a walk. He stepped off to the side of the trail and down into a small arroyo protected from the wind. They were on the trail exactly fifteen minutes, travelled well over a mile, and he hadn't spoken a word.

When he looked back at her, he was glowing. His eyes were bright and it was apparent that he was truly in his element. There was perspiration on his forehead and he was breathing heavily. He seemed to be a different person.

"Man, am I out of shape! That's exactly what I needed," he said with a content sigh.

"Okay, lady, time to check boots and feet! Sit down over there and take off your boots," he told her, pointing to a fallen log without giving her a chance to protest.

He sat next to her and slipped out of his own boots and socks. He rubbed his feet gingerly and then put socks and boots back on but didn't lace them.

"How do your boots feel, any chafing on your feet?"

"No I don't think so... I mean I hadn't thought about it."

"Take 'em off," he said indicating her boots. When she did, he glanced at her socks and then felt inside the boots while she took off her socks. He nodded with satisfaction and then took one of her feet in his hands. That startled her and she wasn't quite sure she felt comfortable about it. He noted a pink spot on her heel and then looked at the other foot.

"I'm fine," she replied sharply. "Just what are you doing?" she asked as he ran his hands over her feet.

"What's this?" he asked when she flinched. "You should have said something."

"I was trying to keep up and didn't think about it," she replied defensively.

From his pack, he took out a small stuff sack, and removed a tube of ointment. "This ought to do the trick," he said as she watched curiously.

He squeezed ointment onto his fingers and then rubbed it into her heel. He had powerful hands but his touch was surprisingly gentle.

"What are you doing?" she asked.

"There's a blister starting here, probably from your sock bunching up. This is pretty good stuff. It'll skin over shortly and protect your heel. Sort of like moleskin, but better because it stays moist. You can't enjoy a hike if your feet hurt. I'll put your socks back on so they won't bunch up."

She laughed, "You mean you don't think I can dress myself properly?"

Rob looked at her with a sheepish grin, "No, that's not what I meant... I just... well, I'm only trying to help."

The daily phone calls during the week made her feel safe with Rob. Judy leaned down and kissed his forehead lightly, "I'm just kidding, Rob. It looks like you know what you're doing. I probably would have kept on going until my foot fell off."

His touch was gentle and the salve soothing as she watched him massage it onto her heel.

"You have nice hands," she said seriously.

Looking up, he grinned, "You have nice feet."

Rob was squatted on his heels and missed the mischievous twinkle in her eyes. With a quick movement that caught him unprepared, she pushed him off balance.

It happened so quickly she was shocked. One moment he was sprawled on the ground. An instant later, both of them were lying in the dirt. He was laughing, but he stopped abruptly.

"I'm sorry," he said and sat up with a worried look. "Did I hurt you?"

"No, but you surprised me," she replied.

"It's the mountain air, this place...it's you," he said gently and brushed a few pine needles from her hair. "I didn't mean to startle you. I forgot what it's like to let go, to allow joy in, to be happy. I," he paused, and added, "Thank you."

"It's okay to be happy, Rob," she smiled, "You have my permission."

Gesturing at her boots, he said, "We should get those boots back on and laced up right."

She watched him while he slipped her socks on and adjusted them comfortably. He was quick and strong, but very careful and efficient. When he put her boots back on, he made her stand as he adjusted the laces differently at each eyelet. It felt strange having someone put on her socks and boots.

"Like I asked before, don't you think I can dress myself?"

He stood up and looked at her, "I'm sure you can, but sore feet can ruin any hike. That salve will skin over and protect your heel. It's better to get something like that early and not suffer later. I didn't mean to embarrass you. It's a habit from my time in the Corps."

"You were a Marine?" she asked.

"Still am," he grinned.

"I've heard that about you guys," she laughed, and shifted on her feet. "You didn't embarrass me, Rob. It feels better already. I'm not used to someone like you. Thank you."

"You're welcome," Rob said and took a moment to look at her. She definitely was not a 'teenybopper' as Dave had described her.

"Okay, now that's done," he said as he led the way back up to the trail. "I didn't mean to push so hard at the start, but I needed to get started, to get the city out of my system. I needed to get reacquainted with what's out here. Thanks for being patient with me."

When he set a slower pace, they found common interests along the side of the trail and in the woods beyond. Now he was talking. He pointed out landmarks and asked endless questions. At one point, he stopped and directed her gaze across the canyon to their left. It was an eagle perched on a tree just below the skyline. If he hadn't pointed it out, she would have missed it.

He talked about the plants and trees they passed and what they could be used for if the need arose. It was practical knowledge, not based on textbook ramblings, and gave her insight into what early people would have looked for. It was no longer the forced march that began their hike. Now it was a pleasant stroll in the forest with a good companion. They were both learning, about the trail, and about each other. A few late and tiny flowers nestled at the base of the giant Ponderosa. Judy discovered that Rob was observant, and missed nothing. He pointed to an elk standing motionless in the trees close to the skyline. It was turning in to her kind of hike and she was pleased.

"Do you hunt?" she asked when they continued up the trail.

Rob flinched, "No!" he replied instantly.

His abrupt reply startled her. After a moment, he continued in a softer tone, "Not for quite a while. There's just too much meat on an elk for me alone so I gave it up. Besides, there's getting to be too many crazies out there."

She looked at him curiously and realized there was still a lot to learn about him. She touched a sensitive area when she asked about hunting and wondered why. He was kind and gentle and yet there was also great strength. There was no weakness in this guy. He could have forced her to take care of her feet, made a big deal about it, or even ignored the situation, but he didn't. He handled that with gentleness, and yet, a subtle firmness. He could have taken advantage of her when they tumbled in the dirt, but he didn't do that either.

She thought back to the night when his daughter was so abusive toward him and the way he handled that situation with restraint and dignity. She was impressed. Very quietly, she slipped her hand into his and continued walking. She didn't know if her gesture affected him, but it made her feel safe and secure.

The steady stream of hikers and joggers thinned out the further they progressed and when they took a narrow side trail there were none. They wandered happily through the tall trees whispering in the wind. Stopping frequently, they discovered new and interesting things. In the distance, they heard the trickling sound of water and came to a small stream that made its way across the trail yet left stepping stones for them to cross. Once they were across the stream, Rob stopped. He glanced at the sky and unlimbered his pack.

"I think we should consider this the halfway point. Are you hungry?" he asked.

"Yes, I am," she replied. "I don't usually eat a big breakfast like we had, but the hike and this mountain air changed that.

"I brought lunch for both of us," she said and reached into her pack.

She took out fresh fruit and thick, hearty sandwiches. Lettuce and tomato slices were in separate sandwich bags. There were carrot sticks and celery in a small plastic container, and two cans of fruit juice. It was a simple lunch. It was what Judy did and she took it for granted.

Rob didn't take it for granted.

"I don't know how you gals do it," he said as he watched her with his hands on his hips. "I can cook a pretty fair steak, but when my friends come over for a barbeque, the salads, and the side dishes their wives make blows me away. This is a real treat. I appreciate you going out of your way like this."

It was no idle comment. It was honest and sincere. This man was not used to simple gestures of thoughtfulness.

"I thought it was the least I could do after you bought breakfast," she responded while she put the sandwiches together.

15

LUNCH ON THE MOUNTAIN

"For an Anthropology major this must be fascinating country for you," Rob said as they sat on the ground munching on their lunch.

"I love it," Judy beamed. "It all started when I was a kid and found this," she said. Taking the pendant from around her neck, she handed it to Rob.

He examined it carefully and then looked at her, "Who made this for you?"

His question startled her, "What makes you think someone made it for me?"

"Nobody makes anything with this kind of quality and then sells it. The person that made this loved you very much."

A soft gasp escaped her lips, and a flood of emotion from happy memories shook her.

"My father made it," she whispered emotionally.

Holding the pendant and observing her reaction, Rob felt he needed to move on, "I'm way over my head here, Judy. Obviously it's an arrowhead, but is it Clovis?"

"How did you know that?"

"I don't... I'm asking you."

Judy was surprised; he wasn't afraid to ask when he didn't know something. Sharing the story of her pendant with Rob was a pleasant experience. He listened intently and was obviously impressed. Stories of her field trips and what she had learned in lectures continued while Rob sat listening.

"There are sites northeast of here that haven't been researched very much," Judy said.

"They're too small to prompt any sort of dig by the Museum or the University, but I'd like to go there some time and see what I can find. It's a pretty rugged area and hard to get to. I don't really want to try it alone, because it's so dangerous."

"Can you show me where it is on the map," Rob asked as he dug out a topographical map and spread it across their knees.

After a series of questions, answers, and speculation, they decided on the most likely area, "It looks like it's only about ten miles round trip," Rob said. "But as steep as that is and with the elevation changes we'd need every bit of eight hours to allow a little time for exploring... how about tomorrow?"

"Are you serious?" She asked in amazement. He was just as excited about exploring the site as she was!

"We could plan it for another weekend but this late in the year the weather gets pretty iffy. Would that interfere with your school work if we made it tomorrow?"

"No, I'm caught up... what about you?"

"I can't think of anything I'd rather do. Six and breakfast again?"

Her hesitation in replying made him realize that she worried about him buying her breakfast.

"Judy, this is several hours driving time each way for me just to get up here. I don't mind the drive, but I'd sure hate for it to be wasted by not being able to check out some of these areas. This is a part of the state I've always wanted to explore but I never took the initiative. There always seemed to be places to go closer to home. Besides, seeing some of the things we've seen today and being able to discover something new just isn't fun for me anymore if I have to do it alone. Like we agreed, it's tough to find a good hiking companion, and like you said, you can keep up, you know the area, and you are good company... well, maybe a pain in the ass sometimes."

It was the same observation she heard from her professors. Judy grinned and looked at him seriously, "You know I don't feel right about you spending all the money."

"I can tell you don't, but I work pretty hard and I make more than you do right now. What's so wrong about spending my money when you can't afford it and I can?"

"I feel like I can't reciprocate."

He took her hand in his and grinned, "I have no idea how I can reciprocate for the hugs. Getting out on a trail discovering new things with someone that can actually hike is a lot more valuable than just money."

There were lots of suggestive comments he could have made in reply to her comment but it didn't seem to occur to him. She was searching for an answer, but she didn't take her hand from his, "You are absolutely impossible! What am I going to do with you?"

"Go to breakfast with me before we go look for your ruins. I'll pick you up at six and let you choose where to have breakfast. How's that for a fair trade?"

He hadn't suggested or even hinted at spending the night together. Many of the girls she knew on campus would have expected that. When they wrestled on the ground, he didn't make any attempt to get fresh with her. He was incredibly strong and could have forced her. That far away from other hikers, she could have screamed and no one would have heard. She wondered if he was even interested.

As they talked, Rob was watching the sky overhead. The small, friendly, white clouds of morning had given way to dark gray thunderheads that were building rapidly against the mountain. He checked his watch and calculated the distance they had already traveled.

"We're going to get wet before long," he told her and pointed at the clouds. "We better have something warm and then get started back. Coffee or soup?" he asked as he rose and went to the stream with a small stainless steel container.

Judy almost laughed at his question but thought better of it. He was serious, and the clouds did look menacing, but where was he going to find something hot to drink way out here? It didn't take long to find out. He set the water on a backpacker stove to boil and rummaged through his pack for packets of soup. As he worked, the wind picked up and brought a chill down from higher country. Judy took her windbreaker from her pack and putting it on zipped it up with a shiver.

"I think soup is a better idea," he suggested. "Too much coffee and we'll be stopping at every tree we pass on the way down."

Judy laughed, "You think of everything don't you?"

They chatted happily until the water was boiling. It didn't take long at the altitude and soon he produced two heavy, plastic cups that he filled with a steaming, rich soup. It tasted surprisingly good and it warmed them against the dropping temperature. When they finished the soup, he rinsed out the utensils in the stream and reloaded his pack. They hadn't gone very far when they saw the flash of lightning and heard the first crash of thunder. It was quite a ways off but the wind promised to deliver it much closer, and soon. The trail was downhill back to the parking lot and they were making good time when Rob signaled a halt. He stooped down and adjusted the laces on his boots and then did the same for her.

"Going down beats your toes into your boots. If I tighten the laces like this, it helps to lessen the shock. Now all we have to worry about is knees," he explained.

It made sense to her; she just hadn't done it that way before. But then she hadn't had several miles of steep downhill travel and it was going to have to be at a brisk pace. She took his hand and squeezed it, "I'm learning a lot, and I thought I knew how to hike. Thank you."

"I learned most of this the hard way, but once I learned, I tried to remember it all. I keep learning though and I like that. Out here all you have is your wits and whatever gear you happened to bring along." He squeezed her hand and smiled, "I think I chose the right hiking partner though. You're good company."

Judy leaned against him and wrapped her arms around his, "I'm glad you brought me... and you're good company too."

They were making good time but the thunder was rapidly getting closer. The first of the rain was large, cold drops that pelted them hard. Rob stopped and went into his pack for rain gear. He could tell by Judy's forlorn look that what she had on was all she brought and wasn't prepared for the rain.

"That windbreaker won't do the job when this rain starts coming down in earnest. Do you have any rain gear or a poncho?"

"No... I didn't think I'd need it. I guess I'll just have to get wet."

"Not at this elevation and at this temperature. It can be pretty serious up here."

"Hey, I'm from Minnesota. I'm used to the cold," she replied, but she knew better. Hypothermia didn't require the brutal cold she knew in Duluth. Just the wet and wind could be disastrous.

Rob looked at her and shook his head. He was grinning and she knew he wasn't trying to belittle her. He put his rain jacket over her shoulders and against her protest told her to put it on. It fit her like a tent and it was lightweight, but it was warm. She could tell it would keep her dry. He pulled on his rain pants then removed a poncho from the pack and slipped it over his head.

"I'd let you wear the pants but I'm afraid you'd trip on them. They're sort of long."

Then they were back on the trail and none too soon. With a thunderous roar, the skies opened up. In no time, the trail was a river of mud. He took her hand and held it firmly as they slipped and slid downhill. The cold rain ran off the rain jacket but it stung her lower body like needles. Her legs were soaked and her boots felt as if they were full of water. Her upper body was dry and comfortable but she felt the numbing cold in her legs. At times, under the trees, there was some protection from the direct intensity of the rain but that was of little consequence.

He stopped once and looked at her. He could tell she was feeling the effects of the cold on her lower body and it concerned him. She was shivering and some of the fire had gone out of her eyes, "We've got two choices, Judy, we can try to find a spot to hole up, build a fire and hope the rain lets up, or we can keep moving. How do you feel?"

"I'm cold," she replied in a weak, trembling voice.

"I'm sure you are. The rain is cold. We better keep moving, but if you start feeling weak, let me know right away. I know you're tough but this is not the time or place for heroics."

Judy looked at him as she continued to shiver and tried to be brave. She was miserable but she couldn't let him know that, "I think I'll be all right," she said weakly.

Rob put his arm around her waist and started back down the trail. He could feel her shivering with the cold but she didn't complain. She was tough!

When they finally arrived at the trailhead, the parking lot was empty except for Rob's Toyota. He opened her door and lifted her in. He put their packs in the back and then slid in behind the steering wheel. He started the motor and turned the heater and defroster on low. Reaching behind the seat, he produced a towel.

"You better get yourself dried off as best you can, Honey. I've got a blanket back here somewhere," he added as he knelt on the seat and rummaged in the back.

She was shivering as she dried her face and hair and watched him. *Honey, that sounds nice... I like it.*

He produced a large woolen blanket from behind the seat and offered it to her, "Put this over you and get out of those wet boots and jeans. You can put them down by the heater so they'll dry. You'll never get warm otherwise."

It sounded so natural and it made sense. She just wasn't sure that she wanted to be wearing nothing but a blanket and it showed in her face.

Rob had a puzzled look on his face as he watched her working the idea through her head and then he laughed, "This is no time for modesty. You need to get dry and pretty soon or you'll get sick. If you're worried about me, I'll be busy driving and I won't look, I promise."

The heater was just now beginning to take effect. The fog on the inside of the windshield was lifting from where the defroster was pushing it up the glass. He turned it on high, shifted into gear, and made his way slowly out of the slick, muddy parking lot. The rain came down heavier once they were out on the road and no longer under the canopy of trees. The low sky was a dull, dark, gray punctuated occasionally by brilliant flashes of lightning that were followed by thunder rumbling across the gloom.

Shivering from the cold, she squirmed out of her wet jeans and boots. She arranged the blanket so she could dry off her legs with the towel. Rob drove slowly peering through the arc made by the wipers and was only partially aware of her movements from the corner of his eye. As they approached town, the rain changed to a steady downpour. Judy wrapped the blanket around her and tucked it in beneath her. The heater was beginning to have its effect and Judy wasn't shivering quite as badly.

"I'm glad we went even if it did rain," she said with her teeth chattering. "And I'm glad you were with me. It would have been scary if you hadn't been prepared and known what to do."

Rob glanced at her, "You did fine under some pretty rugged conditions without complaining, Judy. Lots of people, both men and women, would have just quit. I'm impressed. I'll hike with you any time."

He was serious and she realized he had paid her an honest compliment.

"I enjoyed it," she said. "I really enjoyed it. I think we did pretty well for our first hike together... well after the first part where you almost ran off and left me. I didn't think you were in shape for hiking at this elevation but you sure surprised me. I appreciated it when you slowed down so I could keep up."

He glanced at her and grinned, "I've needed to get out for a long time, and this was just what I needed. I had to get a lot of things off my mind so I could get reacquainted with just being outside. I'm sorry I ignored you at the start. I didn't intend to."

"I was wondering about that. When you stopped you seemed like a completely different person."

"That's exactly what I was feeling. It was like stepping out of a dark place and into the light. I did feel good, and having you along made it even better. I'd like to do it again."

"So would I. In fact if this weather lets up, maybe we could try again tomorrow."

"I doubt if it will. The weather report wasn't promising. In fact, there's a chance that the snow level will drop down pretty low by morning. We'll have to make it another time."

Judy gave an inaudible reply and looked down at her hands. She was hoping to spend a little more time together. He lived so far away and she wondered when, or even if, he might make the trip up again.

Rob glanced at her and continued, "If you don't have too much studying to do I was sort of hoping maybe we might be able to get together for a little while tomorrow. I thought we could check at the library and see if there's any more information on those sites you mentioned. I'd kind of like to get out there and see what we can find… of course if you've got other things going on I'd understand."

Judy's face lit up and her eyes sparkled. "I was afraid you might have to head back down tonight."

"No, I reserved the room for both nights in case the weather decided to cooperate. I hope you don't think I'm being presumptuous… I mean by assuming you might have been willing to go out two days in a row."

Judy laughed happily, "That's not presumptuous, that's just thinking ahead. Here I was worrying about whether or not you would want to try a second hike. Well, if we can't hike, I'd like to spend the time together anyhow," then she looked at him and touched his arm. "I'd like to get to know you better, Rob."

Rob felt a tingle as his cheeks took on a pink coloring. "I thought the same thing… I mean getting to know you better. I already know me," he stammered.

Judy laughed again, not at him, but with him, and she felt good. Her initial observation was correct. This was the man she had imagined him to be, not the meek object of his daughter's wrath. In addition to that, he shared her love of the outdoors and the history waiting to be discovered.

16

DINNER

It was much darker, colder, and still raining heavily when Rob drove into the parking lot at Judy's apartment. There was an awkward moment when she reached for her boots and jeans and found them still soaking wet. She looked at Rob uneasily.

He grinned, "If it won't embarrass you too much I'll carry you in. Grab your boots and jeans. I can come back out for your other things."

He went around to her side of the vehicle, and without a word, picked her up effortlessly and hurried to her door in the driving rain.

"I don't have my keys," she said helplessly. "They're in my pack."

"Go ahead and knock. If someone's there they'll answer," Rob said and looked at her.

Her hair was straight, a straggled mess, auburn streamers plastered to her face with rain dripping off her nose. Any makeup she might have been wearing had long since washed away. She was shivering, wrapped in a wet blanket with no jeans, boots, or socks. She was self-conscious. He thought she was beautiful. She reached out and knocked firmly on the door hoping that one of her roommates was home. After a short pause, she knocked again and heard movement inside.

"Who is it?"

"It's me, Judy. Open the door, Beth, I don't have my key."

It took a moment before the door opened. Beth stared at Judy wrapped in a blanket with her jeans and boots in her lap laughed, "And I thought you were just going hiking."

Rob carried her in and set her on the floor as Judy glared at her roommate. A quick glance told him that their arrival had interrupted something. There was a young man sitting with his back to them but as he rose and turned around Rob recognized him.

"Hello, Jack. So we meet again. I didn't need your help finding out about hiking trails after all."

Jack stepped forward with a broad grin, "Hi, Mr. Simpson."

Before shaking Jack's hand, Rob grinned, "You're not going to crush my hand again are you?"

"I was thinkin' the same thing," Jack laughed and shook Rob's hand.

After trying to explain about getting caught in the rain it was obvious that Judy was going to have to try harder in order to make Beth believe her. Rob excused himself and went back out in the rain to retrieve Judy's pack. When he returned, Judy had changed into a dry robe and was using a towel to dry her hair. There was a section of tile at the door that prevented Rob's rain gear from dripping on the carpet as he waited hesitantly.

"Get out of those wet things and I'll make us some supper," Judy suggested. "It'll take me a minute to get something started."

Rob looked at her and then at Jack and Beth. "I have a better idea. It's been a rough day. Why don't I take the three of you out to dinner? You'll have to suggest someplace good though. I wasn't very impressed with the last place I ate when I was up here."

The reference to the restaurant where they first saw Rob and his daughter made Judy blush. Beth laughed out loud.

"There's much better places than that," Jack said. "One of my friends is a waiter at an Italian place. From what he says, it ain't bad. I'll call and see if we can get a reservation if you want to try that."

"That would be fine with me, how about you, Judy?" Rob asked.

"I can't go anywhere looking like this," she replied. "I need to get cleaned up... I'd like to take a shower. I'm still a little chilled from getting soaked."

"That's a good idea," Rob agreed, "I'll run over to my motel and change into something dry. That'll give Jack time to find us a place to eat. We can take my vehicle. How does that sound?"

Although she hesitated, Judy agreed. Beth and Jack were curious about what had transpired during the day. It was going to be an interesting dinner. As he started to leave, Judy stopped him at the door and gave him a hug. Jack and Beth watched with interest. Judy hurried off to take her shower and Rob slipped out the door with a happy grin.

After a shower and putting on dry clothes, Judy was being grilled by Jack and Beth. A knock at the door rescued her. Gathering coats and umbrellas, they hurried out to Rob's vehicle. When Jack opened Beth's door and helped her in, Rob smiled. Jack was someone he wanted to get to know better.

From the outside, Jack's recommendation didn't look like much. It was an older stone building with a dilapidated sign that needed paint.

"The way I heard it," Jack explained, "It used to be a Catholic Church. I reckon they couldn't make it when the Mormon pioneers settled the area and started preachin'. It was vacant and deterioratin' until some guy brought his family out here from back east and turned it into a restaurant. He's a good cook and they sure do a good business."

There was only a short wait at the entrance, but they were impressed. Their table was close to a warm, inviting fire. While Bart passed out menus, Jack introduced him to the others.

Their meals complemented the elegant atmosphere. Rob and Judy ordered coffee. Jack drank beer. She was underage, but Beth ordered wine. She looked smug when she was not asked for I.D.

It was a time for them to learn about Rob and they were curious about his background, "What did you do before you were a mechanic?" Jack asked between bites of lasagna.

"I always was a mechanic," he began. "I built go-karts when I was a kid and worked in a garage all through high school. After graduation, I went in the service. I thought it was patriotic at the time."

"Were you in the Army?" Jack asked.

"No, I went in the Marine Corps. I figured if I might get drafted it would be better to go where I could learn how to take care of myself. After I got out I stayed in California for a while and then ended up in Tucson at the Mercedes Benz dealer. Been there ever since."

Jack thought for a minute and then asked, "If my guess is right you were in durin' the Viet Nam situation. Did you ever get over there?"

Rob shifted uneasily in his chair and looked at the others before he replied simply, "Yes."

"What was it like?" Beth asked with her wine glass in one hand and a forkful of veal parmesan in the other. She was nosy.

"Was it as bad as some of the stories we hear?"

Rob hesitated before he replied, "No. It was worse than any stories you heard. It was a politician's war. They were making too much money to care about the people they sent over there."

"What do you mean by that? How could it have been so bad," Beth asked.

"Just take my word for it, Beth," he replied and turned to Jack.

"Where are you from, Jack? I kind of had you pegged for a cowboy."

A smile crossed Judy's face as she watched the way Rob tactfully redirected the conversation. She sat quietly listening and watching Rob while the others talked. It was the things he didn't say and the topics he avoided that taught her more than she could have learned if he did all the talking. His eyes, the slightest flinch as he avoided the war told her a great deal. Judy wanted to know his character; his morals and values, but he didn't need to tell them that, he showed it. There was even more to Rob than Judy first assumed.

Jack blushed, "Well yeah, at least I like to think I can claim that as my profession. I'm from Wyoming. Wind River area if you've ever heard of it."

"I have," Rob replied. "One of the men I served with lived near Dubois. He used to tell stories that made me want to go there some day. He was always inviting me to come see him and go elk hunting."

"It is fine elk country. Did you ever take him up on the offer?"

"No, we weren't able to do that," Rob replied.

"That's too bad. How come you couldn't make it?" Jack asked innocently.

Rob swallowed and took a deep breath, "He never came home," he said so softly they barely heard him. Then he looked at Beth, "What about you Beth? Where are you from and what made you choose this school?"

He should have directed the conversation toward Beth much earlier. As the center of attention, she rattled on incessantly and drank more wine. When it was time to go, she directed all of her attention to Jack.

On the way back to the girls' apartment, Rob happened to glance in the rear view mirror. Jack and Beth were oblivious to their surroundings. Their activity made Rob uncomfortable. Then he glanced at Judy. She was watching him with those beautiful blue green eyes and wore a content smile. He had the uncanny feeling that they were carrying on a very private and intimate conversation without speaking a word.

The activity in the back seat concerned him. Was that accepted behavior? No, this lovely girl was different, different than her roommate, certainly different than his daughter, and nothing like his ex wife. It would be a shame to ruin the start of a good friendship with improper advances. Judy was too much fun to be with and far too nice a girl to treat that way. Reaching over he took her hand in his, touched it to his lips, and smiled at her.

"I had a great day today, Judy. Thank you. You're quite a lady."

The glow on her face reflected in the lights of oncoming cars. She returned his smile, "I had a great day too... you made it special," she replied quietly and gently laid her other hand on their joined hands.

When they stopped in the parking lot of the apartment, Beth had a satisfied flush on her face and needed a moment to straighten her clothing. They hurried to the door through the cold rain and knocked once before unlocking the door and going in.

"That was an exceptional spot Jack," Rob said as they waited for Judy to open the door.

"Angie isn't home yet," Judy said with a glance at Rob, "Do you want to come in for a while?"

"Maybe for a few minutes," Rob replied.

It looked like Beth was going to ask Jack to stay. It made Rob uneasy. That could put Judy in an awkward position. Rob wasn't about to subject her to that, "I think I better get back to the motel," Rob said. "It's been a full day and we've got a lot to do tomorrow."

He turned to Judy, "I'll pick you up in the morning so we can go to the library. I figure if I go along, I'll learn something," he said and turned to leave.

"I'll walk you out to your car," Judy said and wasn't about to take no for an answer.

As they approached the 4Runner she took his hand and led him around to the passenger door, "Can I get in with you for a minute? I'd like to talk," she said.

"Certainly," he smiled and opened her door. He went around to the driver's door and found it already ajar.

"Thanks," he said as he climbed in and started the motor. "I'll turn the heater on. It's pretty chilly."

Without hesitating, Judy put her hand on his arm and began, "Rob, I feel I should apologize about Beth. She can be an insensitive, self-centered person at times. There was no reason for her to act the way she did. She didn't need to be drinking in public and I really felt bad when she just didn't pay attention and kept asking about Viet Nam. She's so inconsiderate sometimes... and I was embarrassed for you the way she carried on with Jack on the way home. It's my fault. I should have known better. I'm truly sorry."

"Hold on a minute," Rob said. "You don't have to apologize for her actions. I felt bad for you. Her actions put you in an uncomfortable position. I should have put a stop to it, but I didn't. I'm sorry you had to put up with it. I should be apologizing to you."

She leaned over and laid her head on his shoulder. "You really are different," she said softly.

"Is that good or bad?"

She looked up into his eyes and smiled, "It's good... very good, a lot like my Dad. He was the finest man I ever knew. He would have liked you... and you would have liked him."

Rob slipped his arm over her shoulder and pulled her close, "From what you've said about your family I would say that's quite a compliment ... thank you."

Then Rob changed the subject, "Would you mind getting an early start tomorrow? I can pick you up whenever you say and I'll even buy breakfast. We could go to that little spot on the strip mall where we went this morning. I liked that place."

"I liked it too. You know I feel guilty when you spend all the money like that."

"We can discuss that some other time," he grinned. "Now, what time should I pick you up?"

"Is eight too early?"

"The day's half over by then; how about seven?"

"You talked me into it! Now do I get a goodnight kiss or haven't we got that far yet?"

That surprised him. After hesitating, he turned her face to his with a touch so gentle it made her shiver. He looked into her eyes and she could see his doubts and fears. She touched his cheek and pressed her lips to his. His kiss was so soft and tender it made her head spin.

"That's pretty far for me," he whispered in an unsteady voice.

It took her a moment to gather her thoughts before she put her head back on his shoulder and held his arm tightly, "That was very nice."

"Yes it was... you have no idea how special."

"I think I do, and it meant more to me than I think you realize. Thank you for being who you are, Rob. Now I think I better go in."

She kissed his cheek and opened the door.

"See you in the morning," she said brightly and then hurried through the rain to her door.

Rob sat in a daze as he watched her go.

After sitting for several minutes, he started to drive off. With a look back at her apartment, he was surprised to see Jack hurrying toward him.

17

ROB AND JACK

When Judy stormed into the apartment, there was fire in her eyes. Jack took one look and wisely decided he didn't want to be part of it, "I think I better get goin' too. I want to try and catch Rob before he gets away."

"Hey, man, do you mind stoppin' for a beer?" Jack asked as he approached Rob's Toyota.

His look told Rob that it went deeper than just a friendly drink, "I need to talk to you."

"Maybe one quick one; I'll follow you."

He watched Jack scurry across the wet parking lot to an older pickup truck that had seen better days. Once he started the truck, Jack led the way through the misting rain to a small corner bar off the main road. They splashed through the cold rain, pushed open the door and went inside. This was not a spot frequented by the campus crowd. It was small and dimly lit by the flickering neon signs advertising several different brands of beer. Two older men sat at opposite ends of the bar nursing their drinks and ignoring the world around them. The bartender glanced up and then went back to watching something on TV. Jack ordered two beers, dropped money on the bar, and squeezed into a booth across from Rob.

It was a booth designed for smaller men. He set their beer on the worn tabletop, tacky with the residue of years of beers, and twisted the bottle in his hands several times while he gathered his thoughts.

"I want to apologize for the way I acted tonight," he began.

Rob looked at his companion and waited for Jack to continue.

"I'm not sure where to begin. I sure like Beth, but sometimes she comes on a little strong for me and I don't deal with that very well."

"You're a sharp young man, Jack," Rob said. "Any girl would be proud to be with you."

"The ones I choose just don't seem to work out. There was this girl back home. I was nuts about her. We dated for a couple of years in high school and even talked about gettin' married. What I didn't know at the time and never even suspected was that she was screwin' anythin' with pants."

He took a swallow of his beer and continued, "I planned to go to school in Laramie, get my degree, and then spend the rest of my days on the ranch married to her and raisin' a family. She had other plans that didn't include me. She went off to Denver with some other fella. I was pretty tore up, and just wanted to get away. That's how I ended up here. I kinda avoided girls until I met Beth. She's a pretty girl and smart as hell. She's a farm girl and I'm a cowboy. Ain't too many gals that can handle that life.

"I expect it was the wine tonight, otherwise I don't believe she would've been that way especially with you and Judy right there. I got carried away and after thinkin' about it, I felt pretty stupid. You're a decent man so I figured I better at least try to apologize for my behavior. I don't want you to think that I'm some low-life bum."

"I don't think that at all Jack," Rob interrupted. "Beth's a pretty girl and damned sexy looking. You're both young and full of piss and vinegar. It's pretty hard to control those urges sometimes. Believe me, I know that."

Jack lowered his head and took a swallow of his beer before he looked up and continued, "She's sexy all right," he grinned. "But that's no excuse. She ain't much younger than your gal, and Judy don't act that way. She acts like a lady, and you're a first rate gentleman. I saw that by the way you acted with your daughter the first night I saw you. I just got carried away with Beth and I'm sorry you had to put up with it."

Rob reached across the table and grasped Jack's wrist. "You don't need to apologize to me, my friend. Like I said, I know what you're going through. My ex-wife was a lot like Beth, sexy as hell. We dated in high school and ended up going to bed pretty regular. We got married right after boot camp and then I went off to Viet Nam for eighteen months. She had a boy while I was gone. When I came back from 'Nam I got stationed in California and we tried to settle down to as normal a life as possible. Well, I was sent back over pretty quick. That time she had a girl, Patricia. You saw her in the restaurant. As soon as I got back, my tour was almost up so I figured I'd get settled somewhere permanent for a while. That didn't work out. They gave me a special assignment and I was gone again. When I finally got home after that, I got out and started to work. That lasted a couple of months. I was approached by one of those secret government outfits. They sent me to Africa for a while. After that, they sent me out for more covert assignments. Finally, I decided that was enough.

"We moved to Tucson to be closer to her family. I guess my being gone so much took its toll on her and she started having an affair with one of my golfing buddies. One day at work this little punk came into the shop and served me with divorce papers and that was it. My son Robert disappeared. I think he went in the Army, and Patricia stayed with her mother. It shook me up pretty bad. I was naïve like you were with your high school sweetheart. Later, when she took me back into court wanting more money, I found out that Robert wasn't even my son. She wasn't sure who the father was, but it wasn't me and she never told Robert.

"I haven't dated or gone out with anyone until Judy came along. I wasn't prepared for her, but she makes me feel something I've never felt before. I'm sure she'll get over it in time and settle for someone her own age, but in the meantime, she sure is a good friend. I enjoy her company and I enjoyed our hike today in spite of the weather. The way she handled a miserable situation impressed me... a lot."

Jack sat quietly looking at Rob before he shook his head, "Shit, man, I thought I had problems. You've been through it all. It's amazin' that you don't just hate all women. How do you manage to be so cool?"

Rob smiled, "It's like I told you about Patricia. I tolerate her outbursts and when it's over, I can walk away from it and be myself. I like me, and I'm happy with my life. People like her are stuck with themselves wherever they go and whatever they do. It took a long time to learn that, but it was a valuable lesson."

"I never would have guessed that someone like you had been through all that," Jack said as he squirmed into a more comfortable position and looked at Rob with growing respect.

The conversation wandered after that. Jack was asked about his life at home. He talked about the wilds of Wyoming, the ranch where he grew up, and his family. He talked about the wildlife, and hunting, and invited Rob to go with him sometime. It was nearly midnight when Rob suggested they call it a night. He had an early breakfast with Judy. As they were leaving, Jack stopped him at the door before they ventured back into the rain.

"Rob, about Judy... she's a very special lady."

"I'm very aware of that, Jack, and I intend to treat her that way."

"I know you do. I've seen that, but what I think you don't understand is the way she feels about you."

Rob chuckled, "Hell, Jack, I'm old enough to be her father."

"That may bother you some, but it don't mean a damn thing to her. I've known her a while, but from what I've seen and what I've heard from her roommates she's sure impressed with you. She'd like to keep you around. You just think about that, and don't be playin' games. This is pretty serious for her."

"I'd like to believe that Jack, but I'm sure she'll come to her senses one of these days and find someone just right for her. She's smart and tough, and she's beautiful. I enjoyed our hike today and I hope there'll be time for more hikes like that in the future. I'll always be up front with her, though. I don't play games, and I don't think much of people that do. She's probably one of the finest people I've ever met. I'll take care of her and treat her the way I think she should be treated."

Then he turned to Jack with a deadly serious look and grasped Jack's arm in a vice like grip, "When she does find the right man, if he ever treats her badly, he'll have to deal with me."

Jack was a bare-knuckle brawler, and a good one. It was a hard-earned reputation. At 6' 4" and 220 pounds, he deserved respect. Very few men intimidated Jack, but he knew which ones to avoid. Rob's parting words and the look in his eyes sent shivers down Jack's spine. Rob was undoubtedly the most dangerous man he had ever faced.

18

THE SECOND BREAKFAST

It snowed during the night without any accumulation and then became a light drizzle with a warm wind that indicated a change in the weather. When he drove into the parking lot, Judy was waiting for him with a happy glow that took all the dreary out of the gray, damp morning. She was at his door when he got out and gave him a firm hug. He couldn't help but smile at her exuberance and when he looked at her, she gave him a quick kiss.

"There," she laughed. "Maybe now you'll start to get used to that!"

Nodding his head, Rob smiled, "Yes, I could. Let's go eat, I'm starved!"

Judy brought reference books. While Rob drove, she referred to them with wide-eyed enthusiasm. Once at the restaurant, he glanced quickly through her books. By the time the food arrived, he was hooked. Unfolding the topo map and ignoring his food, he began pointing out terrain features that coincided with the information in her books. The lines and symbols on the map were making sense to her. Indicating a trail, he described what the terrain would look like. Judy sat back and watched his excitement grow. She watched his hands flowing across the map, his eyes sparkling with enthusiasm as he outlined a plan to reach their goal. She stopped listening to his words and smiled at him.

This wasn't a normal date; it was vastly different from anything she could have imagined. This was a comfortable breakfast with an old friend. There were similar interests, and now a common goal.

When he made a comment and looked to her for confirmation, he caught her staring at him. He looked down at their untouched food.

"Sorry, I got carried away," he said.

Judy's pleased smile wrinkled her nose. Her eyes were sparkling and she leaned against him, "You're like a kid with a new toy. Most people just don't get excited about anything."

Rob was about to apologize but she interrupted him, "Being with you is an adventure. Like discovering a whole new world of possibilities... I like that."

Their eyes met and held for a moment. On an impulse, Judy reached up and kissed his lips then quickly turned away as her cheeks glowed.

This time it was Rob that chuckled, "I could say the same thing... and I like that too. Now, we better eat. It's probably cold."

The food was cold but they didn't notice. After eating, they cleared a spot on the table and turned their attention back to the map. With his guidance, Judy quickly learned much more about topographical maps than her superficial knowledge. When he showed her the area where they hiked the day before, and the stream where they stopped for lunch, she was able to understand even better how the lines on a piece of paper translated to ridges, or valleys and flat terrain.

With breakfast, studying the map, and planning the hike, they spent nearly two hours in the restaurant. They were surprised when they went outside. The clouds had blown away, the sun was out and there was a warm, welcome, feel to the air.

"In Minnesota, weather like we had last night would have been the absolute end of summer... or fall. Once it starts to snow back there, it stays until spring. This is very different from what I'm used to."

"It still gets cold and wintry up here," Rob said and held her hand. "It can change rapidly at any time of year. It can snow in the summer at the higher elevations, or have fine days like this in winter. That's why it's so important to be prepared no matter what the weather looks like when you start a hike."

She stopped and looked at him, "You're always prepared aren't you?"

"Absolutely not," Rob laughed. "Some things catch me completely unawares and I have no idea how they came about."

"I find that hard to believe," she replied as they continued walking hand in hand across the parking lot. "Name one instance where you weren't prepared for something," she challenged.

By now, they were back at his 4Runner. He opened her door without answering, and went around to his side. He climbed in and started the motor. He was about to drive off when she asked him again.

"You didn't answer me... tell me one time when you weren't prepared for something."

He glanced at her, "There's absolutely, and positively, no way I was prepared for you."

"Oh."

It was almost dark as they were returning to her apartment. It had been a full day. They found part of the information they were seeking and more. Between some older books and several web sites, they were able to piece together enough facts to answer a few of their questions, but there was still so much unknown or only alluded to. There was nothing concrete in all their searching, just bits and pieces that mentioned the possibility of an area that may have been inhabited at one time. That made them even more curious. If the rumors and stories were true, they could be the first to locate and document it.

"It sounds like we're in agreement on taking a look," Rob said. "Now it's just a matter of finding the time. What's your class schedule like?"

"It's not a problem right now," she replied and hesitated. "But whenever we go, you'd still have the long drive."

"Then let's try it next weekend," Rob suggested without hesitating. "We should get an early start. Can I pick you up at six?"

"Yes, or even earlier if we need to," she said with an excited glow and squeezed his hand. "I can make our breakfast and pack a lunch."

"Cooking breakfast will disturb your roommates. Let's pick a restaurant and let someone else do the work."

It was quiet when they arrived at her apartment. Rob went around and opened her door. The weekend was gone. It was filled with excitement and discovery and Judy didn't want it to end. They were walking quietly to her door when Rob took her arm and turned her to face him. He was looking at her as if there was something he needed to say. She felt apprehensive when she looked up at him. Was something wrong, she wondered? Was he going to change his mind?

He reached out and cradled her face in his hands, and then he kissed her tenderly. When their lips parted, she was radiant. She embraced him and kissed him back. Rob felt her pressing herself against him, holding nothing back. His knees felt rubbery and his mind was spinning. He wrapped his arms around her and held her tightly.

When they parted, she was flushed and breathless. Her eyes wide, she smiled at him, "Wow... that should last me until next week."

Rob was speechless, and there was a very serious look on his face. When he tried to speak, no words seemed adequate. He leaned down and kissed her again.

"I think it might be a good idea to take you in now," he said as his voice cracked.

That was the one thing neither of them wanted to do, but it was necessary. At her door, Judy knocked once and then unlocked the door. Angie was reading a book and looked up when they entered. Beth was studying with open books and papers scattered about, but she stood up as soon as she saw them.

"Mr. Simpson, I'm sorry about last night..."

"It's Rob," he interrupted. "I appreciate that, but Judy's the one you owe an apology to. That sort of activity puts her in an uncomfortable position, especially when we're just getting to know each other. It gives the wrong message."

Angie tried desperately to appear engrossed in her book while Beth's shoulders slumped and she looked down at the floor, "I didn't think about it that way... I am sorry, Judy."

Turning to Angie curled up on the couch, Rob said, "That looks like some heavy reading, Angie."

She looked up from her book, "It's for my business law class. You're right, it is heavy stuff."

"I better get going," Rob said. "You gals have a good week. Good night."

Judy followed him out to his Toyota and stopped him at his door, "I appreciate the way you stood up for me. It made me feel good."

"You deserve respect, Judy. You're an exceptional person," he said as he slipped his arms around her.

"Thank you," she said quietly.

Their parting kiss was tender and meaningful. Then she stood watching with a feeling of exhilaration as he drove off. When she went back in to the apartment, she was oblivious to her roommate's comments. Going directly to her room, she picked up the phone and made her weekly call home.

19

CALLING HOME

"Hello."

"Hi, Mom, it's me. I met a guy, a really great guy," Judy said right away, and Marianne knew that it was serious.

Judy was level headed and mature. If she mentioned anyone at all in the past, it was only a casual reference. To begin a conversation this way meant that it was much more than that. There were a number of questions that came to mind, but Marianne held back waiting to see if Judy would explain further. She did. There were no secrets between them, and never had been. Judy recounted every detail from the first time she saw Rob in the restaurant confrontation with his daughter, right up to the goodnight kiss in the parking lot just a few minutes earlier. Her mother listened carefully to every word and was struck by the realization that this was not a mother-daughter conversation. Her daughter had grown up. This was an intense and very personal conversation between two adult women.

Rob's thoughts were spinning as he pulled on to the freeway and accelerated to the speed limit. He set the cruise control and turned on the radio but he didn't hear it. The situation with Judy had started curiously and then escalated rapidly in the last two days. He wasn't quite sure what to make of it. He thought about it from every angle he could imagine, looking for reasons and trying to understand. The intimacy that went beyond physical, was not the mindless, clinging displays that Beth exhibited on the previous night with Jack. It was a genuine display of sincere feelings, and he had responded in a similar manner. She kissed him without reservation and he returned that kiss. In only two short days, she had become much more than just an excellent hiking companion. It didn't seem to matter to her at all that he was almost old enough to be her father and that puzzled him. He suspected that his daughter was sexually active. He saw that in Beth's actions with Jack. Was that the sort of thing that was common to her generation he wondered?

No, Judy was different. Openly affectionate when they were alone, yet in the company of her peers, she was reserved, more mature. She seemed interested in him but retained her independence. She had a fantastic body, firm and muscular, sexy as hell, but she didn't flaunt it. She easily could have. She dressed and acted conservatively but when she kissed him, he could feel her willingness to give herself to him... completely.

Stopping at a pay phone in Verde Valley, he used his phone card to call. It was time to find out if this was just a game for her. Her phone was busy.

No reason for her to wait for me to call. Maybe I'm taking this whole thing too seriously.

He tried to focus on other things as the miles slipped by but it was no use. He stopped at another pay phone in Cordes Junction.

I'll try her number again... cancel the hike. That'll be better in the long run. This can't possibly go anywhere. If I break it off now, no one gets hurt.

He called her number again.

"Hello."

"Hi, Judy, it's Rob."

"Hi, Rob, are you all right?"

"Yeah, I'm fine..."

"I hope you didn't try to call earlier," she interrupted. "I was talking to Mom."

"That's right... your once a week call home," he remembered. "How are they doing?"

"They're all fine. I always call on Sunday night to catch up on what's happening at school... Rob?"

"I'm still here."

"I told her about our hike yesterday and our plans for next week," she said happily.

That was important to her, important enough that she had to share with her family. It was time to rethink what he had intended to say.

"How did she react to that?" he asked guardedly.

"Naturally she wanted to know all about you. I told her you were a Marine veteran, a mechanic and you had a daughter that was here at school. I told her how I met you and that surprised her. I told her about how you fixed my boots and put that stuff on my heel. I told her about the rain and how cold it was and how you took care of me. She even laughed when I told her how nervous I was about wrapping up in your blanket with nothing on underneath. Then I told her how we did our research for our hike next weekend."

"It sounds as if you didn't leave much out. It makes me wonder how I would react if my daughter called with a revelation like that."

"I'm not sure I understand what you mean by that. Are you upset that I told her about you?"

"Well, the part about having a daughter at your school."

"Oh, now I understand. Are you going to pull that on me?" she asked angrily.

"Now I'm not sure I understand."

"You were going to bring up that bullshit about our age difference weren't you?"

Her use of profanity startled him, "That's a pretty strong choice of words."

"If it got your attention then it's appropriate! I didn't get that reaction from my mother. She was more interested in what kind of person you are than how old you are or what you do for a living."

"And what did you say about that?"

"I told her about the incident with Beth and how you treated me with respect. I told her that you take care of me, and you're a good friend."

"So she was all right with that?"

Judy laughed, and closing his eyes, he could see the way her nose wrinkled when she laughed like that, "Well she did ask me one thing that caught me off guard."

"I can't imagine you being caught without a quick reply. What was that?"

"She asked me if I was sleeping with you!"

Rob was flabbergasted. There was a long period of silence while he took a deep breath.

"Rob, are you still there?"

"Yes, did you say what I think you said?"

"About sleeping with you?"

"Hell yes!"

Judy laughed gleefully, "Now you're the one with the limited vocabulary. Yes, Rob, that's what she asked."

"That must have been an interesting exchange."

"Mom and I are pretty close. She knows if she asks something like that, I'll answer truthfully. There are no secrets between us," then she added, "Just like there's no secrets between you and me. I'd never lie to you."

That part was mostly true. She just neglected to tell him that when her mother asked, rather than saying no, she answered, 'Not yet'.

"Is there anything else that you talked about that I should be aware of?"

"Yes, my brother Brian was excited that you're a mechanic. That's something he wants to learn about and he asked when he'd get to meet you. Sarah, she's my sister, wanted to know what you look like and if you're interested in music. She plays the piano and she's quite good. She wants to meet you too, well, so does Mom. They all do."

"Judy, that's halfway across the country."

"I know," she answered dejectedly.

"We'd have to wait for a holiday... like Thanksgiving or Christmas or something."

Judy couldn't think of a thing to say. He sounded serious. When she was able to reply, she asked in amazement, "Are you serious? No... you wouldn't do something like that... would you?"

"It's something we'd certainly have to discuss... in fact I think there are a number of things we should discuss."

"Like what?"

"Like the idea of wanting me to meet your family. That's pretty serious. So much has happened with us in such a short time. Believe me, I'm not complaining, but I guess I'm just a little concerned. We've never really talked about us. You know, the usual; expectations, guidelines, goals... things like that."

"Rob, this weekend was so unexpected. I enjoyed every minute of it. I never thought just doing the simple things we did together could be so enjoyable and even exciting. Do you want to know something? In getting to learn about you, I know that this was just the beginning. I know that being together whenever we can, doing whatever it is we decide to do, will only get better. I don't feel it's necessary to set guidelines and expectations. I know who you are and what kind of a person you are and I hope you've learned a little about me. I feel like we're comfortable enough together that if one of us does something wrong we can discuss it and solve it right then and there."

Rob laughed softly before he answered. "You've got it pretty well figured out don't you?"

"No, Rob, I don't have all the answers. I just know that we seem to think a lot alike, that we've both got the same values."

"When you kissed me... I just didn't expect that," he said softly.

"But how did that make you feel? Were you embarrassed?"

"No, I was surprised. I didn't expect it."

"I guess it surprised me too... I've never done anything like that before, but it felt so natural with you. I'm glad I did. I'll bet if I had waited for you, I'd be waiting a long time!" she added.

Rob grinned, "That's probably true, but I wasn't sure how you'd react. I wasn't about to mess up a good friendship."

"You seem to learn pretty quickly. When you took me home tonight you kissed me... that meant a lot to me."

When he hung up the phone, Rob smiled and said aloud, "Well I didn't get around to canceling that hike after all... good idea, Rob!"

In Duluth, Judy's mother had a meeting with Sarah and Brian. "It sounds like your sister has found someone that has certainly captured her interest."

"You mean like a boyfriend?" Sarah asked excitedly.

"Yes, I think so, although it might be even more serious than that. He's older than her but she made it very clear that it didn't matter to her and didn't want us to bring it up."

Brian and Sarah wanted more information and continued to inundate Marianne with questions until she had exhausted all the information she had and sent them off to bed. There were serious concerns. She wasn't quite comfortable with Judy's announcement. Was she just infatuated, or was there some merit to this man that was suddenly part of her life? Marianne hoped that this man was not a bum and would treat her daughter well.

"Judy is an exceptional girl," she told one of her co-workers the next day. "I wish she would choose someone that's good enough for her."

20

RAIN GEAR

All week long Rob and Judy were looking forward to their exploratory hike on Saturday, but the weather report was not promising. As Rob drove north after work on Friday, the skies changed from partly cloudy to overcast. When I-17 climbed out of Phoenix, it began to rain. It was not an auspicious beginning to the weekend.

He called Judy from Cordes Junction. She sounded depressed, "It's raining pretty steadily here and it doesn't look like it will clear up. I was really looking forward to it, but if the rain continues, I don't think we'll be able to make our hike."

"It changed to rain when I started up the hill, but don't let it get you down. There's still a chance that it might clear up, but even if it doesn't, I'm sure we can think of something."

"If you like music, there's a concert on campus in the afternoon," she replied half-heartedly. "It's a symphony... but I don't know if you like classical music."

"I love it, but maybe we can do both. Don't get down in the dumps. We can think of something... trust me," he added with a chuckle. "Now don't give up on it until we have breakfast. We'll see what the weather's doing then."

"I could make our breakfast here if you want me to."

"No, let's go to our place in that strip mall. If we eat at your place it'll wake your roommates."

"I suppose you're right. Once they heard activity in the kitchen and smelled food cooking they'd want to eat too. It would be noon before we could get away."

"Good, I'll pick you up at 6:30, how's that?"

"I suppose I can wait that long to see you," she replied and still sounded depressed.

"You don't sound happy... why don't we make it six?"

"It'll probably still be raining, but being with you sounds a little better."

Rob made good time and it was a little after eight when he drove into town and found a motel not far from Judy's apartment. After checking in, he made a quick trip to see if the sporting goods store he saw on a previous trip was still open. It was just off the main street, and still open.

Rob made a quick stop and asked the manager if he would be willing to stay open just long enough to go and get his friend and make a purchase. The manager agreed to hang around for a little while... but not too long.

There was cell phone coverage here, so Rob punched in Judy's number.

When she answered he asked, "Can you come out for a little bit right now? I can pick you up in a couple of minutes. I've got an idea."

"You're already in town?" she asked brightly. "I look a mess, but I can be ready. What is it?"

"See you in a couple of minutes!"

She was watching for him and when he drove into her parking lot, he pulled up to the curb as close as he could get to her door. He barely stepped out into the rain when she ran up and hugged him with a happy, bright eyed, "Hello!"

"We have to hurry," he said as he led her around to the passenger door and helped her inside.

Once they were buckled in, Rob drove off quickly. "What's this all about," she asked curiously.

"It's a surprise... but if you feel uncomfortable about surprises then think of it as an adventure!" he said.

"It sounds like you're trying to keep from telling me something."

"Well yeah, in a way I am. I don't want to get in an argument before you even find out what it is!"

"I don't like the sound of that. Where are we going?"

"We'll be there in another minute... just watch the rain."

"I've been watching that rain all day, and the more I watch it, the more depressed I get," she answered and slumped back against the seat.

The windshield wipers splashed their arc across the glass, and with each pass, her mood deteriorated. It was that cold, wet, rain that was going to prevent them from hiking. The headlights and taillights from other cars mixed with streetlights and multi-colored store signs, glistening in the mist. Rob drove into the parking lot at the sporting goods store, shut off the motor and hurried around to open her door.

"Come on, its closing time but they're waiting for us. We need to hurry!"

"What are we doing here? We don't need anything. Besides, this rain isn't going to quit so we can't hike anyway."

He wasn't listening to her objections. As they approached the door, the manager unlocked it and let them in. He greeted them as Rob hurried past pulling Judy along behind him. He called a quick 'thank you' over his shoulder and went directly to the area he was looking for.

"There," he said to Judy as he came to an abrupt halt in front of rain gear. "Pick your color and make sure you choose a jacket that's a little large so you can layer under it."

She glanced at the racks of clothing and then at him, "Rob I can't afford to buy something right now. We can always wait for a better day."

"I told you I didn't want to argue. Pick out something you like and let me worry about the rest of it. If you get the right stuff, we can hike no matter what the weather throws at us tomorrow. I saw how you handled the wet last weekend. You did great, and if you weren't so cold and wet you would have been fine. All we have to do is be prepared."

Judy looked at him and realized it would be senseless to argue with him. She wandered over to the rack and began looking through some of the brightly colored rain suits. He watched her anxiously for a minute and then stopped her.

"Here," he said as he guided her to a different display. "You need to be looking at something that will do the job and last more than just one hike. This is called Gore-Tex. It's waterproof, breathable, and durable. The colors aren't as bright, but this stuff *works*. Pick something with adjustable sleeves, and a hood, and zippers at the bottom of the legs so you can put it on over your boots."

Judy glanced through the selection and then found the perfect shade of green, just her color, and her eyes lit up. "Can I try this on?" she asked.

Rob nodded, "Sure, that's the only way you can see if it fits!"

She slipped into a jacket that seemed large, but it felt comfortable and well made. Rob checked the fit at the sleeves and made sure it was roomy enough to wear over a coat, or maybe a pack. He pulled the hood up and snugged it at her chin. When he seemed satisfied, he handed her the matching pants.

"Make sure you can put this on over your boots."

As soon as she was outfitted, she looked in the mirror and smiled.

"This is really nice! I like the color and even though it's a little large, I can see what you mean about being able to wear a coat under it. I'd like to get something like this some day, then we could go out in any weather."

Changing the subject, he asked, "Are your boots waterproof?"

"Well sort of, they did get wet last week, but not bad. They're good boots, though. They fit well and they're broken in."

Rob took her hand and started toward the cash register. She was still wearing the rain suit. On the way, he snatched a can of waterproofing.

"This ought to do it for tonight. I appreciate you waiting for us," he told the manager as he handed him his credit card.

Judy looked at him with a concerned expression, "What are you doing Rob? I told you I can't afford to buy something right now."

"It's all right; I'll buy it for you. It's the only way we can be sure of getting on that trail tomorrow. This will keep you warm and dry, and we won't have to worry about the weather."

The manager looked up as he took the tags off Judy's rain gear, "If you're planning on going out tomorrow, I wish you luck. It's supposed to keep raining through the weekend, but if you're going to go out anyhow, then this is the only thing to wear. It'll keep you warm and dry better than anything else I've got, and it's rugged. This outfit will last you for years."

Judy was standing with a forlorn look on her face. She could see the logic in having rain gear but she felt guilty about Rob paying for it. She almost came to grips with her concern until she saw the total come up on the cash register.

She was stunned, "My God, Rob..." she gasped. "This is expensive! I can't let you do this."

"The manager stayed late just for us, Judy. He needs to get home to his family. Come on, we can discuss this outside."

Rob was banking on Judy's shock to prevent her from taking the rain gear off before she had time to react. He signed the receipt and taking her arm headed for the door. His timing was good. They were back out in the rain and the manager was locking the door behind them before reality sunk in.

"I can't let you do this for me Rob!" she retorted. "I can't repay you for this. You didn't even tell me how much this outfit cost! This is expensive, far more expensive than I would buy for myself! I could do just as well with one of those nylon things from Wal-Mart. You're putting me in an awkward position here."

They walked past the 4Runner and beyond the parking lot. Walking down the street in the rain, Judy continued her tirade and Rob listened without response. She was uncomfortable about being put in such a position with no warning. They walked for several blocks before she began to wind down. Walking in relative silence, she continued to fume inwardly. Rob reached out and took her hand in his. She tried to pull away but he wouldn't let her. They walked another block before he spoke.

"Have you got it out of your system yet?" he asked.

She looked at him and most of her anger had subsided, "It just isn't fair Rob. You make the trip up here, drive for hours each way, and then you pay for everything. I feel guilty about that. I don't know how to repay you."

"You can do one thing for starters."

"What's that?" she asked cautiously.

"You can begin by having a higher opinion of yourself. You deserve better than that Wal-Mart junk. Are you warm?"

"What? Yes, I'm warm."

"Are you dry?"

"Yes, I'm dry, but you're trying to change the subject. What has that got to do with anything?"

"Well if you're warm and dry, then this cold rain isn't bothering you at all is it?"

She gave him a strange look, "But Rob... this is an expensive outfit."

He kept walking and he still held her hand, "I don't think of it that way. I look at it as an investment. We've been looking forward to getting out and trying to find that place we talked about. With this weather, we wouldn't be able to go. I'm hoping that with that rain gear you might reconsider. If you do, then it was a good investment. Besides, with good equipment, if you turn me down for an outing in the future then I'll know that I have to worry."

When she stopped and turned to look at him, the moisture in her eyes wasn't from the rain. She put her arms around him and laid her head against his chest.

"Nobody's ever done anything like this for me," she said sincerely. "I don't know what to say."

"You could invite me to your place for something hot to drink. I didn't put on my rain pants and the bottom half of me is getting wet!"

She stepped back and looked at him with a devilish grin, "Does that mean you have to ride back with no pants on and just a blanket wrapped around like you did to me?"

He smiled at her impish look and turned back toward the parking lot, "I'm not that wet."

21

AT THE APARTMENT

When they got to her apartment, Judy unlocked the door and led him in, "Angie's out somewhere and I don't expect her home until Sunday night or Monday morning, and Beth's out with Jack, so they won't be back until later, either. I think they went to a movie or something. I'll be right back; I'm just going to put my new rain outfit in my room."

"Bring your boots with you," he called after her as she disappeared down the hall.

She came back shortly with her boots and several towels, "Dry off with this, and then sit on one of the others. That way you don't get the furniture wet. I'll make us something hot to drink."

He took her boots and the towels but as she started toward the kitchen, he caught her arm and gave her a quick kiss, "Thank you."

Judy shook her head in exasperation, "What for, I haven't done anything."

"Yes, you did. We're communicating," he said quietly and sitting on the towel, started on her boots.

His comment surprised her.

Communicating. What makes that so significant for him? Isn't it obvious, isn't that what people do?

Before long, she returned with two steaming mugs of hot chocolate.

He motioned for her to sit next to him, and handed her the other boot, "Work the waterproofing into the leather and be sure to get some at the seam where the sole meets the uppers."

She laughed, "You must really think I don't know anything. First, you teach me how to put my boots on and now you want to teach me how to waterproof them. I don't know what I'm going to do with you!"

"Just be patient with me. I'm learning."

"So am I," she said and kissed his cheek.

Planning for their adventure in the morning made the time pass quickly. When her boots were waterproofed, Judy got up to put them away, "Would you like something to eat?"

"I'm good, but another cup of hot chocolate if you don't mind."

On her way to the kitchen, she turned on the TV, "I don't know if there's anything worth watching."

After flipping through several channels, he found a movie that was already in progress. Judy brought their mugs and sat beside him. When a commercial came on, he set the mug aside and put his arm over her shoulder. She nestled comfortably against him. Outside an occasional gust of wind drove a smattering of cold rain against the window. Inside it was warm and comfortable. Auburn hair on his cheek was soft with a clean fragrance to it. He turned and brushed her hair with his lips.

"Your hair is so soft," he whispered against her ear.

"Thank you," she said, paused, and grabbed his leg, "But your pants are still wet!"

In an instant, they were wrestling across the floor and laughing. When the rambunctious play subsided, Rob was sitting on her stomach holding her arms. She was helpless and couldn't break free. Their laughter died down when Rob released her arms. He leaned forward and kissed her tenderly. Wrapping her arms around him, she pulled him tightly against her. They rolled off onto their side, then again until she lay on top of him. She felt his hands gently on the small of her back, under her sweater, caressing soft, bare skin. She squirmed against him, her lips pressed tightly to his, her hands in his hair. His hands were lower, exploring tentatively. She was aware of his reaction, felt his passion rising with her own. She was breathing heavily now, responding to his touch, aware of where this was leading and full of eager anticipation.

Rob heard the voices first and sat up suddenly. Judy was frustrated until she heard the dreaded knock at the door and the sound of a key in the lock. She sat up beside him, her face flushed and tried to act interested in the movie when Beth and Jack came through the door.

"Hey, what are you two doing?" Beth grinned. "I didn't think you were coming until in the morning."

"From the look of the weather it doesn't look like you're going hiking," Jack said.

Controlling her frustration, Judy replied, "No, we are going hiking in the morning. Rob got here early and took me out to get some rain gear so we could go."

She rose from her spot on the floor and offered to show them. Rob got up and shook Jack's hand.

When she returned with her rain gear, Beth replied with a disinterested comment. Jack's eyes got big. "Wow, that looks like good stuff! Is that Gore Tex?" he asked.

"Yes it is," Rob answered. "I thought if we're going hiking in this weather she should have the right equipment."

Slipping his arm around Judy's waist, he added, "I wouldn't want anything to happen to her."

He went for his jacket, "Tomorrow could prove to be a rough hike, I better get going."

Judy's crestfallen look was too obvious to miss.

"Come on, Judy, walk me out to my rig and then I'll be off. We both need to get a good night's sleep. We can't do that if we stay up all night and visit." He slipped into his jacket and stood by the door.

Reluctantly, Judy donned her new rain jacket and followed him outside. He took her hand, led her to the passenger side, and opened the door for her, "Get in, Honey, we need to talk."

Judy unlocked his door and then sat anxiously while he came around and climbed in. He started the motor and turned the heater on low before he spoke, "I'm sorry I got carried away in there..."

"I'm not!" she interrupted and he felt the anger and frustration in her voice. "I'm upset that those two came when they did!"

Rob chuckled without humor, "It could have been worse. They could have arrived ten minutes later."

"It's not funny, Rob. That was pretty serious."

Their eyes met before he continued, "You're right, Judy, it is serious. I've been away from the dating game for..."

"This isn't a game!" she interrupted.

"That's not what I meant," he said.

She felt the intensity of his response. With a sharp intake of breath, she held her tongue, realizing that this was not the time to debate, or argue. It was time to listen!

"For some people it is a game, seeing how far they can go, chalk up another conquest. This isn't a game for me. All of this is moving so quickly, and I wasn't prepared for us. There has to be more to a relationship than sex. It should be something that lasts, something that's worth having, keeping, and working for. I see that in others, my friends, but I don't know how to make it work. I tried, and I failed."

She lowered her head while her hurt and disappointment hung in the silence between them.

"I'm not good at this," he said. "I don't know how to describe my feelings in a way that you could understand. I'm not sure I understand myself. I haven't felt this way before."

"You were married, Rob," she said gently. "You must have felt something."

"Yes, at first it was pretty exciting, but that didn't last. There was lots of passion, but there was no intimacy. We never communicated. At the time, I didn't understand that. I thought I was working at it pretty hard, trying to make things all right. Maybe I was just being selfish. I don't know.

"I've had a few years to think about it, but I still don't know what I did wrong."

Pausing, he continued quietly, "But that's just my side of the story. The war, the time away, had to be hard on her and the kids. After the divorce, after it was over, I promised myself I'd never go through that hurt again."

She touched his arm, "I couldn't hurt you, Rob."

"I believe that," he replied, "But, in a way, I'm glad we were interrupted. Sex complicates things. That's when people stop learning about each other and just concentrate on sex. That scares me. I'm still learning about you, and about myself. I don't just want us to make love... I want more."

"What more is there?"

"When we first met you told me you knew the area, you could keep up, and you're good company. That was true. You were honest, and that's 'more'. We have a lot of the same interests, like the same things. What's even more important is that we can talk... communicate. We can disagree and talk it out... like this rain gear," he said and touched her sleeve.

"That's 'more'. It's happening so fast, but it feels like we can become friends, true friends, and that too is another part of 'more'. That's new to me, I'm trying to understand it, and it isn't easy for me. Learning to trust is the hardest part."

He paused and took her hands in his. He continued, his voice hesitant, "I'm enjoying every minute we have together. I wouldn't want to jeopardize that for anything. You're an incredible woman, Judy, but I'm not ready for what you're offering... not yet. I don't know if I'm capable of reciprocating. Things have changed, and I don't know what goes on any more, what's expected between people. I'm afraid of what could happen. I can't go through that again."

Easing his head to her shoulder, she held him and kissed his cheek, "That wasn't easy for you to say was it?"

"No, it wasn't," he replied. "I feel foolish... I don't need to saddle you with my problems."

She touched his lips with her fingertips, "Don't say that Rob; don't even think that... not ever.

"I think I understand now what you mean by 'more'. I always admired my parents."

She spoke softly, past memories, feelings, clearer now, and understanding, "I respect the love they shared. For many years I thought I understood it. I didn't. What Mom and Dad had wasn't a gift that came easily. It was hard work, something they did together and struggled with every day of their lives. It was give and take, mutual respect, and trying to understand, growing to understand. It was not a game and not easy at all. I saw that the result was worth every moment of struggle. Their love and tenderness is the clearest memory, but there were times when it wasn't so easy, the times when one of them had to relinquish pride or selfishness. That wasn't easy. They're both strong willed and independent... kind of like us," she smiled. "But I learned that they were far stronger together than either one of them could ever have been alone."

She leaned back against the seat and sat quietly then, deep in thought.

With a heavy sigh, Rob sat up, "I probably better go. We've got a full day tomorrow."

"It's all right Rob. I think I understand. Everything is okay," she said and reached for the door.

He touched her arm and she stopped, "Judy?"

"Yes?"

"Don't ever think for a minute that I don't want to make love to you."

"I know... and the feeling is mutual."

Judy went back into her apartment filled with powerful and mixed emotions. Their conversation concerned her even more. She was the one acting like it was all a game, not Rob. It was becoming clear. Now she was beginning to understand how serious this was for him.

She went to her bedroom without noticing that Jack was already in Beth's room. Lying in bed, her fear grew. There was no one she could talk to, no one that would listen to her concerns, no one to advise her about what to do.

Suddenly she stopped and smiled. That was not true, she had Rob. She could talk to him. He would listen. Together, they would know how to proceed.

That's what he meant about communicating!

Taking a deep breath, she refocused her thinking.

No, I'm expecting too much, too soon. I'm not being fair, forcing him to make decisions he's not ready for. Too many years of pain in his life.

Rob was worth waiting for, and the more she thought about it, the more her resolve grew. She prepared herself mentally for the morning. Rob's pain and fear were deep. A single night trying to sort things out would not erase years of hurt. It was not going to be easy... she would have think clearly, be strong, and be wise.

Rob made his way to the motel and without even getting undressed, fell into bed. Events were unfolding so rapidly. Helen baffled him completely. She veiled her true character when they had sex and he lost his objectivity. Were other women that way? Was Judy?

The struggle within lasted the night. Everything he believed about Judy, the truth and honesty that he saw in her eyes told him that he was being foolish doubting her character and integrity. She hadn't done anything to cause him to doubt her, but he was getting involved emotionally. When Jack and Beth interrupted them, it was a warning. He didn't want to believe it, but there was the possibility that Judy could do the same thing Helen did.

When the morning came and it was time to leave, he wondered if she would even want to see him after being frustrated last night. She was a strong person and spoke her mind readily. If she did go with him, he felt sure he would be subjected to the sort of tongue-lashing and recrimination that Helen did so well. He would have to prepare himself.

22

THE MORNING AFTER

When Rob arrived on time, it was still raining but Judy brightened immediately. Her first concern was that he might not come at all. She had all her things with her and was wearing her new rain outfit as she dashed out to greet him, confident and wearing her brightest smile. He was bleary eyed and looked as if he had a rough night.

She kissed him quickly, then with a cheery smile said, "You look terrible."

"I didn't sleep very well."

Her reply was gentle, "I didn't think you would. That was a pretty intense night... I know it was difficult for you, but it meant a lot to me that you were able to talk about it. I appreciate you being honest and sharing with me." Then she brightened, "Now, let's get some coffee in you and then some breakfast. There's a trail out there with our name on it, and like John Wayne said, we're burnin' daylight!"

"Come, we burn daylight, ho!" Rob mumbled under his breath.

Judy stopped abruptly and stared at him. She was surprised and impressed; not many people knew the Shakespeare version of that quote.

Rob couldn't help but grin at her bright and cheery attitude. It helped. He gave her a hug and after loading her pack, opened her door. Jack's old truck was still in the parking lot. Obviously, he spent the night with Beth. It was something Judy would know. He imagined she'd say something about it, reminding him that he could have spent the night with her. A woman could certainly make things miserable.

As they drove out of the parking lot, he felt it wisest to bring the matter up first and take his abuse, "It looks like Jack spent the night with Beth."

Judy laughed lightly and squeezed his arm, "Yes he did, but I feel sorry for him. He's a decent guy, but I think that Beth is just using him. She's done that before. She'll get tired of him before long and be on the lookout for someone else. It's all pretty temporary with her as I'm sure you've guessed. She's really smart, but she just doesn't understand anything about people. She never takes the time to find out what a guy's really like. It makes me glad that I know you."

Her tone changed, she was serious now, "Last night was the second time you could have taken advantage of me and you didn't. I respect you for that, and I feel safe with you. When we talked last night, I know that couldn't have been easy, but I learned so much about you."

That was definitely not what he prepared himself for. He dreaded what he felt would be an unpleasant confrontation and yet Judy did not react the way he expected. It was as if she understood. The morning was looking better already!

Because of the cloud cover and rain, it was still dark with only the illusion of potential day. At the edge of town, they found a small diner. Going in, they found a booth along one wall. There were several other customers gloomily drinking coffee or huddled over their breakfast. A group of rowdy young men sat at a table, obviously finishing up their night's partying.

Judy slipped in beside him and they looked over the topographical map of the area they would hike. He explained the details of this part of the map and described what the symbols meant and how the contour lines related to what they were facing. Judy had classroom knowledge of topo maps, but Rob knew them intimately. For years, his life depended on how well he knew and utilized them. He pointed out the area where he suspected the ruins to be based on what they had discovered the previous week.

"If we followed this shorter route," he said, indicating the semblance of a trail, "That might allow more time for exploring when we reach the site. There's a problem though. This area here, where the contour lines are very close together, our route looks to follow the edge of this narrow canyon."

He spread his hand over an area to the east of the narrows, "This is the drainage area that will direct all its water from the rain into the canyon. Depending on the ground cover here to the east, the rain could soak in or run off through the narrow canyon making it impassable."

"What do you think?"

"It's a shorter route, but there's the potential that we might be stopped at this point here," and he tapped the narrow area with his finger. "It could have us in the general area sooner or it could prevent us from making it at all. It's a gamble."

"Let's try it. If we get stopped then we can try it again some other time and take the other route, or the short way in better weather."

Rob grinned at her enthusiasm. It looked like nothing could deter her once she made up her mind about something. They folded the map when the waitress brought their food and ate heartily.

When they finished eating and prepared to leave, one of the young men from the loud group swaggered to their booth. Rob sensed trouble. He quickly surveyed the group and made a mental note. There were only five of them but it could get messy. The one that approached them would be easy. One of the others was big and would have to go down quickly. The others might hesitate. It could end there, or he would have to finish it. It could get nasty with Judy there.

The young man leered at Judy, "Hey red, how's ya doin'?"

Judy sized him up and gave him a cold look without answering.

"Why don't you leave this old man here and come party with us. We could show you a good time."

Rob tensed and was about to get up when he felt Judy's light touch on his leg. For a moment he wondered why. Then she showed her stuff.

When she glanced at the intruder, her look changed to a smile, but it was the look in her eyes that should have been a warning, "No thanks," she replied.

His look changed to a surprised scowl, "Is your Daddy here going to get mad if you come with us?"

Judy continued to smile sweetly but there was ice in her reply, "No, we just came out for breakfast to get away from our children. I certainly have no intention of babysitting someone else's kids. I think it would be a good idea for you to go back to your friends before I have to give you a spanking for being naughty... excuse us," she added, and getting up she brushed past him abruptly.

Fortunately, the punk retreated a step to let them past. As Rob went by, he looked at the kid and nodded toward Judy, "Black belt," he whispered confidentially. "I sure wouldn't mess with her."

His buddies howled with laughter at how he'd been put down. When he returned to their table, he told them all the things he intended to do or say, and some of them were very clever.

A change came over Rob. He smiled and put his arm around her waist as they returned to their vehicle. When they were settled in, Judy was laughing. Rob turned to her, "You handled that pretty well, a lot better than I would have."

"It's not as bad as it could have been. I was just lucky in guessing how far I could push before they all reacted. It could have been uncomfortable, but that kid was still drunk and he didn't look as tough as he sounded. I hope you weren't embarrassed by letting them think we were married," she replied with a smile and a hug. "Now let's go find that trail. It's light enough to see and I want to get started!"

This little redhead had some spunk. The more he thought about it the more he was glad she was on his side. She could be a tough competitor. The kid was right, he could easily be her father, but that didn't faze Judy. She simply gave the impression that they were married...

and had children. He glanced at her out of the corner of his eye. She was an extraordinary woman. Rob resolved once again, as he told Jack, if Judy's future husband ever treated her badly, he would take it upon himself to correct him.

The Simpson method of correcting abusive husbands was frowned upon by most legal systems.

23

ON THE TRAIL

Once they found the starting point, they set out in the rain. It led up a steep, rocky bank and then onto a shelf that was reasonably level for a short ways before it pointed uphill and was lost in the rain and mist. Judy wore her pack under her new rain jacket and was pleased that her jacket was roomy enough to accommodate it. Rob shouldered his pack and started at the same brisk pace he had on their first hike. Rob's gloomy countenance brightened noticeably. After 15 minutes, he stopped and checked their boots. Judy grinned as she stood with one hand on his shoulder for balance while he adjusted the laces. She knew how, but she wasn't about to let him know that.

It was a new trail for both of them and they were enjoying unexpected discoveries. Part of the time, they were in trees and occasionally in open country with sparse vegetation that faded into the rain. Warm and dry, the only exposed flesh was face and hands.

"Getting this rain suit was a good idea, Rob. I'm sorry I made a scene about getting it. You were right and you sure could rub my nose in it if you wanted to."

"I wouldn't do that," he answered honestly.

"I know," she answered with a grin.

Rob knew that she wasn't that way either. It would have been a miserable morning with sarcastic comments about last night.

Although the going was rough, they made surprisingly good time. Not only did she keep up, but she was enthusiastic. Very few people could maintain a positive attitude under such adverse weather conditions. Rob was impressed. He was thoroughly enjoying himself, and she was too.

At one point Judy stopped and looked around. Taking in the trail, the trees, the fog, and the rain, a strange feeling came over her. She had never been here before yet everything was somehow familiar. She tried to shake it off and continued up the trail but the feeling wouldn't leave her. Now, even the rocks and the twisting of the trail were something she was certain she had seen before and it unnerved her. Hurrying up beside Rob, she took his hand.

After several hours of rugged hiking, the trail grew narrower. The rock walls crept out of the fog and rain from both sides and eased toward them. There was another sound above that of the steadily falling rain. To their left the ground fell sharply into a gray void with a vertical wall beyond. To the right the slope was giving way to a steeper wall that funneled them forward. Rob led the way, alert for potential hazards, then he stopped.

"It looks as if this is as far as we go today," he advised and pointed ahead.

The trail went downward and disappeared into a boiling, muddy torrent. The canyon was funneling the rainwater from miles away through this narrow passage. There was no way to tell how deep the water was or where the trail would work its way back out of the treacherous flood.

"This is one trip that will have to wait for another day," Rob said and his dejected tone mirrored her attitude.

"I saw a spot back a ways that might give us a little protection from the rain. We'll look at the map and see if there's any alternative."

Retracing their steps, he led the way up a muddy slope to an area of large boulders. There was a narrow gap between two large rock walls that would afford protection from the rain. The narrow opening widened, then narrowed quickly as it went back into the side of the hill, but it would keep them out of the weather while they considered their options. The floor was reasonably level and surprisingly dry.

They stripped off their packs and sat on the floor in the dirt. Rob took a towel from his pack so they could dry off. He took out the map and studied the area.

"Any alternate routes are even more hazardous. It would be cross-country with no visible landmarks to keep us on course. We could go back to the start of the trail and take the longer route. It's still early right now, but even if we found the site, we wouldn't have any time for exploring. We better plan on making this trip another time.

"How about something hot to drink, I've got some freeze-dried soup or instant coffee."

"Soup sounds good," Judy replied brightly. "Too bad it's so wet. It would be nice to have a fire. Do you think there's any chance I can find some dry wood somewhere?"

"Not much chance of that with this rain unless we can find some deadfalls. Do you know what to look for?"

She shrugged, "No, I don't. We'll have to forego a fire after all."

"Maybe not," he said. "That's a good idea and we might get lucky. Let's take a look and see what's out there."

Donning their rain gear, Rob led the way back out into the rain. A short distance away saw what he was looking for. Several giant pine trees had fallen and were wedged against boulders. The underside would be fairly dry. The stubs of broken branches protruded below the trunk. He kicked several of them loose from the rotting trunk. When they got back to the shelter, he laid them in the dry dirt and surrounded them with rocks while Judy watched his every move. He went to his pack and took out starter materials. Working intensely he coaxed a tiny flame into a larger one. Adding the stubs of branches, he soon had a small fire going.

"I don't know if there's a term for it, but I've heard people call it 'pitch'," he told her as he carefully built up the infant fire. "It's pretty dense and doesn't smoke much. It's good for cooking. I learned this from a pretty savvy friend of mine years ago and it stuck. We were in rain like this and I would have been plenty cold if he hadn't taught me. I felt pretty foolish the way he made it look so easy."

Judy grinned; he could have easily made her look foolish but he didn't. Now that she knew what to do, she was eager to help and soon they had an ample supply of fuel. Back in the shelter, the small fire was burning steadily in spite of the weather. While he made soup over his mini stove, she tended the fire. It cast a cheery glow, taking the chill out of the damp air. When the soup was ready, it quickly became a cozy setting.

"It's too bad we couldn't make it this time," Judy began, "But this is nice. I'm sure glad you're here. If you weren't, I'd have turned back and slogged out in the rain. I never would have seen this spot. You turned a disappointment into something really nice."

Rob smiled at her. In front of them, a river of mud. Raining steadily, visibility was close to zero, and they hadn't reached their goal. It could have been a great disappointment, but she was enjoying the situation... nearly as much as he was.

He leaned toward her and gave her a quick peck on the cheek, "You're something else," he said with a grin. "Most anyone would be miserable and complaining about the weather, the mud, and not being able to reach our goal. I've never hiked with anyone like you. I'm impressed."

She tried to hide her pleasure as she replied, "But Rob, I'm with you. We're warm and dry, what could be better? We could even camp here. This is turning out to be a pretty good day after all!"

"For us maybe," Rob said. "But not for that kid back at the restaurant. You embarrassed the daylights out of him in front of his friends and got away with it. That was a situation that could have been pretty ugly but you handled it admirably."

They laughed about the incident. It was something they would long remember. The fire crackled and spit occasionally, but it was warm and the flickering flames danced shadows across the walls. It was comfortable, the sort of atmosphere that leads to quiet, relaxed conversation. There were more stories about growing up in Minnesota and about her family. It was a pleasant picture filled with happy memories of a close-knit family. She coaxed stories out of Rob that carefully avoided his war experiences or his failed marriage. They paused at intervals to tend the fire. Later, Rob prepared two freeze-dried dinner packets for their lunch. After they ate, Rob leaned back against the rock wall once again. Judy nestled in his arms.

"I like being with you," she said with a content smile.

"I do too, but there's one thing I don't understand."

"What's that?"

"This morning... the way you handled it. That kid made reference to the fact that I was old enough to be your father but it didn't seem to faze you in the least."

Judy tensed and sat upright glaring at him, "It *didn't* faze me! That doesn't matter to me at all, and my family doesn't mind either. The point is that age simply doesn't matter... unless it matters to you. If it does, then we better talk about it and you better have some good reasons for thinking that way!"

"He was right you know... I mean about me being older than you."

"So what," she replied angrily and got to her feet. "It's none of their damn business!"

"That's the only time I've ever heard you use profanity," he said.

"What do I have to do to make you understand? We both like the same things. I've never enjoyed anything as much as I do when I'm with you. Other than the age issue that you keep bringing up, we can talk about anything and *communicate!* You're the best friend I've got and I'm trying to be your friend too. I want you in my life Rob... on almost any terms, but I can't if you keep worrying about something as insignificant as our ages. I don't understand your thinking. You need to tell me and make me understand why you feel that way!"

"I guess you're right, we do need to talk about it."

"Well?" she challenged with fire in her eyes.

Rob stood and faced her. Judy was adamant. This was an issue that she was going to settle *now.*

"Judy, I *am* old enough to be your father..."

"Old enough," she exploded, "but you're *not* my father!"

Rob reached out to touch her but she slapped his hand away sharply, "Yes, maybe you're old enough, but you could be, or at least you *should* be wiser, not like those punks back there," she continued angrily.

155

"Maybe you are old enough to be my father, but you're also young enough that you could be my friend... or my lover," she added quietly as she turned away.

"But I'm concerned about you. Shouldn't you be seeing someone closer to your own age?" he asked quietly.

"You let me decide that!" she snapped and turned to face him. "This is one thing I won't let you decide for me even if for some stupid reason you think you're right! Are you too old, or am I too young? You can worry from your viewpoint and I can worry from mine. Damn it Rob, I'm scared too. I've got my doubts about measuring up to your standards and being good enough for you. My concerns are just as real as yours! I'm not about to make any decision based on the comments from a bunch of drunks! I'm willing... no, I'm *excited* about seeing where this goes. Don't you even care?"

"But I do care. It's just that..."

"Don't you dare say it!" she exclaimed facing him. "Don't you ever say anything about our age difference. It's just not fair!"

He took her in his arms and replied, "I wasn't going to say that."

"What then?"

"I was going to say I don't have a very good track record."

Her anger flared once more, "You mean with someone that didn't realize how special you are and treated you like shit! Don't you think I can see that? Don't you realize how much I hurt when I see your pain?"

Judy's harsh language startled Rob.

Releasing her, he stepped back and lowered his head. Judy feared she had made a terrible mistake, "I'm sorry Rob. That was a mean thing to say," she said and took his hand in hers. "Please don't shut me out."

"I don't think I could."

She looked at him with moist eyes, "Then don't. Don't fight it... just let it happen. Let's see where this can go. Just be yourself, be who you are. I see who you are and I don't think that's who you've been. If you can do that, I'll try to be good enough for you."

He looked at the beautiful young girl standing before him, and her tears were because of him. When he pulled her against his chest, he felt the convulsions of her hurt. He stroked her hair gently, "I can be a real jerk sometimes."

She controlled a sob but couldn't answer.

"I'm sorry, Honey."

She looked into his eyes, "Please don't ever think that... never use it as an excuse."

"I don't want to hurt you."

"You don't have to."

"I'm not comfortable fighting with you like this."

Leaning back, she smiled, "We aren't fighting Rob. We're both pretty independent. We have our own standards, but I think you'll be surprised how similar they are.

"We're not fighting. We're *learning* about each other. It's give and take, the learning when and where to back off. Fighting is when people use the intimate things they know to hurt each other just to come out on top. I'm not that way and neither are you."

Rob looked at her incredulously. Helen used those very tactics to devastate him. Judy didn't play games. She didn't have to. She wasn't afraid to speak the truth... or suffer the consequences.

Rob sat down and released a long sigh. "All right... I understand that it's something you feel strongly about... it's not what I expected. It's hard for me to believe that someone as beautiful and smart as you with your whole life ahead of you would want to gamble on someone so much older. If you think of the long term, and you sure make it sound that way, then it seems to me that being with someone closer to your age would give you more time together."

Judy had calmed down now. She knelt beside him and replied, "But Rob, that's the one thing I thought you of all people would understand. Finding someone my age would be a mistake if they weren't everything you are. It's a matter of *quality* time over quantity. It's what my Mom and Dad had every minute they were together. Please don't misunderstand what I'm trying to say. Helen was your age, but she was the wrong person for you. Doesn't finding the right person matter? Isn't there a chance that I could be the right person for you?"

Rob smiled, "Once your mind is made up you don't quit do you? You're talking about a long-term commitment and you barely know me. I feel the same way, but then I'm not too bright when it comes to matters like this. I didn't do very well in the past."

"That's because you're so committed once you get involved. You aren't a quitter."

"I hadn't thought about it that way. I should have seen what was going on... I wanted to believe that I could make things work," he answered quietly and stared into the fire.

"But you must have learned something from that experience. You saw through Beth pretty quickly. I'm not like she is..."

"I *do* know that!" he interrupted. "You're not like anyone else in the whole world. It's just so hard to fathom what it is you see in me."

Judy laughed, "That's easy, I see who you are. Did it ever occur to you that we just might be worth the gamble? Do you want to look back on a day like today and say to yourself that you wished you had given us a chance? Has it ever occurred to you that this is just the beginning, that it only gets better... as soon as you let it?"

"I've thought about all those things, but I'm not thinking that far ahead," he said as he turned her face to his and looked into her eyes. "I could never talk to Helen like we do. This is new for me. I can say things to you without being condemned or judged. It's something I don't want to end."

Judy's eyes sparkled, "There's no way it can end if we keep talking and you start believing it won't end. My family's that way, but none of my friends are. You feel like my family... safe and comfortable."

When Rob leaned back smile spread across his face. Tension, fears, and doubts slowly drained away and he relaxed. He watched her as she spoke and the impact of her honesty was refreshing. Judy watched the change come over him and she didn't know what to expect.

"That's the way you want it?"

"I want to try."

"No, you weren't talking about *trying*. You talked about *doing*! You need to understand that I won't always be what you want or need. Some disappointments go pretty deep. You'll have to be patient and give me time to learn a new way of thinking. I'll do my best."

She touched his lips to silence him, "I know you will," she said gently. "I'll be patient and understanding, but there's something you need to know."

"What's that?"

She got on to her knees to face him and held his face so he was looking directly into her eyes, "Rob, I'm falling in love with you."

She said it softly with a tremor in her voice and he knew it was true. Breathing deeply, he touched her cheek with one big hand, "Well, that's good," he said and took a deep breath.

"Is that all you can say?" she asked with a hurt expression.

"That's one thing you shouldn't do alone," he said with a look that said much more.

She understood his reservations were honest. She fell into his arms and smothered him with kisses. They tumbled onto the floor of their shelter holding tightly to one another and lay side by side.

"Finally," she whispered as she ran her fingers through his hair. "It's about time."

"We've known each other two weeks and you say 'finally'. That sounds a little quick to me."

Her blue-green eyes sparkled with joy, "It's about a dream that I've had since I was a little girl and never understood."

"I think you better explain that one."

"In the dream I was following a path in the fog and couldn't see where I was going, but I was looking for something very important and I didn't know what it was. Every time I had that dream it was the same; just when I thought I'd found what it was that I was looking for, I would wake up. It was very vivid. I could see the trees beside the path and even feel the rain in my face but there was always something missing. That path was so real that I felt I would know it when I saw it.

"I did. We hiked that path today...you and me."

"Are you making that up?"

"No..." she replied, and then looked into his eyes, "I've been looking for you for a long time and never even knew it was you that I was searching for. Does that sound strange?"

Rob propped himself on an elbow and considered her story, "For some folks, maybe. But strange isn't the right word. I've had premonitions, maybe not quite like that, but similar."

He spoke quietly, but there was a distant look in his eyes.

"My friend Willy, he's the guy from Dubois that invited me to go hunting... he knew the night we went out that he wasn't coming back and I didn't believe him. He was the bravest man I ever knew, always careful, and never took chances so I always felt safe with him. It all happened so quickly, it was an ambush, he was there, and then he was dead, just like he said. There was nothing we could do to save him. I realized then just how fragile life is.

"It was pretty bad. Eight brave men died out there. We carried Willy and the others out. Just because people don't like to believe things like that, there's a lot to them."

He spoke just above a whisper and it came out all at once without a pause. It was only part of the story. He left out the fact that it was where he earned his first Purple Heart... and the Congressional Medal of Honor.

Rob didn't talk about himself at dinner with Beth and Jack. He avoided the war and never mentioned his divorce. Now they were alone. Judy shivered. It must have been a terrible experience. He shared it with her, not to impress, or frighten her, but to find release for that burden, to finally experience closure. She held him to her breast and felt him trembling.

He pulled away and smiled weakly, "I didn't mean to sound so gruesome. I'm sorry."

"You never told anyone else about that, have you?" she asked in amazement.

"No. How did you know?"

"I just knew... my God you're an amazing man Rob," she whispered in awe.

The fact that he told her the story, showed her how deeply his trust in her was. She saw how difficult it was for him to talk about. Judy realized that the horrors of war are not often spoken of to those that are loved. If they are, it is with great difficulty, complete trust, and a desperate need for closure. She gave him that.

"I want to apologize for last night," he said suddenly.

Judy tensed. It was a subject she wanted to avoid, at least for the time being. At the time she was frustrated and disappointed. For him, it rekindled unpleasant memories from his past.

"You don't have to talk about it if you'd rather not."

"No, Honey, I think it's something we should talk about. For several reasons... one, because I got the feeling you were disappointed the way things turned out. Maybe I'm wrong about that, maybe we just got carried away..."

"That's not true," she interrupted. "I was disappointed, but not for the reasons you probably think I was."

He stopped her momentarily, "There's another reason that we should talk about it, and that's because we can... without recrimination, or judgment. You surprised me this morning. I was sure I was going to get an earful... if you even showed up. But you did, without a chip on your shoulder. It's the kind of thing one would hope for, rational, intelligent discussion about an uncomfortable situation. I can't begin to tell you how much I admire you for that."

Judy blushed at his heartfelt compliment, "Thank you," she answered looking down at her hands.

"Unless I'm mistaken, and I don't think I am, your feelings last night were just as intense as mine."

"That's true and my feelings haven't changed," she replied as she looked into his eyes.

"Well mine haven't either."

She smiled and kissed him softly, "I'm glad. You do know that I wanted you to stay with me last night."

"I didn't know that... I only hoped that you felt that way."

"I did... and I still do."

"That's a comforting thought," he said with a grin.

This was a new and totally unexpected revelation for him. It never occurred to him that a woman, especially one as beautiful and desirable as Judy, would actually want to sleep with him. In the past he always felt that sex was a tool that a woman used to get what she wanted. Not this incredible girl. The only thing she wanted was to give her love to him and receive his in return. It had to be mutual or not at all. It was not ever going to be a temporary fling to satisfy desire or passion. It would be for the long term with total commitment and unquestioned loyalty. It never occurred to him that it was something that could be returned.

No, he would not look back on this day with regret for having let the chance slip through his fingers. The struggle to overcome the doubts and fears in his failed marriage would not go away quickly, but Judy's love could erase those feelings with determination and devotion. That much he knew.

He took her in his arms and kissed her, holding nothing back, and felt her respond. He felt her body trembling and pressed tightly against his. Her passion was as great as his. His hand was shaking when he touched her breast, unsure for a moment what her reaction might be. Her trembling stopped; she leaned against his caress and sighed.

They made love in their cave. On the dirt floor, while the rain continued just beyond their fire. What they lacked in skill was more than compensated for by their enthusiasm. The euphoria continued even as they lay together in intimate conversation.

She saw the scars on his body; the ones that had earned him his purple hearts, but she didn't ask. He wasn't ready to talk about that yet, but she knew that in time he would release that burden. Eventually it was the time they dreaded. They had to put their clothes back on and extinguish the fire that had been their companion.

They walked hand in hand, oblivious to the weather, and speaking with intimacy that few ever share. Once back at the vehicle he did not hold the passenger door for her, but rather held open the tailgate. There was no need for explanation; there was a common goal.

It was dark and the windows were fogged up, when they finally put their clothes on again.

When they arrived at her apartment, she looked at him and smiled, "Wait here. I need to get a few things."

24

TUCSON PLANS

For the second night in a row, Rob barely slept, but this night was different. It was the same motel and the same bed, but this night Judy shared that bed. All through the night, he watched her sleep, a content smile on her lips, her soft auburn hair spread out against the pillow. Their lovemaking had taken him to levels that were beyond anything he had ever dreamed of. Now as he looked at her it was not her body, or the passion they shared, but the words she had spoken and the complete trust he felt that filled his thoughts. Even as he felt her warm, soft body against his, it was who she was inside; the person she was, that consumed him. For his entire life, the closeness he shared with this beautiful woman was exactly what he longed for. This was a feeling that he tried in vain to create with his ex wife. It didn't work. It took two.

Now, after only a few short weeks, a woman barely beyond the age of his daughter fulfilled that need. He longed to wake her and tell her of his feelings, just hold her in his arms. He was afraid to wake her, afraid that when she awoke the magic would be gone.

It was early morning when he sensed the flicker of her eyelids. In the dark, he could barely see the sparkling blue-green of her eyes, but there was no mistaking the sleepy smile that slowly formed on her lips.

"You're awake," she said sleepily as she touched his face.

"Yes," he answered cautiously.

"Why didn't you wake me up, Sweetheart? I thought you would be tired... I thought you'd still be asleep."

"I was watching you."

She closed her eyes and nestled under his arm content and happy. "Did I wake you?"

"No... I was just watching you... trying to comprehend it all."

Snuggling closer, she smiled, "And what did you come up with?"

"I'm finding it hard to believe it's not all a dream," he replied.

She shifted to be able to look at him seriously, "Do you really think that? I mean don't you feel that what we've done, what we have is... well, very real?"

"Yes I do."

She kissed him softly and then looked into his eyes, "That's the way I feel too. This *is* real. It's not a dream. I feel like there's direction and meaning to my life now. Before I met you, I was just going through the motions of living and none of it made sense. Loving you, not someone like you, but *you* makes me know you were worth waiting for."

She embraced him passionately before she continued, "I didn't know there could be anyone that could satisfy me so completely," then she laughed softly, "and the sex is fantastic too!"

"I think you're making fun of me," he replied.

"No, I'd never do that," she said as she turned and pressed herself even closer against him. "I have to joke a little otherwise I wouldn't be able to control myself... I never knew I could love someone so much."

Unable to reply, he held her tightly. She felt him trembling. "Are you all right?" she asked.

His reply was a choked sound of affirmation. The admission of her love affected him deeply. It was not that difficult for her. It was a thing that filled her with joy. It was different with him. With insight far beyond her years, she understood. Rob was a man so full of love and patience and understanding, and the need to release it. She could accept that, and love him back.

It was later in the morning as they lay together. Judy touched one of the scars on his chest. She didn't say a word yet Rob felt compelled to explain. The stories he told were of incidents that never made the news headlines. He did not glorify his own actions. He seldom used the word 'I'. It was always 'we' or 'us'. Even in his mild and abridged version she felt the horror of the events he alluded to. She could have stopped him at any time, but these were memories that had to be eliminated from the dark recesses of his mind, and so she listened. It was a different side of him, one she never would have imagined. She saw him in a different light, and her respect and admiration grew. To do the terrible things he had done, to survive the terrors he had experienced and still be able to show compassion and tenderness astounded her. She realized now, even more vividly, the tremendous restraint he had shown that first night she saw him when his own daughter ridiculed him publicly. At the same time, she shivered as she thought about what could have happened in the restaurant when the young punks annoyed them. It was the image of a man capable of deadly violence. It was also the same man with hands so strong and a touch so gentle it took her breath away.

Suddenly he stopped and looked at her, "Forgive me, Honey... you didn't need to listen to all that."

She stopped him instantly, "Yes I did! Those memories are like the story about Willy aren't they? I mean what you told me this morning is the part of your life that no one else knows, except those that were there. That's true isn't it?"

"Yes... but it's long past."

She laid her head on his chest and held him tenderly. She was beginning to comprehend the magnitude of his trust in her. In his total trust, she was seeing a side of Rob that no one else knew. He was not bragging. These were terrible burdens, weighing him down, gnawing at his insides, poisoning his outlook on life, and testing him the limit of human endurance. Simply saying the words aloud began the healing process.

"Thank you for trusting me enough to share that," Judy whispered. "It *is* past, but I don't believe vivid memories ever go away completely. Not the bad ones and certainly not the good ones. We can talk about the bad times and share the burden just as surely as we can create good memories by living them together."

Rob breathed deeply and released a long sigh, "We certainly have made some good memories in a very short time haven't we?"

Judy smiled, "Yes, and we've just begun. It gets better from here!"

After leaving Judy at her apartment, Rob made his way to the Interstate, set the cruise slightly over the posted limit, and turned on the radio. Tall pines stood at the side of the road, indistinct in the light rain, standing like silent guardians, stately and unmoving with their tops disappearing into the low clouds beyond the glow of his headlights.

It was late and there was little traffic. The skiers that in future weeks would be returning to the valley on a Sunday night had not yet filled the Interstate. The silent hum of tires on pavement and quiet music from the radio created a background conducive to reflection.

He still felt the softness of Judy's warm skin against his and the exhilaration of their passion. The intensity of that thought crowded out all attempts at reason. He learned many new things about Judy, but he learned even more about himself. The emotions that filled his mind were feelings he felt were no longer possible. The hurt and disappointment that built impregnable walls around his heart had tumbled down in just a few short weeks. He was in love with a girl that returned his affection without reservation. It was foolish, impractical, and unwise. He tried it once and learned painfully that it just didn't work. A red haired, green-eyed teenybopper changed all that... but she was not that. Judy was mature beyond her years...and wise.

The terrain changed as he descended and wound down across the level and open country, and his mood changed with it. Although she denied it vehemently, their age difference would someday become a major factor and he had to face that fact. Would it be fair to her when age began to affect him? She would still be in her prime with needs he might not be able to satisfy. Could she maintain that love under those circumstances? Surely, she would want children. Could he bring himself to suffer through that once more?

His son, no the boy he only raised and loved as a son, despised him. His daughter, Patricia, made his life miserable. In spite of all his efforts, she only contacted him when she needed money, and even then with her belligerent attitude. Was it possible to overcome the bitterness? He began to doubt his ability to show affection for a child. Judy didn't need to have to cope with that.

It had been an incredible weekend. Rob knew what he wanted, but what was best for her? It would be so easy for him to continue in the direction they were going. For him it could only get better, but what about Judy? Was he capable of giving her what she thought she wanted, and what she really needed?

Then another thought crept in to his consciousness. Unbidden and hateful, the memory of his ex-wife and her unfaithfulness assailed him. He had been so foolish and trusting. The memory of that pain wrenched his gut, poisoning his attitude, and rekindling the doubts and anger. Helen played him for a fool and did it so well.

While Rob was fighting his doubts and fears, Judy was trying to explain her feelings to her mother. None of her words seemed to come out right, but her enthusiasm was clear. Marianne wasn't able to provide much feedback, either positive or negative. Judy wouldn't quit raving about how wonderful Rob was. She didn't mention a single thing about school or her grades and that concerned Marianne. That was one of the things she feared, being infatuated with a man could easily destroy any chances of Judy getting a quality education. For the time being, it was one thought she wisely kept to herself.

At the end of their conversation her mother said, "You sound quite pleased with this man in your life. I'm happy for you, Honey." She tried to sound sincere.

"Mom, I've never felt as safe as I do now. For the first time in my life I truly understand what you and Daddy have."

'Have' instead of 'had' brought a lump to her mother's throat. It was a fact that was painfully true. Not a single day had gone by since

John's death that she didn't feel the comforting warmth and safety of his love.

Marianne heard her daughter's voice, strong and confident, as she shared the recent events in her life. It was the sound of maturity and focus. Marianne felt that she was losing her daughter to a man that she had never met. It all happened so quickly and Marianne was concerned. She felt Judy's love for this man without ever hearing the words. It was only her trust in Judy's wisdom that prevented her from voicing her concerns.

Marianne needed to bring Judy's siblings, Sarah and Brian, up to date on what their older sister was doing. Marianne's abbreviated version of the conversation piqued their interest. What was unsaid was left to their imagination. Their imagination was fertile.

Rob dropped off the dark, twisting highway below Sunset Point and faced the long straight stretch toward the increasing glow of Phoenix lights. Traffic was heavier and his attention was redirected to driving. With the shift in concentration, the unpleasant thoughts began to fade. He looked at the other cars beside him and saw families, couples, and single drivers. He passed a minivan and glanced at the occupants. In the rear, sleeping soundly, were two small children. The driver, intent on traffic, his wife beside him, was dividing her attention between her children and her husband. For an instant, Rob saw the smile on her face as the woman watched her husband. It was a look of complete trust and deep affection.

Rob had seen that look before... only hours ago.

At the northern edge of Phoenix, he took an off ramp and stopped at the side of the road. He looked at the time and almost decided against calling. No, he needed to hear her voice.

He heard the phone begin to ring and then heard her voice, "Hi Sweetheart! Are you all right," she asked happily. "I hope you didn't try to call earlier, I was talking to Mom."

He closed his eyes and sighed. "I'm fine... just driving and thinking about you. How are your Mom and the kids?"

Judy laughed, "I think Mom's getting concerned. She didn't say anything, but she sounded a little cautious. I talked to Sarah and Brian too. They're both excited and want to meet you. I can't wait until they all meet you."

"I am a bit wary about meeting your mother. I wouldn't want to alienate her, especially if she's anything like you. You can be a frightening adversary!"

Rob was thinking about the punk in the restaurant and Judy's unrelenting drive to discuss the things that concerned him... and ease his doubts.

Judy laughed, "You don't have to worry. Mom's very perceptive. You'll get along fine!"

He imagined her eyes; he could see the way her nose wrinkled when she smiled. Every detail of her came sharply into focus. He could see her face and feel the soft texture of her hair; he remembered the incredible softness of her skin and the unbelievable curves of every part of her body. He could feel her in his arms, taste her lips, and hear her voice. He thought of the things she said and the way she said them. She was no ordinary woman.

On Monday, Dave started in on Rob, "All right man, what the fuck's going on? You've been up there every weekend since you met this chick and haven't said a thing."

"She's a pretty amazing woman," Rob answered, "But then I used to think Helen was and you know how that turned out. I sometimes wonder if I'm thinking clearly, and I'm not sure what to do about that."

"That's easy, bring her down here and let Sandy check her out. Can't put nothing over on my old lady."

Rob chuckled, "That might not be a bad idea, but if I did that, I'd have to keep an eye on you. This gal is even better than perfect."

"Go ahead and invite her down," Dave said. "We can have a barbeque at your place, invite Chuck and Samantha. If your lady can get past those two, she'll have to be damn good."

"You just want a free steak dinner."

"Yeah, if she turns out to be nothing, it won't be a wasted week-end," Dave said with a wary eye for Rob's reaction.

Rob relented, and invited Judy to come to his home in Tucson and meet his friends. It would be an interesting event. Each member of his group of friends and acquaintances had a picture of her in their minds. Some of them were in poor taste and none of them were accurate. Rob was careful to forewarn her, describing the eccentricities and in some cases downright obnoxious nature of these folks. Judy knew that she would be scrutinized and tested by them. She hoped for Rob's sake that she wouldn't embarrass him.

Rather than drive up to get her, he arranged for her to fly down on Thursday after class. She was uncomfortable with him spending so much money on her behalf, but it meant more time together. Judy agreed.

Flagstaff was cold and clear when she boarded the plane wearing a warm coat and carrying her bags.

It was a small plane and her seat was next to the window. As the flight made its way south, she watched the changing landscape in fascination. There was so much open space that looked dry and barren, so few houses. Occasionally she saw patches of a weak green color but mostly it looked like barren red rock mountains or brown stretches of sand with the twisted shape of dry watercourses. The sprawling mass of Phoenix was hidden under its hazy brown glow of pollution in the late afternoon sun.

Rob forewarned her that he was a bachelor and lived alone leaving the condition of his home to her imagination. As the flight neared Tucson, she formed a mental image of plain adobe looking buildings surrounded by rocks, dirt, and cactus.

When the pilot announced their final approach, Judy felt nervous. She was excited about spending the weekend with Rob in his home, but she was concerned about the impression she would make on his friends.

In the terminal, Rob was pacing anxiously, alternating his attention between his watch and the flight monitors. He felt a surge of emotion as soon as he saw her and burst out of the crowd. He ran to greet her with a great bear hug.

The Phoenix terminal that she was familiar with was concrete and steel, the desert lost beyond buildings and teeming traffic. Outside this terminal, saguaro cactus, palm trees, and green grass in tended areas! It was late afternoon and the western sky was preparing itself for another superb sunset. To the north was the long stretch of Mount Lemmon with its glowing palette of colors in the twilight. On the ground, it was different than from the air. On the ground, away from the concrete and steel, the desert introduced itself.

25

ROB'S HOME

The drive to Rob's home was filled with the necessity of catching up on all the latest events and trying to take in all the new and different scenery.

"Have you ever heard of the Amerind Foundation?" Rob asked.

"Yes I have. It's very highly thought of by most anthropologists. It's not too far from here, is it?"

"Less than an hour east of here," he replied. "While you're here I want to show you something I found. It's something I was going to take out there, but I figured you'd want to see it before I did."

"Are you going to tell me what it is," Judy asked with a twinkle in her eye.

"No, I have to show you. I don't know for sure what it is, but you will."

Rob's home was not far from the airport. It was a modest house with simple yet tasteful landscaping. Nothing like she expected, and different than homes in Duluth. Next door, an elderly neighbor was watering plants.

"You must be Judy," he hollered and started toward them. She wondered if he was nosy or just being friendly.

"You're sure pretty. I've heard about you and it feels like I already know you," he said, extending his hand. His handshake was warm, smiling as looked her over carefully.

"I'm the nosy neighbor Sam Whitborn, but just call me Sam. Rob says you'll be here a couple of days. If you need anything, just holler."

Nodding to Judy, he went back to his watering. He looked very pleased.

Rob took her bags and stopped at the front door. He set them down and unlocked the door. As it swung open, he swept her off her feet and took her in his arms.

"I want to carry you in," he said.

Smiling at the implication, she laid her head on his shoulder, "Good."

Glancing around, Judy was surprised. It was clean and neat, for a single person, tastefully furnished. Setting her down, he began to show her around.

"You have a beautiful home. It's not at all what I expected from your description," she said.

"Thank you," Rob said. "I'm glad you're here."

When they got to his bedroom, he showed her the space he had cleared for her things in his closet and the drawers in his dresser, "I hope this will be all right for you. I cleared some space in the bathroom for your things, too."

She was stunned by the preparations he had made on her behalf and wasn't sure how to react. It was a very humbling feeling.

"Sit down for a minute, I want to show you something," he said.

He went to his closet and returned with a box covered with a towel. "I think this is pretty valuable to some people, but you'll know much better than me."

Removing the towel, he handed her the finely crafted, airtight display case that encased the Hohokam pot. Judy gasped and stared in amazement at the perfectly preserved artifact.

"Where did you get this?"

"I found it in a section of the Santa Cruz River after a rain. It was pretty close to some houses and I thought that someone would find it and sell it. I made the box. I thought we could take it to the Amerind, or you could take it back to school with you."

"I'd be afraid to do that no matter how much Dr. Kenmore would love to have it for the University. Maybe we should go to where you found it and document all the information."

"I already did that. I saw some of your notes. I didn't do it as well as you do. I thought you could look them over before we went to the Amerind and make corrections," he said and handed her his notes.

She looked them over and grinned, "I don't see anything wrong with this, Rob."

The back yard was accessed through a patio door from the bedroom. A covered patio extended the length of the house. The barbeque grille and a large table with benches and chairs were at one end. Judy kicked off her shoes and stepped into the grass. It was soft and luxurious, a reminder of summer grass at home.

Glancing at the trees and wall that surrounded the yard, she smiled and embraced him, "We could make love in the grass."

Going through the door to the kitchen, they sat at the table. The kitchen reminded her of something she had seen in a magazine, neat, orderly, and efficient.

While she was admiring her surroundings, Rob stood, "I've got something for you. I'll be right back."

He was only gone for a moment before he returned. Reaching into his pocket, he took out a cell phone like the one he used and handed it to her, "Actually it's for me," he tried to explain.

She raised her head with a troubled look, "I can't afford something like this."

"It won't cost you anything. It's like an extension on my house phone. As long as there's reception, we can be in contact anytime, day, or night."

She liked that idea, "Maybe I can try it for a month."

"Let me show you what it can do."

Rob explained the functions of the phone. She wanted to try it out right away. When she called his number, his phone responded immediately and they both laughed.

"Maybe you should call your Mom," Rob suggested.

"But that's long distance."

"That's the beauty of this setup. It's only air time, not the distance."

"I think it snowed today in Duluth. I'll bet Mom and the kids are cold."

Rob smiled, "Why not give them a call and warm them up?"

Although apprehensive at first, Judy finally relented and made the call.

"Hi, Mom, it's me."

"Is everything all right, Honey? You don't usually call until Sunday."

"I'm at Rob's home in Tucson. I'm calling from a cell phone. Rob got it for me. It means you can call me any time without worrying if I'm at home, and I can call you even if my roommates are on the phone."

"It must be terribly expensive."

"No, it's like an extension on Rob's phone. It's even cheaper than long distance if we don't talk too long."

"He must think a lot of you," her mother said.

"He does," Judy said and smiled at Rob.

There was a long silence on the Duluth end of the phone before her mother continued, "Is there any chance we'll ever get to meet this lucky guy?"

"We've been talking about coming there for Christmas. I'll be out of school and Rob can take some vacation time."

Marianne replied cautiously. "Christmas is so far off, but we miss you and we'd like to meet him. We'll set a little extra aside so you can fly..."

"Don't worry about the money," Judy interrupted. "We've been saving up so we could make the trip. It's important to both of us."

When she hung up, she smiled, "All right, you've made your point. Mom's pleased that we can come for Christmas, but she worried about the expense. Can we really afford it, Honey?"

"Yes, we can. My friends, Ralph and Cathy, have a travel agency. They'll get us the cheapest fare.

"Now, are you hungry? Let me take you to dinner to celebrate."

"No, I want to stay here. I'll cook something for you."

She made herself at home in his kitchen, and with the barest of essentials put together an excellent meal. She seemed to know where everything was. He set places on the patio and they ate in the romantic glow of candles. After cleaning up their dinner dishes, they returned to the patio. It was a pleasant evening, much warmer than what Judy had left behind in Flagstaff.

Rob had his arm over her shoulder. He grinned, "I have to work tomorrow and it's getting late. I can make you up a spot on the couch."

Judy's eyes sparkled with mischief, "I didn't come all this way to sleep on your couch! I want to take a shower and I need someone to wash my back. Do you think Sam would mind coming over to help?"

Rob sat on the edge of his bed and watched as she undressed. It took his breath away. At first, she was self-conscious until she saw the look in his eyes. A growing feeling of content crept over her as she realized how deeply he was affected. His look was not one of lust, but one of deep and overpowering love. She stood watching him as he undressed and realized that she felt that same thing.

They showered together and then went to his bed. He turned out the lights, but a dim glow filtered in through the closed curtains. He lay at her side and touched her face gently. She smiled happily at him and whispered, "I'm happy to be here with you."

"I'm glad you're here, too," he said and kissed her.

They made love tenderly and then lay nestled together sharing their feelings. When Rob fell asleep, there was a content smile on his face. Judy laid her head on his chest and eventually slipped into peaceful slumber.

The dark of night had barely begun to lighten when she awoke. She looked at Rob and smiled. He stirred lightly and his eyes blinked open.

"How long have you been awake?" he asked sleepily.

"Not very long."

"Is everything all right?"

"Everything is great, Honey," she smiled mischievously and glanced at the clock beside the bed. "I think we have a little time before you have to get ready for work. I'll make your breakfast while you shower."

She prevented him from taking his shower right away, but he didn't mind.

Once he showered and dressed, he followed his nose to the kitchen. Judy met him with a cup of coffee and a kiss. She was wearing one of his old flannel shirts. It barely reached her thighs, but that didn't matter. She didn't bother to button it.

"That's not fair," he said and held her close. "Maybe I should call in sick,"

"No, you can't do that. You make me study so I'm making you go to work."

"Damn!" Rob uttered with a sense of frustration.

"Of course you could come home for lunch," she smiled.

As they were eating their breakfast, Rob offered to leave the 4Runner with her so she could look around town. The idea was a pleasant surprise for her, but she declined.

"I'd rather just be here among your things. I know it sounds silly but it would be more comfortable than driving around fighting traffic. Besides, I'd be afraid of denting your new car."

Rob laughed, "New car? Sweetheart, that thing is several years old and has over a hundred thousand miles on it. It's not new by any means!"

Her surprise showed, "But it looks new."

"I try to take care of it."

Judy's searching gaze caught him unprepared. Then she smiled, "You take good care of lots of things don't you?"

"I try to. At least the things that are important."

He pushed away from the table and pulled her down into his lap, "You're important to me, Judy."

Rob did come home at lunch and Judy was waiting for him. When he went back to work, he looked very content. He ate the sandwich that Judy made while he drove.

Judy spent the afternoon visiting with Rob's neighbor, Sam. He told her as much as he knew about Rob, which was plenty.

"I didn't know him when he was married, but I've heard enough stories from some of his friends to make me shudder. She didn't deserve someone like him. I can tell you're a lot different. He's changed a lot since he met you. You sure do make him happy. You look pretty content, too."

Judy glowed, "I am,"

Sam laughed heartily, "You two are good for each other. That brings up a question, though."

"What's that?"

"Age... I'm sure there's folks that look at you strangely. Is it a problem for either of you?"

Judy hesitated before replying, "Not for me, but I think Rob feels uncomfortable. He's more worried about it than I am."

"He's worried that he might not be good enough for you."

Judy stared at Sam, "Are you serious?"

"Yes I am."

"Sam, he's everything any girl could ever want in a man. It's me that's worried. He could have his pick of..."

"Judy," Sam interrupted, "He chose *you*! Now that I've met you, I can see why."

26

MEET THE FRIENDS

Meeting the Saturday morning coffee group would be a challenge. Only casual acquaintances, they were not Rob's closest friends. Stories found their way back to the group and they speculated about the significance of Rob dating a much younger woman. Reluctantly, Rob agreed to let them meet Judy.

Rob dressed in a polo shirt, jeans, and tennis shoes. Judy opted for shorts and sandals with a long sleeved blouse. It was a simple and inexpensive outfit, but auburn hair curling at her shoulders and slender figure made people notice. Men took note of her long shapely legs. She attracted attention and increased heart rates.

One look at Judy, and out of courtesy, the men stood. Judy ended up seated next to Eddie McGonical, a sharp dressing car salesman. His quick mind and aggressive manner helped make him successful at his chosen occupation. He considered himself quite the ladies man. Women with an IQ greater than their shoe size wouldn't give him the time of day.

He eyed Judy approvingly and was certain that he was a far better match for her than an old man like Rob. Flirting with her began with subtle and quiet conversation. Courtesy for what she assumed to be one of Rob's friends caused her to listen to his line. The first time he laid his hand on her leg, she tried to ignore it. The second time, she had enough.

Leaning toward Eddie, she smiled. Under the table, she grasped his hand on her leg and dug her fingernails deeply into his flesh, "If you touch me again I'll tear your eyes out," she whispered.

Sitting up calmly, she used a napkin to wipe the blood off her hand.

At her side, Eddie was turning white, struggling to ignore the pain, "Hey guys," he said in a choked voice, "I hate to run, but I've got to meet a customer."

With his handkerchief wound tightly around his hand, he departed quickly.

"Wonder what got into him," one of them said.

"I think he just discovered something about people that he didn't realize before," another said and nodded his approval at Judy.

Leaning back in his chair, Rob grinned. Once again, Judy handled a difficult situation far better than he would have. If it was a test, she passed.

A quick trip to the Amerind Foundation was next. On the road, Judy expressed her concern, "I hope I didn't hurt him," she said and Rob laughed.

"Guys like that need a reality check once in a while. You did fine and impressed everyone at the table."

Their trip to the Amerind Foundation was shorter than either of them wanted. The director was waiting curiously. The strange phone call earlier in the week describing an artifact was interesting. Would this be just another hoax? It was not. Even Rob's description over the phone paled in comparison to reality. He knew what he was talking about and his lovely companion was even more knowledgeable.

"You could be a valuable asset to the Foundation," the Director told Judy. "If someone doesn't snap you up after you graduate, I'd be very pleased to talk to you. I have no doubt we could make a place for you here."

Returning to Tucson under a cloudless sky with the endless landscape and layered mountains shimmering and shifting in the desert air, gave Judy time to ponder what she observed.

"Stop," she said suddenly.

"Can you see it?" she asked pointing at the sky when Rob pulled to the side of the road.

"What," he asked with a puzzled look.

"Nothing, no end, no clouds, no trees to limit your view, or comprehension," she said.

"That's how my parents love each other! In Duluth, the clouds always limited my view. I can't see the stars in daylight, but they're there... always. Endless and eternal," she beamed.

"It wasn't until I came here that I really understood those concepts. That's what Mom and Dad had and still have. It's what we have... it can never end."

"Never is a long time."

"So is forever," she smiled and held his arm. "I like that better."

Rob stared at her... the most beautiful, brilliant, strong, loving, and tender living thing he had ever encountered. And she loved him.

It was time for some grocery shopping and then back to Rob's home. The afternoon barbeque would be Rob's closest friends, people that knew him well and shared a deep mutual respect. They were anxious to meet the person responsible for the drastic change in him. They also had legitimate concerns about someone so young being involved with an older man. They had every intention of looking out for his better interests. Judy would be under close scrutiny not only from the men but from their wives as well.

"I'm a little worried about meeting your friends," Judy said. "What if they don't like me?"

"Honey, all you need to do is be yourself. If you don't, they'll see through it right away. Besides, I didn't invite them here to approve of you. They're here for your approval."

Then he smiled, "If you don't like them, I'll throw them out."

The first to arrive was Rob's co-worker and long time friend Dave Grierson with his wife Sandy. With long black hair and a day's growth of beard, Dave was normally a little rough around the edges. Today he was clean-shaven, wore a clean shirt, and pressed slacks. His wife Sandy had short auburn hair and an open friendly face. Judy liked her immediately but she wasn't sure about Dave. He looked her over carefully and although he certainly approved of her appearance, she knew that she would have to earn his acceptance. That wouldn't be easy. Rob probably shared more of his feelings with Dave than any of the others.

The guttural roar of a motorcycle announced the arrival of Chuck and Samantha Stuart. They made a most unlikely pair. Longhaired, with a scraggly beard, and mustache, Chuck was more than a little frightening. He was the ultimate biker with his filthy jeans, leathers, and tattoos. In contrast to his appearance, his wife was dazzling. Under her helmet, she had short blonde hair and a pretty face. Her stunning figure was accented by the tasteful blouse and slacks she wore. They simply didn't fit together. Samantha looked Judy over carefully and reserved her judgment. Chuck threw her a quick glance and asked for a beer, but there was something in his glance that told Judy he knew more about her in that instant than the rest of them would learn in the entire afternoon.

They adjourned to the patio and were just getting seated when the doorbell rang. It was Ralph and Cathy Jorgenson. They were nondescript compared to the others. They were pleasant, and after being introduced to Judy, exchanged pleasantries with the rest of the group.

The final arrivals came in a dark Mercedes sedan. J.J. and Doreen Rabinowitz were not dressed for a barbeque. He was still in a three-piece suit. Although he had removed his tie, that was not his usual nature. Doreen's dress would be acceptable at a formal dinner. Judy felt a little intimidated until they were introduced. J.J. was very polite and gracious but he did look her over rather carefully. Doreen was surprisingly warm and friendly and made Judy feel at ease.

It was still too early to eat so they gathered on the patio and eased into their interrogation of Judy. After listening to their grilling, Doreen had enough.

"I think it's time for you to let up on this poor girl! We've got her outnumbered and cornered and that's just not fair! I know it would scare the daylights out of me to be thrust into a group like this. Hell, it scares me already, and I know all of you!"

Her profanity was completely out of character and aptly chosen. It drew a guarded laugh and eased the tension. She continued by re-introducing Rob's friends and telling a little about each of them.

"Dave is probably Rob's closest friend. They've known one another the longest, and they work together daily."

"Dave's wife Sandy teaches school and puts up with Dave." She winked at Sandy, "Both are a full time job."

"Ralph owns a very successful travel agency," Doreen continued. "But most of its success is because his wife, Cathy, runs the office. My husband, J.J., is an attorney and he has ambitions to move into politics. Actually, our reason for being here is to solicit your votes," Doreen added with a twinkle in her eye. That drew a stern look from J.J. and laughter from everyone else.

"Now as for Chuck, the biker, all he's ever told anyone is that he's got a job with the government. You know how those civil service workers are! He says he likes it because he can dress the way he wants and gets paid enough to support his Harley. I guess that's why Samantha had to get a job. She can support the kids and pay for the house!"

Chuck scowled harmlessly and everyone else laughed... including Samantha. Doreen tactfully and successfully loosened up the entire group. From that point on, the atmosphere was relaxed. The questions directed at Judy were no longer probing, but curious. She had her questions also, and they were answered honestly. When it was time for the food, Judy tried to excuse herself to make the final preparations. Rob stood up to help her.

"Sit down, Rob," Sandy laughed. "You don't know anything about kitchens. Let us professionals help Judy!"

The men took their drinks and gathered around the barbeque grille while Rob started the steaks. He enjoyed the idea of cooking out in the back yard with friends. Now, with Judy here, it took on new meaning.

It surprised him when J.J. put his arm around Rob's shoulders, "Congratulations Rob. Judy is a very fine young lady. I'm happy for you."

The others nodded in agreement, "Yep, she ain't bad for a girl," Dave laughed. "Too bad she gets stuck with you, though."

Inside the house was a different atmosphere. There were 'girl things' to talk about, making sure that Rob treated her well. Judy was reserved in the company of the older women, but she glowed when they brought that up.

"He's the most incredible man I've ever met. He treats me with respect, like I'm something special. Mostly it's the little things he does, like opening doors, or taking my hand, or understanding my moods. He's so much smarter than I am and yet he makes me believe that he's learning from me."

Sandy smiled, "We know all about him, Judy. We just want to make sure you know how to keep him in line!"

"Yes, if you worship him too much he'll get a swelled head," Cathy added pleasantly.

This was a more mature, wiser, and sassy group of women with one thing in common, they all adored their husbands and respected Rob. Judy understood that, but she was still in awe of them and unsure of how to react to their flippant comments. In order to direct the discussion away from herself, she commented on the variety of foods the women had brought.

From recipes and favorite dishes, the subject changed to exotic (or erotic) foods designed to entice their men, "Cathy, why don't you demonstrate how you serve guacamole to Ralph?"

Cathy glowed bright red and tried to avoid the question. She turned to Sandy, "Tell Judy about how Dave likes his ice cream sundaes."

That was a subject Sandy absolutely refused to discuss. The antics of these women made Judy grin; they were a fun group and didn't hesitate to include her. Doreen had long since given up trying to moderate the discussion and stood to one side shaking her head.

In spite of their antics, these ladies were skilled and willing workers when it came to feeding their men. Disguising their mirth, and with armloads of food, they started outside. Doreen touched Judy's arm as a signal to wait just a moment.

It was just the two of them when Doreen took Judy's hands in hers and gave her a warm smile, "I'm genuinely happy for you both, Judy. We've been quite concerned about Rob for a long time. The divorce was very hard on him. I don't know how much he told you about it, if anything. He stuck with a terrible marriage long past the time any normal person would have out of loyalty and commitment. I know she never loved him and I'm not sure if he ever really loved her. I don't think he even understood what love meant... but he does now. Thank you for what you've done for him," and with moistness in her eyes that she couldn't help, she embraced Judy warmly.

Judy wore an astonished look and was at a loss for words when Doreen released her. These were his true friends. They were genuinely concerned about him. Mrs. Rabinowitz seemed to be a bright and astute observer. What had Judy done to merit her vote of confidence she wondered? When the two of them took the last of the food out and rejoined the others Judy felt a little awkward, as if all eyes were on her. When she took Rob's hand, he gave her a quick kiss on the cheek and held her chair for her. Much to her surprise, everyone remained standing until she was seated.

The dinner was excellent. Everyone was content as they settled back and the conversation flowed. Dave was watching and waiting for an opportunity to make a point. At a lull in the conversation, he made his move.

"Hey, Judy, did Rob ever show you his ring?"

Judy's puzzled look answered the question while Rob tried to redirect the subject. Dave was insistent, "Naw, man, go get it and show her. The rest of us would get a kick out of it too."

Reluctantly, Rob excused himself and went into the house while Judy watched him curiously. Dave held up his hand and showed his ring. It was huge. A stunning gold ring with an onyx stone that bore the Mercedes insignia.

"Next to my old lady and the kids, this is my proudest possession. There ain't a whole lot of them around. The Mercedes factory tests their mechanics regularly and rates them on their test scores as well as their proficiency and productivity. I worked damned hard for this and it took a lot of years to earn it. The whole point of this is that I think you know that Rob's pretty prone to understatement. Judy, did he ever tell you how good a mechanic he is?"

Judy looked around and then replied, "Well, not really. He says that he's all right but whenever he talks about work he usually gives you the credit."

Dave laughed, "I figured that. Well, he told me that he thought you were the most incredible woman he ever met."

Looking down, Judy blushed while Dave continued. "When you see his ring, remember this; he says he's *just* an okay mechanic. That's an understatement. If that's his idea of an okay mechanic, then what does he think of you if he says you're the most incredible woman he's ever met?"

They were pondering Dave's remarks when Rob returned with his ring. He set it on the table in front of Judy. It glistened in the flickering light of the lanterns. It too was big, and heavy, and gold like Dave's, but when she turned it over to look at the setting, it sent glittering rays of intense blue-white sparks. At each point of the tri-star was a small diamond while in the center was a large, perfect stone that nearly blinded them. Its magnificence took their breath away. They turned to Rob for an explanation. He looked embarrassed and didn't say anything.

Dave had to explain, "When I earned my ring it was a big deal. If I ever receive the recognition again, I'll get got another ring with a single diamond in it and a second diamond for the next time. I'm not that good yet, but maybe someday. Rob got the ring, then three diamonds. The big stone is for five years in succession so that means a total of nine years that he's been honored by the factory as one of the top technicians in the country," and he paused to let the significance sink in.

"Do you know how many rings there are like that in the whole damn world?" he asked.

They looked at Dave and then at Rob waiting for an answer. Finally Dave held up his hand with a single finger extended and said, "One."

There was a subdued silence as all eyes turned to Rob. What Dave said about Rob's tendency to understatement regarding his abilities as a mechanic finally sunk in. They turned to look at Judy. She was getting up from her seat and went to Rob with a look of admiration. She put her arms around him and hugged him.

Puzzled, he looked down at her, "What brought this on?" he asked.

"I hope I never disappoint you," she said.

Their friends realized they were sharing an intimate moment and responded with a nervous laugh. They barely heard Rob's reply; "That's probably the only thing you're incapable of."

At the head of the table, J.J. stood. Picking up his glass nodded to Rob and Judy, "It pleases me to propose a toast to you, Judy, and to you too, Rob. I was blessed with finding the right companion very early in life," and he took his wife's hand in his. "I don't think I could ever find a way to adequately express the love I have for this lovely lady here. I see that I am not alone in feeling such a deep affection for another person. Thank you both for allowing us to share this time with you. I consider it an honor to know both of you," and he raised his glass.

Everyone else stood and lifted their glasses in a toast to Rob and Judy. It was an emotional moment until J.J. spoke again, this time with levity, "Now if you will excuse us, we have to leave. There's an election coming up and we're running for office. I hope you'll vote for us," then he smiled, "That makes this an official visit, tax deductible and all."

Everyone escorted J.J. and Doreen to their car. J.J. was holding the door for his wife when Judy stepped forward and embraced Doreen, "Thank you for your kind words, Mrs. Rabinowitz."

"Please, Judy, call me Doreen. Nothing has been said that you didn't earn."

Judy turned to J.J. and hugged him warmly, "Thank you sir. I can see how much you love your wife. Thank you for helping me understand how lucky I am."

J.J. smiled down at her, "No, Judy, I didn't make you understand anything. The way you look at Rob makes it very plain that you already knew that, and the way he looks at you says that he knows how fortunate he is. God bless you both," and he kissed her lightly on her forehead.

Rob followed him to his door and shook his hand, "I'll never be able to thank you for what you've done for me, J.J."

J.J. put a hand on his shoulder, "Rob, you're a fine young man. You deserve something better than what you've had in the past and I believe you've found it. As for thanking me, you did that by inviting me to share this day with you and your friends. I hope we can do this again."

He paused and then put his arms around Rob and hugged him, "Good night, my friend."

Ralph and Cathy were the next to leave. They thanked Judy for what she had done for Rob, "He's not the same person he was before he met you. We've never seen him happier or more relaxed."

Chuck and Sandy shared their pleasure at meeting Judy, and both of them hugged her. Judy still didn't understand Chuck. He just didn't fit with Samantha, but it was apparent that she loved him.

"I'll call you later," Chuck said as he shook Rob's hand, then with an ugly roar, the Harley thundered to life and they were gone.

Dave and Sandy stayed for one more beer. Rob sat beside Judy while they visited. They talked about work and some of their special customers. It was apparent to Judy that Dave and his wife both adored Rob and would do anything to protect him. These few private moments together were what Dave needed to observe Rob and Judy together and see for himself that she was everything Rob said she was.

Once he was satisfied, he staggered to his feet and draped an arm over Sandy's shoulder, "C'mon babe. Take me home, I want to play with the baby's mother."

Sandy grinned and led him off to their car. She poured him into the passenger seat and then turned to Rob and Judy, "Thanks for having us. Judy, I'm so happy we finally got to meet you after all that

Dave has said about you two. I hope we can get together again real soon!" She hugged them both and then drove off.

Going back into the house, Rob and Judy sat at the kitchen table facing one another, starry eyed and content. For Judy, the past days had been intense, but not stressful. Sipping her tea, she studied Rob. There was no physical contact, only the look that passed between them.

Powerful emotions filled Rob as he looked at Judy. Reaching across the table, their fingertips met, "For the first time in my life, this is home" he said softly with a sweep of his hand, "With my soul-mate."

27

CHUCK'S REVELATION

The sun was not yet up when Rob came out of a deep sleep with the feeling that he was being watched. He opened his eyes to find Judy propped on an elbow watching him. She was smiling and her eyes held the special sparkle that she reserved for him alone. He turned on his side and draped his arm across her waist pulling her close, "Good morning," he said sleepily.

"Good morning... I've been waiting for you to wake up," she answered with a mischievous grin.

He was going to ask her what she had on her mind but that would have been a foolish question.

It was mid-morning when Chuck called. He had several hard questions for Rob. He asked very pointedly how well he really knew Judy, if she could be trusted. Chuck Stuart was the only man alive that could question Judy's integrity.

Rob's reply was abrupt, "Yes."

"We'll be over in a little while. I want to talk to her."

Rob briefed Judy. Of all his friends, Chuck was the one that disturbed her the most.

When Chuck and Samantha arrived, they joined Rob and Judy in the living room. While the others sat, Chuck paced ominously. He questioned Judy about school, her classes, her friends, and her roommates. She answered his questions with apprehension. Once he seemed satisfied with her answers, he handed her a scrap of paper. There was a phone number scribbled on it.

"If you need anything, call me, 24 hours a day, seven days a week. I'll be in Flagstaff, but if you see me, don't do anything to show that we've ever met."

Judy gave Chuck a puzzled look. It made no sense that he would make an offer like that and it frightened her. She glanced at Rob, then Samantha.

"Chuck's with the FBI. He's working undercover," Samantha explained.

"There's criminal activity up there, Judy," Chuck said. "It involves nasty people and some pretty dirty business. We're trying to bring it down. The people involved have no qualms about violence. I'm not saying that to frighten you, just to make you aware. We've got a lot of undercover agents up there, men and women that fit into the community. If you get into a bad situation, call that number immediately. If I'm in the area, I'll come. If not, I'll make sure someone does, but don't hesitate. Response time may be six or eight minutes."

Frightened, she turned to Rob, "What's this about, Honey?"

Rob took her hand. "Like Chuck said, there's some criminal activity up there. He's working it. It would take me several hours to get there... but I would come, you can bet your life on that."

Samantha smiled reassuringly at Judy, "You don't have to be anxious, Judy. These guys can take care of anything. All you need to do is be alert. Pay attention to what's going on around you and don't hesitate to call either one of them."

Chuck smiled for the first time, "If you have any doubts about this man of yours, or his ability, just ask him to show you his uniform and make him tell you about it."

Dave talked about Rob's propensity for understatement. Thinking about Rob's war stories, Judy wondered if the truth was even more horrifying. She turned back to look at Chuck. There was no doubt that Chuck was tough and capable. He was in a business that demanded that, but the look he gave Rob made it obvious that he knew Rob's capabilities exceeded his own.

With his message delivered, Chuck touched briefly on some of the things for her to watch for. Judy watched Samantha as Chuck spoke and realized that if she hadn't been there the warning would have been far more frightening. Chuck had a dangerous job but his wife radiated confidence in his ability to be careful, and to come home safely to her after every assignment. Samantha was a beautiful woman, but incredibly strong. Judy watched her and knew that she would have to be that way too.

As they prepared to leave, Judy handed the scrap of paper with the telephone number back to Chuck. When he gave her a puzzled look, she said, "I've already memorized it. It wouldn't be a good idea for someone to find it."

Chuck nodded at Rob, "This is quite the lady you've got here! You better take good care of her."

Rob wasn't smiling when he replied quietly, "I intend to do just that."

It had been an intense meeting. Judy's mind was spinning. She sat with Rob on the patio while he reiterated what Chuck had disclosed, "Somewhere in Flagstaff, there's a key figure dealing with drugs, pornography, and disappearing kids. The two Interstate highways make it a transient area with tourists and travelers passing through. It's a logical place for any number of illegal activities."

The day was winding down now and she would soon have to return. She remembered Chuck's comment about Rob's uniform. Over his objections, she asked to see it and hear the story.

Reluctantly he took her to his bedroom. From the back of his closet he removed a clothing bag. He unzipped it and took out his neatly pressed Marine Corps dress blue uniform. It is a uniform that has earned and deserves the respect for all that wear it. On the sleeve were the stripes of a staff sergeant, on the chest were brightly colored ribbons, and around the neck was a single medal on a star-studded blue ribbon.

She looked at the uniform and then touched the single medal, "This one is special isn't it?"

"Yes it is."

"I'm sorry, Honey, I don't know. What does it signify?" she asked sincerely.

"It's called the Congressional Medal of Honor." He answered simply.

Judy gasped. She had never seen one before, only heard stories. It was the highest honor that could be bestowed on an American fighting man and indicated the greatest respect a grateful nation could bestow on an individual. The man she loved was an American hero.

With a trembling hand, she touched another of the ribbons, "What's this with the four little stars?

"It's a purple heart," he replied quietly. "It signifies wounds received in combat. The stars are for subsequent incidents."

"You were wounded five times?" she asked in awe.

"Yes."

"Is it difficult for you to talk about, Sweetheart?"

Rob smiled warmly, "No, not with you. You understand, and that means a great deal to me. When people talk about that sort of thing, they just see the glory, or the blood and guts. John Wayne stuff, and they don't realize that there are real human beings in uniforms like this, guys and gals, kids mainly, that are scared to death, trying to do their job and praying to God that they can just go home alive."

Judy shuddered and held him as tightly as she could, "I'm glad you came home to me," she whispered softly, unable to hide the depth of her feelings.

Then it was time to go. Rob drove her to the airport and watched as her plane lifted into the afternoon sky. Long after the plane was out of sight, he drove home. His heart was full of pleasant memories spent with the woman he loved. He felt at peace with the world.

He parked in the garage and went into his house. The moment he passed through the doorway, the silence and the emptiness hit him like a physical blow. A large portion of his life was spent alone, yet he never felt loneliness. When he took Patricia to school after spending the summer with him, the feeling was not loneliness, but one of peace. When his wife left him, he had felt a sense of loss, but never loneliness. He understood that it was a terrible thing to be alone... and be with someone. It was what his marriage had been.

He fell into a chair, somber and depressed. She was still on the plane. He couldn't salve the emptiness with her voice. He went to the kitchen, took a beer from the refrigerator, then wandered aimlessly through an empty building filled with her memory. He went to his bedroom and stopped abruptly. There on his dresser was a framed picture of Judy! His spirits lifted at once and he smiled. She put it there without a word. How could she have known how much it would mean to him? When he went to his closet to make sure he had a clean uniform for the next day, he smiled again. All the clothes she brought with her from Flagstaff were hanging neatly next to his, and in the bathroom, a hairbrush, makeup, and the toiletries that belonged to her.

He breathed a deep sigh of satisfaction; his house was no longer empty. It had changed. It was their home.

Judy used her new cell phone as soon as she was off the plane. She needed to hear his voice. Sitting in the empty terminal, waiting for one of her roommates, she listened while he told of coming home to an empty house. When he described his pleasure at finding her picture and her things in his bedroom and bathroom, she felt a warm glow. She closed her eyes and knew that they were together; no matter how many miles were between them. Now, in listening to the things he said, she was beginning to understand how great her impact had been on his life.

In the following weeks, Marianne listened to her daughter's phone calls that had become more frequent and longer lasting now that she had a cell phone. She heard glowing reports of Rob and although she kept her thoughts to herself, she grew more concerned. Judy was very special in her eyes and she wondered how any man, let alone an older man that was just an auto mechanic could ever be good enough for Judy.

Rob and Judy shared a relaxed Thanksgiving with their friends and families in his backyard. Dave and Sandy brought their two young children. In spite of their father's antics, they were well behaved. Ralph and Cathy brought their three youngsters. Chuck and Samantha's daughter had her mother's good looks and her father's fascination for motorcycles.

The youngsters were fascinated by Judy, and kept her occupied. She was now a welcome and accepted part of that group of friends.

After Thanksgiving, Rob drove Judy back to Flagstaff. There was research to do and a paper to write. The long drive allowed then to firm up their plans for visiting her family at Christmas. Gathering her reference materials, they went to the motel where he stayed when he visited. In order to make sure he didn't distract her while she studied, Rob spent part of each day familiarizing himself with Flagstaff.

Chuck's information bothered him. According to Chuck, there were agents in the area, but did they really know what to look for? Rob had his own ideas. It was unlikely that someone dealing drugs and involved in prostitution and pornography lived in an apartment. Still, he looked them over and picked up on Chuck's surveillance people. He became intimately familiar with the area surrounding the apartment where Judy lived.

Parking the 4Runner he sometimes strolled around various neighborhoods, observing the people that lived there and what they did. Other times, he rented a plain sedan or U-Haul truck and drove the streets looking for anything that might indicate the presence of illegal activity. Finding houses or businesses that looked suspicious, he noted the location and surrounding area. On future weekends, he would look them over after dropping Judy at her apartment.

Gated communities were a problem. That necessitated waiting for a resident to enter, and follow them in. U-Haul trucks were ideal for that. If someone was on the street, Rob stopped, and looking lost, he asked directions. Residents were often helpful, providing the information Rob needed about their neighborhood without realizing it.

Back home in Tucson, Rob compiled all the information, and plotted the suspicious homes and buildings on a detailed street map of Flagstaff. If it ever became necessary to act, Rob was prepared.

28

MANUEL'S NEW GIRL

The informal business meeting was held in Manny's home, "The rock group's concert is in Phoenix this weekend. I need to replenish their supply of product and maybe allow them to sample something new," Manny said. "Why don't you arrange for a couple of college girls to join us."

"I know just the girl for you, patron," Hector grinned. "She's blonde, big hooters, very pretty, and smart, but naïve as hell. I think you'll like her."

"Is she one of our customers?" Manny asked.

"No, not yet," Hector replied with a grin.

"Can she be trusted?"

"I wouldn't introduce her to you if she couldn't be trusted."

Manny nodded, "Then you make sure you bring something for her to sample. It doesn't hurt to have a new customer. She might even have a few friends that could prove useful."

The girl Hector had in mind was a devoted fan of the rock group. She knew about the concert, but she couldn't afford to go. An opportunity like this was something she couldn't miss. She was eager to accept a blind date with someone as wealthy as Hector described him.

When she was introduced to Manny, she was impressed. Not only was he wealthy, but he was good looking. While Hector drove the Lexus, Manny sat in the back seat with his date. Entertaining gullible young girls was an area where he excelled.

"Would you like something to relax on the long drive to Phoenix?" Manny asked politely once they were out of town.

He showed her a joint, "This is smooth and relaxing. There's no hangover, and no after affects. I think you'll enjoy it."

She hesitated, "I haven't done that before, and I'm not sure how it would affect me."

"It's nothing to worry about," Hector said over his shoulder. "It won't affect you as much as a beer or glass of wine."

Hector's date agreed, "Try it, you'll probably like it."

At first, she was reluctant to join the others, but before they reached the Verde Valley, she changed her mind. She was pleased to discover that, like Hector said, the effect on her was pleasant. In the relaxed atmosphere, she cuddled with her date.

Their reserved seats for the concert were the very best. The concert was everything she hoped it could be. When it was over, she was exhilarated, and thanked Manny with a firm hug and a promising kiss.

"We aren't ready to leave yet," Manny smiled. "I have another surprise for you."

He led his companions toward the mob of fans waiting for a glimpse of the band. It seemed a futile effort. The tightly packed throng was being restrained by the large contingent of security people. One of the security guards met them. He escorted them past the screaming mob, through the gate in the chain link fence, and back to the band's familiar coach.

It was the thrill of a lifetime to be introduced to her favorite group in person. It was even more exciting with the reception they received. They knew Manny. They treated him and his guests like family. Manny's date received autographed copies of their latest albums. One of them even gave her his distinctive 'doo rag'. She was too distracted to observe the business transaction between Hector and the band members.

When they left the coach and made their way back to the Lexus, Manny suggested that rather than return to Flagstaff that night they should stay at his condominium in Phoenix. The condominium was in a gated community, tastefully decorated and very luxurious. His date was delighted.

With the excitement of the evening and the effects of the marijuana, she was willing to do anything he asked. Satisfying a man was something she knew how to do well. She took excellent care of Manny that night. The silk negligee that he provided saw very little use.

In the morning, Hector drove Manny and the girls to several exclusive women's stores.

"If I date a pretty girl like you, she should be able to dress properly," he said.

He suggested that she choose from among the most expensive outfits in each of the stores they visited.

When it was time to return, she placed her new wardrobe on top of several other packages in the trunk of the Lexus. Once back in the car, she devoted all her attention to Manny.

On the trip back to Flagstaff, Manny took advantage of her accommodating nature. He liked the combination of soft warm flesh and leather seats.

Hector was right. This girl was his type... big busted, plump, and smart, but naïve. It might be a good idea to keep this one around for a while.

29

To Duluth

With Christmas break coming up the girls were studying diligently in order to be prepared for the holidays. Judy was having a hard time concentrating on her studies. Her mind was on visiting her family with Rob. Angie was looking forward to spending the
holidays with her family in Douglas. Only Beth seemed indifferent.

"It's the weather," she told her roommates. "Mom and Dad said
it was brutally cold and snowy. I thought I'd just stay here."

Outside it was snowing, but their apartment was snug and warm.
Judy sat at the kitchen table with reference books and maps covering
the table and overflowing onto the floor. She was taking notes and
had been for hours. She was wearing down.

Angie was curled up in one of their chairs, halfway through a
thick textbook. Beside her on the table, were the notes she had been
jotting down as she read. Her eyes were getting heavy and her head
nodded on occasion. She was ready for bed.

Beth was sprawled on the sofa. She was reading, just not taking
as many notes. She had a photographic memory. Her roommates en-
vied her. They needed to rely on their copious notes to jog their
memory when it came time to write reports or prepare for tests.

Beth looked bored. She put her book aside and yawned, "It looks
like things are going well for you and Rob."

"They are," Judy smiled, ready for a break. "I'm excited about
him meeting Mom and Brian and Sarah. I know they're going to love
him."

Angie looked up from her book, "Maybe, but it might take them a while to get used to the idea that he's older." When she saw the angry flash of Judy's eyes she quickly added, "But I know they'll get over it pretty quick. I'm sure they'll realize what he means to you. You aren't anything like the girl I first met, and it's all because of him."

Judy smiled, "I've got my guy, Angie, what about you? You haven't mentioned anyone special. Have you got someone hidden away down there in Douglas?"

Angie shifted in her chair. "No... no one," she answered and then turned to Beth. "How about you, Beth, are things still going hot and heavy with your cowboy?"

"Well, I suppose so," she answered indifferently.

Judy gave her a surprised look, "I thought you liked him."

"Oh, he's all right, but he's still just a cowboy. That's all he'll ever be. I grew up with farmers and cowboys and I've had enough of them. I want someone a little more exciting, someone that knows what's going on in the world and knows how to have a good time."

Her roommates were shocked at Beth's comments. "But, he's a decent guy, Beth," Angie said.

"If he's so great, why don't you go out with him?" Beth challenged.

"He's a nice guy, and I respect him, but he's not my type," Angie replied. "I don't play games, and I wouldn't lead him on knowing that."

Judy intervened before the situation became even more heated, "You've never talked about it, Angie. Just what kind of guy is your type?"

Angie put her book aside and smiled at Judy. "I'd want to find someone like you did. My parents wouldn't want me to marry an Anglo. Unless he was like Rob," she grinned. "Mom wants grandkids, and I like that idea. I've got three sisters, but I wish someday I could have a big family. Lots of kids of my own and a man that loved me," then she paused and a change came over her. "But that's just what I want. I don't expect it will ever happen," she ended with distant look.

"I never knew that about you, Angie," Judy said. "You're a pretty girl. You could easily find someone like that."

"It's not that simple," Angie replied quietly. Putting her books aside, she stretched her arms over her head and yawned, "I'm tired. I think I'll go to bed."

After watching her go, Beth spoke, "What's the matter with her?"

Judy sat quietly thinking about this insight into Angie. It simply didn't make sense. Angie was a pretty girl and she had been on dates. She just didn't bring any of them to the apartment to meet her roommates. The revelation about her parent's opinion of Anglos was also an eye opener. If there was any similar prejudice in Angie, she had never shown it. Was it possible that her boyfriends were Hispanic and she didn't want them to know, or worse yet, she was ashamed of that? That didn't make any sense. Angie was intelligent and the three of them were pretty close... or were they? Suddenly Angie's private life took on a puzzling air that did not make sense.

Beth returned to her studies and Judy's thoughts shifted. It gave her an uncomfortable feeling the way Beth had dismissed Jack as 'just a cowboy'. It seemed that Beth and Jack were still getting along. It was only a week ago that Beth asked Jack to spend the night with her again. Had something changed in that short period of time?

But those were someone else's problems. She smiled and thought about Rob and their prospects for Christmas. Things were happening so fast and yet she felt as if she had known Rob forever. She thought about Angie's dream of a husband and family. She wished that was something she could dream about with Rob, but the subject never came up. His marriage had been painful and she often felt that the difficult relationship with his children was tearing him apart. She knew he would talk about it if she asked him. No, that was one issue she was not willing to force. Maybe in time he might change and think about marriage, but that didn't matter. It would be his choice. Judy would not push the issue. She would simply be herself. She would love him, support him, and be there for him.

That thought made her pause. She *was* there for him. He shared things with her that no one else knew, not because he was bragging, or trying to impress her. He told her those terrible things from his past because the burden was too great to bear alone. He trusted her... she swallowed hard with the realization and tried to concentrate on her studies.

Angie was already on her way to Douglas when Rob arrived to pick up Judy for their drive to the airport in Phoenix. Beth was still there, but he got the distinct impression that she wasn't going to spend the holiday alone. He left the gifts for Judy's roommates and they were off.

On the drive to Phoenix, Judy shared her thoughts, "In spite of what Beth said about Jack I think they still might spend Christmas together. He's a pretty decent guy, and he likes Beth a lot. If there's any problem between them, he'll try to work it out."

The pilot announced their final approach to the airport and Judy was excited.

"Are you anxious to see your family?" Rob asked.

Judy wrapped her arms around his and smiled, "Yes I am. It's been a while and a lot has happened since I was last here... I hope you like them."

"That's not important. I hope they'll accept me!"

"They will," Judy said confidently.

"Why don't I get our bags and you get our car. Ralph made the arrangements, all you need to do is sign the paperwork and have them send it up for us."

"Right... how will I do that?"

Rob reached inside his jacket and took out his pen, "Here, you'll need this."

"What am I supposed to do with this?" she grinned.

Taking a credit card from his wallet, he handed it to her, "You'll need to sign this. It's not valid without your signature."

It was a brand new Visa card with her name on it, "I don't understand... I didn't apply for a credit card."

"It's on my account, and it's yours. You'll need it to get our car. Make sure it has front wheel drive and can handle the snow. Get one that's big enough to haul all of us, in case we go out somewhere, and don't let them talk you into the extra insurance. My insurance will cover anything that could happen."

Shocked and bewildered, she turned to him, "I can't accept this Rob. It's... it's..."

"It's yours," he interrupted. "You might need it."

"But Rob... what if I bought something expensive and never told you?"

"We both know you wouldn't do that. I trust you," he said simply.

"But..."

"There'll be other times when you'll need it. If you sign the card, you can get our car when we land. That'll get us on the road sooner."

'I trust you' was still ringing in her ears. She looked at the credit card and then at Rob. She was concerned about potential problems. As the plane bumped down on the frigid runway, a thought occurred to her, "But what about Patricia? What if..."

"She gets an allowance. She doesn't have a credit card in my name."

"But I don't understand."

"Simple. I don't trust her."

Providing her with a credit card was a significant responsibility. Rob showed no concern. 'I trust you' was all that mattered to him.

In his travels in the service, Rob had endured many drastic changes in weather between points of departure and arrival. None were quite like this. They flew out of Phoenix with the temperature in the low 80's and no humidity. Duluth would barely creep above zero during their visit and the bitter dampness that came off the lake cut like a razor.

He found Judy standing beside a brand new, all wheel drive Chrysler minivan with 27 miles on the odometer. It wasn't from the rental agency that Ralph had reserved.

"The guy at the counter tried to give us a car we didn't want," Judy said with a worried look. "He said the insurance was mandatory. I told him I'd check with one of the other places, but he said I couldn't do that because the car was prepaid and non-refundable.

"I asked for his name and wrote it down here," she said showing Rob the slip of paper. "The other agency was at the next counter and the lady there was very helpful. Her car was more expensive so I told her that I wanted to check another agency. She said she'd see what she could do for us."

Rob was trying to keep a straight face as she told her story. It made her self-conscious, "Did I do something wrong? I thought Ralph could help us get the charges taken off the card," she said nervously.

"You did exactly right," Rob said with a smile. "You got us a better deal and a better car."

30

JUDY'S FAMILY

"**T**his is your hometown, Honey," Rob said and handed her the keys for the van. "If you drive, we won't get lost."

While she drove, Judy pointed out significant places and told him about her family, "I'm not worried about Sarah and Brian, but I think Mom still has reservations about us."

The home where Judy grew up was a small, two-story, older house in a quiet residential area surrounded by similar houses. The walkway to the front porch was recently cleared of snow leaving a welcome pathway. As soon as they stopped, the front door burst open and Brian, unable to conceal his excitement, flew toward the car. Sarah followed more discreetly, zipping up her coat as came. Standing in the doorway was Judy's mother, Marianne. A quick glance showed where Judy got her good looks. Marianne was certainly anxious to see her daughter, but her concern about this man in her life held her back.

16-year-old Brian darted around the car and slid to a halt at Judy's door. He was slender, solid, with a mop of unruly red hair, and blue green eyes like his sister. Rob stood facing him.

"Hi. Do you want to open her door for her or can I?" Rob asked.

Rob was a lot bigger than Brian was prepared for. Stepping aside, he looked up at Rob without a word. As soon as Rob opened her door, Judy burst out and hugged her brother.

Sarah remained on the curb until Judy came around and made the introductions, "Sarah, Brian, this is my friend, Rob Simpson," Judy beamed.

"How do you do, sir," Brian said tentatively and extended his hand.

Rob removed his glove, took Brian's hand, and looked him over before he replied, "I'm fine, Brian, but I'd be more comfortable if you called me Rob."

The smile was genuine and the appraising look that accompanied it caught Brian off guard. The look was measuring Brian on his own merits, not the word of others. He stood a little straighter.

"Too short for basketball... I imagine you play football," Rob said.

"Yes sir..."

"Rob."

"Oh... yes sir, I mean, Rob, but I guess my sister told you."

"No she didn't, but you have the look of a football player and probably a pretty good one. Are you fast?"

"Well, sort of. I've been on the varsity team since my freshman year."

Rob tested his shoulders and looked into his eyes, "You'd be a great defensive safety, but I'll bet you're a wide receiver. Good hands?"

"Yeah, I don't drop many."

Watching the interchange, Sarah couldn't help but notice how Brian was overwhelmed by someone taking an interest in him. She was impressed. The whole family knew how much Judy liked Rob and now Sarah understood why. He was very good looking, but he was a decent person too. When Rob turned to look at her and extended his hand, she suddenly felt very self-consciousness. No one had ever looked at her quite so intently before.

18-year-old Sarah had brown hair and brown eyes. She was nearly as tall as her sister and very pretty. Even with her bulky jacket, it was apparent that she had a nice figure. She was going to be a heartbreaker... if she wasn't already.

"Hi Sarah, Judy has told me a lot about you, but she didn't say how pretty you are. Are you as smart as she is?" Rob asked.

Sarah was blushing, "I don't think anybody is a smart as Judy."

"And you play the piano?"

"A little."

"Is there a chance I could hear you play while we're here?"

His interest was sincere.

"We usually do Christmas carols. I play the piano for that," she blushed.

Turning to her big sister, Sarah was pleased and understood that Judy had found an extraordinary guy. Sarah was happy for her and even a little jealous. His age had not affected Sarah in the least.

The meeting at the car only took a few minutes, but it was bitterly cold, "Why don't we continue this inside where it's warmer," Judy suggested and started toward the house where her mother still stood in the doorway.

Watching how Rob interacted with her children surprised Marianne. It was not what she expected, but then she didn't know what to expect. Was his interaction with Brian and Sarah just an act for her benefit? Judy glowed and hugged her mother, "Mom, this is Rob Simpson."

She looked at him unemotionally and extended her hand.

"How are you, Mr. Simpson?"

"To tell the truth Mrs. Whitby, I'm nervous," Rob replied as he took her hand. "I'm sure you're more than a little concerned. I appreciate you allowing me to visit with you and your family."

"Why don't we get in out of the cold? It would make it easier to get acquainted."

Once inside they removed their coats and congregated in the living room. Mrs. Whitby stiffened when Judy joined Rob on the couch and held his hand. It was a natural thing and not an act of defiance. That concerned her even more.

Judy talked about school and her roommates. She told them about some of their hikes.

"What about school?" Marianne asked."How are your grades?"

"She's the top student in all her classes," Rob interrupted. "She even tutors her classmates. You can be proud of her, Mrs. Whitby."

"How do you know all this?" Marianne asked while Sarah and Brian stared at him.

"He knows more about my grades than I do," Judy interrupted. "Lots of times I'd rather take a break and hike, but he makes me to stick with the books."

"Of course I do, Honey," Rob said. "Your education is more important, and you know it."

Obviously, this was not the first time the subject had come up between the two of them. Marianne was impressed.

"I'd like to take you folks to dinner tonight if that's all right," Rob suggested as they visited. "Judy tells me there are lots of good places to eat here."

"That's a kind offer, Rob," Marianne replied nervously, "But I thought we might put something together here."

"Aw, she's just worried because our car isn't working right and she doesn't want you to have to drive," Brian interjected.

"What's the matter with it?" Rob asked.

"It doesn't start very well when it gets really cold," Marianne replied. "It's an old car but it's usually reliable. I made an appointment at the garage to have them look at it next week."

"But Mom," Judy asked with concern, "How do you get to work and the store if the car isn't working? In this weather you'll get sick... or worse."

"Maybe I should take a quick look at it," Rob interrupted.

"Rob's a great mechanic, Mom," Judy said proudly.

Marianne relented after being assured that he would take a quick look and offer an opinion. Brian volunteered to go with Rob. He said he wanted to learn more about cars. The truth was that he simply wanted to be with Rob. They bundled into warm coats, hats, and gloves and went back outside. The frigid air made Rob wonder if it was such a good idea after all.

The Whitby car was an older Chevrolet sedan. Rob slipped in behind the wheel, pumped the accelerator pedal, and gave the starter a turn. It ground slowly but it was apparent that it wasn't going to start. Opening the hood, he made a quick appraisal. It was the small block V-8 with a carburetor. He removed the air cleaner with fingers rapidly becoming numb and looked. As he suspected, the choke had not set. He felt the linkage and saw the buildup of sludge. No wonder it wouldn't start. He set the air cleaner back loosely in position and closed the hood.

"Any auto parts stores close by?" he asked Brian.

"There's one over near the car dealerships."

Rob looked at his watch, "They should still be open. Let's tell those ladies where we're going and we'll see if we can fix your Mom's car."

Brian looked at Rob in awe. He was going to fix the car and take Brian with him. Once back in the house, Rob explained what he intended to do. It took several more minutes to overcome the objections, then Rob and Brian were off. There was an auto parts store right where Brian said and they went inside. Rob located the things they needed and they were off.

"Do you have a pair of pliers, a screwdriver, and some old rags we can use?"

"I've got a few tools," Brian answered, "But they aren't real good."

They pulled to the curb behind the Whitby's Chevrolet, "Why don't you run in and get the tools we need, Brian. I'll get started out here."

As he hurried through the house, he exclaimed proudly, "Rob and I are going to fix the car, Mom."

Gathering his precious tools, Brian rushed back outside. The spray cleaner that Rob used to free up the linkage barely worked in the cold air. Working quickly and efficiently, Rob explained everything he did. He described how the choke was supposed to work and what it did when it was operating properly.

"When it comes to tools you should get the best you can afford," Rob said. "If you take your work seriously, and you should, you'll find that the best tools allow you to the do your job easier and quicker."

Brian's meager supply of tools weren't the best, but they were all he had and he didn't really know the difference. There was no one to teach him.

"These are all I got," he said quietly.

Realizing that his comment embarrassed Brian, Rob explained, "I guess I didn't make myself very clear, Brian."

Putting the tools aside, he concentrated on Brian. "Your tools are fine for getting the job done. It's obvious you take care of them and that's important too. They're more than adequate for most people. I get the impression that, like football, you strive to be the best. You can learn the basics with average tools, but when you become a professional, you won't be satisfied with anything but the finest. When I first started as a mechanic I used tools just like these, but as I learned, I found that only the very best would do."

Something in the way that Rob talked about tools impressed Brian. His tools, while not the best, were satisfactory for learning. Waiting for the best and putting older things aside when something better came along made sense. Leaning across the icy fender, he looked at Rob differently.

"That's true about other things too isn't it, Rob, I mean things besides tools?"

It was not a simple question. It required more than a simple yes or no answer, "That's pretty profound, Brian. I think you're looking for a lot more wisdom that I've got."

"No, I don't believe that," Brian replied.

The time for fixing cars could wait. Rob put the tools aside. In spite of the numbing cold, matters that are more important needed to be addressed. The two of them spoke earnestly with a dirty air filter and stuck choke between them. Ignoring the cold, he tried his best to answer Brian's questions.

Inside the house, Judy was visiting with Sarah and their mother and they lost track of time. When she looked out the frosted window, she could see Rob and Brian extending out from under the hood of her mother's car. Her mother joined her at the window and looked out into the fading daylight that cast a cold, bitter blanket across the frosted snow.

"I hope they're all right," Judy said with concern. "It's really cold out there."

"What's he trying to prove anyhow?" Marianne asked sharply.

"He's not trying to prove anything, mother!" Judy retorted defensively. "He doesn't need to prove anything to anybody. He's helping you because that's the way he is. He's a good man, just like Dad!"

She wasn't about to back down.

The intensity of her outburst surprised Marianne. Reaching out she took Judy in her arms, "I'm sorry, Honey. It's just that I wasn't quite prepared for this. Losing his father was hard on Brian. He doesn't have many friends or any adult role models he can look up to."

"But, what about the guys on his football team?"

"I thought that might make a difference, but when the coaches saw how good he was, they put him on the varsity team."

"Isn't that good?" Judy asked.

"Not really. The upper classmen don't associate with him because he's younger, and his classmates think he's stuck up because he's on the varsity team. He's stuck in the middle."

"Well then, he's got Rob now, and Rob needs a boy that looks up to him," Judy said.

"You really like him don't you?"

Judy didn't hesitate, "No, Mom, I'm in love with him."

"Well then, maybe we should make something hot to drink for when those two finally decide to come back in," Marianne suggested.

The intensity of the conversation under the hood of the Chevrolet had lessened. It was time to go back to fixing cars.

"Let's see if we did any good," Rob said with his teeth chattering.

Opening the door, he slid onto the cold, hard seat. He pumped the stiff accelerator pedal several times and then looked at Brian who had joined him on the other side of the car, "Cross your fingers, buddy."

The motor ground slowly when Rob turned the key, coughed once and then chugged to life! It ran for a minute and then died. Rob pumped the pedal again and turned the key. This time the car started readily and after feathering the throttle several times, it ran smoothly at a fast idle.

Rob smiled at Brian, "Well, Brian, we did it. Let's put the air cleaner back on and take a spin around the block to see how she runs."

Brian was elated. Watching a master mechanic at work, Rob performed a miracle and shared the credit with him! Back under the hood, Rob instructed Brian in the procedure for safely replacing the air filter with the engine running and then let him do it. Once again, it was a simple thing, but Brian took pride in what he did, even more so under Rob's watchful eye. When they were back in the car, Rob looked at the gauges and listened for any unnatural noises. He carefully explained what he was doing and what he was listening for. He used the same procedure when he put the car in gear and drove off. He watched for correct shift points as he accelerated, and with a delicate hand on the wheel tried to ascertain any potential problems in the steering and suspension. It was second nature to him; the things he did daily and instinctively. He kept up a steady monologue of what he was doing and what he was looking for. Brian listened intently, devouring every word.

With their road test completed, Rob eased the car to the curb and turned off the motor. Their efforts paid off. Judy's mother wouldn't have to worry about a car that wouldn't start. Darkness was descending from the bitterly gray sky when they climbed the steps to the house.

31

GETTING ACQUAINTED

Although she would rather have joined the family for dinner, Sarah had a date and changed clothes while Rob and Brian worked on the car. She joined the others warming up in the kitchen. Dressed in a sweater, plaid skirt, and matching stockings, her attire was conservative. Not suggestive, but it could hardly disguise her figure. Her hair was brushed out straight and she had tastefully applied a minimum of makeup.

"You look very nice, Sarah," Rob said. "Tell me about the lucky guy."

"He's one of the guys from school," Sarah replied. "He's been bugging me to go out with him for a long time and I finally agreed to see a movie with him."

They were sitting in the living room when a horn announced her date.

"There he is," Sarah said and went for her coat.

It was not his place to say anything but Rob was seething inside. He chose his words as carefully as he could, "Sarah, what are you doing?"

"I don't want to keep him waiting," she replied and stood holding her coat.

"Why is that?" Rob asked as her siblings watched and Marianne hid a grin.

"I don't want him to think I'm not ready."

"What do you think is going through his mind right now?" Rob asked.

While Sarah stood uncertainly without answering, he continued, "If he was thinking about you he would come to the door and escort you out even if he didn't take time to meet your family."

"But what if he gets mad and just leaves?"

"That's a measure of *his* character, Sarah, not yours. It's important for you to demonstrate the kind of person you are, that you deserve something better than waiting for the honk of a horn. It's not a matter of thinking you're better than him. It's a matter of being treated with respect. If you don't respect yourself then he has no reason to treat you that way either."

There was a long and uncomfortable silence while Sarah stood with her coat in hand debating Rob's words. The silence was suddenly broken by the doorbell. Sarah looked relieved and began for the door.

"Don't you think its best that your mother answers the door?" Rob asked quietly and then turned to look at Mrs. Whitby.

With an effort to control her smile, Marianne arose and answered the door. Sarah's date was somewhat bewildered by this turn of events. Marianne invited him in and introduced him to the others. Daryl was Sarah's age, the same age as Rob's daughter, Patricia. He was slender with long black hair, and an earring in one ear. His jacket was too big for him. It hung loosely over a baggy sweater with pants slung low on his hips. When Rob stood to shake his hand, he towered over Sarah's date. Daryl was the sort that his daughter associated with and Rob knew what they were like.

"We're going to dinner while you two are at the movie," Rob said pleasantly. "It shouldn't last much later than that. Why don't you come back here after the movie? I'm sure Mrs. Whitby would like to get to know you better."

It was not a request or a suggestion. In spite of Rob's casual tone, it was the law.

Brian knew the withering gaze that Rob fixed on Daryl. He experienced a milder version of it earlier and would not have wanted to be in Daryl's position for anything. Brian saw the reaction in Daryl's eyes.

Whatever happened that night, whatever he planned, Daryl would ultimately have to answer to the man who stood before him right now. Whatever he thought Sarah was, whatever he thought he might get from her wasn't quite as important as he previously thought. This was one chick he had no intention of messing with.

Watching with delight as the situation unfolded, Judy sat with a pleased grin. Rob *had* changed. This was not the same man that endured his own daughter's abuse the first time she saw him. This was the man she knew he really was.

Daryl actually helped Sarah into her coat and departed with a nervous glance at Rob. The look he received left no further doubt in his mind. If he didn't have Sarah home within 15 minutes of the end of the movie, he would suffer the consequences.

Once they were gone, Marianne grinned, "You handled that quite well, Mr. Simpson."

"Rob... please call me Rob," he said self consciously, and then added, "I'm sorry, I didn't mean to intrude."

"Very well, Rob then, but thank you. That's what I should have done."

"I don't like him," Rob said with a disgusted shake of his head. Then he turned to Marianne, "You've got two beautiful daughters Mrs. Whitby. I'm doing the best I can to treat Judy with the respect she deserves and I hope I don't ever let either of you down. Sarah deserves that same respect. I don't think she realizes what a special girl she is or what a great family she comes from."

Then Rob added through clenched teeth, "That worthless punk doesn't deserve to be in the same town as her."

The intensity of his words startled Marianne.

Judy hugged him and smiled, "Mom's right, you did handle that pretty well," she added proudly.

He kissed Judy's forehead and looked at her mother, "I learned that restraint from your daughter, Mrs. Whitby. She would have handled it better, but that punk upset me."

Sitting quietly on the sidelines, Brian was watching, listening, and learning. Rob treated women with dignity and respect. Their discussion about tools came back to him vividly. Rob talked about making do until one could get the very best. He waited for Judy because she was the very best. There was something else too. Rob was her protector and the guardian of all she held dear. Brian firmly believed that Rob was a man that would willingly and without hesitation lay down his life for those he loved. That observation was absolutely correct.

Their dinner was pleasant, a relaxed occasion that allowed Marianne and Brian to know Rob better. They were home only a short time when they heard a car drive up. Sarah's date did bring her home right after the movie.

Daryl brought her inside and without looking at Rob, mumbled, "I'd stay and talk but I have this other thing I got to do. Bye Sarah," he said and hurried out the door.

Once he was gone, Sarah put her jacket away while Rob waited for her to berate him for interfering. Much to his surprise, she reentered the room where they all sat and went directly to him. After hesitating for a moment, she bent over and gave him a hug.

She stood with an embarrassed look at Judy, "Sorry," she said then looked back at Rob.

"Thank you for standing up for me like that. I really didn't want to go out with him but I already promised."

"Don't give me all the credit, Sarah" Rob interrupted. "Your Mom would have done the same thing; I just butted in before she got a chance. She raised you kids, and she's done a pretty good job. You've all learned good values and you're smart. I had nothing to do with that. Your Mom is the one that deserves the hug, not me."

Later that evening, Marianne was shocked when Judy brought out bedding and made up a spot on the couch for Rob. She felt relieved that it was an issue she didn't have to address. Once everyone was settled in, Marianne went to Judy's room and sat on the edge of her bed.

"He's a lot different than I expected, Honey. I can see why you're so happy. He treats you pretty well doesn't he?" she began.

Judy sat up beaming, "Yes, he does lots of nice things like the cell phone and now the credit card, but it's the little things he does every day."

Then she smiled, "After what he did for Sarah tonight, I think she has a crush on him."

"You're probably right," Marianne agreed, "But it's the car thing. Rob spent so much time with him and treated him as if his opinion mattered. Brian really needed that."

"I think Rob did too. I know he misses his son terribly. That's a pretty bad situation. I wish there was something I could do."

Marianne hugged her daughter, "I think what you do is good enough for him. You certainly can't replace his children but you've made a big difference."

Marianne paused and took a deep breath, "Honey, I want to ask you something and I don't want to upset you."

"It's about our age difference, isn't it?"

"Yes, I just wonder if you've thought it through."

"I have," Judy smiled. "Everyone I ever dated was close to my age and none of them could ever measure up to Rob. He worries about it more than I do. I don't know what will happen or how long we'll have, but for now, I have what you and Dad have."

There was a lump in her throat when Marianne replied, "Your father and I had a lot of wonderful years. It's hard to be young and alone."

"I'm sorry, Mom. I don't want you to feel bad. It's just that I want to spend as much as I can with him."

"Then I don't understand something."

"What's that?"

"Why did you make up the sofa for him?"

Judy grinned, "Well, I can tell you it wasn't my idea! We talked about it before we came and he suggested it. He was concerned that if we slept together under your roof it would validate that sort of behavior. He didn't want to offend you or give Sarah and Brian the impression that it was all right."

In the morning, Judy was the first to arise and slipped downstairs in her robe and pajamas to wake Rob. He was already up, coffee was ready, and he was searching through the kitchen for ingredients to make breakfast.

"You got up early," she smiled and embraced him.

They were drinking coffee at the kitchen table worn from happy years when Marianne joined them. Her kitchen had the warm smell of breakfast cooking and it embarrassed her, "What have you two done? I thought I'd be up early and get breakfast but you've already started."

Rob stood and held a chair for Marianne. He poured her coffee, "I thought I better do something to repay you for letting me stay here. I appreciate it."

The three of them drank coffee and visited while Rob prepared omelets with a Mexican flair, juice, and toast. After she ate, Judy excused herself, gave Rob a quick kiss, and went upstairs to dress. Rob and Marianne continued their dialogue until there was a momentary lull. Taking a deep breath, she looked at him earnestly and asked, "Have you been sleeping with my daughter?"

Rob was caught completely off guard.

Shifting in his chair, he looked directly at Marianne, "Mrs. Whitby," he began softly, "If anyone but you were to ask that I'd deck them. But Judy is your daughter, and coming from you it's a legitimate question. It's also one that can't accurately be answered with a simple yes or no."

"You're right; it isn't that simple... if you answer at all," she replied.

"Before I say anything else, I want you to understand that Judy is the most wonderful person I've ever met and I'm deeply in love with her. Sleeping together is simply not accurate. To answer your question in another way, yes, we have made love. For me, it is the first time in my life that the 'we' part of that statement applies. For me it is the most magical, intimate, and incredible thing I have ever experienced. It goes so far beyond sex that I can't begin to describe it. I hope that doesn't offend you, but it's the truth. I've tried and will continue to try to do everything I can to be worthy of her love and your respect. Both mean a great deal to me."

Marianne's eyes were misty as she listened to him. Finally, she smiled and interrupted him, "Please, Rob, call me Marianne. I love my children, all three of them, and I only want what's best for them. I'm sure you understand that. Judy is the oldest and I have to admit she's my favorite. When she first told me about the two of you, I was concerned. She sounded serious and I didn't want her to get side-tracked from her education. I was worried that eventually she would have to choose between school and you. You've made it very clear that she doesn't have to make a choice. I didn't realize that before."

She was about to continue when Brian and Sarah stumbled into the kitchen, still half-asleep. After greeting their mother with hugs, they hesitated and glanced at Rob. He solved that problem with hugs that pleased Brian, brought a glow to Sarah's cheeks, and made Marianne smile.

After breakfast, the five of them gathered around the kitchen table, "You haven't spoken about your family, Rob," Marianne said. "Do you have any brothers or sisters?"

Judy knew the answer could be difficult for Rob. His reaction surprised her.

"I have a brother," he said with a faraway look in his eyes and a pleasant smile as the memory returned. "He was killed in action in Viet Nam while I was still in high school."

Marianne was about to speak but he continued, "He was sent home to be buried. My parents arranged for the funeral. It was a pretty sad affair because we were all very close. Mom and Dad went on ahead to get things set up. On the way to the funeral home their car was struck by an impaired driver."

Marianne caught her breath as she listened to his tragic story. Sarah and Brian sat wide-eyed. Judy reached under the table and held his hand. He gave Judy a quick smile and continued, "Mom died at the scene and Dad died on the way to the hospital."

"Oh Rob," Marianne gasped helplessly. "I'm so sorry they're gone."

Rob turned to Marianne, "No, Marianne, they aren't gone. I feel them with me all the time... here," he said and held his hand to his heart. "But then, you understand that. They may be gone, but the relationship we had, the love we shared will never end.

"I have to thank Judy for teaching me that. It took meeting her to realize the profound difference between that and my divorce. My brother and my folks are dead, but our relationship continues. It's permanent. That can never die. I knew the same thing was true when my friend Willy died in Viet Nam.

"The divorce was the death of a relationship and any affection that may have existed. That too was permanent."

32

CHRISTMAS IN DULUTH

By Christmas Eve the house was decorated. Everyone participated, decorating the tree with simple handmade ornaments that survived many memorable years. Piled beneath were brightly colored packages. Gingerbread men, sugar cookies, rum balls and other sweets packed the plate on top of Sarah's piano. The tang of spiced apple cider, eggnog, and Christmas carols filled the air. For the Whitby family it was a tradition, for Rob it rekindled pleasant memories.

Very early on Christmas morning Judy crept into the living room, turned on the tree lights, and nestled with Rob on the couch, "This is our first Christmas together," she whispered.

Rob kissed her hair, "Yes, and for me it's like a fairy tale that came true. How soon will the others be down?"

"If I know them it won't be long."

"Then we better get the coffee going."

The coffee was almost done when Brian hurried down the steps to make sure he didn't miss anything. Marianne and Sarah followed shortly after him with excited looks and found the coffee ready. Gathering around the tree in pajamas and robes, they waited for Marianne to do her duty passing out gifts. Most of them were simple, homemade items intended specifically for beloved family members.

They felt embarrassed by the small homemade tokens they gave Rob until they saw him blinking the tears from his eyes, "This means so much to me... I've never received gifts that came from the heart like this... thank you."

Rob's gift for each of them was different. For Marianne, he chose a cutlery set to replace the old and worn knives that sufficed for too many years, and a warm sweatshirt with NAU emblazoned across the front. Sarah received several CD's of her favorite Artists and sheet music that she didn't know was still in print. Much to Brian's delight and amazement, his gift was a select set of Snap-on tools. Judy opened her gifts to find a warm wool sweater, slippers, a book of Curtis photographs, and a small box that contained a key.

"What's this?" she asked with a puzzled look.

"I worry about you getting to and from school on your bicycle," Rob explained. "I was able to pick up a little economy car from work at a pretty decent price. They wouldn't let me bring it on the plane so you'll have to wait until we get home."

All too soon, the vacation had to end. While Rob was taking their luggage out to the rental car Marianne had a few quiet moments with Judy, "Rob is fine man, I'm so pleased you found each other. You take good care of him, Honey."

"I will, Mom."

"You sure look happy," Sarah said. "I wish I could find someone like him."

"I like him, too," Brian said as he joined them.

The conversation might have continued, but Rob returned from the car. Everything was loaded and it was time for the last goodbyes. There were hugs all around and then Rob and Judy started for the door. With one hand on the doorknob, Rob paused and turned.

He hesitated, and then asked, "If we sent plane tickets, do you think you all could come and visit us in Tucson for spring break?"

Marianne might have protested, but she never got the chance. Her children's enthusiasm overruled her objections, and that was settled. With one last round of hugs, they watched sadly as Rob and Judy got into the rental car and drove off.

Sarah looked at her mother, "Mom, why did you make Rob sleep on the couch? Shouldn't they sleep together?"

It was Brian that dumfounded her with his version, "Yeah, why didn't Rob sleep in Judy's room? Did they have a fight or something?"

Marianne shook her head in exasperation, "What in the world are you two suggesting? I thought I taught you better than that! Where are your minds?"

Brian shook his head, "Boy are you ever old, Mom, this is the 90's! It's one thing if a guy wants to score on a chick, but those two are in love, or didn't you notice?"

"Yes Brian, I noticed, but for your information it was their decision. They didn't want to give you two the wrong idea."

"They must think we're stupid or something," Brian mumbled.

"Brian!" Marianne commanded as he turned to leave.

"Yeah Mom?"

"They made that decision out of respect for all three of us. What they do in private is one thing, but they weren't about to flaunt that right in front of you as if it were perfectly normal. It's something that's too meaningful for them and they wanted to convey that to you. Can you understand that?"

Both Brian and Sarah looked at their mother with shock. The high regard they had for their sister and the newly acquired respect they shared for Rob made a quantum leap.

"Wow!" Sarah exclaimed. "That must have been hard on them."

"I'm sure it was," Marianne agreed.

Chasing the setting sun and returning to Arizona was a strange feeling for Judy. In the past, it was the sadness of being separated from her family. Now it felt like coming home. There was a short layover in Phoenix, the quick plane ride to Tucson, and then the drive to Rob's home. When they pulled into the driveway, Sam came out to greet them. He was curious to learn how their trip had gone. The events they related pleased him.

"I kind of figured your family might like this boy," he said with a twinkle in his eye. He turned to go and then stopped, "Oh, by the way, Judy, I have something of yours over here."

Holding Rob's hand, she followed Sam to his carport. There parked next to Sam's older car was a shiny white import with a large red ribbon taped across the hood. There was a small card attached that said *'Merry Christmas Judy. With all my love, Rob.'* The car gleamed in the fading light. Judy stood dumbfounded.

"I thought you said it was an old car... this looks brand new!"

Sam laughed, "It looks that way now, but you should have seen it when he towed it home! It was a wreck. Couple of fenders, rebuilt the motor, and then he painted it. That boy of yours is pretty handy. He's been working on it in all his spare time." Then he turned to Judy with a grin, "But he hasn't had much of that since he met you."

With an excited glow, Judy hugged Rob and then went to the car. It was locked but when she took the key from her purse, it fit perfectly and the door opened easily. The inside looked just as new as the outside. "Can I drive it?" she asked.

"Of course you can, it's your car."

He climbed in beside her, "I hope you can handle the five speed. I couldn't find an automatic transmission."

She threw her arms around him and kissed him, "Oh, Honey, its perfect! I love it! Are you sure it isn't new? It's so clean and fresh, it even smells new!"

"It's three years old, a Nissan Stanza that was wrecked and had a blown motor. Go ahead and take us for a spin, make sure you like it."

The little car started instantly. Judy let it warm up while she looked at the instruments and adjusted the mirrors. She located all the controls and then eased it into gear and drove off leaving Sam standing in his carport with a satisfied smile. The instant response amazed her.

"As powerful as this is, it must be hard on gas," she said with a glance at him.

"It has a four cylinder motor. You should get about 30 or 32 miles per gallon."

Judy drove and felt comfortable with its handling right away. She might address his extravagance later, but for now, she was too thrilled to think of anything except her new car and the man she loved.

When they returned home and unloaded their things, Judy wanted to call her roommates and tell them the news. There was no answer.

"Angie's not home yet and Beth and Jack are probably out."

"Maybe Beth is at Jack's place. I've got his number; let's see if we can catch her there."

When Jack answered Rob barely recognized his voice. "Jack, its Rob, are you all right? What's the matter?"

That was a complicated question for Jack's muddled mind. He sorted through the haze of recent events to see if they had any bearing on what Rob asked. He sort of remembered. It wasn't much of a fight, just something to do on a boring night and it took his mind off Beth. He got his ass kicked by a big fat punk that he could have handled easily, but that night his heart just wasn't in it.

Flagstaff wasn't a big town and there were mountains and open country all around. Still, Jack felt it closing in on him and missed the ranch. There he could ride in any direction on a good horse and see nothing but open range with damn few fences, just cows and lots of wildlife. Even a knockdown brawl with his older brother would have been more fun. He rented a case of beer, recycled it, and nursed a hangover. When the hangover subsided, he got in his truck and drove aimlessly around town wondering why he was even here in the first place. Once Jack had those events more or less organized in his mind, he gave Rob an abbreviated version in hopes that the questions wouldn't get more difficult.

Judy sat upright and looked at Rob with concern. Jack was in the process of recycling more beer and his speech was slurred. He mentioned the fact that Beth dumped him for a guy with more money. Rob turned away from the phone and gave Judy the sad news, "Beth left him. Some guy with big bucks."

"That bitch!" Judy fumed as she got to her feet and began pacing angrily. The additional expletives were uttered under her breath and none of them were complimentary of her roommate.

"Tell Judy it ain't Beth's fault," Jack said when he heard her reaction. "I ain't nothin' but a low down cowboy... I'll never amount to much... she deserves better than anything I got."

"Bullshit!" Rob fumed.

Judy overheard Jack's comment and took the phone away from Rob, "That's not true, Jack!" she fumed. "You've got more character, morals, and ethics than she'll ever have! She doesn't deserve someone as good as you. I'm sorry for what's happened, and I'm sorry you feel so bad, but I promise you that you're better off with her out of your life. She would have done nothing but drag you down to her level and you're a better man than that!"

Rob and Judy took turns speaking to Jack and it was a chore. If they called a few beers earlier the conversation might have been more coherent. It was over an hour before they finally hung up.

"I'd say you reacted rather strongly, Sweetheart," Rob said with a grin.

"Of course I did! It makes me angry when some girl treats a decent guy like Jack that way. It makes guys think all girls are like that and it's just not true."

Rob kissed her hair and grinned, "Sounds like you're talking about someone I know."

"Well it is true, Rob. When something like that happens it scares me because I don't know what you're thinking."

"Would you like me to tell you what I think?"

"Yes, I need to know if I'm doing the right thing, that you believe me when I tell you I love you."

Rob laughed, "You're doing everything right and then some... the things you do for me, the way you act, just the way you are says more than any words could ever say. I don't doubt your love and I know you will always be faithful to me, to us. I just feel sorry for guys like Jack. There's lots of them out there... and girls too. Women haven't cornered the market on deceit. There's just as many deceitful men as there are women.

"Let me illustrate my point in another way. Do you have your purse?"

Judy looked at him curiously. Her purse was next to the sofa and she handed it to him. He opened her purse and took out her wallet. From the wallet, he removed her new credit card and held it up.

"Do you remember what I told you when I gave this to you?"

"Yes... you said you trusted me."

"Sometimes love isn't enough," he said quietly. "I've learned that to be trusted is far more important than to be loved."

He took her in his arms and held her tightly. He stroked her hair and kissed her cheek, "I have no idea what I ever did to deserve you. I feel Jack's pain and I remember that same feeling years ago... I simply don't know how to tell you or show you how much you mean to me, how complete my life is now that you're part of it. I guess I've known that all along... but now, when the memories of all that pain come back to me I have your love to sustain me, your words to help me through it.

"What happened to me then and what's happening to Jack right now isn't the way it is with every woman. I learned that from you, and I saw that same honesty and faithfulness in your mother. I may need my quiet time to come to grips with those feelings sometimes, but more than that, I need *you* to be able to talk to, to sort things out, and to understand. You did that for me when I talked about Willy and my family, and you did it again when I talked about the war and those medals on my dress blues. Those were things I needed talk out for a long time. I never had anyone that understood or even cared. Now that I have that, I don't know how to tell you how important you are to me; how much I want you in my life."

Judy touched his face gently, "You just did."

When Marianne returned to work, Judy's boyfriend was the single topic of conversation, "What do you think of the guy, Marianne," one of her co-workers asked. "Is he any good or is he just another older man with an ego problem?"

Marianne's reply shocked them, "I just hope she's good enough for him."

33

A Chance Meeting

It was a brisk winter day, but with the sun shining and no wind, it was pleasant. Judy had studying to do but Rob drove up so they could spend time together. Judy didn't mind. They took a break for lunch at a nearby restaurant to allow for a change of atmosphere before going back to the books. After a pleasant lunch, they were returning to Judy's car.

Rob's daughter Patricia and several of her friends were in the parking lot. This was the first time Rob saw her face to face since bringing her up to school in the fall. Any thoughts of a pleasant encounter and the opportunity to introduce Judy quickly disappeared.

Patricia's anger flared up instantly, "What are you doing here? Are you spying on me?"

Judy was startled by the venom of Patricia's greeting. It was even more hateful than what Judy observed the first time she saw Patricia. She looked at Rob with concern. He changed since that first encounter she and her roommates observed, but she wasn't sure how he would react.

"No Patricia, I'm not spying on you, I have an important reason for being here." Rob replied mildly with a smile.

Then Patricia became aware of the pretty redhead on her father's arm. Interrupting Rob, she turned to Judy, "Who the fuck are you?"

Judy was shocked at the vehemence in Patricia's voice, but she held her tongue.

Rob spoke up, this time firmly, "Patricia, this is my friend Judy..."

He didn't get to finish the introduction. Patricia grinned knowingly, glared at him with an insolent look, and snarled, "Like fucking that young stuff, do you?"

It happened so quickly that neither Patricia nor her friends saw anything. She suddenly felt the burning sting spreading across her cheek where the red welt of Rob's hand was quickly forming and it took her breath away. He had never spoken harshly, raised his voice, or struck her. She was too stunned to react.

He caught her eyes and continued in a soft, controlled voice, "As I was saying, this is Judy Whitby. She's the reason that I'm here, not checking up on you. Now, once you apologize to her we can continue our conversation or you can be on your way. The choice is yours."

The choice of staying or leaving was obvious. There was no choice as far as an apology was concerned. Patricia felt the burning of tears forming in her eyes. She looked at her father in shock. No man had ever struck her, and she was always in control. She was not in control now. Memories of his calm and quiet reaction to all her outbursts came flooding back to her in a rush. He always maintained his control, and always treated her fairly. No... more than fairly. She didn't understand this change. She glanced at Judy and did not see a challenge, but pity. With a lifetime to learn about her father, Patricia never knew him. She was learning fast.

"I'm sorry," she uttered quietly in Judy's direction then turned to look at Rob. It was the first time she saw him for who he really was and it shook her visibly.

She stood looking at him with the brassy taste of blood where she had bit her cheek and could not find words to say. There would be many unpleasant words later when surrounded by her friends. For the moment, in this instance, she felt something unfamiliar... respect. Then she did something she didn't know she was capable of. She stepped up to Rob and hugged him. At that moment, she meant it.

"We need to go, Dad... I'm sorry I don't have more time," she gave Judy a strange look and added, "Nice to meet you... Judy."

Patricia quickly turned away and with her friends falling in behind her, walked off. Once she had regained control of herself, she turned to her followers, "I'll get even with that son of a bitch," she told them in an effort to save face and regain the leadership role she played so well.

"I have my ways and he'll regret that."

One of her friends asked, "What about the chick? Should we take care of her?"

"No, leave it to me, I'll handle it."

As Patricia continued walking away, she became aware not only of the welt on her left cheek, but a stinging sensation on the right. She had never seen the first slap coming and yet he had slapped her twice! Past memories flashed before her eyes non-stop. Was it possible that some of the stories she had overheard about her father being a hero in some war were true? All the times he was gone, was he really fighting for his country and not just staying away from his responsibilities as her mother always said? Did her mother lie to her all those years?

Patricia glanced over her shoulder quickly to see her father and that redhead still standing arm in arm and watching her retreat. He never looked that happy. He never stood up for her, or Robert, or her mother that way either. Or did he? Could it be possible that he actually cared about her? She thought back to the last time she saw him when he brought her things to her dorm. She asked for money and he gave it to her without question. Was it because he was a pushover, or was it because he actually loved her? Now she knew, and the truth hurt.

As Patricia and her friends walked off, Judy looked at Rob with apprehension, "Are you all right, Honey?" she could feel him shaking.

"I never touched her before... never, I hope I didn't hurt her," he replied but it was almost as if he was speaking to himself.

"Her pride was hurt maybe, but she's all right. It shocked me when you slapped her," Judy replied with concern. "Why did you do that?"

Rob didn't reply at once, he was still looking at his hand and trying to determine how such a thing could have happened.

"I don't know," he answered absently.

"It was a lot of things that happened in a rush... maybe I was afraid of what she might do to you, maybe I didn't like what she said or how she said it to you. I should have taken a firmer stand a long time ago, not physically, but giving her direction, teaching her right from wrong."

He lowered his head in shame, "I'm not much of a man... even less of a father."

Judy lifted his chin. She looked into his eyes and responded honestly, "That's simply not true. You never had a chance from the very start. Look at the way you treated Brian, and the way you handled that situation with Sarah at Christmas, just like she was your daughter. You taught her to respect herself. The difference is having someone listen to you... and believe in you. Maybe I shouldn't say anything, but I believe that if you had raised Patricia alone she would have turned out differently. You're a fine man, Rob, and you *are* a good father. I truly believe that, and even Patricia is just now beginning to understand it."

Rob had a strange look on his face when he turned to Judy, "She hugged me," he said in a choked voice. "The last time she did that was when she was seven years old..." and his eyes were moist.

"And she... she called me Dad."

When he held Judy, she felt him trembling with emotion. In his anguish, he turned to her. He never had an understanding companion before, and Judy realized that.

Rob was very quiet and obviously troubled as Judy drove them back to the motel where they stayed when he was in town. She wanted to comfort him but wasn't sure how to do it or what to say. She touched his hand and asked, "Is there anything we can do for her?"

"I don't know... I hit her... she'll never forgive me."

"No, Honey, I think she already has. You need to be able to forgive yourself, and I believe that's harder."

It was deep into a restless night when Judy awoke and found Rob was still awake. She snuggled against him and kissed him softly, "Do you think it would make any difference if we tried to talk to her away from those girls she hangs out with?"

"I don't know... I hadn't even thought about that. It's something I should deal with. I can't burden you with my problems."

"Anything that troubles you is not your problem alone, Rob," she responded gently. "Not any longer. We're in this together, you and me. I can't solve my problems alone; I need you to help me. I want to help you too."

Rob held her tightly and breathed deeply, "I know you do. Oh God, how I love you."

It was mid-week and Patricia was making her way back to her dorm. Her classes were done for the day. She would have a few hours quiet time before her followers got out of class and joined her.

"Hello Patricia."

She turned to see who was speaking to her. It took a moment for the face to register.

"I'm Judy Whitby, your father's friend. We met last weekend."

"I know who you are," she snapped insolently. "What do you want? Did *he* send you?"

"I'd like to talk to you, if you'll let me... are you aware of your Dad's reaction to what happened?"

"You mean when the son of a bitch slapped me?"

Judy looked at her warily and continued, "No, when you hugged him. Do you remember the last time you hugged him?"

"No, but it's no big deal," Patricia responded, her reaction softened by the way Judy spoke.

"It's a big deal to him Patricia. You were seven years old... he remembered."

"Well, so what?"

"You called him Dad."

"Yeah, I know... so what's the big deal?"

"He didn't tell me when you last referred to him as Dad, but judging by his reaction it must have been a long time."

"So what did he do, laugh about it?"

"No, Patricia, your father cried."

That was more than Patricia was willing to hear. She turned and started to walk off but Judy touched her arm gently and stopped her, "How much do you really know about him, Patricia? Did it ever occur to you that he loves you? Your father is a strong and brave man."

"Is that what he told you?"

"No, he never did, but I've talked to his friends and he has some pretty spectacular friends. They say some remarkable things about him, and they have no reason to lie. Did you know that he earned the Congressional Medal of Honor in Viet Nam?"

"What's that?"

"It's the Nation's Highest Military Award, the bravest of the brave, an honor that can only be awarded to someone who risks their life above and beyond the call of duty in a war serving his country and those he loves. Your father is an American hero."

"How do you know that?"

"I saw the medal; it's on his Marine Corps uniform. I didn't know what it meant either until I looked it up. He was presented his medal in person by President Ford. That medal goes back to the time of the Civil War. Of all the millions of brave men and women that have fought and died for our country, only a little over 3400 of them has been honored like your father."

"I saw it when he came home. Mom told us it was a door prize, that everybody got one."

Judy shuddered hearing those words and she thought of the terrible life that Rob tolerated with his ex wife. Yet he remained loyal to his family. He never shared that event with Judy.

"Do you remember what it looked like?" she asked Patricia.

"Probably."

"Look it up, Patricia. Read about what that medal means. You don't have to believe me, or believe your Dad. His name is on the list, and his story is there too; the kind of man your father is. It's in the library and on the Internet, but even with all that, it doesn't mean as much to him as when you hugged him and called him Dad."

"Why are you telling me all this, what's in it for you?"

Judy looked at Rob's daughter carefully and paused long enough to be sure that Patricia was listening, "Your father is the finest man I've ever met, and I'm in love with him."

It was a very matter of fact statement but the look in Judy's eyes said that it was true even more profoundly than her words.

"He doesn't know that we're talking, but I felt that you needed to know a little about him. You need to know that he cares about you, that he loves you in spite of all the hard times. You can do what you want, Patricia, but you do need to know that. You will always be his daughter."

"All right, you've done your thing," she replied with a trace of scorn. "I've got to go."

With that, she turned on her heel and walked off. Her arrogance might have worked if only she turned away a moment sooner and Judy didn't see the tears that were starting. With bleary eyes, Patricia went to her room and fell on her bed sobbing.

Judy made the effort she promised herself she would. But deep inside she had an uncomfortable feeling. She simply did not trust Rob's daughter.

The following day Rob received a call at work.

"Hi Dad, it's me, Patricia."

Rob leaned heavily against his workbench and took a deep breath, "Hi, Honey... I'm sorry... I didn't mean to slap you."

"Well, I probably deserved it," Patricia laughed. "I never noticed her before, but I ran into your friend Judy on campus yesterday. She seems like a nice lady, and she didn't deserve the things I said. I'm sorry, Dad... about that and a lot of other things."

"There's no need to apologize, Honey... it's just such a surprise to hear your voice. Is everything all right?"

"Yeah, everything's fine. I just wanted to call and tell you I was sorry for acting the way I did. You know she loves you, don't you?"

"Yes I do, and I love her too. I guess that's a bit of a surprise."

"No, like I said, she seems like a nice girl. It's something you finally deserve."

There was along quiet pause before Patricia continued, "I hear my friends coming... I gotta go."

"Thanks for calling, Honey."

"Dad?"

"Yes, Patricia?"

"I didn't know a lot of things... I'm proud of you," and she hung up.

Rob stared at his phone and smiled. The years of waiting and being patient were finally going to pay off.

"Hey, what are you looking so smug about?" Dave called from under the hood of the car he was working on.

"That was Patricia," Rob answered. "She called to apologize. She ran into Judy and they talked. She said she was proud of me and didn't even ask for money."

"Shit," Dave muttered under his breath so Rob wouldn't hear. "Just when you're getting your shit together that worthless kid has to call and stir things up."

Then he spoke up, "Good for her, I hope things work out."

Patricia grinned at her friends, her hand still on the phone, "Well how did you like that... he bought the whole line. He'll be an easy mark from now on."

In the meantime, there was a more pressing situation. Patricia's stash was depleted, and her friends counted on her for a solution. Without ready cash, there was a simple alternative. Patricia was a very attractive girl with a pleasing shape. It was something that she often used to her advantage. She knew who to contact. All that was required was to turn on a little charm.

34

BAUMGARTNER'S PLAN

"There's a situation that I think we should take advantage of. It would be beneficial for both of us," Baumgartner began.

"Tell me about this situation," Manny replied.

"There's a demand for pornographic video using very young girls. It's extremely lucrative, but obtaining the girls is difficult. However, a solution presented itself. One of my regular customers, Rachel, works at a private institution in Sedona that provides schooling, counseling, and a place to live for troubled young girls. She owes me a lot of money, so I suggested there was a way for her to pay off that debt. Those girls are rebellious and prone to running away from home. I told Rachel those girls would be happier in foster homes with more freedom.

"I explained that there are people willing to pay to have a daughter to raise as their own. If she could arrange for those girls to escape, we could transport them here. I would see that the girls are taken care of. If she did that, it would settle her debt and I'd be willing to extend her more credit."

Baumgartner grinned, "She liked the idea and she's willing to cooperate."

Manny nodded, "That sounds so easy, it just might work. What do you want from me?"

"I have access to a large van to transport the girls, but I need a driver, someone that could be trusted."

"I can arrange that," Manny replied. "When do you want to make the transfer?"

"I need to make a video first. My customer has some specific requirements, so I'm looking for someone now. As soon as I set that up, I'll contact Rachel and make the arrangements."

Manny considered Baumgartner's proposal. It was a gamble, but had the potential for a substantial return, and maybe some youthful entertainment.

"All right, I'll supply your driver," Manny agreed.

At the same time, another opportunity presented itself. The intended buyer of a substantial shipment was careless and contracted a fatal case of lead poisoning. Those drugs were available. Manny contacted the source in Mexico and arranged for the shipment. This load was too large for mules. It would have to come up through Nogales by truck. That meant bribe money for the Border Patrol supervisor in that area. For a small fee, Hector's father agreed to handle that.

The transaction was arranged through a contact in Phoenix. Manny delivered the cash and waited for his shipment. When the cash and the shipment disappeared, Manny was in trouble. In Mexico, the source adopted a tolerant attitude; Manny had ten days to come up with the cash.

Lead poisoning was contagious.

Desperate times call for desperate measures and Manny was in a business where desperate times are common. He had a solution and made his plans accordingly. Without a word to anyone, he left Flagstaff that night.

Jorge Martinez, Manny's adoptive father, was found murdered in McAllen, Texas. His widow left a message with the Ortega family in Douglas. They would notify Manuel.

Manny arrived in McAllen looking tired and distraught, driving an older Dodge van with Louisiana license plates. Wearing old clothes, he told a story of hard times.

"It's hard to find work, and what I can find doesn't pay well. I had to borrow this van from someone I work with. I have to go back soon so I don't lose my job."

Mr. Martinez' widow sympathized with Manny, "I told Jorge many times you could have stayed here. Why don't you stay with us now?"

"But I would have to find a job and I don't have any skills," Manny lamented. "There is no work here. At least I have a job in Louisiana."

"We have a little money saved, Manuel. Let us give you some so you can get a suit for the funeral and a little for the trip back to your job."

Local law enforcement had no evidence. They assumed it was a mistaken hit by one of the drug cartels. Senor Martinez had a single bullet wound in the back of his head. It had all the earmarks of a professional assassination. Because of Jorge's standing in the community, local, state, and now Federal authorities were pursuing the matter diligently.

The family was questioned at great length, but they knew nothing. No one could imagine why a deacon in their church and upstanding community leader would be victim to such a crime.

As soon as the questioning was completed, Manny was allowed to leave. Before departing in his borrowed van, Manuel demanded that he be kept informed of developments. He wanted to be sure that the perpetrators were found and held accountable.

When the authorities searched Senor Martinez' warehouse for clues, they discovered automatic weapons, crates containing ammunition in various calibers, and sophisticated explosives. Removing the boxes, they discovered the tunnel that led directly to a similar warehouse in Reynosa, Mexico. Mexican authorities found drugs in the second warehouse.

Stopping outside of McAllen, Manny looked into the dust-covered boxes in the rear of the borrowed van and smiled. The bills were large, nothing smaller than a twenty, many hundred thousand dollars of untraceable, unmarked bills. He transferred the money to several suitcases and destroyed the cartons. It was a profitable trip.

He swapped the aged van for a Ford sedan in San Antonio and transferred the suitcases to the new vehicle. There was a cell phone in the glove box. Manny loved cell phones. Although they were expensive, cost was no object in his business. He smiled as he thought of the advantages of modern technology. He could call from almost anywhere and no one knew for sure where he was. Cell phones could eventually be traced if one used them too long. But they were disposable. Just like cars... or people.

He made a quick call to his creditor and arranged to deliver the money. With that pressing problem handled, he could concentrate on recovering his drugs.

It took several days. Not hindered with Miranda warnings and civil rights, Manny was an unpleasant and persuasive visitor. He remembered the lesson he learned long ago. Anyone that caused trouble could be silenced. The survivors were willing to help Manny recover his shipment, and eager to inform him of the men responsible for his inconvenience. They had offices in an older building in downtown Phoenix.

The drive back to Flagstaff allowed Manny to plan his next moves. Recovering the drugs would require outside help, but that was easily financed and would only take a few days. The girls in Sedona would soon be ready for pickup. Hector would handle that. There was an electrician in Phoenix that owed Manny a favor.

Picking up the Phoenix newspaper several days later, Manny allowed himself the luxury of a content smile. The headlines told of an unexplained fire that destroyed one of the older buildings in the downtown area just off Central Avenue. The fire resulted in the tragic deaths of several businessmen trapped on the fifth floor. It was assumed that the fire was the result of faulty wiring. The media focused on the lack of enforcing building codes and fire department inspections. It was an election year and the current administration held views that contradicted those of the newspaper. It was obviously the fault of the mayor and city council. That removed the focus from the actual event and concentrated on politics.

Baumgartner was having difficulty finding a suitable prospect for his video. None of his regular girls matched his customer's required profile, until he received a surprise caller. It was an attractive college student.

"Hello, Mr. Baumgartner," she said as she shook his hand and then got right to the point. "I was wondering if you could help me."

"I don't recognize you from my class young lady, so I assume you weren't in need of tutoring," he answered.

"No, it's something mutually beneficial."

"You have me at a disadvantage," he replied with a puzzled look. "I'm not sure what you mean, Miss...?"

"You can call me Patricia," she said as she looked around to make sure they were alone. "I need some stuff but I don't have any money, and spring break is coming up. I figured we could work out a deal."

Baumgartner looked offended and replied indignantly, "I'm sure I don't know what you're talking about. By stuff, I assume you mean some sort of illegal drugs. Well you've come to the wrong place and I resent the implication."

Patricia's attitude changed abruptly, "Cut the bullshit, dude. We both know you have access to a new shipment and now you're looking for girls for your movies. Word gets around."

She dropped a few names and silenced any doubts he had. She was far too obnoxious for an undercover cop. It didn't take long to complete their negotiations after that. Patricia agreed to perform for one of his sex videos in exchange for a supply of drugs for her and her friends.

Baumgartner watched her go and grinned. In a few days the girls from Sedona would arrive, and this girl would make his video. As soon as he received his portion of Manny's latest drug acquisition, he would provide them for Rachel and this obnoxious new girl.

Patricia showed up at the agreed time. She made his movie and took her drugs. Returning to her dorm, she arranged for a party the next night with her friends.

The first group of girls, aged 11 thru 15, arrived from Sedona that same night. Baumgartner paid Rachel with drugs and housed the girls in the basement of his home. Securely housed, isolated, and suddenly aware of the dreadful mistake they had made, they realized the potential for matters getting even worse.

It was a while since her last fix, so Rachel made use of the drugs she received as payment from Baumgartner that same night. Because it was common for Rachel to sleep in late, her roommate didn't discover her lifeless body until almost noon.

35

JUDY'S FRANTIC CALL

Working under the hood of a new Mercedes, Rob was trying to determine the cause of an erratic problem when his cell phone rang. It was Judy, and she was frantic, "Are you all right, Honey," he answered with alarm. "What's the matter?"

Judy was trying desperately to sound calm and hide her anguish. It wasn't working, "Rob, it's Patricia... something's terribly wrong. They took her to the hospital in an ambulance, there's police everywhere."

Rob glanced at the clock that hung on one wall and calculated the time it would take to drive to Flagstaff. He would be delayed by rush hour traffic in Phoenix.

"Is she all right?"

"I don't know...they wouldn't tell me anything. I was going to call Chuck's number but I thought I'd better call you first," she said on the verge of tears.

"Can you go to the hospital for me? It'll take some time to get there. I'll hit Phoenix at rush hour."

"I'm on my way now... I'll call you as soon as I can, as soon as I hear anything."

"Thanks, Honey, I love you."

"I love you too... Rob, please drive carefully... I'll do everything I can at this end."

Rob was calling the airlines when Dave approached with a concerned look, "What's up, man?"

"Something with Patricia... I've got to get up there as quick as I can. They just took her to the hospital in an ambulance."

After making several frantic calls to the various airlines, Rob found that there weren't any flights that could get him there before tomorrow, but they were all booked. He called Chuck's number and got a message. His office wouldn't give out any information. Rob's frustration was increasing when Dave interrupted him.

"Here, buddy, it's J.J." Dave said and handed Rob another phone.

The calming voice of J.J. Rabinowitz came on the line, "Hello Rob, Dave said there's an emergency. I might be able to help you, but I'll need a few minutes. Stay on the line, my friend. I'm going to put you on hold while I make a few calls."

J.J. didn't need any explanation from Rob. Dave's call had covered enough of the details. J.J. understood the need for immediate action. It took two calls to find a private jet that could make a trip to Flagstaff immediately. He got back on the phone with Rob and gave him the information. Rob never even closed his toolbox. He was in his 4Runner and speeding to the airport even as he continued talking to J.J.

How J.J. arranged it didn't matter. At the airport, Rob parked as close to the terminal as he could. Grabbing a duffel bag from the rear of the 4Runner, he ran to the area where he was to meet the small plane. Someone was waiting. They rushed Rob out to the waiting plane. The plane was more than he expected. A sleek corporate jet, eager and capable of putting many miles behind it very quickly, was warmed up and waiting. The thought of how he would ever be able to pay for the flight crossed his mind briefly and then disappeared... it was his daughter. His heart was pounding as the plane took off and made its way to Flagstaff with two bewildered passengers dressed in expensive three-piece suits. They looked at Rob, still in his uniform from work, and wondered who he was and how he managed to get on their flight.

As soon as they were airborne, the pilot announced that they were going to make one quick stop before continuing on to Las Vegas. The flight was incredibly fast and the quick stop in Flagstaff was even quicker. Flagstaff has a short runway at high elevation, not the ideal conditions for larger, quicker planes. The plane was already moving as Rob made his way to the terminal. The taxi that waited for him had been summoned by the pilot while enroute and began its trip to the hospital as soon as Rob got in.

While the cab was making its way to the hospital, Rob called Judy. The anguish in her voice frightened him, "She's in the ICU... they're working on her... how long before you can get here?"

"I'm in a cab on the way from the airport. Five minutes," he said.

When the cab stopped at the hospital, Judy was waiting. Her eyes were red with tears as she hugged him, and then rushed him to the ICU. He forced his way into Patricia's room and went to her bedside. He called her name. Her eyes fluttered weakly. He heard a tone and looked up at a monitor to see the once ragged line go to a steady flat signal. She was gone.

It was nearly an hour with Judy at his side before Rob was able to pull himself together. He made a call to Chuck's wife, Samantha. It took several minutes before Samantha was able to find the most recent number in her records. Rob thanked her and punched the number for his ex-wife.

"Helen... it's me, Rob..." he said when she answered.

"What do *you* want, and how did you get this number?" she replied arrogantly.

"It's bad news," he said somberly, "It's Patricia... she's... she's gone..." his control was at its limit.

"Well what do you want me to do about it? She's a big girl. If it's so important to you, then you go find her!"

"No, I mean... Helen, I'm at the hospital in Flagstaff... Patricia's dead..." he was barely able to control his anguish. He would have broken down were it not for Judy comforting him.

There was silence for a moment on the phone before Helen continued, "Well then, what happened?" There was still a bitter edge to her voice.

"I don't know any of the details yet. Judy called me at work... they took Patricia to the hospital in the ambulance. I just got here... I thought you should know."

"Who the hell is this Judy?"

Holding the phone away from his ear, Rob stared at it for a moment and glanced at Judy.

His voice was cold and hard, "Helen, your daughter is dead. I'll see to things as best I can from here," and he terminated the call. He sat quietly seething before he turned once again to Judy.

The look on his face frightened her. She feared his wrath would be directed at her and she prepared herself for the worst. Rob put his arms around her and held her tightly as he breathed heavily and she felt the gradual easing of tension. When he released her he looked into her eyes, "I wouldn't be able to handle this without you here," he told her in a choked voice. "Wait for me... I need to talk to the doctor."

Judy kissed his cheek and tasted the salt of his silent tears, "I'll be here, Sweetheart."

Rob went to the nurse's station and asked who the doctor was that had treated Patricia. The nurse was reluctant, but Rob was insistent. It took him several minutes to locate the doctor.

"My name is Rob Simpson... Patricia's father. What... what happened to her?"

"I'm sorry for your loss, sir, but I won't be able to provide a cause of death until there's an autopsy," the doctor said in a cool, professional voice.

That wasn't the answer Rob wanted. Grasping the doctor's arm in a vice-like grip, he ushered him into an empty room and closed the door ominously behind them. The look on Rob's face convinced the doctor that this man was serious. Speaking quietly and firmly he repeated his question, "What happened? Why did she die?"

"Well, we're not really sure, sir, but we should know in a few days."

Grasping the doctor's collar Rob forced him against the wall. His calm, controlled voice was even more frightening than the rage in his eyes. He asked once more, "If you're not sure, make a fucking

SWAG... that's scientific wild assed guess. You're supposed to be a professional, what do you *think* caused her to die like that?"

The doctor considered his options. Even if he was able to summon help, no amount of hospital security would prevent this distraught father from getting answers.

"I would guess that she died from a dose of bad drugs... probably laced with some other chemical... maybe rat poison," he answered nervously.

"What makes you say that?"

"There's been several similar cases among students recently. They're being investigated by the authorities."

Glaring at the doctor, Rob let go of his collar and left the room. He made another stop at the nurse's station and determined what needed to be done to take care of Patricia's body. He left his contact information, gathered Judy, and left the hospital. The pain he felt was put aside. Now he needed some answers. He briefed Judy on his conversation with the doctor while he called Chuck's number.

"Yeah," a surly voice answered.

"Chuck, its Rob. Patricia's dead. I'm just leaving the hospital now. What do you know about this?"

"I'm sorry, Rob... I just heard... where can I meet you... someplace private where we won't be seen?" Chuck answered quickly.

"There's a park of some kind, south... just off the freeway."

"Twenty minutes," came Chuck's reply and the call ended.

"I'll take you," Judy insisted and Rob paused.

The cold determination in his eyes was made more frightening when he spoke quietly, "I'm going to get to the bottom of this. It could get ugly. Are you sure you want to come along?"

Judy swallowed hard. This was a frightening situation that she knew nothing about, but she couldn't leave Rob now, "I don't know what I can do, but I have to be here for you. Please don't shut me out."

They got in Judy's car and drove to the spot where they would meet Chuck and parked off the road under the trees. It was dark and they would not be seen readily. Rob sat quietly as he leaned back in the seat. Long forgotten memories and training were slipping back into his consciousness. Rob looked dazed, but his every sense was alert. He heard Chuck's Harley long before Judy was aware of it.

"Stay in the car while I talk to Chuck," Rob said. He took something out of his duffel bag, gave Judy a quick kiss and disappeared.

There were two Harley's, chopped and noisy. They rode past Judy's car and stopped about 20 yards beyond where she was parked, shut off their bikes and waited. They expected Rob to drive up in another car and join them.

A sudden, quiet voice from the darkness shook them, "Who's that with you, Chuck?"

Chuck and his companion were tough, experienced, and cautious, but the voice sent chills through them both. Chuck hardly recognized Rob's voice. The sound was like ice. He had no idea where it came from.

"It's my partner... Cervantes... Tony Cervantes. He's all right, Rob. Do you want to come out where we can talk?"

They never heard a sound yet suddenly he was standing in front of them. He was still in his uniform from work, his hands hung at his sides. In one hand, he held a knife.

"I'm sorry about your daughter, Rob. I had no idea she was doing drugs."

"What's going on up here, Chuck? It was bad stuff that did it to her, and she's not the first."

"What are you talking about?" Cervantes interrupted, but stopped at a signal from Chuck.

Over his partner's objections Chuck related as much as was currently known, "A couple of weeks ago DEA was tipped about a shipment of drugs coming up from Mexico. They were ready to intercept the shipment when it disappeared. DEA figured it was a rival group in Phoenix that intercepted the shipment. They found out where the drugs were located and were about to close in when people started turning up dead and the stuff disappeared again.

"It's my guess that the Phoenix people assumed the drugs would be recovered by the person or persons it was initially intended for. They probably altered the drugs with some kind of poison to destroy the credibility of the distributor.

"We wanted to talk to them, but there was a fire and every one of those bastards died.

"Like I told you before, Rob, these are some pretty ruthless pricks, every one of them. They don't give a damn about the users, not even kids. We do know that one of the dealers is here in Flag, but we aren't sure who the head of this operation is or where he is."

"Who's the dealer?" Rob asked unemotionally.

"I can't tell you that, Rob. We have him under surveillance, but at the moment, our hands are tied. We can't get a search warrant without more evidence. We want to get his guy clean, because as you know if anything at all goes wrong in our procedure, the son of a bitch will walk. These people have lots of money to cover their ass. It's just a matter of time..."

"What about the head man?" Rob interrupted coldly.

"We're hoping to use the dealer to get information... maybe scare the shit out of him, or as a last resort, a deal."

"You mean turn him back on the street if he talks."

"This guy is our only lead to the head man right now. We're doing everything we can... within the law."

"The law didn't protect my daughter, Chuck. You know as well as I do that there's ways to make him talk. Give me ten minutes with him and he'll tell us everything he knows."

"You know we can't do that, Rob. We're a nation of laws, meant to protect everyone. Let us do our job, and for God's sake don't you go and do anything stupid."

There was no one there when Chuck offered his admonition. A few minutes later, they heard a car start up and drove off. Tony Cervantes turned to his partner, "Who in the hell was that guy? I never even saw him come up to us and didn't see him leave. He was just gone."

"He's the father of one of the dead kids."

"Do you think he'll try anything?"

"I certainly hope not," Chuck replied quietly.

"Don't worry," Tony grinned. "We'll get that drug dealing bastard."

"Tony, if we don't get him before some irate father does, he'll end up going through somebody's garbage disposal in little pieces."

"Are you hungry," Rob asked when he rejoined Judy.

"I could make us something if you feel like eating," she replied and squeezed his hand.

"No, let someone else do the cooking. You've been through enough already."

She drove to a small restaurant that was nearly empty and they found a booth that afforded some privacy. While they waited for their food, Rob took her hand in his.

"I'm sorry you had to go through this, Honey, but thank you for being with me. I don't know what I would have done without you."

"I wouldn't want it any other way," she answered sincerely. "I'm so sorry about Patricia."

"She had a hard life, but now she's at peace. You heard the conversation with her mother. Helen was more interested in who you are than what happened to her daughter."

"You did what you had to do, Rob. It took a lot of courage to make that call, but now it's up to her. We'll take care of Patricia, just you and me. I only wish we would have had more time to help her."

"We did our best, that's all we could have done. I'll have to make the funeral arrangements and get Patricia taken care of."

"Let me help, Rob. That's not something you should have to do alone... even if I just follow you around while you handle all the details. I know it won't be easy on you."

Never once in their conversation did Judy say anything negative about Patricia or Rob's ex-wife even though she felt bitterness toward them both. Her only job at this time was to support the man she loved. She knew how to do that.

It was later in the evening when Rob's cell phone rang, "Hello, Rob, this is Marianne Whitby, Judy's Mom. I just want you to know how sorry we are about your loss."

Her voice touched him deeply. He took Judy under his arm and after a deep sigh responded weakly, "Thank you, Marianne. Your call means a lot to me."

"Is there anything we can do for you?"

"Marianne, you've already done it. You raised an incredible daughter. She's here with me now. If she wasn't here... she's so strong."

Rob choked up and handed the phone to Judy.

The next day was spent making arrangements for Patricia's remains. Her body would be returned to Tucson where there would be a quiet funeral. At the end of the day, Rob took a bus back to Tucson. There were things in his bag that would never pass airport security. Judy would gladly have driven him but he insisted that she stay at school.

The funeral was held in Tucson and attended by Rob, Judy, and their friends. Helen showed up late with her current boyfriend. Helen was callous and cold. Her companion looked to be in worse shape about the death of Patricia than her own mother. Helen was more interested in who Judy was. Casting aside the remnants of Patricia's life that had been offered to her, Helen made a point to corner Judy after the memorial service.

"Who do you think you are intruding on my daughter's funeral when you're nobody," Helen snarled. "You think just because he's her father and he's showing you a good time that you have some right to be here? You're nothing! I'm the mother here."

Judy listened patiently to Helen's wrath. When she paused, Judy responded calmly and quietly in spite of the broken hearted, righteous indignation seething inside.

"That's true, you are the person that fulfilled the biological function of giving her birth, but you're no more a mother to Patricia than you are to Robert. Rob isn't even Robert's biological father and the truth is that you don't even know who his real father is. Rob fulfilled his role as father to both of them in the only way he knew how, by giving them his name and his love without question. He never stopped loving them... you never started. You stole the joy of raising and guiding those children from the one man that could have made them into something. You don't know where Robert is or what's become of him. The quality of your love and guidance for your daughter lies over there... a beautiful young girl that lost her life to drugs and prostitution. *That* is your contribution. If that's what you consider being a mother, then the world will have to change the definition of what is the most revered and honorable task a human being can face."

Judy had spoken so quietly that very few of the others in attendance were aware of the dialogue between the two women. Judy's chosen words cut deeply and cruelly. The things Judy said made Helen wish she had never begun the conversation. Without another word, Helen took her boyfriend's arm and leaving Patricia's personal belongings behind slithered out of the room.

There was a somber gathering at Rob's home after the funeral. Before it was over every one of the guests approached Judy with heartfelt thanks for supporting Rob. She was his source of strength in his time of need and they knew that.

Dave was one of the last to speak to her, "I knew the whore before," he said, speaking of Rob's ex-wife. "She had a way of cutting him to pieces with that sharp tongue of hers. But she sure met her match today. Just watching you handle that bitch was worth waiting for. I sure hope you never get pissed off at me!"

Judy smiled in return, "Then don't ever mess with my man."

Dave wasn't sure if she was serious or not, but he had no intention of finding out.

36

Plan Problems

With the sudden rash of student deaths on campus, Baumgartner was fortunate. Only two of the victims, Rachel, and the obnoxious little blonde, got their drugs from him. They were both dead, so they couldn't divulge their source.

Still, he was concerned. He obtained two vicious dogs, killers, not barkers, to supplement his extensive security system. On the streets or on campus, he carried a loaded revolver, constantly looking over his shoulder. He took alternate and unpredictable routes as he went about his business.

The Sedona girls were securely confined in his basement. Soon they would be willing to do whatever he asked to gain their freedom. He would make the videos, get his money and pay Ortega his share. Or maybe just disappear.

After making a routine check of his security systems Baumgartner went to bed alone. That wasn't his preference, but he wasn't ready to trust any of the girls from Sedona yet. Another few days and it would be a different story. By then they would be grateful to be out of their rooms.

Late that night Baumgartner awoke from a troubled sleep. There was something wrong. He couldn't move his arms or legs! An ominous shape was sitting on the edge of his bed, holding a very sharp knife to his throat. He glanced at the security monitors. They were blank. It must be a dream, but it was not.

"Who... who are you, what do you want?" he asked hysterically.

"A name."

"What name... what do you want? Who are you looking for?" Now there was terror in his voice as the blade remained at his throat.

"Where did those drugs come from?" the voice asked quietly.

"I don't know what you're talking about," Baumgartner replied and then cried out in pain. His left ear lay on his pillow and blood streamed from the open wound.

"Where did the drugs come from?" the voice, entirely devoid of emotion, repeated.

"What drugs... I don't know anything about any drugs," Baumgartner answered and then screamed in agony once more. A severed finger dropped to the floor.

He was unable to concentrate, unable to move, and petrified by the apparition that was the cause of his pain. When the figure stood and pulled back the sheets on his bed, Baumgartner's terror increased. The razor sharp blade was in a more private location. The voice repeated the question one more time. The knife was next to his skin.

"No... please, not that... I'll tell you anything you want to know... anything."

There was no reply and the knife did not move. Baumgartner had a well-founded fear of Manuel Ortega, but the blade at his groin was an immediate concern. If he implicated Manny, maybe this assailant would go away.

I've got ample resources now. I don't need Manny any more. To hell with that Mexican bastard, let him suffer... let these people get him.

"Ortega," he called out in his pain. "Manuel Ortega."

"Where is he?'

"Here... here in Flagstaff. He has a place north of town," Edward gasped and felt the pressure of the knife increase slightly.

"Address?" the voice questioned once more and Baumgartner gladly provided the information.

The knife went away and Baumgartner felt a sense of relief. Now he could concentrate on the excruciating pain where his ear had been and his missing finger. He didn't understand why someone was rolling up his sleeve. He looked up and in the dim light saw the hypodermic syringe and a numbing fear overwhelmed him.

"This is some of yours, and it's a terrible way to die," the voice said evenly as Baumgartner struggled in vain against his restraints. "In a minute or two you will experience the same thing you did to those children. The only difference is that you'll have someone with you to the end. Just to make sure... but that won't be long."

Baumgartner felt the syringe enter his arm and felt the excruciating pain. The voice was correct; it was an unbelievably painful way to die. The only mercy was the massive dose that acted quickly before the grotesque shape that once was Edward Baumgartner lay stiffened in the agony of a painful death.

Tony Cervantes hated the night surveillance work. It was boring and uneventful no matter how necessary. He was told to watch the dark, quiet house for any activity. They knew about the dogs and the surveillance systems. They certainly didn't need him there too. No one could get in or out of that impregnable fortress without being detected. He felt drowsy and dozed briefly. He jerked awake. How in the hell was he supposed to be alert sitting in a cold, dark car a block away from the house. No help, no music, and no coffee.

"This really sucks," he said. "The least they could have done was give me a partner. We could take turns sleeping." He took one more glance at the dark, ominous fortress and sat upright. There was something different, something that was not there before. It was on the heavy iron gate that secured the entrance. Something was there... something hanging inside the gate. He lifted his night vision goggles and then dropped them into his lap with a sickened gasp. He snatched his radio to report even as he started the car and drove closer.

Agent Cervantes was new in the department and in his short career he had not had the misfortune of dealing with corpses. He was unprepared for the grotesque sight. Suspended head down from the gate was the form of what had once been a man. This form did not have a head. That lay on the ground beneath the body in a fresh pool of blood.

His radio crackled softly, "Get the hell out of there... NOW! I'll call it in to Flag P.D. If they don't screw up too much evidence they'll call us or DEA."

The first officer on the scene was an alert veteran. He swept the gate with his spotlight. This was no ordinary homicide. He called for backup with a SWAT team. He turned off his lights and took a position behind his car, alert, his weapon ready, and waited for his backup.

Within the hour, building and grounds were secured while specially trained forces heavily armed and with specialized equipment cautiously entered the building. Chuck Stuart was in contact by radio. He knew the agony associated with the tainted drugs they found. That didn't prepare him for what was discovered in the locked and filthy rooms below the main floor. There they found hysterical young girls ranging in age from 11 to 15, unfed, and chained to iron beds lying in their own excrement.

By sunrise, the area was sealed. Ambulances were being loaded with young girls carried on stretchers. Forensic teams were searching for evidence. They found a great deal of information related to a series of crimes, but not a single clue that explained what had happened during the night.

Once Chuck had enough information to determine the magnitude of Baumgartner's operation, he scaled back the efforts of the forensic teams searching for evidence about the intruder.

When the team leader asked the reason, Chuck replied, "I don't see any reason to spend a lot of effort looking for whoever did our job for us. Even if we caught Baumgartner in the act, even with all this evidence there's enough money behind people like him to beat the rap in court. We don't have the resources, backing, or commitment at higher levels to put someone like him away. He would have been back on the street in a matter of months... if that long."

It was a comment that could have ended a brilliant career if word had ever reached higher authorities. Those in hearing range looked at the children on stretchers and they knew it was true. Chuck's comment would never be repeated.

Later in the day Chuck placed a call to Tucson, "Hello, Rob, it's Chuck Stuart. Do you have a minute?"

"Is Judy all right?" Rob asked instantly.

"Yeah, she's fine. I've got people watching out for her. This is about another matter. I told you we had a suspect in the dirty drug situation. We were getting close, but someone beat us to him. He was decapitated and the body was hung on the gate."

Rob was silent for a moment before he asked, "Any idea who did it?"

"We're working on it. We think it might have been a rival drug group, maybe one of the cartels."

"If he's the one responsible for my daughter's death, and if you ever find them, do me a favor and let me know."

"Why would you want to know that?" Chuck asked curiously.

"I'll send them a 'Thank You' card," Rob replied bitterly.

Days later in Phoenix, Chuck Stuart briefed his superiors on the report he filed relating to the Baumgartner murder, "Nothing; not a single shred of evidence to show who killed the bastard, I'd almost say it was a hit by one of the Cartel people, but that doesn't explain why nothing was missing. The money, the girls, all the porno movies, even the drugs were still there, untouched. Baumgartner kept meticulous records, and we've got all of that, just no way to put a name or organization to any of it, yet. If it was a professional hit to send a message, it certainly did that, but I don't understand why there was no evidence. We had a man outside who didn't see anything. The surveillance video that should have shown an intruder was wiped clean. That took some damn good handiwork. Baumgartner had some pretty sophisticated equipment but there was no sign of tampering, and no damaged cameras. The dogs were attack trained, not barkers. They were both dead; their throats cut."

Chuck's superior grimaced, "You paint a rather ominous picture. Any idea how many there might have been?"

Chuck looked at his boss, "You want my opinion or the forensic boys'?"

"I want your opinion, Chuck, how many?"

Chuck held up a single finger, "One."

37

MANUEL'S LEXUS

Manny realized he was overzealous in forcing information from the underlings in Phoenix. The word got out and the damage was done. Doctoring the drugs made sense. He would have done the same thing. The dead students were simply an inconvenience, but the loss of his shipment and loss of credibility was serious. It would take time to overcome that. The other problem was finding out who provided the information that resulted in the initial theft of his drugs. Manny had a good idea who that was. He would deal with that when the time came.

Now, the Baumgartner execution created perplexing questions for Manny. Were the two events related? Who did it? It was not law enforcement's style. Could it be one of the major cartels sending a message, a competitor moving in, or maybe even a new player? Was it retribution for exploiting the underage girls? What became of Baumgartner's drug supply? Did he keep records that could implicate Manny?

There was also one minor matter that required his attention. He called Hector and told him to come to the house.

The extensive law enforcement activity following the Baumgartner murder didn't concern Hector. That was merely a nuisance. Given the timing, being summoned by Manny could be serious. Manny didn't trust anyone. When he stopped trusting, accidents happened.

"There's no need to worry," Manny said as he greeted Hector. "They found those little girls in his house. Abusing children stays on the news for days and makes everyone angry. The FBI will investigate that and make lots of noise. The drugs they found mean nothing. Drugs are everywhere and not newsworthy."

Hector breathed a sigh of relief. Manny still trusted him.

"I think it's time that we dispose of the Lexus," Manny continued. "When they investigate Baumgartner's assets they will find his name on the phony corporation you set up. Eventually they will look for the Lexus that the corporation leased."

Hector laughed, "That dumb gringo owned the corporation and didn't even know it!"

Manny smiled paternally at the younger man, "That was well done, Hector. What you learned in your business law class is protecting us. The money I spend on your education is paying off."

Then he changed the subject, "What are your plans for spring break?"

"I thought I might take my girlfriend to Rocky point."

Manny waved to a chair and smiled at Hector, "Sit down, my friend. I have a better idea. You've done well for me, watching my interests, delivering those girls to Baumgartner, the Lexus, and introducing me to the blonde girl."

"I'm glad you like her, Patron. A man should have a woman to entertain him," Hector replied with a smile.

"That's true," Manny smiled and nodded toward the bedroom. "She's sleeping, but that's another matter. I want to reward you for all you've done for me."

Hector relaxed and smiled.

"If you go to Rocky Point, you would have to find a place to stay, or sleep on the beach with your girlfriend. I have a better idea. Maybe I should give you the condo in San Carlos. You always seemed to like that one. You could drive the Lexus and leave it there."

Hector was astonished, "Are you serious?"

"Yes I am. With the Lexus at the condo, we would have something to drive whenever one of us went there, and the FBI would never find it."

"Thank you, Patron," Hector smiled. "That's a good way to take care of the car, and San Carlos isn't so crowded. We have a good thing going, and I do my best to protect us."

"Then that's settled," Manny said and stood, the meeting was over.

Manny watched Hector leave and something his adopted father said came to him; 'Watch your enemies closely, but watch your friends even more closely'. It was a wise concept and one he had followed diligently. Hector was a good man. He was smart and ambitious.

He made one fatal error.

When he said *we* have a good thing going, it alerted Manny where those ambitions lay. If Hector went to the condo at San Carlos, Manny had friends in Guaymas that owed him a favor.

But enough of business, Manny thought as he made his way back to his bedroom. When he entered, the girl looked up through bleary eyes and smiled. She was already undressed and waiting for him. Golden hair flowed over soft skin, with large breasts, and the smooth plump body that he favored. He undressed and went to her. She was good, Manny thought... if only she hadn't learned so well about the drugs.

Once she satisfied him, he lay against the satin sheets in the dark and thought about Hector's ambition. If it became necessary to replace him, it would be difficult. A replacement might be needed, but who could step in and take over what Hector had done?

He was about to drop off to sleep when suddenly a thought occurred to him.

Mi Querida will do anything I ask. She's just as capable and she knows what my business is. I don't like the idea of trusting a woman but she has proved loyal for a long time.

In the morning, it was time for his guest to leave. Manny picked up his phone and called Hector.

"Si senor," Hector answered.

"Come and give Beth a ride back to her apartment."

Shortly before spring break, Hector met with Manny, "My girlfriend wants to go home for a quick visit with her family. She can drive her car to the condo after she sees her family."

"That's good," Manny said. "If she's going to drive down, you can ride back with her. It'll be easier coming back across the line in her car.

"So what will you do in Mexico?" Manny asked.

Hector smiled, "The beach is like sugar, the sand is so white, and the water in the Sea of Cortez is cool and refreshing. San Carlos is quiet and private because most of the students party at Rocky Point. It's so warm at night; we'll lie on the beach after we eat the fine food in the restaurants," then he grinned. "My girlfriend wears those tiny bikinis... they come off so easy."

Hector saw the longing in Manny's eyes, "You should come with us, Patron. You've been under too much stress. It would help you relax."

"Maybe I could come down for a few days. I could fly into Guaymas as soon as I finished my business here."

He gave Hector a stern look. "My friend Beth would like San Carlos. She's never seen a real beach or that much water. If she was there it would be easier to conduct my business here. Can I trust you to take her with you?"

The request showed how much trust Manny had in him, "I'd be happy to do that for you, Patron. It would make both girls happy to have another woman to talk to. Beth will be waiting for you when you arrive."

His response made Manny smile, "Yes, I think you're right. It'll be good to lie on the beach with her. Yes, mi amigo, that's a good idea. You take Beth with you. I'll call you when I'm going to arrive. You can pick me up at the airport in the Lexus."

38

SPRING BREAK IN ARIZONA

As the miserable winter in Duluth continued to drag on, the idea of visiting Judy and Rob in Arizona sounded even more appealing than it did at Christmas. Other than Judy, none of the Whitby's had ever been outside of Minnesota.

After his breakup with Beth, Jack was feeling miserable, so Rob and Judy invited him to join them in Tucson. As soon as school was out, Jack and Judy drove down in his truck.

"I'll feel more comfortable havin' my truck," Jack said. "If I get in the way of you guys visitin' with your family, I can just bug out."

Dinner was waiting when Rob came home and the three of them ate together on the patio. It was a pleasant meal with Rob and Judy making Jack feel at home, unlike the 'third wheel' he feared. The change of atmosphere and good friends was like a tonic, and Jack began to act more like himself. After describing her family, Jack he felt that he knew them already.

In the morning, when it was time to go to the airport, Jack remained behind while Rob and Judy went to pick them up.

First-time visitors to Arizona from snow country are easily spotted at the airport. They arrive pale, overdressed, and in a state of shock. Everything is new, different, and warm. Their first view of the saguaro cactus outside the Tucson terminal and the majestic range of mountains to the north become eternally etched in their memory. Judy's family was no exception.

The thrill of arriving in a warm climate was tempered initially. It was the first time they had seen Rob face to face since the tragic death of his daughter. He put them at ease immediately.

"It's over and done with," he told them. "I've got Judy here for support. You all were a big help and I appreciate that."

Marianne, Sarah, and Brian were barely able to contain themselves. Even the hugs of greeting lost some of their enthusiasm with all the fascinating things to see. The drive to Rob's home was an adventure in itself. In addition to cars without rust, there were motorcycles, and convertibles that actually had the tops down! When Rob pulled into his driveway, Marianne was quietly impressed. It was a beautiful house with a nice yard. Rob's home was not what she expected.

When they stopped, Jack came out to help with luggage. Rob made the introductions. Sarah heard his name before, but no one had said he was so tall... and so good-looking! When he shook her hand, she felt a tingling sensation as her cheeks turned pink. Brian was equally impressed. He had never met a real live cowboy before. As soon as he got a chance, he would have a million questions.

Judy showed her family around the house while Rob and Jack put away their luggage. There were three bedrooms so Rob explained the sleeping arrangements, "Marianne, you and the girls will each have a bedroom of your own. We set up my tent in the back yard. Jack and I will camp out," then he turned to Brian.

"You can join us if you want, or we'll make up a spot for you on the couch."

"No way I'm gonna sleep in the house with the girls," Brian said. "If there's room, I'll sleep in the tent, or on the ground outside if there isn't. I want to be with the men!"

Once their things were put away and the travelers took time to freshen up, they all gathered in the living room to plan the rest of their day.

"Why don't I take you folks out for dinner," Rob suggested. "I'm sure you're all hungry."

"Let's have a barbeque in the back yard instead, Honey," Judy said. "I'm sure eating outside will be more fun after coming from the snow and cold."

"That sounds like a good idea," Marianne agreed. "We've had enough travelling for one day. It'll be much nicer to be able to relax and visit."

"Are you going to cook steaks?" Brian asked. "Judy said you make the best steaks in the world."

"She might be a little biased, but if that's what you want, we can handle that."

Sarah noticed the small piano nestled off to one side of the living room when they first arrived, "I didn't know you played the piano, Rob," she said.

"I don't. I enjoyed your playing at Christmas, so I rented this one. I was hoping you might find some time to play for us."

Sarah went to the keyboard and fingered the keys lightly. After a moment she looked up, "This really sounds good!"

"Why don't you play something for us, dear," Marianne suggested.

The others gathered around the piano while Sarah played several exploratory chords. Pleased with the quality of sound, she played several pieces, then stopped abruptly, "That's enough for now. I'd rather be outside in the sun!"

Rob and Jack brought cold drinks out to the patio, "You're pretty good at that," Jack said and handed a glass of lemonade to Sarah. "I enjoyed listenin' to you play."

Jack's voice was an easy sort of drawl. It was pleasant, but she was annoyed with herself for being so intrigued by him. "Thank you," her reply sharper than she intended, "And what can *you* do?"

The cool response was a challenge that Jack ignored, "I play the guitar a little," he answered nonchalantly.

"Rob said you were from Wyoming. You look like one of those cowboys. Are you?"

"Yes, I reckon I am. I mean my family raises cows and when I'm home that's what I do."

"So I suppose you like that country and western stuff?" she challenged.

"Well, yes, I can play that," he answered as he looked at her with a smile. They were testing one another and enjoying the subtleties.

"I don't suppose you've got a guitar with you do you?"

"Yes I do."

"I've done my part," she said maintaining her haughty attitude. "Why don't you see if you can entertain us?"

Turning away, Judy winked at her mother. This would be the first time Sarah wasn't able to intimidate someone with her good looks.

"Excuse me," Jack said and went out to his truck.

He returned shortly with a battered and well-worn guitar. After finding a spot to sit, he took a moment to tune the strings and strummed a few chords.

He started playing 'Cool Water', then stopped and looked at Sarah, "This ain't really what you meant by a country western song. It's more of a cowboy song, and that ain't what you asked for."

He gave Sarah a cool look, "How about this?"

The tempo changed to a popular country western tune. He played and sang that fairly well, and then stopped again. He looked at the group, "You've had to listen to me sing and I can't carry a tune in a bucket. Let me give your ears a break... like Sarah did."

The double meaning made Sarah flinch. They were even.

When he played 'Under the Double Eagle', his fingers fairly flew across the strings. His skill impressed them.

When he finished, he nodded at Sarah, "That ain't country western music either, but I sort of like it."

Jack was one up.

Fuming inside, Sarah could not think of a fitting reply. She just smiled politely. Intrigued by a self-assured member of the opposite sex, she had no idea of how to deal with it. It could prove to be an interesting matchup after all... if they ever stopped sparring.

The barbeque was a welcome treat for those shut in by the long winter. Marianne and Sarah helped Judy with salad and side dishes. Rob's steaks were everything Judy said they were. When they finished eating, they were rewarded with another breathtaking Arizona sunset that filled the balmy evening sky. Pleasant conversation added to the atmosphere as they shared their thoughts and enjoyed the company. Before long, it was time for bed. After a long day, the guests welcomed the idea. Tomorrow would be another day and they were excited to see what it would bring.

When Judy went to Sarah's room to bid her goodnight, it was apparent Sarah had something on her mind, "When did you know Rob was the one for you?" she asked.

Sarah's choice of subject confirmed Judy's suspicion. Sarah was infatuated with Rob since their visit at Christmas. However, watching her reaction to Jack this afternoon, that was changing. Her date at Christmas and some of the others that their mother alluded to weren't the same caliber as Jack. He was mature, steady, honest, and reliable. Sarah was out of her league.

But that was not what she asked, so Judy told her story. When she finished, Judy paused and asked, "What made you ask that?"

Sarah looked away, "I was just curious... good night, Judy."

"Good night, Sis," Judy replied and went to the door. She paused and looked back, "Jack's a pretty decent guy."

Sarah grunted and turned to her pillow.

Then Judy went to her mother's room. Marianne smiled at her daughter, "You seem very happy, Sweetheart."

"I am, Mom. I've never been happier or more content in my life. It makes me wonder what I ever did to deserve someone like Rob."

"You did it by being yourself, Honey. That's more than enough for him."

"How do you know that?"

Marianne smiled, "Because that's what he told me... many times."

Brian was in his glory as he settled in the tent with Rob and Jack. He looked up to Rob with a feeling bordering on reverence and yet Rob treated him like a good friend. Now there was Jack, a real cowboy. He treated Brian with respect, too.

Rob explained about cowboys, "People in that occupation and in that part of the country are either stark raving mad or that hardy breed that provides the very backbone and substance that makes our country great."

Brian had a million questions he wanted to ask them but narrowed it down to a select few that kept them talking for hours.

Rob arose early the next morning to prepare for work and went into the house to get cleaned up and dressed. The pleasant aroma of fresh coffee greeted him. Judy joined him at the table while they ate. Then it was time for him to leave.

"I'll drive Jack's truck," Rob said. "Take the 4Runner and show your family around the area. They'll enjoy that, and there's plenty to see with you and Jack for guides."

In order to make the trip to San Carlos in a single day, Hector and Beth left Flagstaff early in the morning. Hector drove steadily while Beth slept for the first part of the trip. When she awoke, Hector found Beth to be a pleasant traveling companion. As the miles flew by, he began to understand why Manny was so taken with her.

"So, when we get to San Carlos, it'll just be the two of us?" she asked.

"At least until my girlfriend arrives later. We'll pick up Manny at the airport when he calls," he replied and glanced at her. Wearing a short skirt, she lounged seductively on the seat beside him.

"Then we'll be alone tonight... just the two of us in that big condo?"

"Yes."

Beth stretched and put her hand on his leg, "That sounds nice," she added with a smile.

There was no mistaking the invitation in her actions. She didn't want to waste her first night at a romantic seaside spot in Mexico sleeping alone. Hector didn't either.

Once they crossed the border into Mexico, Hector began to point out familiar sights. It was just barren and lifeless desert, but his narrative made the drive interesting. The highway was good and the traffic was light, so he pushed the Lexus harder than he did while driving in the U.S. He knew that expensive cars going very fast were ignored by the Mexican authorities. It wasn't good to antagonize wealthy Americans headed for the resort areas. On their way home, it would be different.

It was late in the afternoon when Hector brightened. He pointed to the rugged range of dry, rocky, red mountains to their right and told Beth to look at the sky. If he hadn't pointed it out, she would not have noticed the subtle change in color.

"Just over those mountains is the Sea of Cortez. The water makes the sky look hazy like that," he explained.

"A few more miles down the road, we turn off the main highway at Cabalito. Just beyond that and we're in San Carlos. I know a good place for dinner. You'll like the food here. Everything is fresh and well prepared. Then we'll go to the condo. It's very private and right on the beach."

Beth grinned and leaned across the console, close to Hector. She laid her hand on his thigh, "Good... I like private," she said with a bold smile that confirmed what he was thinking.

Driving steadily at 85 miles per hour for so long felt much slower. Manny liked the leather seats in the back, but Hector loved the power. It was a personal affront for any lesser vehicle to pass him. There was a pickup truck approaching rapidly from the rear. He wasn't about to allow it to pass him. About one and one half miles before the turnoff, a wash crossed under the highway. Just before the bridge, the truck pulled up on Hector's left. He glanced into his side mirror just in time to see the truck's fender make contact with the rear of the Lexus.

Hector was arrogant. He ignored the laws of both the U.S. and Mexico with impunity. He always felt himself to be above the law. There was one law that even he could not ignore.

That is the law of physics.

The Lexus is a fine, well-built vehicle. It has numerous safety devices as standard equipment, seat belts, and air bags, none of which were designed for some events. One of those events is the rapid deceleration from over one hundred miles per hour to zero in the space of about 18 feet. Beth never did get to see the water. Her purse containing her identification followed her through the windshield. Most of her remains were discovered some distance from the concrete embankment where the Lexus was impaled. Hector remained securely fastened in the car as it collapsed on itself and burned fiercely. The investigators discovered material remnants in the wreckage, but were they from leather seats, or was there another occupant?

39

TUCSON VACATION

After breakfast, the adventure began. Judy drove and Jack was tour guide. He kept the Whitby family on the edge of their seats asking endless questions. Meanwhile, the subtle sparring between Jack and Sarah continued throughout the day. Sarah didn't relent in her rivalry with Jack. He didn't respond with anything but courtesy. However, he didn't pass up an occasional opportunity to put her in her place, and that delighted Judy. He was a gentleman, but not a pushover.

One night Rob suggested a Mexican food restaurant.

"There's only room for five in our vehicle," Judy said. "Sarah, do you mind riding with Jack in his truck so he won't feel left out?"

The others were already gone when Sarah followed Jack to his old truck. When he opened the door for her, she looked up at the seat, "How am I supposed to get up there with a dress on?"

"If you'll let me, I'll give you a hand," Jack offered.

He grasped her waist, effortlessly lifted her into the truck, and placed her on the seat. Sarah blushed. He was very strong. When he climbed in, she turned away to conceal her delighted smile.

The Mexican restaurant was on the west side of Tucson in an older adobe building. The surroundings set the mood for an exciting evening. The strolling mariachi band added to the atmosphere of excellent food and service.

"I've heard that margaritas are the perfect combination with Mexican food," Marianne said and ordered one with her meal.

Combination plates with beans, rice, something different for each one of them to sample, and an endless supply of chips and salsa provided an unforgettable experience.

"This is really good," Marianne said as she ate and sipped her drink. "I think I'll have another one."

"The first one goes down pretty easy," Rob grinned. "The second one will get revenge tomorrow."

"It couldn't be that bad," she replied. "It's so smooth."

Much to the delight of her children, margaritas loosened Marianne's tongue and lowered her inhibitions. They had never seen her so relaxed and happy. By the time they got home, Marianne required assistance to find the ground let alone the front door. Finally, Rob lifted her up and carried her into the house and back to her bedroom.

Judy followed them and helped get her mother into bed. Marianne was a happy drunk, delighted that she had the opportunity to experience Mexican food and margaritas. Grinning at Judy, she slurred, "Ish it aw right if Rob shreeps wif me?"

"Mom!" Judy replied in a shocked voice. "No, you can't do that!" she replied laughing.

"I sought I'd ask," Marianne giggled and was asleep when her head hit the pillow.

Jack and Sarah were seated side by side during dinner. They were getting to know one another and enjoying the process.

Standing at the door of Jack's truck, Sarah smiled, "Are you going to lift me in again?"

"It's an old ranch truck and it's a ways up there. Makes it difficult for a lady with a dress on to get in gracefully," then he stopped. "You are a lady aren't you?"

"Usually," Sarah replied with a mischievous twinkle in her eye. "It just depends on who I'm with."

Jack grinned and easily lifted her onto the seat, "Well, tonight you're with me."

When he settled in his seat, he found Sarah close at his side. "That was a nice restaurant and good food," Sarah told him and looked at him with an inviting smile.

Jack was no dummy. Sarah was a beautiful girl, and her glance was an invitation that he accepted willingly. It was a very pleasant kiss, one that she returned enthusiastically.

With Marianne safely tucked in bed Rob, Judy, and Brian went out on the patio. It was a balmy night with a light breeze. Overhead the stars were twinkling merrily in a jet-black sky. Lanterns sent a dancing glow across the area and gave it an intimate atmosphere.

They were chatting quietly when Jack and Sarah joined them. They looked like they stopped sparring and got to know each other better. At home, Sarah was gregarious, usually surrounded by girlfriends. Jack was much more interesting...and fun than a bunch of girls. Sarah liked that.

When the others went off to bed, Jack and Sarah remained behind with only the flickering lantern light for company.

Leaving the others on the patio to enjoy their final night in Tucson, Rob joined Marianne in her room. She was doing some preparatory packing.

"Can I talk to you for a minute, Marianne?"

"Certainly, I'm just trying to get a few things organized so I don't have to do it all in the morning."

Setting aside her packing, she smiled warmly, "What's on your mind, Rob?"

Rob seemed uneasy, "I want to ask you something, but I'm a little nervous."

"I think we know one another well enough by now that you can ask me anything," Marianne smiled. "I've found that when something difficult comes up, the best way to deal with it is just go ahead and say it the best you can and sort it out as you go along."

"That's true," Rob said and took a deep breath. "Mrs. Whitby, I want to marry your daughter."

Marianne's face lit up with a radiant smile, "It sounds like you're asking my permission."

"I know you're close to Judy. It's important to me to have your approval."

"I'm pleased that you'd ask me, Rob. Of course you have my blessing. I'm so happy for you, both of you! Have you set a date for the happy occasion?"

"Well no, not exactly," Rob replied. "I haven't asked her yet."

Marianne chuckled, "Why doesn't that surprise me.

"You are old fashioned in some respects, Rob. I know John would have understood your reasoning and he would have been as pleased as I am. Judy is a lucky girl to have found you. You love her very much, don't you?"

Rob eased into a chair and faced Marianne, "I think that's a term that has lost a lot of its significance. It's overused, but because of her, I've come to understand the true meaning. Yes, I do love her. I respect her, too, and I admire her for who she is. Most of all, I trust her completely, and that's important to me. My only concern is making her happy. I didn't do very well with Helen."

Marianne smiled warmly and held Rob's hand, "Judy told me about meeting her at your daughter's funeral. I don't know her, but I know you. I don't believe anyone can make Helen happy, but Judy has never been happier or more content. She's lucky to have found you, and wise for understanding that. She's strong and independent, but she loves you unconditionally.

"I still remember that night she called. It was the first day you met, but the way she talked about you, I knew she was in love. I have to admit I was worried at the time, but now that I know you, I understand why she felt that way. She's far more perceptive than I am."

Watching his anxiety, she continued, "Rob?"

"Yes..."

"When were you going to ask her?"

"As soon as I get her ring from my room."

Marianne gave Rob one of her bear hugs and although she smiled, there were tears of joy in her eyes, "Thank you. That means I won't have to get the news over the phone. I'm so pleased that I can share this with both of you."

"I just hope she'll say yes!"

That brought a hysterical outburst from Marianne, "I don't think you have to worry about that!"

While Marianne joined the others on the patio, Rob went to his room. In a corner of the closet, he took a small velvet box out of the toe of his hiking boots. He stuffed it in his pocket and went to the patio door, "Judy, can you come in here for a minute?"

"What's this all about?" she asked, and followed him into the bedroom.

"I needed to ask you something," he replied reaching into his pocket.

"Well make it quick, Sweetheart. This is their last night here and I want to spend a little more time with Mom before she goes."

"All right, I'll be quick," Rob said and dropped to his knees before her.

"Judy, I love you. Will you marry me?"

He said it quickly and held out the ring.

The ring was a simple gold band with a single diamond. It sparkled with elegant simplicity. It spoke of commitment and radiated a sense of lifelong love and companionship.

Judy was speechless and stared in disbelief, first at the ring and then at Rob. Her momentary hesitation shook him. He realized it was not fair to her; it was something they never discussed.

But Judy recovered.

From the patio, they heard Judy's squeal of joy, "Mom! Oh Mom," Judy cried as she burst through the open door.

"Mom, he asked me to marry him! Rob wants to marry me! Sarah, Brian, Jack, we're going to be married! Mom," she cried, "Look at this!"

The ring that sparkled on her finger, as simple as it was, spoke volumes, not too simple and not too extravagant. It fit Judy, and for those that knew him, it was Rob.

A few minutes later, the doorbell rang. When Rob answered the door, Judy was still clinging to his arm with stars in her eyes. It was Sam.

He took one look at Judy and grinned, "I figured that's what the noise was for. Well, I'm mighty pleased! Congratulations to both of you... here," he said and offered a bottle of champagne. "I went out and bought this the first time I met you, young lady, bought it just for this occasion. I didn't think it'd take your man here so long to get around to it."

They took Sam to the patio and introduced him. Sam's eyes twinkled merrily as he looked at Marianne and Sarah, "I might have known your sisters would be almost as pretty as you are."

"Sam, this is my mother!" Judy exclaimed.

Sam looked closely at Marianne, "I think you'll need to show me your birth certificate before I'll buy that, young lady."

Marianne blushed at the compliment and invited Sam to join them for the champagne. They were toasting the newly engaged couple when the doorbell rang again. This time it was Dave and his wife Sandy. They had another bottle of champagne, a couple of six packs of beer, and a small package for Judy. Then there was a steady stream of friends. Rob only mentioned his intentions privately to his friend. Dave had done the rest. Every one of the unexpected guests brought champagne... and a small gift or card for Judy. She was overwhelmed.

"You all brought me something, but nothing for Rob. I don't understand."

J.J. Rabinowitz smiled, "He doesn't need anything else. He's got you!"

Later, when J.J. and Doreen Rabinowitz were preparing to leave, Judy had a request, "Mr. Rabinowitz, I know it's asking a lot, but would you consider filling in for my Dad and walk with me down the aisle?"

J.J was a decisive man. He agreed to Judy's request without hesitation.

Later that night J.J. sat quietly on his bed, lost in thought. Alone with his bride of 42 years, he showed his sensitive side. They had two sons and always wanted a daughter.

Doreen sat beside him and gave him a comforting hug. "I can tell you're pleased that Judy asked you to be with her."

J.J. could not reply. His heart was full and he was overcome with emotion.

40

BACK TO FLAGSTAFF

After leaving Tucson, Jack drove Judy to her apartment. When he carried her luggage in, they found Angie curled up on the couch. She was sobbing, and looked terrified.

"Angie! What's wrong? I thought you were going to go home for the break," Judy exclaimed as she went to her roommate's side.

"It's Beth... she's dead," Angie sobbed, "Killed in a wreck in Mexico."

Her revelation was staggering. Judy sat in stunned silence while Jack fell into a chair and buried his head in his hands. It took Judy a few minutes to recover.

"Has anyone notified Beth's family?" she asked as she went to the kitchen to make coffee.

"Yes," Angie sniffed. "They know."

While the coffee was brewing, she called Rob and broke the news to him. His first concern was for Judy, and then he asked about Jack and Angie. Judy had things under control.

Angie related the details of the horrible accident, "The Mexican police contacted U.S. authorities. They notified Beth's family and they called me yesterday with the news.

"I came right home," Angie sobbed. "Someone had to be here to let her parents in to get... to get Beth's things."

It took a moment before Angie could continue, "I didn't want to call you... I couldn't ruin your time with Rob and your family. I'm sorry... but I know that was so important to you," she sobbed and held Judy's hand.

Then, through her tears, she saw Judy's ring, "Oh Judy," she cried. "You're engaged... I'm so happy for you. He's such a fine man!"

The situation had gone as well as could have been expected. Judy's engagement temporarily allowed Angie to concentrate on something beside her own grief.

For his part, Jack was stunned by the news. Beth was a friend. She treated him badly, but didn't deserve such a tragic end.

Through her tearstained eyes, Angie looked at Jack and tried to smile. She held up Judy's hand with the diamond ring, "She did it didn't she... in spite of all our warnings."

She turned back to Judy and continued, "This is a happy time for you. It feels like we've all played a part in it. Who would have ever suspected this would be the result of that silly disagreement about whether or not he was a wuss?"

Jack joined in the conversation then, "Well I'll tell you one thing about that guy, he sure ain't that."

He nodded at Judy, "You two are a perfect match. You've got what everyone wishes they had a shot at."

"I know... and I'm grateful. I've loved him since that first night when we all saw him in the restaurant with..."

Judy had to pause before she continued, "Patricia...she was alive then."

"That had to be hard on him," Jack said.

"He's incredibly strong," Judy said.

"He was heartbroken but he managed to call his ex wife and inform her... she is even more of a bitch than her daughter. He handled all the arrangements. He made sure that Patricia was properly cared for and had a respectable funeral. He gave me all the credit for supporting him. He told me he never could have managed without me. I'm not sure that's true."

Jack told them what Rob said when he stopped with Jack for a beer after their first meeting. It was the first time they heard that story. Jack shook his head, "He is plenty tough, but you've given Rob more than he feels he deserves. You're there to support him. He never had that before... never."

"I love him," she said softly.

Jack and Angie sat in silence as they watched Judy. Hers was a relationship strong and full of love and commitment. It was the kind of thing stories are written about, fairy tales mostly, but the kind of relationship people dream about and want for themselves. It caused them to look inwardly, to examine their own commitments to those they thought they cared for. The tragedy of Hector and Beth brought those emotions close to the surface or they might not have understood the significance of what Judy was sharing with them.

They ate together in the apartment, and then Jack went to his own apartment. Angie went to her room and Judy went to hers. She sat on the edge of her bed looking at Rob's picture and her heart was full. She picked up her phone and made a call.

"Hi, Honey," Rob answered as soon as he heard her voice.

Judy felt the glow simply from the sound of his voice. Their call lasted for over an hour and it was a comfort to both of them.

Judy's next call was to Beth's family in Nebraska. It was a difficult call but a necessary one. Judy met Beth's parents when they brought Beth to campus in her sophomore year and they talked on the phone many times since then. There was little Judy could say to lend comfort, but she was a good listener.

The next call was to Duluth. Judy's mother was already in bed when the phone rang. She answered with concern. Judy relayed the information about Beth and described how Angie and Jack had reacted. With the unpleasant topic out of the way, Marianne changed the subject and expressed her pleasure at the visit to Arizona. It gave Judy the opportunity to tell her mother what Jack said about Rob.

Marianne smiled, "Honey, I thought you knew that. Rob loves you very much."

"I know, Mom. I guess I never realized *how* much. Hearing it from Jack that way made it even clearer. It makes me wonder if I can ever live up to being the person Rob thinks I am."

"You already do," Marianne answered firmly. "Rob has both feet on the ground and he's got his head screwed on. He sees who you really are. He probably knows you better than I do. You are a treasure,

Honey... just by being yourself. You will never have to do any more than that. He loves you for who you are. All I can say is treasure every moment you have together."

"I do, Mom. He's hundreds of miles away but I can feel him here with me. Can you understand that?"

Marianne was quiet before she answered, "Yes, Honey, I understand that perfectly. It's the same feeling I have with your father."

Alone in his apartment that night, Jack tried to sort out his troubled thoughts. Most of his thinking revolved around the women in his life, and the mess he made of those relationships. His friend Rob personified the attributes of patience, understanding, and commitment. Jack felt he didn't have any of those qualities. His high school sweetheart and Beth both left him for more exciting lifestyles. He shook his head in disgust; he just wasn't too bright when it came to women.

Then a thought struck him. There was Judy's sister, Sarah! She was beautiful and she was Judy's sister. Their affair was in secret with stolen moments when they found ways to be alone. The only thing that troubled him was the similarity of the three girls that he had fallen for. Putting that thought aside, he drifted off to sleep, content with dreaming of Sarah's physical attributes and Judy's faithfulness.

Angie's thoughts were more troubled. She did not possess Judy's character. Her relationships with men were arranged and forced on her. Those men used her. Angie would be a disgrace to her family if they ever discovered the truth. Even her close friends did not suspect the depths to which she had fallen. The tears she shed when Judy returned were an inward glimpse of what she had become. The brutally honest self-appraisal sickened her. She was trapped with no idea how to escape the bonds that confined her.

In the days that followed, Angie observed Judy on a daily basis, from a different perspective. Judy was in love with the man of her dreams. He loved her, and now she wore his ring. It happened because Judy believed it would happen. When the opportunity came, she was ready.

Angie felt she could learn from that. It meant believing that it could happen to her too. It would require drastic steps on her part. That terrified her... but there could be no change until she took charge of her life and made it happen. She resolved to do that.

41

A Surprise Visitor

It was Thursday night and Rob was waiting patiently for Judy's arrival when the ringing doorbell startled him. He hadn't heard her car drive up. Did she have her arms full and couldn't open the door?

The young man at his door was unshaven, looked haggard, apprehensive, and wore a well-traveled Army Ranger uniform. Rob hesitated for an instant to be sure.

"Hello, Dad... it's me, Robert."

Staring in disbelief, Rob felt an immediate rush of emotion.

"I had a hard time finding you," Robert began, his voice shaking. "I heard about Patricia and what you did for her... I was on maneuvers when I found out...it was too late to do anything. I even talked to that miserable bitch you used to be married to. She wouldn't tell me anything."

"That's pretty strong language to use about your mother," Rob said gently.

Robert's hands were shaking, trying to control his emotions. He could no longer do that. He stepped forward and hugged Rob, "I'm sorry... a lot has changed, I've learned a lot... I've missed you, Dad."

Rob heaved a tremendous sigh and held the man that once was a part of his family, the son that was not his, the boy he loved. Come in and sit down," he said. "This is a surprise; I never expected to see you again."

"Yeah, I know," Robert replied and followed Rob inside. "I was a real asshole. I'd like to think I've grown up a little since the last time I saw you."

"Would you like something to drink, soda, a beer, or maybe something stronger?"

"I've been on the road a while... just a glass of water."

"What are you doing, besides being a Ranger that is, and what brings you to Tucson?" Rob asked as he went to the kitchen with Robert following.

"I came looking for you. I wanted to get some things straight between us."

Rob tensed for a moment, wondering what that meant. He handed Robert a glass of water and leaned against the counter watching.

"I've learned a lot in a pretty short period of time."

Seeing the remains of a very black eye and a split lip, Rob pointed and asked, "How did you get that?"

"Part of my education," Robert grinned. "You Marines are tough!"

Rob grinned, "When the Navy wasn't around, we were always more than happy to tangle with the Army. Hell, we're all on the same side. So what started it?"

"In a way, you did. He saw my nametag and asked me if I was any relation to you. I told him you were my Dad. He said you were pretty brave."

"How did he know me? Was it someone I was stationed with?"

"No, he never met you. He was in one of the outfits you were in and knew about some of the things you did. I told him I thought you were some kind of scumbag leaving your family alone while you went off on your travels around the world. He took exception to that. That's when I found out how tough you guys are. I thought I could hold my own in a brawl, but that dude kicked my ass. When I gave it up, he educated me. I bought the beer and we had a long talk. I didn't know you earned the Congressional... I didn't know that it wasn't your idea to keep going back overseas, or why they kept picking on you. I'm ashamed for the way I've been."

"You never really had any reason to look for me. I suppose your mother told you that I'm not your father," Rob said without emotion.

Robert replied angrily, "That's just some overrated biological bullshit! You were more of a Dad to me, and to Patricia too, than any man could have been. No, maybe you aren't my biological father, but I don't think of it that way. I don't even know or care who it was that impregnated her. What I do know is what I remember growing up. No, you weren't there all the time, we were stuck with her, but when you were home, you gave us every bit of your attention and affection. I was young and stupid. I spent too much time listening to her bullshit and actually believed that lying bitch!"

Rob led Robert back into the living room where they continued their discussion. By the time Judy arrived Robert learned much more about the man that served as his father. His respect had grown. Most of Rob's talk was glowing descriptions of Judy. When her car drove up, Rob met her at the door with an affectionate greeting that dispelled any doubts Robert might have had about their feelings. With his arm around her waist, Rob introduced his visitor, "Honey, this is Robert... my son Robert." He turned to Robert and his face glowed, "This is my fiancée, Judy."

Robert stood and approached Judy with wide eyes, "How do you do, ma'am. I'm very pleased to meet you!"

Judy shook his hand warily, "We've talked about you often, Robert. What brought you here?"

"I was looking for my Dad. I've made a lot of dumb mistakes in my life. This is one I want to see if I could do something about. It doesn't do any good to blame that... that... my mother for the things she told me. Being too young isn't much of an excuse either. That's not what my father taught me... it's not what he would do. I've come here to apologize for my past behavior and to try to earn Dad's forgiveness."

Robert hung his head, "I need to apologize to you, too. Knowing about us, Patricia and me, couldn't have been easy on you either. You must have wondered what kind of man my father is."

"No," Judy answered instantly. "I never questioned your father's integrity, his loyalty, or his devotion as a father. I knew that the first time I saw him. But..."

"Yeah, I know. She told me," Robert said. "But he's my Dad even if I never treated him that way, and I'm his son because that's the way he treated me and my sister all our lives."

"Then you know about Patricia?" Judy asked carefully.

"Sort of... I know she died, and I know Dad took care of her. That woman told me a little about it, but mostly she talked about meeting you at the funeral. The things she said weren't very nice. I sort of figured by the way she talked about you that you didn't put up with her sh...uh, behavior. It made me understand a lot. I realized that something good had finally happened in my Dad's life. Patricia and me, we made things pretty tough for him, and even if he had every reason to be, he wasn't bitter."

As their conversation continued, Rob worked in the kitchen putting the finishing touches on dinner. Robert realized that and stood up to leave, "I better go... you two are almost ready to eat."

"No," Judy said, "I think it would be better if you stayed for dinner." She turned to Rob, "There's enough isn't there, Honey?"

"Of course."

Judy looked back at Robert, "Then that's settled. You'll stay for dinner. I think we have a lot more to talk about."

Robert told how he hitchhiked to Tucson and spent a good part of the day, mostly on foot, searching for Rob's house. He was on leave but had to start back the next day. Even in uniform people were reluctant to pick up hitchhikers and he was short on time.

"Where were you planning on staying tonight?" Judy asked.

"I thought I could get a room at the 'Y' or maybe on the Air Force base." Robert replied.

Judy laughed, "Nonsense! You'll stay with us. We've got an extra room and I think we all need the time together. You and your Dad have a lot of years to catch up on, and I'd like to be part of that too."

While they ate, Robert watched Judy and his father. She was the one that asked him to stay, but she spoke for both of them. Rob and Judy were not two separate people, they were one single unit, the family that Rob never had.

With dinner over and the kitchen cleaned up, they adjourned to the patio and continued the conversation. Robert wanted to know the circumstances of his sister's death, but he was not fully prepared for the truth. Without a single negative word about Patricia from Rob or Judy, Robert was still able to discern the way Patricia had treated their father up to the very end and he was ashamed.

"I wish I could get my hands on the person responsible for killing her," Robert muttered.

"That's already been handled," Rob said quietly.

That night as she lay nestled in Rob's arms, Judy asked, "Do you mind if we asked him to stay longer? I think we both need to get to know him. We could give him a plane ticket so he wouldn't have to leave so soon."

Lying in bed, Robert didn't know what sort of reception he would receive from his father. He expected the worst. To be welcomed by Rob and accepted by the lovely lady that was to be his father's wife was an unsettling experience.

Running away to join the Army, and not the Marine Corps where Rob served, was an act of rebellion. When Robert learned the reality of military life, his attitude changed. His father's absence was not his choice. It was a term Robert had grown to despise; 'Convenience of the Government'.

Hidden memories surfaced of his father returning from war, leaving those bitter events behind. Now Robert understood the daily challenges of military life. He understood what Rob tried to do as a husband and father. Now he knew who and what his father really was. Men that never met Rob, men who knew him by reputation only, revered him. They defended him unconditionally. Rob was a living legend among brave and honorable men. It sickened Robert to realize what a fool he had been. His tour in the Army had been a disgrace to his father's name.

In the morning, they asked Robert if he would stay a little longer. It surprised him to be accepted back into his father's life so readily. But that's the way Rob always was with his children. Robert was never close to his mother. She worked hard to gain that hatred and she succeeded. His Dad worked hard to earn Robert and Patricia's love in spite of everything they did. Patricia never learned the truth. Robert did.

When it was time to leave, Robert felt that he was now part of a real family. Judy was only a year or two older than he was, but she was going to be his father's wife and he liked that.

"What are your plans for the future?" Rob asked as they drove to the airport.

It was several minutes before he replied, "I never did anything in my life to be proud of. I could never be the man you are, but I'm going to try to do something, anything, to make you proud of me. If they'll let me, I thought I might stay in the Army. If I could do that one thing successfully, I might feel that I deserve your name."

At the airport, Rob touched the paratrooper insignia on Robert's uniform and spoke softly, "I am proud of you, son."

When it was time for Judy to return to Flagstaff Rob stood at the end of his driveway and watched her drive off. Back inside the house, he sat looking at Judy's picture. She accepted Robert so readily. He was a grown man and could now take care of himself. Rob did his best for Patricia but it was not enough to save her life and that troubled him. He wondered how Judy would manage if anything happened to him. They were not married, yet. If he was gone, Judy would be saddled with responsibilities and he didn't want that.

On Monday, he contacted J.J. Rabinowitz and made an appointment to speak to him. When they met, Rob outlined his concerns. They drew up a will that named Judy as the sole beneficiary. J.J. suggested a stipulation that would care for Robert, but beyond that, all Rob's assets would go to Judy.

Rob left his attorney's office feeling much relieved. There was still one matter that required his attention. In the event that went badly he wanted to be sure that Judy was taken care of.

42

MANUEL'S SOLUTION

Unable to discover who was responsible for the Baumgartner execution, Manny was concerned. It was too close to home. Who was responsible? When the cartels eliminated competition, it left an unmistakable message, but there was no word on the street.

He sat down and tried to plan his next moves. He had ample resources so he could simply drop out of circulation for a while. Then he shuddered. No, the cartels were patient and had long memories. If they were after him, there was no place he could hide that they couldn't find him. He pursued that thought. There were places one could disappear. Europe had possibilities, as did the Far East. No, the language problems would attract attention. Someone would find him.

Then he grinned, Australia!

He could live a long time on the money he had accumulated. The only difficulty was the cash. Cash was a problem in his trade. The vast sums he dealt with simply took up space, and lots of it. It was not easy to transport or hide truckloads of large bills. There had to be a way to transfer some of that to a secure location and still have access. He wondered if the one he referred to as *Mi Querida* would know how to do that.

He would risk a call to her. He punched her number on his cell phone and when she answered, he hung up. She would know his number on her caller I.D. and call back when it was safe to do so. It took several hours before his phone rang with her number and he answered.

"Si senor," she said when he took her call.

"*Mi Querida*," Manuel began in his most condescending voice. "How are you?"

"I'm all right. I was afraid to call you. I didn't know where you'd be."

"You have nothing to worry about. I've been thinking about you a great deal. You're the only true friend I have, and you have been for a long time."

"We have been through a lot, haven't we," she replied.

"Yes we have," he said. "We need to talk. Can you come here... please?

It was not the cold, heartless Manuel she was used to. He was pleading with her, but she was afraid. Could he be trusted?

He sensed her hesitation and asked again, "Please... I need you."

It was a request she could not ignore, "I can be there in an hour."

"Bueno... I'll watch for you," and he hung up.

It was less than hour when he saw her on his monitor and in spite of the precautions he usually took, he hurried out to meet her and embraced her warmly. Leading her back into his house, he reset the intrusion devices, and took her into his living room. He sat facing her from another chair.

"Thank you for coming," he began. "Would you like something to drink?"

"No, thank you, but you sounded so... so different on the phone. Are you all right?"

Manny smiled, "You're the only person I know that would ask that... and mean it. Yes, I'm all right now that you're here. I want to ask you something, something I could not say on the phone... have you ever thought of going to Australia?"

She laughed "Australia? Whatever made you ask that?"

"Because that's where I'd like to go."

"You mean take a vacation?"

"No, *Mi Vida*, to live there. I want you to go with me. I want you to go with me as my wife," he said watching for her reaction.

At first, she looked surprised and then a smile slowly spread over her face, "You almost sound serious, Manuel."

"I am. I've thought about making you my wife many times. I can take care of you. We have money. You could have anything you wanted. We'd be safe away from this place. I want to marry you and have lots of children. It would be a different life for both of us. We'd be happy."

"I never knew you thought of me that way."

"I always have, but it's too dangerous to let others see my true feelings. They'd come after you if they understood how important you are to me. I'd never put you in such a dangerous position. Can you understand that?"

She laughed softly, "Yes... it makes sense. I thought about the pictures you have, the way you said you would use them if ever I proved to be a danger to you."

Manny stood and went to a safe on the wall. It was a large safe, filled with lots of cash. There were three envelopes, one addressed to her family, one to the local police department, and the last one addressed to the newspaper in Douglas. He handed them to her.

"I forgot about them," he said and gave them to her. "Here, do with them as you wish."

She opened the envelopes. Inside, she found negatives and the incriminating pictures taken when she was younger. There was a description of what she did. She looked up at Manuel in disbelief.

Taking her hand, he led her to the fireplace and handed her matches. She watched as the fire consumed the one hold he held over her and smiled. When the fire died, Manny stirred the remnants with the poker. Nothing remained but a pile of unrecognizable ash.

"Thank you," she said.

He lifted her chin to look at her, "Now that you no longer need to be concerned with that, will you come with me to Australia... as my wife?"

"Yes, but when can we go?"

He returned to his seat and taking her into his lap outlined his plan.

"First, I have to find a way to take care of my money. Once that's done, we'll go. We'll leave everything behind because we won't have to worry about money. Your family could visit, or they could move to Australia with us."

As he talked, she sensed his excitement at the prospect for what lay ahead. She was surprised when he asked for her advice on how to handle the money and gave her details that staggered her. She never suspected that he had so many assets in so many places. He was telling her things that no else knew. His trust in her was complete. She had some ideas, things she had learned in her classes in business law.

"I think I know a way to hide your money," she said.

Manny stroked her hair gently. He felt a sense of relief. This girl was a beautiful girl, smart and loyal. She could be trusted and they would be happy in a new country with a new life and more money than they could ever spend.

When she looked up at him, he kissed her and felt his desire rising. Taking her hand, he led her back to his bedroom.

Later that night Manny sent her out for the groceries he needed to remain out of sight. After that, she returned to her own apartment.

Manuel Ortega watched as she departed. She was at least as smart as Hector and far more pleasant. She knew how to accomplish things that Manuel did not know. His guardian in McAllen and his stepfather in Douglas both had wives that were loyal and cared for their men. They knew nothing of their husband's business dealings. This girl knew everything about Manny and his business.

Angie Romero could prove to be a problem.

With every visit, Angie grew more concerned. As long as Manny needed her, she would be safe, but how long would that last? After doing her research, Angie explained it to Manny, "There are financial institutions in foreign countries, like Panama, that can manage large amounts of money discreetly."

There were details, terms, and concepts that Manny didn't understand. When she explained, Manny was pleased.

"You'll need a passcode for the secret account," she told him.

"A secret account?" he asked.

"Yes."

"No one would have access but the one who knew the code?"

"Yes, all you need to do is supply a passcode known only to you and make the deposits. The deposits would be verified to you electronically. No one would have access to those funds except you, because you would be the only one that knew the passcode."

Manny wore a bewildered look, "That's far too complicated for me. You know how it's done. You should set up the accounts for us."

The simplicity of the concept and the magnitude of the details were mind-boggling. Treachery and deceit were tools of his trade. It never occurred to Manny that the same tools were used in the world of high finance with subtle alterations in terminology, but every bit as ruthless. The people in that business wore expensive suits, walked the streets freely and were admired and respected. They didn't live with the constant threat of assassination. Manny looked at Angie and smiled. Angie was not just smart, she was brilliant. There was so much she could teach him.

Laughing suddenly, he took Angie under his arm, "I'm proud of you, *Mi Vida*. You've solved a major problem for me. I want to show you my gratitude."

Fear struck at Angie's heart with those words. There were ways people such as Manuel showed their gratitude. Most were fatal. His show of gratitude shocked her.

"You've made all the preparations, done all the work to make this happen. You'll be the only person who knows how much money we have and how to access it. The only thing you don't know is the passcode."

"But Manuel, you haven't chosen one yet."

"No I haven't. I'll leave that up to you. I trust you to take care of our money. You're not as extravagant as I am. I'm sure there'll be times that we'll argue about it when we're in Australia, but those will be good arguments. Of course you'll have to allow me to buy things for you."

She hugged Manny and kissed his cheek, "I think it would be better if we both knew the passcode," she smiled. "It would be embarrassing for you to have to ask me for your own money."

They both laughed at that. Manny felt relieved. "Maybe you're right, but you'll have to teach me how to use it."

When Angie left, Manny watched her in his monitors and smiled.

She fell for it. Her name will be on the paper trail. If anything goes wrong she will be the one investigated. I can change the account and I'll still have my money.

Documents for Manny were easily purchased with a new name. The birth certificate in Texas for Manuel Jesus Martinez, and school records for a different Manuel Jesus Ortega, were meaningless. Manuel Jesus Ortega no longer existed. There was no property in his name, no house, no car, and no income tax records. His new name had a social security number, passport, visa, drivers' license, voter registration card, and even college transcripts.

The cash Manny had secreted in multiple locations was carried to Mexico by the same mules that brought drugs into the U.S. They were carefully selected, well known, and wise enough to know the consequences of stealing. With help from his stepfather in Douglas, pilferage and bribes were kept to a minimum. That expense was simply a part of doing business.

Once the funds were safely across the border, they were deposited in a Mexican bank. For a small fee, the money was quickly transferred to the designated accounts. Nine and one half million dollars, and drawing interest, was safely out of the country in a numbered account. Only two people had access.

With her good credit, Angie purchased the tickets to Australia on her credit card. A college student on a trip to Australia was an adventure that would not attract undue curiosity. They would leave as soon as school let out for the summer.

43

ANGIE'S CONFESSION

"Angie asked if she could hike with us this weekend," Judy said when Rob called.

"That might be a good idea," he said. "After Beth's tragedy, the outing might do her some good."

Given the timing of her request, Rob wondered if it was more involved than just a friendly hike.

The girls agreed on an area south of Flagstaff and east of the Interstate for their outing. Judy dressed as she always did for hiking, but Angie looked different. Normally well dressed, but today she wore baggy jeans, a flannel shirt, and a floppy wide-brimmed hat with dark sunglasses.

After parking, they shouldered their packs and struck out through the forest. A brisk 15 minutes later, they stopped to adjust boots. Angie had not spoken a single word. The next hour was at a slower pace. Rob was watching Angie for any signs of fatigue or discomfort, but something was driving her. It was her silence that concerned him.

"I have some pretty bad friends," Angie began when they stopped.

"We all do, Angie," Rob replied kindly.

"Not like these," she continued without looking up. "These people are dangerous."

"It sounds like you want to talk about it. What can we do to help?" Rob asked.

"I don't know if there's anything you *can* do. I don't even know why I'm telling you, except that you need to know."

Judy was sitting next to Angie on a dirt ledge beside the trail. Rob stood in front of them with his hands on his hips. For all outward appearances it was a relaxed posture, yet every one of his senses was acutely aware of their surroundings and alert to Angie's words and actions.

"Just tell it like it is, Angie, and we'll go from there."

"I have to start at the beginning... about me. Maybe it will help you understand. I've done a lot of things I'm not proud of. I can make up excuses or blame someone else, but that doesn't change anything."

"You're among friends, Angie," Judy spoke up for the first time.

Angie's story began with her high school years when she first met Manuel Jesus Ortega. He made the sort of promises that capture a young girl's attention and her life deteriorated after that. She was foolish and willing to do anything he asked, hoping that Manny would change and fulfill his promises. She suffered physical and mental abuse at the hands of Ortega as well as from the men he forced on her.

"He promised that one day we'd get married and have a family. I believed him. I gave up a scholarship to Arizona State and followed him here to Flagstaff. He made me provide him with contacts on campus."

"You introduced him to Beth," Judy gasped.

Angie took a deep breath and when she continued, her voice was filled with remorse, "Yes," she whispered. "He arranged for her... her accident."

"There must be something we can do... can't we go to the police?" Judy asked with a fearful look at Rob.

"That wouldn't do any good," Angie interrupted in a lifeless monotone. "He has too much money. He could beat or delay anything that came up in court... in the meantime he'd get his revenge."

Rob leaned forward and gently took Angie's sunglasses. She looked up at him with eyes swollen and red, "Is he that well connected?"

Angie hesitated, nodded, "Yes…"

Angie's story was terrible, but what concerned Rob was her lifeless resignation, "I don't understand why you're telling us this now. You didn't need to tell us. If he found out he would come after you."

"That doesn't matter anymore."

"Why is that?"

"He started asking about Judy."

Taking a step back, Rob asked sharply, "What did he say?"

"Nothing specific… he just knew that the three of us were roommates… Beth, Judy, and me. He doesn't trust anybody. He's thinks that one of us might have said something to Judy," Angie said and turned to Judy, "You have to get away from here!"

Angie wasn't trying to forget a terrible past or unburden herself of those memories. Angie was not seeking forgiveness or understanding. This was the desperate confession of a terrified woman that knew she was about to die. She had no one to turn to, no one to protect her.

Rob knelt in front of Angie and took her hand in his, "Has he said anything specific… mentioned any time frame, or how concerned he is about what Judy might know?"

"No… he just asked about her, if she knew or suspected anything."

"So you don't think he has any immediate plans?"

"No, not yet… but I don't know."

"When are you going to see him again?"

"I don't know. After what happened to Mr. Baumgartner, he's paranoid. He's not even going out of the house. He's just using me. My only chance is to remain subservient to him, valuable enough that he won't eliminate me the way he did to Hector… and Beth.

"Do you think we have four days, Angie? There may be another solution. I'll give you an answer by Wednesday at the latest. Can you hold out that long?"

Angie looked at Rob with a brief flicker of hope. It quickly vanished. "It just doesn't matter anymore."

Then she turned to Judy, "I just needed to warn you so you could get away… try to hide someplace he couldn't find you. I'm the one responsible for... for Beth. I couldn't bear for anything to happen to you."

Judy embraced Angie and felt her shaking, "Don't you worry, Angie. We'll take care of you."

"Yes, we will," Rob answered absently.

If Judy was in danger, there was no alternative. Manny's fatal mistake was mentioning Judy's name. With that single word, Manny's fate was sealed.

"I want both of you to call me every day. If you even suspect something, let me know immediately."

On Sunday night, after he left Judy at her apartment, Rob stopped at Jack Randolph's apartment.

"I need your help, Jack. I want for you to keep an eye on Judy. I think someone may try to harm her."

The intensity of Jack's immediate reaction surprised Rob. Going to his closet, Jack took out a scoped 300 Weatherby magnum. Loading it with 165-grain hollow point hunting rounds, he pushed the safety into position.

Rob and Jack understood one another. They spoke the same language, "If any son of a bitch even looks at her crossways, he's dead," Jack said without hesitation.

Rob called Judy from Verde Valley and tried not to show his concern for her safety. He tried to talk about ways that they could help Angie. Judy didn't buy that, "What are we going to do?" she asked pointedly.

Rob grinned; there was no way to placate Judy, "I paid a visit to Jack and asked him to keep an eye on you girls. Chuck has at least one agent covering you. I'm going to look into another alternative and I'll let you know."

The simple truth was that there was only one way to deal with the situation. Rob knew it was up to him. There was no doubt about his ability to resolve matters. What needed to be done had to be accomplished unemotionally. Strong emotions could make him overly confident and careless. Manuel Ortega was a dangerous man. There was no room for carelessness.

44

MANUEL RETIRES

The call from Manny came on Tuesday, "I've been cooped up in this place too long with nothing but the TV, no one to talk to. I want you to come and stay with me tonight."

Angie was scared. There was no word from Rob, no one to help her.

"I'll be there," she replied, and now it was up to her... alone.

But then it always was.

Shortly after midnight, Angie slipped out of bed. Barefoot, she went to the kitchen and selected a heavy, razor sharp carving knife. She stole back to his bedroom and paused over him with the knife raised.

Hesitating was a dreadful mistake. Manny was not sleeping.

Manny was big, quick, and brutal. Angie was just over five feet tall and slender. The blow that he delivered to knock away the knife shattered her arm. Leaping from his bed, he struck again. Senseless and limp, her body flew across the room and crashed into the wall. She fell to the floor, a battered heap. A vicious kick fractured her ribs. He stood over her motionless body, seething with rage. This was not a job for a hireling. Killing Angie with his bare hands would be a pleasure.

He bent over her and caught a glimpse of the security monitors. The screens were blank! Had she done this too? Manny stood with uncertainty. Movement! Someone else was in his house! He reacted quickly, but too late. The intruder came from the side, driving his shoulders into Manny's knees. With a shriek, Manny's bulk crashed to the hard tile floor, his knees shattered, his legs useless and unmoving.

While the intruder went to Angie's side, Manny groped for the knife. It had to be close. He felt the knife with his fingertips. Stretching further, his fingers closed around the handle. The knife arced through the air and made a brief slashing contact with his assailant. Manny's follow-up was an instant too slow. A heavy foot descended on his wrist pinning the knife to the floor. The kick that followed destroyed his elbow. The ragged pieces of splintered bone that glowed white in the dim light were soon hidden by blood spurting from a severed artery.

A crude tourniquet, torn from the bed, was cruelly tightened around Manny's arm. Manny lay on his back, his body twitching, as he cried in pain. A second wad of bed sheet forced in his mouth silenced the cries. Stepping on Manny's free arm, pinning it to the floor, the intruder knelt heavily on his chest. Manny saw the hypodermic syringe and he reacted with horror. He struggled in vain despite the excruciating pain in his legs and arm. He knew what the syringe contained. The contorted bodies of those that had died that way were familiar to him. His pain was nothing compared to what he was about to experience. With tears flowing from his eyes, Manny cried like a child and begged for his life.

The man kneeling over him slapped Manny's face violently. An iron grip held Manny's face so their eyes met. The man's eyes flamed with rage and hatred.

"This is from your stash," he said and held the syringe in front of Manny's face. "There are ways to keep people alive for weeks while they pray for death."

Unlike his eyes, the voice was calm and unemotional, "You aren't worth the effort."

Without another word, he released Manny's face and prepared the syringe. He plunged it into Manny's arm and pressed the plunger, slowly sending the deadly fire into his bloodstream while Manny struggled to break free.

"That's for the children," the cold, hard, voice said just loud enough to be heard over Manny's muffled screams.

There was a distant sound of movement, a scraping sound, and then more pain as a heavy oak chest of drawers dropped across his legs and hips securely pinning him to the floor.

"That was for Angie," the voice said, unheard over Manny's muffled wailing.

The dark figure knelt at Angie's side and surveyed her injuries. Immobilizing her arm quickly and efficiently, he dressed her and carried her and all her belongings to a waiting car outside the building. She lay unconscious on the seat as he reentered the building.

He returned much later and found her beginning to stir. She was barely conscious of someone that was not trying to hurt her. Her broken arm throbbed and it was hard to breathe. Her face was swollen painfully and she could still taste the blood but she could not comprehend what was happening, only excruciating pain.

"Ortega," She mumbled through split lips.

From somewhere in the fog of semi-consciousness she heard a voice, almost familiar, but just out of reach, "It's over Angie. He'll never hurt another living soul. You have to go to the hospital now."

The calming voice came from a big man. Dark, mottled clothing and a mask that covered his face... and gloves... she lost consciousness again.

For a moment she was lucid... in a strange car outside the emergency room of the hospital. The dark clothed stranger was gone, replaced by a different face... a face beyond the periphery of recognition.

"I'm going to take you inside now, Angie," he said. "I'll leave you in good hands. Try to forget who brought you here. It's better that way."

He went around to her door and gently carried her in the emergency entrance. He called for help as he burst through the door and found bedlam. It was early in the morning and the emergency room was chaos. Ambulances were bringing in the severely injured survivors of an accident that had just occurred on the Interstate. He carefully lowered Angie onto a gurney and grabbed the first nurse he saw.

It was easy to disappear in the commotion once he saw to it that Angie was being cared for. No one would remember who it was that brought her in, not even Angie. In the flurry of activity, she was treated as one of the accident victims.

Judy was awakened in the dark by a gentle caress on her cheek. At first, she thought it was a pleasant dream, but it was real.

"Rob! What are you doing here? How did you get in? Is everything all right?"

He leaned down and kissed her tenderly, "I'm sorry to startle you, Honey, but we need to talk."

Judy sat up and listened in horror as Rob explained what he had done.

He told her about Angie, "Ortega tried to kill her. I stopped him. I took her to the hospital."

Slowly and with difficulty, he told her the rest of the story. Judy stared in shock at the man she loved and tried to digest what he was telling her.

"In the war they gave me medals for this and I was ashamed. I was only doing a terrible task against people that were trying to do their job. That was because of useless and cowardly politicians.

"What I did tonight was personal, retribution for what he did to those that I love. I have no shame for that. This is what I'm capable of doing. It's something you need to know. I don't want you to wonder or hear stories from someone else... I have to be the one to tell you the truth. If knowing this changes what you feel, I can understand. It's not something easy to live with... I know that."

As Rob told his gruesome tale, Judy sat staring at him. She was speechless. When she didn't say anything Rob stood up. In the dim light, Judy could see the agony it caused him to tell her what he had done.

He hung his head and went to the door. He accomplished what he set out to do. He told Judy what he had done to Baumgartner and now Ortega. There was no reason for her to accept that. She would be better off without him. A woman could not be expected to live with someone like him. His house was in order. In the past days he had done everything he could to provide for her and now he must go. She was young and in time, she would get over him.

Without Judy, his life no longer mattered.

45

Judy's Decision

Rob reached the door when he heard her anguished cry, "Don't go!"

He heard footsteps running to him. She flew into his arms, crying frantically, "Don't leave me, please don't leave me," she pleaded. "I love you... I love you!" she cried as she held him tenaciously.

He touched her hair and kissed her tear stained cheek, "Do you know what you're doing?" he asked gently.

"We've come so far," she cried. "*You've* come so far, changed so much. I don't know what to think, how to react to what happened, all I know is that I love you! I need you, Rob. Don't shut me out, don't leave me. I *know* who you are. I *know* what made you do what you've done. You didn't need to tell me, but you did. That had to be terrifying for you, not knowing what would happen, but it's over now. Please... let's face this together no matter what happens."

The next hour was an emotional time for them. Her level of comprehension and the strength of her love overwhelmed him. Dressing his wound, she listened in spite of the horror and any misgivings she felt... and she accepted him. It was more than he could bear. He cried unashamed as she held him in her arms and comforted him.

Wiping away his tears, she understood the terrible burden that Rob and so many others like him carried for so long. Her eyes filled with compassion and she spoke softly, "That's what war is all about, isn't it... men like you killing men like him to protect others that don't know or care what it does to you."

Rob swallowed hard and buried his head on her shoulder. Finally, someone understood.

The muddy red streaks of cloud and sky were signaling the approach of another dawn when Rob slipped out of Judy's apartment and made his way to the parking lot. Chuck's agent sat in his car and watched Rob through his binoculars and smiled. He had been on the detail covering Judy long enough that he understood Rob making the trip all the way from Tucson to spend a single night with her. Judy was a woman worthy of Rob's affection. The agent hadn't seen Rob's arrival and the visit did not go in his report.

Sitting in an apartment directly across from Judy's, Jack Randolph watched as Rob left. Replacing the safety on his rifle, Jack turned his attention back to the agent in the unmarked car. As long as he stayed in his car, the man would be safe.

When the first officer responded to an anonymous call that morning, he found Manuel Ortega's remains pinioned under a chest of drawers with both legs and his arm broken. A severed head lay beside the mangled and distorted body. The officer was staggered at the brutality of the scene before his eyes. The smell of blood, urine, and feces from the victim overwhelmed him. Falling to his knees, he vomited violently.

Chuck was livid when he arrived, "Who puked on my crime scene!"

Manny's surveillance tapes were wiped. The phone and a knife were wiped. The building and floors showed no signs of entry. As in the case of Edward Baumgartner, there were no clues. By the time forensic experts arrived from Phoenix, there had been enough traffic through the crime scene that any chance of recovering viable evidence was impossible. According to the Flagstaff Police Department, it looked like another cartel assassination. They wanted no part of this investigation and promptly turned it over to the federal agencies.

When Judy went to pick up Angie at the hospital, she was surprised to see Jack drive up behind her.

"What are you doing here?" she asked.

"I just happened by, and saw your car. I wondered what you were doin' at the hospital."

There was a moment's hesitation before she replied, "Angie had an accident...I came to take her home."

Jack nodded in reply and waited until Angie was brought out in a wheelchair. When he lifted Angie into the car, Judy noticed the bulge under his jacket. It was a very large handgun. Without comment, he followed them to the apartment and carried Angie inside.

Gently lowering her onto her bed, Jack stood and forced a smile, "You'll be all right now."

Before he left, he spoke quietly to Judy, "If you two need somethin', give me a call. I'll be close by."

The media carried gruesome stories that linked both Baumgartner and Ortega to the drugs responsible for the deaths of several students. There were the sordid details of kidnapping and pornography. Federal authorities were investigating, and measures were being taken to apprehend the perpetrators.

With their part completed, Chuck Stuart and his partner were returning to Phoenix in a government vehicle. The long drive allowed Tony Cervantes to quiz his mentor.

"Do you think we'll catch the cartel people that did this?"

When Chuck didn't reply, Tony tried a different approach, "Do you think it was the cartels?'

With a non-committal grunt, Chuck replied with a question, "What do you think?"

"I don't know, but it sure dried up the drug activity. Whoever did this should have moved in by now. Who else could do something like that?"

"Pretty basic police work, Tony, motive."

"Someone related to one of the victims?" Tony asked.

"That's the logical answer, but let me ask you this, what would happen if we caught those two corrupt bastards before they were killed?"

"They'd spend the rest of their lives in jail!" Tony said confidently.

"Do you really believe that? Between the two of them, they had several million dollars in cash. With that kind of money, they'd be back on the street before we got to Phoenix."

Chuck remained quiet while his partner considered the implications. Finally, Chuck continued, "With a little investigation we might be able to discover who did this, but would Justice, not the law, but Justice be served? Society is rid of two degenerate criminals... permanently. Is there any conceivable good that could come from prosecuting someone that, in taking the law into their own hands, accomplished what the legal system is incapable of doing?"

It was a long time before Tony replied. He looked at his mentor, "But, if you know something, shouldn't you speak up? Concealing evidence is something that could ruin your career."

Chuck's reply was bitter, "You saw those children. As long as those two bastards are gone, I don't give a damn about my career."

When she came home from the hospital, Angie needed help, both physical and emotional. Judy provided both.

While Judy was loading her car to drive to Tucson for the weekend, Jack appeared. He helped transfer Angie and her wheelchair to Judy's car. Angie was still terrified, barely able to care for herself and she could not bear to be left alone. Her arm was in a sling and her ribs were tightly wrapped. Her once pretty face was swollen with ugly purple bruises. Her battered lips were puffed up and she had lost a tooth. She needed Judy's help to dress and fix her hair.

When they arrived in Tucson, Rob met them in his driveway. After an affectionate greeting for his fiancée, he went to Angie's door. Lifting her gently, he carried her inside. After putting their luggage away, he rejoined them, "I made soup and sandwiches."

While he was in the kitchen Angie looked at Judy and attempted to smile, "You were right about him all along weren't you," she said quietly. "Rob is everything you told us he was that first night."

"Maybe even more," Judy said and looked toward the kitchen where Rob was preparing their lunch.

Watching the tenderness between Rob and Judy, Angie began to cry, "He said he wanted to have children," she sobbed. "All I ever wanted was to have a man I could love and to have babies of my own. He destroyed that. Because of the things I've done, the things he made me do, no one could ever love me."

Rob spoke tenderly, "That's not true Angie. That's all behind you. He's gone... gone forever, and took the past with him. You can still have your dreams as long as you don't give up on them."

As the afternoon progressed, Angie relaxed. She was dozing peacefully when Rob's phone rang. He went to another room to talk. When he returned, he was laughing, "That was Jack. He's parked down at the corner. I told him to come in."

"What's he doing in Tucson?" Judy asked.

"He followed you," Rob smiled. "I asked him to keep an eye on you. It looks like he did."

"That's why he showed up everywhere I went, isn't it?" Judy asked.

Rob nodded, "He's a good friend. I'm glad we know him."

When Jack came in, Judy embraced him and kissed his cheek, "You look like hell," she said with a smile.

"I ain't had much sleep lately."

After shaking Rob's hand, Jack went to the extra bedroom. Fully dressed, he fell onto the bed and was asleep immediately.

When Angie woke up, she was puzzled, "What's Jack doing here?" she asked.

"He's our guardian angel," Judy smiled.

46

THE REST OF THE STORY

In spring, friends and family gathered in Duluth for Rob and Judy's wedding. Ralph and Cathy arranged an inexpensive charter flight for the Arizona group. Chuck Stuart cleaned up nicely, and with Samantha at his side, they made an attractive couple. Rob's neighbor, Sam Whitborn, needed a walker to get around, but he came. Mary Jane was delighted when she was asked to be Judy's maid of honor. She arrived on the charter flight with her husband and her parents. Dave's wife, Sandy, was there to make sure that he was clean-shaven for his duty as best man. With Doreen's support, J.J. Rabinowitz would give away the bride.

Jack drove in from Wyoming. There wasn't much contact with Sarah since spring break, so he wasn't surprised when she introduced her current boyfriend. Jack was there for Rob and Judy's wedding, and that was more important.

Brian changed since spring break. His personality bordered on arrogance. He bragged about his new girlfriend, Dana Metcalf, and kept a close eye on her. Bright eyed, petite, and lovely, Dana was the same age as Sarah.

The only one missing was Angie Romero. The two tickets for her flight to Australia were non refundable. She took a friend.

On the day of the wedding, the church that Judy attended in her childhood was filled to capacity.

Wearing his Marine Corps dress blues with his Congressional Medal of Honor, Rob created quite a commotion when he took his place at the front of the church near the pastor. There was a sudden intake of breath and then silence when Judy appeared in her wedding gown. Auburn hair curled down over tanned shoulders and her eyes sparkled. She was stunning.

Wearing a tuxedo and glowing with pride, J.J. took Judy's arm and they made their way forward. Judy's eyes were fixed on Rob. When she could no longer restrain herself, she burst forward, ran to Rob, and hugged him.

J.J. stepped forward quietly and taking her arm once more, the ceremony resumed. When the Pastor asked, "Who gives this woman to this man?" it was J.J.'s moment.

He placed Judy's hand in Rob's and for J.J. time stood still. Looking at those two hands, he understood the significance of the commitment they were making. The hands and hearts that from this day forward would be one. Always dignified and poised, it was the only time in his life that J.J. Rabinowitz was speechless.

Rob and Judy looked at their friend and understood his emotions.

Slipping her arm around Sarah's waist, Marianne stepped beside Brian. They looked at the Pastor and together they replied, "We do."

The reception that followed meant creating or renewing friendships.

After the ceremony, the newlyweds made a leisurely trip to the Randolph ranch in Wyoming. Jack's family was prepared for their visit. Not far from the ranch house, nestled in the trees, was a small, rustic cabin built from native rock. It was quiet, private, and ideal for the honeymoon.

On a cool, clear day with the golden glow of summer in the air, Jack saddled three horses and rode out with Rob and Judy to show them the countryside. Riding to a high vantage point, they dismounted and sat below the crest of a windswept hill. Below them, a wide green valley was laced with streams and dotted with sparkling ponds. Beyond, trees carpeted the distant mountains up to tree line.

"This is some of the finest huntin' in the state," Jack said as he swept the area before them with a wave of his hand. "If you come up durin' elk season, you'll have your pick, and we won't even have to leave the ranch."

With the wispy flags of clouds above them, the perpetual wind buffeting the ridgeline behind them, the conversation turned to the first time they met in Flagstaff. There were many memories, some pleasant, and some tragic.

Leaning on his elbow, Rob was studying the windswept silhouette of ancient trees on the skyline behind them. They were short and tough, all their branches growing on the downwind side of their trunks. Barely six feet tall, they survived in a harsh environment. They were far older than the giant Ponderosa where he and Judy shared their first outing together.

He studied them for a long time before he gestured, "Those trees up there, they're like people," he said, "At least the strong ones. Bent and twisted by outside forces, wearing their scars, and yet firmly rooted in what they believe in and stand for. The limbs are formed by the outside forces, wind, and weather. The roots grow deep and the trunks are strong. They're determined, bent by the forces around them, yet rooted and steadfast."

He sat up an put his arm over Judy's shoulders, "I've done some terrible things in my life, but the one thing I always wanted was exactly what I have now with Judy. She's like those trees too. Maybe even stronger because she had to support me in the hard times," he said sincerely and kissed her cheek.

"Next year she'll have her degree and a future in her field. That was one of her goals..."

"You're the other one," Judy interrupted with a content smile and leaned against him. "Finding the right man, someone to love that would love me back, was something I dreamed about even before I found this," she said and touched the pendant at her throat. "That first time we met face to face, I knew."

Rob took a deep breath before he glanced at Jack and continued, "You're the same in many ways, Jack. You're true to what believe in. This land, this life, is who you are. You might have given that up for some skirt, but you know who you are. That would never have worked, and you were wise enough to see that."

After sitting quietly for a few minutes, Rob turned and pointed once more to the scraggly and ancient trees he had been studying, "Life shapes us like those trees up there," he said. "It's the way the wind blows."

* * * * * * * *

END NOTES

Clarification of several facts and incidents portrayed in this story are provided for a better understanding of the time frame. For example, the Westbound Santa Fe did not pass through Flagstaff during daylight hours in 1987, only the eastbound trains did. The Mercedes factory did recognize and reward exceptional technicians with a ring similar to those that Rob and Dave earned. The location of the site that Rob and Judy wanted to explore is fictional.

Cell phone use and coverage was analog until 1993 when digital service became available. Rob's cell phone was the Motorola Micro TAC 9800X, an early flip phone. Reception areas have been exaggerated.

In the early 90's there were a variety of opinions as to the origin and extent of the Clovis influence. Sherd is the accepted term for broken pieces of Native American Pottery (a.k.a. shards). The distinction between the two terms is related to the broken edge. Shards tend to be sharper and more recent. In the Walnut Canyon area, sherds are usually located up to 17 cm (6.7") below the surface. Charcoal is usually located 88 cm (34.6") below surface.

Mt. Humphreys, at 12,637 ft, (3852 meters), is the highest peak in Arizona. It is in the Kachina Peak Wilderness (San Francisco Peaks) north of Flagstaff. Aaloosaktukwi is the Hopi name, and for them, it is a sacred site.

Rob's comment - "Come, we burn daylight, ho!" is from Shakespeae's Romeo and Juliet, Mercutio, Act 1, Scene IV.

Manny's terms for Angie:
Mi Querida (my love)
Mi Vida (my life)
Mi Corazon (my heart)

The characters represented are a combination of traits associated with real people that I have known. With very few exceptions the action is based on actual events. Locations, names, and dates have been changed.

ABOUT THE AUTHOR

'*The Way the Wind Blows*' is Geoff McLeod's first effort at a full length novel. This revised edition has been shortened. With minimal assistance from the author, the characters have been allowed to express their own opinions.

His second novel, '*Unfinished Business*' is the story of a young man seeking Justice for his father's murder. It is available in both electronic and paperback versions from Amazon.

A third novel, '*Home on the Range*' follows the lives of characters introduced in '*The Way the Wind Blows*'. Confronting Dana Metcalf's abusive past, tests Jack Randolph's grit. When her past becomes personal, Jack's family and friends face an armed attack on the remote Randolph ranch.

Born in Ontario, Canada, Geoff's family moved to Wisconsin when he was too young to offer an opinion. Following a four-year hitch in the U.S. Marine Corps, he worked as an import auto technician for many years. Geoff has lived and worked in California, Wyoming, Colorado, and finally settled in the high desert of southeast Arizona. An area conducive to creativity, this setting provides an outlet for photography, painting, and writing.

The author lives in the foothills of the Huachuca Mountains south of Sierra Vista with his dog Lady. He teaches and paints watercolors, paints murals, hikes, and gathers ideas for future novels.

Made in the USA
Middletown, DE
23 May 2023

30834184R00189